TOWER OF BABEL

TOWER OF BABEL

MICHAEL SEARS

SOHO
CRIME

Published by
Soho Press, Inc.
227 W 17th Street
New York, NY 10011

Library of Congress Control Number: 2020932922

ISBN 978-1-64129-195-8
eISBN 978-1-64129-196-5

Interior design by Janine Agro

Printed in the United States of America

10 9 8 7 6 5 4 3 2 1

to Rudy, who taught me the game

and Ruby, without whom...

TOWER OF
BABEL

LITTLE RICHIE WAS A hard man to like. Though if Ted had known Richie was going to be dead in three days, maybe he would have tried a little harder.

Or maybe not. Richie Rubiano was a nasty weasel with a long list of annoying habits.

It was a warm Friday in May, the Mets were at home, three games up on .500, and the bookies were predicting a sweep. Four hours till game time. Ted Molloy was having a late lunch in the back booth at Gallagher's Pub on Grand Ave.—and anticipating a pleasant weekend at Citi Field— when Richie dropped a stack of marked-up file folders on the table. "I got you some grade A today, bro," he said. "Check this out."

"Nice to see you, Richie. You hungry?" Ted rescued his iced tea as the pile of folders began a slow-motion avalanche across the table.

Richie made no effort to assist in heading off this disaster. He looked at the remains of the house pad thai in front of Ted and shuddered. "How do you eat that grass?"

"I'm offering to buy you lunch." Richie was bone thin everywhere except for his gut. He always looked both undernourished and overweight. He also had a drooping eyelid and wore a greying ponytail that looked like something you might find on the rear end of a very wet squirrel.

"No, man. I don't eat Chinese food."

Gallagher's Pub, a short walk from Ted's apartment and a quiet place to get work done in the middle of the day, had been a faltering business when Henry Zhang bought it four years ago. He'd made only two important changes. First, he fired all the bartenders who had been robbing Gallagher blind, installing in their place a troop of his female cousins. Then he upgraded the menu to better reflect the changing neighborhood, adding Asian, South American, and Middle Eastern dishes. The weekend dim sum brunch was a hit. And the place still made a great cheeseburger.

"How about a beer?" Ted asked.

"Well . . ." Richie twisted his face into a reluctant frown. He wanted the beer, but he mistrusted hospitality.

Lili, the twentysomething-going-on-forty day-shift bartender, was watching the talking heads on one of the two televisions over the bar. A grinning real estate developer with a glistening, almost reflective bald pate was holding forth on the local economy of Queens. From what Ted had picked up, the guy was taking credit for job creation, tax reduction, and resodding the soccer fields in the park. The cameras liked him.

Ted managed to catch Lili's eye, a not terribly difficult feat considering that the only other customer was Paulie McGirk, who occupied the last barstool against the far wall every day from opening until dinner rush, or until he passed out, whichever came first. When Henry bought the pub, Paulie had been included with the other fixtures.

She raised an eyebrow in response. Ted pointed at Richie and she nodded.

Ted turned to Richie. "What've we got?"

Richie had a penchant for committing short cons and other small-time property crimes, but Ted had kept him marginally, and legally, employed for four years. Richie was almost old enough to be Ted's father and had grown up in one of the least diverse enclaves in Queens, the United States' most ethnically and culturally diverse county. This perspective gave him a singular belief in his innate superiority and catholic ability to understand—and hoodwink—anyone from any background. The fact that he had repeatedly failed at this—and had the police record to prove it—was testimony to his true talent: self-delusion.

In their work together, Richie did the research. Ted closed the deals. They were not partners. Neither would have allowed it. Richie because he had never learned to play well with others, Ted because he knew better. Richie looked through public documents for foreclosure auctions that resulted in "surplus money." When, for whatever reason, an owner walked away from a property—commercial only; Ted avoided the heartbreaks of residential foreclosures—and stopped paying the mortgage or taxes or water bill, the building was eventually sold at auction. If some Trump wannabe paid more than the claimants were demanding, the resulting funds were called "surplus money." If the original owner did not claim these funds, they went to the government and were eventually absorbed by that great maw. These kinds of opportunities were neither common nor rare. Ted made a living off them, but only because he worked at it.

His part of the job took over where Richie's left off. Ted examined the files and attempted to locate and cut a deal with the original owners, taking a hefty finder's fee for reuniting these hapless businessmen with the last recoverable scraps of their failed real estate empires. Sometimes it worked; more often it did not. Not everyone wanted to be found or, when found, appreciated being contacted regarding a painful and destructive phase in their lives. Ted managed to have more good years than bad by concentrating on hitting singles and doubles. There were few home runs.

The bartender arrived with a Bud Light and a chilled glass.

"Put that on my tab," Ted said.

Richie ignored the glass and took a hefty swallow from the longneck. "She's always trying to get me to up my game. You see that? Trying to get me to show some class."

"Yeah, well, she's young. She'll get over it."

They had met four years earlier when Ted was coming out the door of the Capital One bank near the courthouse and Richie had approached him with his sad face and a story. Ted had let him spin his whole pitch about having lost his wallet and needing help to cash two checks from his employer and how he'd gladly pay 10 percent—$200—for assistance. It was an old con, and Richie, though glib enough, was unlikely to inspire confidence in anyone in possession of either eyes or brain.

But Ted was new to the surplus-money game and already disheartened by the amount of time he was spending on research, both online and at the courthouse. He bought the hapless con man a few beers, and by the end of the day, they had arrived at a working arrangement. A year later, when Richie was arrested for scamming senior citizens with an IRS spiel, Ted bailed him out, found him a good lawyer, and put him back to work. Ted didn't think of it as either altruism or heroism. He didn't want to waste time finding and training some other researcher.

"What do I owe you?" Ted asked.

"I got eleven. All winners."

"So, that's two seventy-five." Ted passed him the cash and reached for the top case file. "Anything I should know about these?"

"The one in your hand. You read that and tell me it's not solid gold."

He flipped it open. The top page listed the property address, the defendant, the claimant, the amounts sought by claimant, and the sale price. Ted slammed it closed.

"Gimme back twenty-five," he said. "You know I don't hunt elephants."

"You gotta read it first."

"I read it. It's a million-two. That's all I need to know."

There were no guarantees in his business. People who fail to appear at their own foreclosure hearings may be confused, angry, disorganized, broken, or, in some cases, just nuts. It could be a little like juggling rattlesnakes. The process itself could be devastating for the defendants, or for any number of reasons, they could be victims of their own design. Early on, Ted had made some rules to protect himself, and he observed them more religiously than he had ever followed the Ten Commandments.

One of those rules was "Thou Shalt Take a Pass on the Big Ones." Normal people don't leave a million dollars lying around. There's always a story. A divorce, trouble with probate, criminal activity, people fleeing the country or disappearing into the wind. The really big ones were a waste of time. The sweet spot was fifty to a hundred thousand. In a stretch, he would go as high as a quarter million, but he had regretted it every time.

"There's got to be an army of lawyers circling something this large, Richie. It's a sucker bet."

"You're a lawyer. You could work your magic and get by 'em."

Ted had a law degree but no license. He'd let it lapse and no longer gave much thought to it.

"It's the property. The family owned it since the 1880s. One heir. Some lady who never married. She's like ninetysomething." Richie was excited. That was never a good sign.

"You mean 1980s."

"No, like since the Civil War. You know where they started clearing that big lot in Corona? You hear about this?"

About a mile from where they sat, a full four-block area was to be razed and cleared in preparation for the transformation of the neighborhoods surrounding Flushing Meadows Park. There would be a new on/off ramp for the Grand Central Parkway, luxury hotels with views of both the Mets' ballpark and the tennis stadium, and a combined shopping mall and mixed-use high-rise that would throw a late-afternoon shadow as far as the Nassau County line. The three-letter name of the development corporation, LBC, was chiseled into the cornerstone of dozens of projects around the borough, a brand as recognizable to Queens residents as IKEA or Con Ed. Members of the local community had been fighting this monstrosity in the courts for months. But a day did not go by without an appearance on television of the Chairman and CEO, Ronald (Ron) Reisner, smirking at their failure to stop him. Whether Reisner and his family owned the company or simply acted as if they did was a source of constant speculation in the New York press. Nevertheless, Ted was not surprised that Richie seemed to have only recently become aware of the project.

"I heard someone mention it," Ted said.

"It's a big deal," Richie assured him.

"Mr. Reisner was on the television not two minutes ago." Ted saw that Reisner had been replaced by a photo of the mayor shaking hands with a parking lot tycoon, who had recently been indicted for extortion, defrauding employees, failure to pay sales tax, and witness tampering.

Richie glanced at the set. "Nah. That ain't him."

"I'm sure you're right." Conversations with Richie often took these veering turns, and Ted had learned that the only way to keep his sanity was to allow his mind to float above the words and focus on the horizon.

"This was the whole northwest corner," Richie said,

stabbing the file folder with a finger. "This old lady owned *six* lots. She lost it all for two years' water and taxes."

"And interest and legal fees and—"

"Yeah, yeah, I know."

"I'm not interested," Ted finished.

The weasel pouted. "Okay, but if I go after it myself, will you back me?"

"Back you? You mean with cash?" Ted cut off a laugh. Richie was serious.

"If I can cut a deal."

"Why don't I just take the money and burn it?"

"Not to buy her out. Just enough to show her I'm for real. Say, fifty grand. Or a hundred."

"You're dreaming."

"I got some ideas."

"Really?" Ted flipped open the file again. "How do you propose to find a ninety-three-year-old woman named Barbara Miller? That's like looking for John Smith. According to the docs, she never once appeared in court."

"Yeah, but . . ."

"And if, by some bit of magic, you do locate this lady, and she's not so far into dementia that she can't understand the words you're saying, how are you going to keep her from running to her lawyer here? What's his name?"

Ted shuffled pages until he found the settlement page listing all of the parties involved and their representatives. The name jumped up and smacked him between the eyes. Jacqueline Clavette. He slammed the file closed.

"What?" Richie cried.

"Nothing. Look, Richie, keep the twenty-five bucks. I don't care. But leave this alone. Can you?"

"You know this lawyer." Richie tried to take the file.

Yes, he knew the lawyer all right. Jacqueline Clavette was married to Ted's ex-wife.

Richie snatched the file. "We'll talk again, and when we do, I'm gonna show you how this shit gets done."

The talk never happened. Three days later Richie was dead.

2

THE REFRIGERATOR HUMMED IMPATIENTLY. Ted had been staring at the near-empty shelves for long minutes, imagining a carton of eggs, some cheese, butter, a red pepper or maybe a few mushrooms. He slowly closed the door on the remains of a six-pack of Stella, a near-empty container of steamed brown rice, and a carrot. If he wanted breakfast, he would have to put on pants and shoes and go find it.

It was raining lightly but enough to sway his decision. The Honduran bodega was closest. He pulled his sweatshirt up to cover his head and dashed down the street.

There was a line at the counter, and the three tables along the wall were already full. It took an agonizing fifteen minutes to get his to-go order of two foil-wrapped chorizo *baleadas* and a medium black coffee.

As he fumbled with his key at the street-level door to his building, a familiar voice called, "Molloy, my friend. He's gone."

Israel Ortiz was peeking out the door of his storefront office. Ted was wet, hungry, and in no mood for cryptic conversations. "Who? What the hell are you talking about?"

"The policeman." Israel waved him in.

Mr. Ortiz, Ted's landlord, accountant, mail drop, and some-time lawyer—he filed documents that the no-longer-licensed Ted could not—ran his law, real estate, and accountancy office out of the storefront of a two-story taxpayer. He also used the space to sell Bibles; incense; framed images of white, black, and Hispanic Jesuses and Madonnas (separate and together); and Santeria candles. His secretary and bookkeeper—a woman named Phateena whom Ted had never seen wear anything but brightly colored caftans and flip-flops—also did palm and tarot card readings.

Ted shook the rain off his shoulders and rested one hip against Israel's desk. "A cop was looking for me? What for?"

Israel stood uncomfortably in the middle of the room, thrusting his hands into his pockets and then jerking them out again. "A detective. Big man. Are you in trouble, Mr. Molloy?"

"Did he say why he was looking for me?"

"I can't have no trouble here. You are good tenant. You pay, no noise, no complaints. But I don't want no police. I got clients."

"I understand, Israel. I have no idea why a cop—a detective—would want to talk to me. Did he leave a card? A name?"

"No. He's got your card. He said he'd call you."

Ted thought of his breakfast getting cold. "Then we'll just have to wait and see."

"But no trouble? Okay?"

THE HEAD OFFICE OF Molloy Partners—Gallagher's Pub being merely a satellite—was the IKEA kitchen table in Ted's second-floor apartment. Though the apartment had been advertised as a one bedroom, the kitchen, living room, and bedroom all flowed into a single space. It was all Ted could afford after his stumbling descent from Park Avenue and a brief plateau in a Lexington Avenue sky pad—which should have been a bachelor's dream but had felt more like a lonely monk's cell for the recently divorced. But now that he had enough money in the bank to get something better, he realized that he didn't need to.

He had returned to his roots, though this was a neighborhood he had spent his first twenty years trying to escape. But both he and Queens were much changed. He rarely saw a face he knew from his youth, but he at least recognized himself on these streets.

His living space consisted of a queen-size bed with night table and matching dresser; an amateurishly constructed closet protruding from one wall that predated Ted's tenancy by a generation or two; an ancient metal two-drawer filing cabinet that served as repository for dormant deals and the few nearing resolution; an IKEA table and two chairs of which he was ridiculously proud, having put them together himself; and a television, precariously hanging on to the far wall, on which Ted watched old movies on TCM and *Law & Order* reruns on four different channels. His cave, his castle.

The phone was ringing as he came up the stairs. The landline. A minor event. Ted did most of his business on a cell phone but kept a landline because it came with the cable/Internet package. Sometimes he even used it. The number had found its way onto his business card along with the cell phone number, but as he hardly ever handed cards out, incoming calls were few.

He took a breath before answering. "Molloy Partners. Edward Molloy speaking." There were no partners, but maintaining the fiction reassured some of the customers.

"Good morning, Mr. Molloy. This is Detective Duran. NYPD. Do you have a moment for a couple of questions?"

Like all mostly honest people, Ted had a great reluctance to speak with the police on any subject. "Questions" sounded ominous.

"I was trained as a lawyer, Detective. I'm happy to assist in any way I can, but I have to ask: Am I the target of an investigation?"

"Not at this time, but if you feel a sudden urge to confess to anything, I would be glad to caution you." The cop chuckled as if they were old friends joking and sharing pleasantries.

Ted wasn't buying. "That's reassuring, but as I check my schedule, I find that I'm in meetings all week."

"My mother says I can be overly persistent."

Ted was curious. In a fit of escapist desperation, he had once gone on a shark-feeding excursion in Cancún; answering a few questions from the police couldn't be any more dangerous than that. "You were just by here. My landlord was a bit spooked."

"Five minutes," the detective said. It was both a pledge and a request.

"Five minutes," Ted agreed. "How can I help?"

"Do you know a man named Richard Rubiano?"

That was an easy one. "I do. I helped Richie out of a jam a few years back. I don't represent him, though. I'm no longer licensed. Is he in trouble?"

"How would you characterize your relationship?"

Another floater over the plate. "He does odd jobs for me from time to time." This was met with an expectant silence. Wary of swinging at a slider, Ted added, "And when he needed a lawyer, I helped him find one. Does he need one now?"

"No, sir. Mr. Rubiano will not need a lawyer."

"So are you ready to tell me what this is about?"

"Mr. Rubiano was the victim of a homicide, Mr. Molloy. He had a few business cards in his wallet. Yours was one."

A flicker of grief surprised Ted. A shooting pain that was gone even as he put a name to it. Richie was not a friend and never had been. But since his divorce, Ted's world had continued to shrink to the point that now any regularly repeated human contact had significance. He would miss the weasel.

The shock of how Richie had died took a moment longer to register.

"He was murdered?" Incredulity beat all. People in his life died by disease, rarely by accident, and never before by murder. Ted sought words to define or explain it. "He was a not very successful con man years ago, but I can't imagine any of his marks showing up to take revenge."

"Would you be willing to come down and give a statement?" Detective Duran managed to make the request sound casual.

Sirens and flashing lights went off in Ted's head. The shark was inviting him home for dinner. "Only with my lawyer present. And that would cost me money, and you would learn nothing that might be of use to you."

"I would think you'd be more cooperative. We're looking for the person who killed your friend."

Ted noted the feeble attempt at inducing guilt and ignored it. Bitterness had long replaced guilt as a motivating factor in his life. But people he knew were not murdered. He felt himself being pulled in despite misgivings.

If there was any chance that Richie had stirred up some hornet's nest by looking into the old lady's surplus money, there was also a chance of that trouble leading back to Molloy Partners. A chance only, but Ted did not want to take that risk. He needed to know more, and if that meant trading information, he was willing.

"I have a proposal, Detective. If you're willing to answer a few of my questions, I will try a little harder to be more open. But only if the conversation is one-on-one and on my turf."

The cop sighed, signaling that Ted was making his difficult job more so. "Counselor, I am an overworked civil servant just trying to make a living. Cut me a break."

"I'm trying. Listen, I'll go you one better. Let me buy you a burger. Lunch. Tomorrow. Do you know Gallagher's? On Grand?"

3

TED FOUND HE HAD no appetite for his now ice-cold breakfast. He told himself that he had to eat and took one bite. The rest went into the trash.

The possibility that Richie had been killed because of something related to their business together made Ted feel queasy. The business model consisted of picking up the scraps ignored or forgotten by real estate moguls or wannabes. Those people were the predators; Ted barely qualified as a carrion feeder. And Richie? A dung beetle.

Disagreements and disappointments were not unusual—having suffered already, Ted's clients could be angry, suspicious, or belligerent—but there had never been anything beyond occasional strong words and hollow threats. No one got murdered over surplus money. But the doubt clung to him.

He did not feel the passage of time as he sat staring at a blank laptop screen until his cell phone intruded on this bleak reverie. Jill. Though they had been divorced for ten years, he always took her calls.

"I'm late. I'm late. I'm late. I'm late."

"Hi, Jill." He checked the time on the wall clock and was shocked to find that it was already early afternoon.

"I've got to run."

"You're not late. The game's not till Wednesday." Not a date. Just two friends going to a Mets game. Saving a rocky year or two immediately following the divorce, they'd been attending games together since their second date.

"I am late. But that's not why I called. We're on, right?"

"Unless you tell me differently. Why are you late?"

"Because I'm still at the museum, and Teri agreed to fit me in for a blowout in seven minutes." Teri was a tyrannical refugee from Macedonia who happened to have a hair salon on Fifth Avenue with a view of Saint Patrick's Cathedral. Ted had never understood how wealthy Manhattanite women allowed this monster to come near them with sharp objects in his hands.

"At this time of day, you'll get a cab out front with no trouble."

"And if there's no holdup in front of the Trump building, I'll get there in ten minutes. Goodbye. See you Wednesday."

"I'm being grilled by the NYPD tomorrow about a murder investigation."

"What are you talking about? Don't. Stop. Tell me Wednesday."

"Goodbye, Jill."

"Wait! What time?"

"Seven. It's always seven."

"No. They're always changing it."

They had once seen the second half of a doubleheader that started at eight. Once.

"Goodbye, Jill."

She was already gone.

GILLIAN FITZMAURICE AND EDWARD Molloy had been the perfect match. Everyone thought so.

They'd met at a Whitney Museum fundraiser. Jill was a twenty-two-year-old intern, preparing for the life of a privileged docent. Ted, four years older, was the new hire at the family law firm, having clerked for a year with Jill's grandfather on the New York State Court of Appeals. She was tall and willowy, blonde, with eyes the color of lapis lazuli. Ted was also tall, but broad shouldered and round of face. Black Irish with dark hair, dark eyes, and a complexion that tanned easily. They complimented each other.

"You must be Jill Fitzmaurice," he said.

"Why must I?"

"You have the Fitzmaurice look." She moved with a fluidity that could have been the result of good genes or years of ballet lessons. She wore almost no makeup or jewelry and didn't need it. She wasn't conventionally pretty, but Ted thought she was beautiful.

She frowned. "Are you sure? I love my grandfather, but he's got a nose like an ax blade."

"I meant you have a regal look. You hold your head in such a way that mere mortals, such as myself, must stand in awe."

She laughed. "Bullshit."

"Admittedly."

"But you get points for both originality and chutzpah."

"I write all my own material."

"It's a good line. Does it often work for you?"

"I don't know. This is the first time I thought I might be able to carry it off."

"I know who you are."

"Oh?"

"The golden boy. Grandfather 'discovered' you. You're being groomed."

Ted was very aware that his presence at the venerable law firm of Hasting, Fitzmaurice, and Barson was an abnormality. Though he had been top of his class, his degree did not come from an Ivy League institution. The Judge had championed him, giving him a chance, but also putting a target on his back. "Local boy makes good."

"I bet you've always made good."

"I'm not sure how to take that."

"Any way you want."

"Then I'll assume it's a compliment," he said.

"You're a fast learner."

Ted laughed. "I think I'll have to be to keep up with you."

"I'll assume that's a compliment."

"Touché."

"Ooh. And he speaks French."

She was enjoying herself, but Ted felt she was holding back. Hiding behind the sass. Rather than put him off, this made him more determined. He wanted to learn her secrets. "Would you like to continue this conversation over dinner?"

"I know it doesn't look like it, but I'm working."

"Another time?"

"Attaboy. Sure."

"Then I'll need your number," he said.

"I'll call you."

"Then you'll need my number."

"No. I think I've got your number."

TED TAUGHT HER TO ice-skate and introduced her to the joy of watching old black-and-white movies on television. Jill persuaded him to eat oysters and educated him enough for him to not get bored in an art museum. He was ambitious, proud of his proletarian roots, work ethic, and stamina for putting in the necessary long hours. Jill was most content in the moment and wore her Beekman Place heritage like a comfortable old sweater.

They agreed on all of the important things. Both wanted children but not yet. Vacations abroad or in the mountains and never at the beach. Steaks should be rare. Brussels sprouts without bacon were an abomination and inedible. Golf was not a spectator sport. And baseball—Mets baseball in particular—was America's pastime. She was a Mets fan in a family of Yankee worshippers. Ted had grown up a bus ride from Shea Stadium and still refused to wear any garment with pinstripes.

He was a working-class hero, a rebel in a tie, champion of the underprivileged, confident and forthright. What you saw was what you got. Jill had secrets.

A secret.

4

TED WAS SITTING IN his booth at Gallagher's waiting for inspiration or Detective Duran—whichever came first—when a shadow fell across Page Six of the *New York Post*. He looked up in time to see a skyscraper shaped like a man peering in the window, squinting fruitlessly. Gallagher's had been built on that spot in the long ago when privacy and anonymity were prized above all in a neighborhood bar. The lighting, the recessed windows, and the canvas canopy all conspired to make it impossible to identify anyone inside through the window. But when the sun was strong, the reverse was also true. Ted could not make out the facial features of the man glaring so intently. All he could really be sure of was that the guy was bald, white, and big. XXXL plus. Definitely a Big-and-Tall shopper. The giant turned the corner and disappeared from sight. Ted had the impression that the man was not alone, but he was too startled by his size to be sure.

A moment later, a petite woman with hair wound into a towering bun and dyed the color of fresh lemons came through the door. She wore sunglasses that seemed to cover half her face. Even before she saw Ted, he knew she was coming to ruin his day.

"Eddie Molloy?"

The voice was straight out of Astoria. It stabbed through the blather of Fox News emanating from the television over the bar and set his teeth on edge. There are a thousand accents to be heard every day in Queens and very few that could make his sinuses ache in sympathetic rebellion.

"Who's asking?" he said.

She carried a purse the size of a duffel bag over one shoulder, and she let it drop onto the banquette opposite Ted, following it and placing her elbows firmly on the table. "You're him, aren't ya? You're Eddie Molloy."

At the end of the bar, Paulie, too sober this early in the day, began cursing at the television. Lili shushed him and poured him a fresh glass.

"Ted. Edward Molloy to judges and tax collectors. But everyone else calls me Ted."

"Richie called you Eddie."

"Not to my face. Why didn't you ask your friend to come in? Or were you afraid he wouldn't fit through the door?"

"Excuse me? Do I know what you're talking about?"

She was a good liar, but he had caught her by surprise. He'd been right. She knew the giant and didn't want Ted to know that she did. Ted stored this in his mental file labeled "Enigmas" but decided not to press it. "So you knew Richie?"

Lili called across the room, "Youse need anything ovah theh?" She had learned her English in Rego Park. Ted shook his head. The lady wouldn't be staying around long.

"Say what?" the angry blonde said. "I was married to him for ten years." The sunglasses came off, revealing an intelligent face that caught Ted by surprise.

He was, for a moment, speechless. This woman was half Richie's age. When had they married? When she was fifteen? And even with the retro hair and overdone makeup, she was an attractive woman—though definitely *not* Ted's type—and Richie had distinctly not been an attractive man.

"I'm very sorry for your loss," Ted said. "But I have to tell you, Richie never mentioned a wife."

"And?"

"And . . . I don't know. I'm surprised, that's all." The

ancient Ballantine clock over Lili's head—set to bar time, ten minutes fast—showed that noon was approaching. Ted had no idea when the police detective might show up, but he didn't want to be found chatting with the widow of the victim. Cops made assumptions all too easily.

"We didn't always get along, but I want to know what was so friggin' important that some bastid wanted to kill him over it."

"I'm sorry, but what is your name? Or shall I call you Mrs. Rubiano?"

"That's my name. But it's Cheryl. Not Sheryl. Cheryl. Like in 'cherry.'"

"Or 'charming,'" Ted said, hoping to slow her assault.

"Exactly."

"Well, Cheryl, Richie did odd jobs for me. A bit of research at the county clerk's office and the courthouse. That's all."

"So what got him killed then?"

Was she accusing Ted? "Richie made some enemies in his time."

"Yeah, I know all about that. Guy was the worst grifter I ever seen."

"Ah," Ted said, smiling to indicate he was joking. "It's a family business then?"

"You mean me? I'm not bent that way. I got a good job—city government, thank you very much—and benefits. But Richie was done with all that. He quit cold turkey when he partnered up with you."

Ted ignored the misuse of the word "partner" and focused on the subtext. "Forgive me for being dense, but are you implying that Richie's death had anything to do with his work for me?" Though he had entertained the same suspicion, hearing it from another interested party forced Ted into denial.

"Whatta ya talkin'? You two were cooking up a big deal. I know all about it. He told me."

She *was* accusing him. Ted retreated to firmer ground. "Richie searched through court documents for me," he repeated. "I paid him in cash. People don't get killed over what I do."

"Oh yeah? He left me a copy of the file the two of you was working on." She dove into the gargantuan bag and came up with a pristine manila folder that she slapped on the table.

Ted flipped it open. "Ah, no," he said, sighing. Richie had not included the full file, only cover pages for each section, but the first sheet showed $1.2 million in surplus money. It was the elephant. The white buffalo. Moby damn Dick. Ted was not surprised.

"What? This is it, Eddie. This is what you guys were working on. He said you called it an elephant. Huge. You two were going to clear a mil or more out of this. I want my share."

"Have you read this? Do you know what this is?"

Her face twisted into a grimace of distaste. "It's legal stuff."

"Cheryl." Ted paused. How could he make her under-stand? He sighed again and began. "This is nothing. Pixie dust. It is not real. He said he was going to work on it himself. I suggested that he not do that—strongly. I don't take on these kinds of cases for the same reason I don't buy lotto tickets. They're both sucker bets." Ted slid the file in her direction.

She ignored it and tried to stare him down. Ted was immune to this tactic. He'd been stared down by masters. Nonchalance was the best defense. He checked the time on his phone—the real time, not bar time. Ten of twelve.

"What? I'm holding you up? Keeping you from some-thing? My Richie's dead!" The tears began to flow. They were quiet tears, but copious. Her body, a moment before taut with anger, shrank in defeat.

"I don't know what you want from me, Mrs. Rubiano. Richie told you some things that simply don't apply. I'm sorry for you."

"You gotta help me," she said, rallying. The tears were gone, and her body had transformed again. The fireball was back. Ted might have admired her tenacity if he hadn't begun to think she was nuts. One moment all she cared about was the money; the next she was weeping uncontrollably for the dead husband.

"What do you think I can do for you?"

"Get me that money."

"If I thought you would leave me alone, I'd agree to almost anything."

"And you can find out who killed him."

The best way to proceed with crazy people is to stick to facts, speak cautiously, and make no sudden movements. "Actually, that's not something I can do. That's for the police to handle. We should let them take care of that."

"No way. The cops don't care. I talked to one of them. Duran his name was. Guy acted like I did it, fahchrissakes."

And Duran might walk in the door any minute. Ted was starting to wonder whether facing a suspicious police detective might be preferable to continuing this conversation. He tried the direct approach.

"Mrs. Rubiano. Cheryl. That detective is coming here to interview me. If he sees us together, he is going to make some assumptions."

"What assumptions?"

"That's what the police do. It will look bad for both of us. Can you and I talk another time?"

"I know where you live."

It wasn't exactly a threat, but it was close. "I'm not going anywhere."

"That's good, because I want answers. You find who killed him, and I'll pay you for your time outa the money I get from this deal." She slid the file across the table again.

There is no money. The words screamed in his head, but he kept them from spilling out. The path of least resistance was clear. An hour or two of research at the courthouse would give him enough documented facts to convince her of the futility of proceeding further. It would not break a commandment, only bend it.

"Fine. This deal. This one deal. Anything I make off of this, you get half." Negotiation was as much a part of him as his gender. He added, "After expenses."

"Agreed. Now go find who killed Richie."

"Not happening. I'm not a cop."

"You got to."

"Why?" Why wouldn't she just leave?

"'Cause he was your friend."

That was the price of getting her to leave. Ted had to acknowledge Richie Rubiano as a friend. That's what she needed. Then she would go. He would pay the freight. "I'll do what I can. Maybe I do owe him that. But Richie and I worked on a cash basis. No promises. I want to be paid up front. One thousand dollars. In cash." Ted thought he could fend her off with an outrageous demand.

No such luck. Cheryl reached into the bag and pulled out a plain white envelope from which she extracted ten crisp one-hundred-dollar bills. She tucked them into a second envelope, which she pressed into his hand. "Now you work for me."

She'd called his bluff and then some. It felt like a devil's bargain. Already he regretted it. But he crammed the money into a jacket pocket and sealed his fate. "I'll call you next week."

"No way." She took his newspaper and scribbled a phone number across the cartoon of the mayor being pursued by junkyard dogs while a line of real estate developers smiled in approval. "That's my cell. You call me tomorrow. I want daily reports."

He wanted to shake her up, even if only to show he hadn't been bought. "Who's the big guy waiting for you?"

Cheryl stood, hoisted the big bag onto one shoulder, and started for the door. Before she reached it, she turned once more and said, "Tomorrow, Eddie."

"Ted," he said, but the door had already swung shut behind her.

5

DETECTIVE DURAN WAS NOT what Ted expected. He had pictured a balding, overweight middle-aged version of the kids he had known in high school. Trained by Jesuits to be proficient in both obedience and skepticism, they became excellent investigators and administrators.

This broad-shouldered man topped Ted's six-two by an inch or so and appeared to have all his hair. If he carried any excess weight, it didn't show on his chiseled black face.

"Edward Molloy? You still look like your picture." Duran held out a big hand.

There were three images of himself that Ted had found on the Internet: a smiling Ted in the official wedding announcement from the *New York Times* twelve years earlier; an uncertain young man of twenty-five, broad shouldered and lean faced, standing with the half-dozen other new hires at Hasting, Fitzmaurice, and Barson; and a fierce wrestler in a one-piece St. John's uniform, being honored for leading the team with twenty-two falls competing at 165 lbs. in his junior year.

"What picture is that?" Ted asked, taking the proffered hand and giving a brisk shake.

"You were a wrestler."

Ted didn't think he looked much like that boy anymore. He was twenty-five pounds heavier, and the fire in that young man's face had burned out years earlier.

Ted nodded. "A long time ago. Call me Ted. Please." He gestured for the cop to sit.

Duran sank onto the bench opposite. "Okay. Ted."

"You came alone. I'm surprised," Ted said.

The detective waved away the comment. "You are not now a target of this investigation. If that changes, I will be back with my partner and enough uniforms to overwhelm any resistance you might exhibit. Till then." He turned up both hands and raised both eyebrows in an expression of openness and lack of guile. "Now. Tell me about your business dealings with the deceased."

"And then we trade, right? You answer my question."

"Let's see how things go."

Ted described the surplus-money model, making it clear that Richie's part in it had been purely as a researcher in county records. "I paid him twenty-five dollars for every decent lead he brought me. You want that burger now?" He signaled to Lili.

Duran took a menu from behind the salt and pepper. "What's good here?"

"I usually get the pad thai."

Duran gave him a skeptical look.

"Or the burger," Ted said.

"Make mine cheese. Cheddar, if they've got it."

"Two heart-stoppers, Lili," Ted called out. "Medium rare."

Duran pulled the conversation back on track. "Sounds like a sweet deal for you. He does the legwork, and you make a few phone calls. He makes maybe a grand a week, and you get the big payoffs."

"Yes and no. Richie never had the work ethic to bring me forty cases a week—if there were that many to be found, which I very much doubt. And out of those forty good possibilities he found, I'd guess that at best one would lead to any kind of payoff. Most weeks they all turn out to have problems. I'm not the only guy chasing these deals."

"But you make a nice living."

"I'd have trouble getting a new car loan. But it's legal."

"Maybe a bit shady, though."

Ted could tell Duran was pushing buttons, hoping for an

unguarded response, but he didn't like it. "I provide a service. I find people who have been through tough times, and I put some money in their pockets. I can't force people to work with me, but when they do, they walk away happy. It's not altruism on my part, but it's not stealing."

"Suppose Rubiano cut you out of a deal? Maybe he found something juicy and kept it for himself."

This was uncomfortably close to Cheryl's version of reality, but Ted could see no way this might be related to Richie's death. He shrugged. "He was always free to go his own way." Finding possible deals was a boring, repetitive, by-the-book operation. Closing deals was an art.

"But that would have pissed you off."

"No. Richie was a crook. I knew that when he came to work with me."

"But . . ."

"My turn. How did he die?"

Duran paused, feigning to consider whether to answer or not. Ted wasn't impressed with the act. The detective must have been prepared to answer some questions.

"He was shot," Duran said.

The news should have been chilling, but Ted realized that he had expected it. Murder in America. Four out of five assaults involved a gun.

"Do you know the widow?" Duran hunched forward, forcing himself into Ted's space. It was the kind of move the hothead detective on *SVU* always tried when the pace of the interview was getting him frustrated.

Ted wanted to distance himself from Cheryl Rubiano as much as possible without straying too far from the facts. He was well aware that police always looked to the spouse first—and with good reason—but explaining the half-assed plan he had agreed to not ten minutes earlier would clarify nothing. "I didn't know the guy was married until today."

"I asked if you know her."

"We've met. Once. I wouldn't say I *knew* her."

"She's young," the detective said, as though that would be reason enough for Ted to find her attractive. But as it wasn't a question, Ted ignored the comment.

"Did he suffer?" Ted asked.

"I wouldn't think so. When's the last time you saw Cheryl Rubiano?"

The cop knew, or he wouldn't have asked. Or he would have asked differently. *Tell the truth or tell them nothing.* Too many old movie plots hung on an unnecessary lie. "She was here about ten minutes ago. That was the first and only time we spoke. I didn't know there *was* a Mrs. Rubiano until she showed up. Uninvited."

Duran nodded.

"You saw her leave," Ted said.

The detective nodded again.

"Did you see the guy she was with?" Ted asked.

"She walked out of here alone," Duran said.

"He would have been waiting for her." Though this was pure speculation, Ted had a strong feeling that he was right.

"I must have missed him," Duran said, though he made it sound like this was unlikely in the extreme. He was the kind of cop who didn't miss much.

"You missed him? He's the size of an offensive lineman. He's like two of you."

Duran shrugged indifference. "What did you talk about?"

The ten crisp one-hundred-dollar bills in Ted's pocket felt like a signed confession. "Wait up. My turn."

"You wasted your turn. What did you talk about?"

Honesty was one thing, full disclosure something else. The cop could have the truth, but Ted was going to skimp on the portions. "She wants to know who killed her husband."

"And she suspects you?"

"No. For some reason she thinks I can find out who did it. She's delusional. It's grief talking."

"Watch yourself. She's gaming you," Duran said.

"Could be," Ted said. "Explain."

"She has a JD file. Her parents made their living scamming people. She was in court six times before she turned sixteen."

Juvenile Delinquent status was determined by a judge. The arrest and conviction files would have been sealed but available to the police and justice system.

Ted thought back over his conversation with the woman. Certain moments now made more sense. "She claims she's a model citizen."

"If she told me the sun was shining, I'd look up before I took her word for it."

Ted was warned but not alarmed. He would continue to filter anything Cheryl told him.

"She say anything else?" the detective asked.

"It's got to be my turn by now."

Ted could see Duran struggling. The cop didn't like Ted breaking the rhythm of his questions, but he needed cooperation. "One question," he agreed.

"You said on the phone that Richie had other cards on him besides mine. Have you spoken to any of those people? Anyone I might know?"

"I can't answer that."

"First to refuse to answer loses. Sorry. Next contestant."

"Ask me something else."

"You say he was shot. Did he see it coming?"

"The first one, for sure. Two bullets. One in each eye. Twenty-two caliber, heavy grain. Probably subsonic ammunition—it's quieter and more accurate. With a head shot, they tend to go in and not come out. They bounce around in there, turning the brain to soup. The first was sufficient. The second was a message."

Lili dropped two heaping plates on the table. The burgers were the size of two stacked hockey pucks. Lettuce, tomato, two spears of pickle brined in the liquor vault in the basement, and hand-cut fries cooked twice.

"Ketchup? Mustard? Mayo? Hot sauce?" Lili offered.

"Bring 'em on," Duran said.

Ted wasn't hungry anymore. Richie's murder had become real. He couldn't lose the image of two bloody holes where there had once been eyes. And if someone was sending a message, who was the intended recipient?

6

THERE WASN'T A LOT of overhead in Ted's life, either in the business or in his personal affairs. Neither was there much long-term financial security. He had developed a good-sized war chest, but dipping into it to cover expenses violated another of his commandments. Work couldn't wait. There wasn't going to be a wake for Richie—there wouldn't be enough mourners. It was time to move on. Ted needed a new researcher. Also, his promise to Cheryl Rubiano, though made chiefly to get rid of her, was nagging at him. He needed to do something, if only as a sop to his overworked conscience. Stopping by the courthouse would cure a pair of headaches.

The Supreme Court of Queens County soared behind a plaza facing Sutphin Boulevard. While it was the grandest building on the block, with fluted Ionic columns and balustraded balconies, it always seemed to Ted a bit neglected. The scaffolding over the entranceway was a near-permanent fixture, and streaks of grime hung like bats beneath the windows. One or another of the trees planted along the curb always seemed at death's door. Ted tipped the Uber driver in cash and darted across the plaza, avoiding the small crowd of ever-present protestors. Once through the security line, he turned to his left and headed for the records room.

Title insurance investigators were busy on most of the computer terminals, checking lis pendens, mechanic's liens, and any other evidence of potential problems that might affect a real estate closing. They generally worked freelance, and there was no dress code, though the guards at the door fitfully maintained an ever-changing set of arbitrary rules regarding flip-flops, short-shorts, tank tops, and headwear. Most of the workers were younger than Ted by a decade or more; it was piecework and the burnout rate was high.

He was looking for someone a little older, maybe down on his luck, but also someone with a functioning brain. Twenty years of staring at screens and checking real estate records might take the shine off the brightest apple.

And then Ted saw the recruit. The man was hanging back, not engaged with the screens, though from his interactions with the others, it was obvious he was a regular. Unlike the younger investigators, he wore a jacket, tie, and dress shirt that might once have been white. He was dressed for a job interview, Ted decided. A slope-shouldered black man in his late forties. Greying. His pants pressed but shiny. Comfortable shoes. Slip-ons. Scuffed up. Ted edged up to him.

"You've got the air of someone who knows his way around here."

The man looked Ted in the eyes when he answered. "I've worked title if that's what you're asking." The man had more self-confidence than Ted had expected. There was a touch of attitude in his reply. Ted liked that.

"I'm looking to hire somebody, and I don't have the time or inclination to train him from the ground up."

"I know you," the man said. "You're the money guy who was teamed up with Richie Rubiano. I knew Richie. Everybody's been talking about what happened."

Ted processed this. He had no problem hiring a crook, as long as the man got the job done. But he wanted all the bad news up front. He started slowly. "You were friends?"

"Nah. He wasn't a bad guy, but he kept to himself. A scammer is always waiting to be scammed."

Good answers. Ted relaxed. A little. "He served time."

"Never been there myself, but I don't hold it against a man. Is it a job requirement? Because I'm afraid I'm going to disappoint you."

Ted liked him. "What's your name?"

"Lester. Lester Young McKinley. My father knew him."

Ted was confused. "Your father knew Richie?"

The man looked insulted. "No. He knew Lester Young. That's who I'm named for. He knew all those guys. I have a letter he got from Nat King Cole congratulating him when I was born."

Ted had heard of the Lester guy, but everybody knew Nat King Cole. He did that Christmas album. But Ted now revised his estimate of the man's age up a decade. Cole had been dead for fifty years or more. "Was your father a musician?"

"No. He sold sheet music. He worked at Colony in the city. On Broadway? It's gone now. Worked there his whole life almost. He's long gone now, too."

Ted was now close enough to notice the combined scents of breath mint and vodka coming off the man. "And you? You work here?"

"I'm semiretired. On a disability. I pick up a little of this and that here. I know the drill."

"Are you interested in doing a little of this and that for me?"

"I don't know the kinds of cases you look for, but I'm a quick study. I know the system. It can't be that much different than doing title. Am I right?"

"Let me walk you through it, and then we'll see if we can cut a deal." The whole exchange had been a touch too easy. Lester had been waiting to be found. Not merely for any job but for this one. Ted reminded himself to be cautious until he was entirely sure of the man.

"Sounds like a plan," Lester said.

They pulled a pair of chairs over in front of an empty computer kiosk. The banks of florescent lights overhead washed out colors so that the ancient green screen appeared a matte black. Ted walked his recruit through the first stages of identifying a potential surplus-money case. Lester took notes and seemed to catch on quickly. Ted used the Barbara Miller property to demonstrate so that the next time he had to speak to Cheryl Rubiano he could truthfully say he had looked into the matter.

The glacial pace of justice flicked across the screen at speed. *Motion. Motion Answered. Judgment. Appeal.* And so on through to Sent to Auction. It took only a few minutes more to reach the bottom line. *Surplus.*

"Sweet Jesus, that's a lot of money," Lester said when the number appeared on the screen. *$1,200,000.*

"This case is not my usual thing," Ted said. "It's big, for one thing. And I don't believe in big for its own sake. But it'll do for training purposes. You'll pick up my likes and dislikes. I'm not picky, but I am particular."

"But anybody can just come along and claim this?"

"No," Ted said. "That money belongs to someone. In this case, this Miller lady, if she's alive."

"So how do *you* get paid?"

"More research. I track down the person who's owed that money and convince that poor soul to pay me a cut for getting him or her some cash he or she didn't even know was there. Once I've got their signature on paper, I petition the court for release of funds and wait. It takes about six months for the judge to sign off and the checks to get cut."

"You get the court to hand over the money? You're a lawyer?" Lester asked.

"No." Ted still hated answering that question, and he got it all the time. "I used to practice, and if you ask around, someone will tell you why I don't anymore. But no. I write up the contracts, the petition to release the funds, all of that, but I'm not a lawyer. My landlord is a lawyer. He also does my taxes. I pay him a few bucks to file the paperwork, and if he has to show up in court, I pay him a few bucks more, though I usually show up with him."

"Sweet. You're a fixer. A finder. What's the catch? There's got to be one; it's too easy."

"Right," Ted said. "The catch is that a lot of people don't want to be found or can't be found, or when I find them, they tell me to get lost or just say 'Thanks' and go get the money on their own."

"But you must do all right."

Ted could see that the million plus was still having an effect on Lester. A change in venue was in order.

"Let's take a break." After a half hour hunched over the terminal, Ted needed to stretch—and he wasn't about to share his financial status with this stranger. "We'll meet down in the file room in ten minutes. Next thing we need to do is get the case file. The physical file. It'll tell us who all the players are and whether I have a chance of getting paid."

Ted made a quick trip to the bathroom and stopped at the water fountain when he came out. He was bent over swallowing cool water when a tall woman with severely cut blonde hair walked out of the women's restroom six feet away. She strode past quickly—impatiently—without taking notice of him. But Ted recognized her, his whole body tensing. Jacqueline Clavette. She hated being called Jackie. The woman who was married to his ex-wife. She had survived the firm's purge years ago—the purge that had none too gently ushered Ted out the door. The first step in his fall. She still worked there, handling estates, trusts, and real estate. Her wedding four years earlier had made the front page of the Style section in the Sunday *New York Times*. JACKIE AND JILL, had run the banner over the picture of the two women holding hands while posing in front of Turtle Pond in Central Park with Belvedere Castle in the background. Both brides wore white. Both were stunning.

Ted watched her disappear down the hall. There was no reason to be surprised at her presence in the courthouse; she was a lawyer, one of scores, no doubt, in the building at that moment. But seeing her there while he was researching a case that had her name on it felt like more than happenstance. At some point, if he was going to continue following this case, he would have to have a conversation with her. The thought threatened to give him a migraine.

Jackie Clavette was a tough, infighting opponent. He'd seen her in action. He needed to know a good bit more before confronting her.

7

TED BEAT LESTER TO the file room by a long five minutes. Lester smelled like he had spent at least part of his break sucking on another breath mint. As it turned out, there was no reason to hurry. The line at the counter was barely moving, and the clerks seemed slower than usual.

"Hey, people! Listen up, everybody. I'm gonna say it again. No more than three case files per request. We are shorthanded today—everybody gets the flu on the same day for some reason." The speaker was a bearded clerk who must have weighed in at 350 plus.

"They're supposed to let you take five at a time, but it's not worth pushing it," Ted said. "The clerks will never be your friends, but it's very easy to become their enemy."

Lester nodded. "I've dealt with them before."

"So you know." Ted was becoming more comfortable with the decision to have Lester work for him. The man was quick and confident.

Ted filled out the request form with name, address, and the case file number, and they shuffled along together as lawyers, litigants, and investigators of all stripes took the blue-covered files from the clerks and retired to the long tables to examine them. The records of every civil case in the borough were held in this room. If you were suing, being sued, divorcing, or representing a party involved in any of the above, you could find all the pertinent details here. A cross section of the demographics of Queens was present, some people with hope, some with desperation, and many with boredom.

When these dogged searchers found, or despaired of finding, the nuggets of information hidden in these court reports, they dropped the files into a wire box at the end of the counter where another clerk returned them to the stacks. No files left the room unless a judge requested them. Two guards sat on stools at the door checking briefcases as people exited. The process was neither efficient nor satisfying. It had not been designed to be either. The stacks were a cemetery for hopes, dreams, disputes, mistakes, and failures. A museum of unhappy events that, more often than not, had left some poor soul in tears.

Finally, Lester and Ted were first at the counter.

"Edward Molloy. Do I know you?" the bearded man asked, reading the top line on the request form, beginning the foot-dragging dance of the practiced bureaucrat.

"Everybody knows me," Ted said, handing over his driver's license. "I used to date Paris Hilton."

Lester leaned in and whispered conspiratorially: "Ask him about the tattoo."

The bearded face scrunched up in distaste. "That's okay," the clerk said. "I'll pass. Wait here." He made a note of Ted's driver's license number and lumbered off to retrieve the file.

"Tattoo?" Ted asked.

"First thing that came into my head," Lester said with a shrug.

"Well, it got him moving."

"All part of the service."

The clerk was back in two minutes.

"File's out," he said, handing back the form.

"Really?" Ted was surprised. "Can you see if it's signed out to a judge?" If a judge had requested the file, it could mean that someone else was already working the surplus-money angle. He needed to see the file to be sure, but there would be no urgency. Judges and their clerks could sit on files for months—or years—with no repercussions.

"We're a little busy, my friend," the clerk said.

"If it's out to someone here in the room, we'll wait for it."

The man blew out an aggrieved sigh, causing his whiskers to flutter in sympathy. "Give me a minute to look it up."

Ted explained to Lester, "Sometimes the judge's clerk requests a file for one reason or another. Usually not on a case that's already gone to auction, though. That would be unusual unless—someone has beaten us to this one. We wait and see."

The clerk returned with a thin blue folder. "Got it. Someone must have just turned it in."

Ted turned to see who was leaving the room. Two black-frocked Hasidim were being given the full treatment by the guards. A young woman in jeans and a Mets jersey waited her turn. None of them looked familiar. Ted realized that the person he was looking for might already be long gone; the clerks were running well behind.

He took the file to a table, surprised at how thin it felt—and soon found out why.

"Look at this!" Someone had sliced out page after page from the court record. He ran a finger over the cut. It was sharp and fresh. Razor sharp. You couldn't get a knife past the metal scanners at the entrance, but a small, thin blade might pass if it were tucked into a briefcase. The guards upstairs looked for weapons, not miniature tools.

The damage was not random. The court record of motions and proceedings had been gutted. It was impossible to determine from the remaining pages what the main points of contention had been in the case—if any. The names of all participants, other than the presiding judge, the plaintiff, and the defendant, were gone. The Honorable M. Mandel, *New York Bank v. Barbara Miller*. No lawyers for either side. No information at all. What was left was a cover sheet, a description of the properties involved, and a copy of the tax map for the area with some scribbled numbers in one corner.

"Someone sat right here in the records room, with a couple

of dozen lawyers surrounding him, two uniformed guards and who knows how many other citizens looking over his shoulder, and took a razor blade to this whole file."

Lester's face did not register the same outrage that Ted felt. Lawyers, even the defrocked ones, maintained a reverence for documents that was not always shared by other members of society.

"This is wrong," Ted said. The arrogance of the act floored him. Distracted him.

"I can see there's pages missing, but what's left must tell you something," Lester said.

"Yes," Ted said, forcing patience. "Only it's bare bones. I can see that this woman, Barbara Miller, was sued for non-payment of taxes by New York Bank, the proxy for the city. What we don't see is who represented her, what motions they made, the judge's rulings, and all the meat that might explain why Miss Miller lost her property."

"This is that thing Richie was all in a lather over?"

There were other copies of the file. The lawyers for the bank would have a complete record. It wouldn't require much more research to find out who they were, but they would never hand over a file containing client information to Ted. That left only the lawyer for this Miller lady. And the one thing Ted remembered from his momentary glance at Richie's copy of the file was the name Jacqueline Clavette. And he had just seen her leaving the building.

The vandalism was bizarre. Criminal. Was he being played? Conned somehow? The thought that finding Lester had been much too easy—too perfect—came again.

"He was working this on his own," Ted said. "What are you thinking?"

Lester shrugged again. "People talk. Everybody knew Richie was on to something big."

Lester was holding back—Ted could feel it. He looked

down at the useless papers and slammed the folder shut. "Hand this in. We're out of here."

The bottom line was that Ted was in violation of his own rule. The big ones were always a waste of time.

Lester put a hand on his arm. "Hold up. We can't turn in the file like this. You've got to report it."

Ted stood. "I want nothing to do with this. This case was bogus from the get-go. It's cursed."

"You have to report it. Otherwise you're the last one to have the file. If somebody else takes it out, you get the blame."

Ted sat down again. Lester was right and had saved him from possible embarrassment—at the least. A fine and a harangue from an outraged judge would have been equally as likely. "Of course. Thank you." Ted relaxed, his fears of Lester's true intentions fading—for the moment.

"Yup. Be cool. Go up there and complain, but don't get up in their faces about it. See if you can find out who had the file last."

Ted thought it through. There might be a way to finesse it. "And what will you be doing?"

"I'll see what I can get out of the guards. We can meet up outside."

The heavy bearded man wasn't at the counter when Ted stepped up, cutting the line and braving the outraged looks. A harried-looking woman in a turtleneck and winged eyeglasses gave Ted the kind of scrutiny made to make a mendicant feel like a sinner. It worked. He considered abandoning the plan and simply leaving the file in the returns box.

"Watcha got, hon?" Having won the stare down, she softened ever so slightly.

He showed her the butchered file. "The other guy gave me this a couple of minutes ago. Who would have vandalized records this way? Who had it out last?"

"Oh, jeezy-peezy. I don't have time for this today." She turned away and shouted over the filing cabinets: "Hey, Jimbo! Get out here. We got a problem."

The bearded face appeared around the end of an aisle. "What?"

"Come look at this!"

"What?"

"I said come heah!" The accent may have been Queens, but the authority was regal.

The man shuffled up to the counter. "What?"

"Show 'im," the woman ordered.

Ted held out the damaged file.

"What's this?" Jimbo asked.

"You just gave me this file," Ted said. "Look at it. I want to know who had this out last. This is obscene."

Jimbo turned to the other clerk. "I didn't let this go out this way"

"Oh, for the love of Pete. Go find the paperwork." She faced Ted and fake smiled a brush-off. "Thank you for bringing this to our attention. We'll take care of it."

Ted took a strengthening breath and fake smiled in return. "I'd like to know who was responsible." The line behind him was beginning to grow again.

"We don't give out that information," the woman said. "Who's next?"

He was saved by the return of the bearded clerk, who held a stack of request forms. "Give me a minute. It'll be in here."

The woman's attention was split between dealing with Ted and the twentysomething title investigator with an eyebrow ring and studs in his cheek. She glared in frustration while Jimbo sifted the forms.

"Here it is," Jimbo said, pulling one out and placing it on the counter.

She shot a hand out and covered it. "I'm sorry, sir," she said, stressing the last word to remind him who was in charge. "I told you, we do not give out that information."

But Ted had already read—upside down—the name on the file request form: Barbara Miller.

- 8 -

"WHAT DID YOU FIND?" Lester was waiting in the hall outside.

Ted didn't want to talk there. He was spooked. "Let's get outside first." He needed space to think. It wasn't merely the vandalism that had him reeling; it was the audacity of it and what that might mean in terms of scope. Someone had taken a great risk, one that could be easily discovered, if not connected to the perpetrator. That someone was protected. And protection meant power.

Lester took the lead going up the stairs, climbing them two steps at a time. Ted followed, matching his urgency as they sped out past the police and metal detectors in silence. The small group of protestors on the sidewalk chanted, "Keep the light! Kill the spike!" They carried signs: STOP THE TOWER. An earnest young woman with a wild mane of red hair blocked Ted's way and thrust a flyer at him.

"The developers are at it again, and we are the ones who will pay. Your neighbors are being evicted to make room for luxury condos. Again!" She was fired up and speaking much too fast, but she had a voice like a young Lauren Bacall. Or Barbara Stanwyck. Ted almost stopped to hear her say something else. A voice like that worked directly on the more primitive parts of his brain.

He forced himself to keep going. Beautiful women were a distraction at the least and potentially dangerous. He stuffed the flyer in his pocket.

"Hey. Where're you going?" she asked.

"Sorry, I don't speak English." Her mouth dropped open. He stepped by her before she could close it. "Let's go, Lester." Ted took his elbow and propelled him down Sutphin Boulevard.

"If you're not part of the solution," she yelled after him, "you're part of the problem!"

A bodega near the corner was doing a good business in Powerball tickets. A half-dozen believers were queued up for the window on the street. The faces, though ranging in color from pale white through various shades of tan and brown to deep black, all shared the same expression—stony acceptance of defeat combined with the anxiety of hope. Ted passed them and pulled Lester aside outside a stationery store that specialized in LEASES, DEEDS, WILLS, LEGAL FORMS.

"Where did you come from?" Ted asked, pushing Lester back against the building. "Who the hell sent you to me?" Ted didn't know exactly what to believe at that point, but finding Lester was no coincidence.

"Take your hands off me," Lester said, though after the initial push, Ted had kept his hands at his sides.

"Answer me," Ted said, leaning in and over the smaller man.

"Nobody. I heard about this deal Richie was working, and I wanted in. That's it."

"Who tipped you to it?"

"Are you kidding? Richie bragged to anyone who would listen. He was finally hitting a homer, he said."

Ted backed off. It made perfect sense. That was exactly what Richie would have done; he had always talked a better game than he played. And Lester? Ted couldn't blame him for having the balls to insinuate himself once Richie was gone.

And Lester had already shown he had potential. Ted needed him. He made a decision.

"I'll pay a hundred a day—that's a lot more than Richie ever cleared—and if there is a payout at the end of this, I'll see you get a cut. Don't ask me how much, because I don't want you wasting time calculating it in your head. Odds are, we work this and end up with nothing. Are we good?"

"You pay expenses."

Ted smiled. Exactly what he had told Cheryl. "Agreed."

"We're good," Lester said. He stepped away from the wall and shrugged the tension out of his neck and shoulders. "And one thing. You don't ever put hands on me again. Clear?"

"Clear. Let's walk."

They hustled toward Hillside Avenue, Lester matching Ted's longer strides.

"The file's a dead end. It was signed out to Barbara Miller. She's in her nineties. I very much doubt that she was down in the records room today destroying her own case file."

Lester nodded. "I talked to the guards. They said anybody could walk out with a bunch of loose pages. All they check for is the blue folder. And I don't think they're too careful about that either. They ask to look in briefcases, backpacks, and bags, but anyone could tuck a case file down their pants and walk out with it."

"Whoever did this was smart. She must have used Barbara Miller's ID. If we hadn't shown up, that file would have gone into the stacks with nobody checking it. It might never have been discovered."

"You'd think all those records would be scanned and kept online," Lester said.

A semi with a long trailer was trying to make the turn and had traffic blocked in all directions. Lester marched into the intersection, holding up one hand to part the waters. Ted stayed close on his heels. Whatever juju was keeping Lester from getting run over might not extend to a lagging follower.

"Where we going?" Lester asked when they had landed safely on the far corner.

"Down the block," Ted said, pointing toward a strip of storefronts. "It's always about money. Property records are all online because there's real money involved. Civil case proceedings? Nobody cares. That's why I'm able to make a buck at this. If it was all on the web, anybody could do it."

"Are those the only records? No copies?"

"The lawyers would keep files," Ted said.

"How do we get a look at them, then?"

Ted imagined calling Jacqueline Clavette and begging to dig through her files. "Not gonna happen."

"So what will you do?"

He weighed the question. He owed no one a thing. Not Cheryl, not the cop, and not Richie. He could walk away and feel no responsibility. That was the smart move. But someone had taken a big chance just to hide information. He had a strong urge to kick the hornet's nest.

"We follow the money."

9

THEY TOOK A TABLE in the Dominican restaurant on Hillside. It was early for the lunch crowd; the waiter was setting tables. Ted ordered coffee. Lester asked for a screwdriver.

"Just a little something for the arthritis. And go easy on the OJ. I've got to watch my sugar."

Ted opened his iPad and began to search. "Give me the address on one of Miller's properties. Any one. Or block and lot if it's there."

Lester checked the tax map and read off the block and lot. Ted typed in the information and waited.

"What are we looking for?" Lester scooched his chair around so that he could see the screen.

"Recent sales. We start with ACRIS. New York City property records. I know it usually takes you title guys a month or more to get the paperwork in and another month or two for the clerks to enter it into the system. But I'm betting that with a project this large they streamlined the process."

They had. Records for the property went back over a hundred years. Barbara Miller was listed as the owner beginning in 1974 on a deed transfer. She had inherited the property. Prior to that, there were other Millers, all men. The most recent transactions, though, were the forced foreclosure sales to an LLC that went by the name of Corona Partners, followed three months later by a purchase by the LBC Development Corporation, a wholly owned subsidiary of La Bella Casa Hotels, itself a division of LBC International, Inc.—the same LBC whose initials were stamped on controversial developments all over Queens.

"There's something missing," Lester said. "The seller doesn't match."

Ted stopped and checked. Lester was right. The ultimate seller was not Corona but a blind, a cutout—One-Hun-dred-Fourteenth-Street LLC. The practice of hiding ownership was not illegal as long as it wasn't used to evade the taxman or to operate an illegal enterprise. There were legitimate reasons for developers to keep their interest hidden from competitors, and that could have been the case in this instance. But Ted didn't buy it. His faith in the basic goodness of man did not extend to real estate devel-opers. "So who are they? And why hasn't Corona posted the sale?"

"That's an easy one," Lester said. "Corona owes the transfer tax. They don't have to pay until they post the sale. They'll want to take their time."

The drinks arrived. The vodka and orange juice was as pale as winter sun. Lester downed it in two swallows.

"They can only put it off for so long," Ted said. He waved away the waiter's offer of cream and sugar.

"Right. But these guys are flippers. One or one and a half percent paid out every month or so starts to add up."

"Run this by me again," Ted said.

"They never hold a property very long. The transfer tax is owed on every sale, no matter how long you hold it. If they turn over properties once a month or so, they're paying fifteen percent in taxes—on the same capital. That's a hefty bite. So they only file when they're flush with cash."

Ted was impressed that Lester understood this much about Corona and their business. "You know them? These Corona Partners?"

"I don't know them. But I know the name. They're at the auctions every week. They're lowballers. They only bid when there's no legitimate buyers, and they never pay a dollar more than rock bottom. I doubt they own anything for longer than a month or two. It's all about turnover."

"They paid up this time," Ted said. "There's a million-two in surplus money."

"I find it hard to believe that Corona Partners left a million-two on the table. Not those guys."

"How do we find them?" Ted asked. "It can't hurt to ask."

"They should have someone at the auctions on Friday."

"Then we'll be there, too."

10

TED JOINED THE LINE of blue-and-orange-clad fans shuffling toward the gate at Citi Field. He didn't bother trying to find Jill in the melee; she would already be in her seat watching batting practice, her program open, with freshly sharpened number two pencils at the ready, one tucked behind each ear.

"Will you step this way, sir?" The wand-bearing security officer flagged Ted and waved him to the side. Again. Ted could not imagine what profile he matched that got him tagged for extra treatment as often as he was. Possibly it was the fact that he always arrived at the gate sober that made him stand out.

"Are you carrying any liquids?" the officer asked. "Knives, firearms, or other weapons?"

Ted held up a half-empty bottle of seltzer.

The guard took it and dropped it into a plastic tub. "Any other liquids?"

Ted thought of this as the IQ portion of the test. If you were carrying any of the things on the list, why would you admit it?

He raised his arms in crucifixion pose and waited for the burly man to finish his examination. Why did a security officer need to wear a bulletproof vest under his jacket to keep rowdy teenagers from sneaking in bottles of strawberry-flavored vodka? Confrontations with arbitrary authority often left Ted with such questions.

"Go right ahead, sir," the officer said. "Thank you."

"You're welcome," Ted answered without thinking. He swiped his ticket at the turnstile and passed through.

THE VENERABLE FIRM OF Hasting, Fitzmaurice, and Barson had been simultaneously generous and controlling in its treatment of first-year associates. In addition to such amenities as a personal shopper, livery-cab commuting, and free dinners delivered from an approved list of top steak houses and sushi restaurants for anyone forced to work after 8 P.M., the firm had offered gratis season tickets at Yankee Stadium. As a Mets fan and Yankee hater, Ted acted out his rebellion against this political arm-twisting by using a small portion of his signing bonus—earmarked by most new hires for appropriate Brooks Brothers attire—for the purchase of two season tickets for the Mets at Shea Stadium. Why two tickets? Blind optimism.

That spirit paid off wildly when he discovered that Jill was also a rabid fan, the sole heretic in that clan of Yankee worshippers. He and Jill were married eighteen months later. Ted did not propose via the scoreboard, but Jill wouldn't have minded if he had.

"HELLO, DARLING. I BOUGHT you a beer." Jill held up a tall plastic cup.

Ted squeezed into his seat and swapped a cardboard tray for the drink. "And I've got the hot dogs." Nathan's—despite the recent competition, the best tube steaks offered.

They preferred the bleacher seats to the boxes along the baselines, which were packed with lawyers, stockbrokers, bond traders, and the technology gurus from Long Island City. Ted had chosen the left-field section, where they could enjoy the antics of the 7 Line Army without being in among them. The Army was more entertaining at a slight distance.

"I'm glad you could make it," Ted said. Jill managed to join him for eight or ten games each season. Thanks to his lack of any structured schedule, Ted made it to more than twice as many.

"I've been abandoned. Jacqueline left for Albany this morning."

"Oh? I thought she was at the courthouse out here this morning." He felt only a touch of guilt at using Jill's friendship to snoop on her partner's whereabouts.

Jill shrugged. "Maybe. She's never been so busy."

"How's she doing? Are they ever going to make her partner?" The firm had had only two female partners when Ted was there—neither of them openly gay. Ms. Clavette had survived the demise of the Commercial Real Estate department by accepting a reassignment to Trust and Estate. Ted had not been offered a berth. He'd been shown the door.

"I hope so. This thing she's working on now might get her there."

"Then she must be branching out from estate and trust work." T&E was a service department, not a profit center. Partners were rarely chosen from its ranks.

"This is some big real estate deal she brought in. And why are you so interested in Jacqueline tonight?"

"Who's pitching?" Ted said, trying evasion over admission.

"The rookie. He's two and one. Throws nothing but heat. And why are you asking me about Jacqueline?"

"He needs a sinker," Ted said.

"Francesa said they've got him working on it. Are you deliberately not answering me, or have you gone deaf?"

"You're relentless, you know that?"

"And proud of it," she said with a grin.

"I might have to give her a call. Our paths converged. Something that I'm working on."

"I don't know if she'll take your call. If a partner found out she was talking to Edward Molloy, she could get her butt kicked."

Ted knew that if he asked Jill to intercede, she would. They may have failed at marriage, but they were friends. He had precious few of those, and so he did not ask.

"Do you want me to ask her? I don't know if she would do it, even for me, but I can try."

He felt himself capitulating to her kindness. A mistake. Their relationship depended on two things—giving and forgiving as much as possible and taking only what was absolutely necessary.

"I didn't offer lightly, my dear," she said. "If you want my help, you've got it."

"No," he said. "I'll call her. If she won't talk to me, I'll drop it."

"I'll give you her cell phone. Not the firm's phone. Hers."

"You want another hot dog? I'm buying."

"If that's a thank-you, I'll take it," she said.

"Thank you. Now, do you want the dog?"

"No. I want the short rib grilled cheese sandwich from Pressed."

"Will do." Ted rarely took advantage of the fact that Citi Field had possibly the best food court anywhere on the planet. When they served Nathan's in a ballpark, his epicurean needs were fulfilled. Jill, however, reveled in the diversity.

"And another beer."

"All that for a telephone number?"

"Are you going by Box Frites?"

"And fries? Aioli sauce?"

"Hurry back. First pitch is in four minutes."

11

THEY LET THE FLOW of the crowd carry them out of the park. The night had grown cool.

"Do you know that guy?" Jill asked once they'd reached the parking lot.

As Jill had failed to indicate which guy out of the thousands streaming by them, Ted asked the obvious: "Who?"

She looked over her shoulder. "Now he's gone. Which is weird, because he's big. Monument big."

Ted didn't see anyone who fit that description or anywhere such a person could have hidden. "What did he look like?"

"I can't believe you didn't see him. He was sitting in the next section, and he kept staring at you instead of the game."

Ted flashed back to the man outside of Gallagher's. The giant who he was sure had accompanied Cheryl. He scanned the crowd again. "Why didn't you say anything then?"

"Because he wasn't creepy until he followed us outside."

There were any number of "big" people around but none who qualified as monument sized. And none who appeared to be paying any attention to Ted or Jill.

"Maybe he was just walking to the nearest exit," he said. "Like everybody else here."

Jill dismissed the possibility—and the subject—with a toss of her hair. "Can I drop you somewhere?"

Jill always asked and Ted always refused. Usually he took the 7 train to Broadway, where he could grab a gypsy cab. It beat sitting in a Town Car waiting to get out of the parking lot for half an hour or paying blackmail rates to an Uber driver. But that night Ted had a different plan. He wanted to see the site of the planned La Bella Casa tower, to walk those streets, and to get a feel for what the project would mean to the community. And maybe find a clue to understanding how and why Barbara Miller had let her real estate portfolio drift away.

"I need to stretch my legs," he answered. "Can you get away again anytime soon? Tomorrow?"

She scrunched her face into a show of disappointment. "Not likely and definitely not tomorrow—Jacqueline's back tomorrow, and I hate to push it. She does not approve of our shared passion for baseball."

"Your wife does not approve of *me*," Ted said.

"True," Jill said with a sad smile. "But call me."

He did not point out, as he had many times before, that phone calls could be made in both directions. "I will. Give my regards to the family."

She rolled her eyes in response. Wasn't going to happen.

Citi Field sits a few blocks north of Flushing Meadows Corona Park, an expanse larger than Manhattan's Central Park but only a third the size of Pelham Bay Park across the East River. The park is the showpiece of Queens, with facilities for a wide variety of sports, both professional and amateur. It is surrounded, bisected, and overlooked by highways and subway and railroad lines. The remaining structures from the 1964 World's Fair, still standing, though showing some signs of age and neglect—a mammoth globe, the pavilion, a skating rink, and the odd mushroom-shaped towers—are features deliciously out of time.

Ted saw Jill safely into the chauffeured Town Car and gave a short wave before walking out of the lot. Roosevelt Avenue crossed over the Grand Central Parkway with the occasional train rattling overhead, drowning out the honking horns of disgruntled drivers heading home. He found himself sharing the sidewalk with a mixed group of tired fans—all men or teenage boys, all smiling in the wake of an unexpected win.

From snatches of conversations he overheard, he thought there had to be three or four continents and a dozen countries represented, all on a ten-foot length of New York sidewalk.

Suddenly the group slowed. Just ahead walked a group of four young male Asian Americans—Vietnamese, he guessed—all speaking English with heavy Latino accents. They wore team jerseys and flat-brimmed ball caps and took up all of the sidewalk and then some. Despite the fact that they were moving in a slow, exaggerated saunter, none of the other homeward-bound fans made any move to get around them. Ted hung back. The four guys didn't act threatening—they seemed to be in quite good spirits—but this was not his neighborhood, and he had no wish to break some cultural taboo or do something that could be interpreted as disrespect.

It wasn't fear—it was good judgment.

The young men sauntered into the bar on the corner, and the group's pace returned to normal.

The first block after 114th Street held a mix of commercial and residential buildings. The streetlights and the store signs made the sidewalk almost as bright as in day. There were car repair shops, a church, two hotels, and a group of three-story multifamilies. Ted stopped in the middle of the block, letting the straggling crowd pass by, and stood with his back up against the front of the church.

Queens was his home. He had abandoned it for the celestial promises of Manhattan, but it had taken him back when his flame had sputtered out and he had fallen to earth. That was practically the definition of home. The place that had to take you in. He had no living family, no particular childhood friends who would welcome him, and yet, it was home. But as he stood there contemplating the view across the way, Ted realized that he had never seen this neighborhood before. He'd walked through it on his way to somewhere else, but he had never taken the time to really look. Queens, more than any other borough, is a collection of disparate communities. Though it is a stew of cultures, each maintains an individual identity. Geographic lines are fluid, but Hollis and Howard Beach could be separated by light-years for all the contact between them.

The proposed development project would be to the south. Ted tried to gauge how high one hundred stories would look. Impossible to tell. And didn't all developers lie about the number of stories? Trump Tower on Fifth skipped a dozen floors. He'd read of a fifty-six-story building in Hong Kong where the penthouse was listed as the eighty-eighth floor because the number eight was considered lucky. Yet that seemed no more unusual than omitting the thirteenth floor in American high-rises. Number of floors was a poor measure of height. The new residential high-rise on Park was 150 feet taller than the Empire State Building but was listed as having fourteen fewer stories.

There was a tall chain-link fence on the far side of the street where someone had attached a four-by-eight color poster. Despite its size, Ted couldn't make out anything but the banner across the top: SPIKE THE SPIRE. He waited for a break in the traffic and dashed across.

The poster was lit by streetlamps that turned every reflective surface into a mirror. It took his eyes a moment to adjust. There was a second line of letters, smaller than the first, below the main message: CITIZENS UNITED FOR SUSTAINABLE GROWTH. A few sentences of print followed. He scanned the paragraph without really reading it, taking in the stock phrases "rampant overdevelopment," "environmental impact statement," "community dislocation," and others. The banner ran along the top of an artist's rendering of the proposed LBC project.

Painted from a street point of view, the building looked menacing, stretching upward into a dark grey cloud. He stepped back for a different perspective and tried to fit the image into the skyline. One World Trade would still be taller, but there was an elegance to the varied planes of that structure. This thing, on the other hand, was to be a series of cubes set atop one another, diminishing slightly at regular intervals but overall a mass so great it would have its own gravity field. The structure wasn't ugly—nor was it distinctive for anything other than size—but it would be an eyesore from any angle. It would be taller than everything east of Manhattan and located in a borough where the overwhelming majority of structures were one to three stories tall. Air traffic to LaGuardia was already routed away from this area, but controllers would have to take the building into account in emergency situations. The influx of vehicular traffic would make the streets impassable. The increase in number of residents would overwhelm current police, fire, sanitation, schools, and public transportation. The sheer arrogance of the project was impressive.

"Tower of Babel," the man said in a hoarse voice, rhyming the last word with cable or label. This was a first for Ted. In his experience, native New Yorkers—and most transplants— pronounced the word to sound like rabble or babble. Or Babylon, for that matter, the last express stop on the Long Island Railroad before the Hamptons.

He looked over his shoulder. It took a moment to find the dark shape huddled against the subway pillar. The shadow emerged into the light and took form.

The man was impossibly thin, dressed in a long dark over-coat more appropriate for January than May. His skin was mottled, and his hair was covered by a ragged grey knit watch cap. A long grey beard, surprisingly well-groomed, cascaded down his chest. On his feet he wore tattered boat shoes, the toes wrapped in duct tape, the backs broken down flat so that he shuffled as though wearing slippers.

"Do you know your Bible?" the man asked.

Tower of Babel. Ted knew the story. Twenty-some years of

Catholic education had not been wasted on him, but he had spent more time studying the Acts than Genesis. "I'm more of a New Testament guy," he said.

"The Lord punished the people for their arrogance. They tried to build a tower to heaven, and he destroyed them by creating different languages, so that when they spoke, they couldn't understand each other."

"I remember something about Nimrod," Ted said.

"An arrogant king."

Ted didn't remember that part. "A mighty hunter?"

"The god of the Hebrews will return and stop this abomination. Look around you here. The confusion of tongues has already begun."

"Yeah, well, I think that's been going on for quite a while now."

The man straightened to his full height and glared angrily. His hands became apple-sized fists. As Ted was a full head taller and at least thirty years younger than the man, the effect was more comedic than threatening.

"Ron Reisner is the devil!" the man bellowed.

"You'll get no argument from me."

Somewhat mollified, the man relaxed his stance and took a step closer. "You carry a world of troubles, son. Lay down your load."

"Are you a preacher?" Ted asked.

"One does not need to be ordained to see the light."

Ted needed a guide. "You know the neighborhood?"

"My flock."

There was no profit in being coy. Ted plunged ahead. "How about a lady named Barbara Miller?"

"The name is not unusual."

"She owned property on the next block."

"I don't know her, but I can introduce you to people here who might. Why do you seek her?"

"She's owed some money. I'd like to see she gets it. I can make it worth your while."

The man shook his head in disbelief. "There is more to that story."

Ted nodded in agreement. "And I plan on taking a cut. That's what I do."

"An honest thief."

"Maybe. Maybe I'm only a mercenary."

"Meet with me tomorrow morning, and I will introduce you to some of the people I watch over."

Ted handed him a twenty. "Eleven o'clock all right?"

He took the bill reluctantly. "I don't ask for handouts."

"It's not a handout. It's payment in advance for services rendered. If this pans out, there will be more."

"It will go to a good cause."

Ted hoped that meant the man was going to get a hot meal rather than a cold drink.

Uber would be backed up taking Mets fans home. "Where's the best place for me to get a cab around here?"

12

THE NEXT MORNING, TED grabbed an egg sandwich on the corner and ate it while waiting for an Uber. Why was it tougher to get a ride after rush hour than during? He checked in with Lester after giving the driver his destination.

"I don't know how long this is going to take," Ted said. "I'll call again when I'm done."

"I'll be at the courthouse." Cell phone use was restricted in parts of the building. "If I don't answer, I'll get you right back."

The Preacher was waiting on the corner of 113th Street. Ted was five minutes early.

"I told my people you mean no harm to this woman you seek. I hope that is the truth."

"Usually the people I am looking for are very happy when I find them."

"Come with me." He led the way down Roosevelt Avenue to a pizza joint that also offered Mexican food. The breakfast rush was long over, and the staff behind the counter was getting ready for lunch. A thin brown-skinned man with multicolored tattoos running down both arms reached across and vigorously shook the Preacher's hand before giving Ted a skeptical look.

The Preacher raised both hands, palms out. "I am here as this man's guide. You do me honor to hear him speak."

Ted introduced himself. "I won't take much of your time. I'm looking for an older woman. A local landlord named Barbara Miller. I don't know if she lives around here or just owned property."

"Miss Miller is good people, yo. What you want to bother her?" The man talked in a full-speed, overanimated fashion, like a late-night TV shill for Ginsu knives or the Hurricane Spin Mop.

"You're a friend?" Ted said. "Then you'll understand that I have to respect her privacy."

"She's my landlord. Not for the business. My apartment."

New Yorkers rarely evinced positive feelings for their landlords.

"She must be special," Ted said.

"She takes care of her buildings. She got a management company that does all that, but she tells 'em to do it right. Something breaks? They fix it. Like, yesterday. No lie."

"How would I find her?"

"I can give you the management company."

"That's a start," Ted said.

The man checked his cell phone and rattled off a number. "They're in Brooklyn."

"But you don't know where I might find her?"

"Like where she lives? I don't know. I mean she's here in the neighborhood. Or she was. She gets the *sopa de lima* sometimes. To go. I ain't seen her, though, in a long time."

"Months? Years?"

He thought about it. "More than a year. She liked to shop in the neighborhood." He turned to the Preacher. "You gonna take him to Manny's?"

"Manny has the fruit market down the block," the Preacher explained. "We'll go there next."

"Yeah, you talk to Manny," the counterman said. "She in trouble?"

"I hope not," Ted said. "She's owed some money, and I'm trying to get it to her. That's all I know."

"What are you, then? Like an angel or something?"

"Something."

Ted and the Preacher stepped out into the checkered sunlight filtering down through the subway tracks above.

"Tell me about Manny," Ted said.

"A good man."

A train passed overhead, killing any chance of continuing the conversation.

To call Manny Singh's emporium a "fruit market" was akin to calling Trump Tower a multiuse high-rise. It was accurate without being descriptive. The store was Costco-sized, and though fruit bins were the prominent feature outside the entrance, inside one could purchase comestibles from dozens of cultures. There was a team of sushi chefs preparing plastic trays of fish, seaweed, and rice; across the aisle was a halal butcher. The aromas of spices, teas, coffee, and flowers melded into an exotic cloud that spilled out onto the sidewalk, luring in shoppers. Manny, in crisp white shirt and tie and a deep maroon turban, kept watch over his domain from the front door, greeting everyone who passed inside.

A huge grin broke out on Manny's face as the Preacher raised a hand in greeting. "Welcome, friend," Manny cried.

"*Sat Sri Akaal,*" the Preacher replied, his arm also raised, as in tribute.

"*Sat Sri Akaal,*" Manny echoed. "You bring the sun."

"I bring a stranger."

Manny examined Ted sternly for a moment. "Strangers are welcome here. This is the seeker you mentioned?"

"I am," Ted answered. "I'm looking for a Barbara Miller."

Manny's face betrayed nothing, but Ted felt a slight chill of suspicion. "Follow me." Manny took them into a tiny office, where the Preacher and Ted sat on pallets of canned soda. Manny faced them across an ancient green industrial metal desk.

"Barbara Miller?" he said. "A very nice woman. Gentle. Polite. I have known her many years."

"I'm trying to find her," Ted said. "Has she been around lately?" He knew he was pushing it, moving too fast, but

Manny's suspicions irked him. He tried to swallow his impatience.

"She is also very wealthy. What do you want with her?" Manny did not squint skeptically or allow an incredulous inflection to come into his speech, but he managed to convey the fact that he was not going to be satisfied with a bullshit answer.

Ted's only option was to trust the man. It was the first step in getting the guy to trust him. Ted told him about the surplus money.

"This does not make sense. The Barbara Miller I know owns many properties in Corona. She hires a good management company to run them. Why would she let any of them be taken this way?"

"I don't know. She's old? Old people do these kinds of things. I see it all the time. Can you give me some of the other addresses? I'll check them out."

Manny rattled off the locations of three other buildings. None of them were anywhere near the site of the proposed development project.

"Have you seen her lately?"

"No. She told me she was moving to a condo on the ocean. Rockaway? Long Beach Island? I don't remember."

"When was this?"

"At least three years ago. Maybe a little more. It was very cold. January or February. I asked her why she wasn't going to Florida or someplace warm." He laughed. "She said she didn't like big bugs."

-13-

IT WASN'T MUCH, BUT it was far from a wasted morning. Ted had something to work with, and that beat trying to weave fog into mittens. He left the Preacher with a hefty contribution and called Lester. There was no answer, but Lester called back in less than thirty seconds.

"What's up?"

"You're at the courthouse? Take down these addresses. Find out whatever you can, and text it to me. Then go down to the county clerk and check tax records. I'm getting a slice, and I need to hear from you before I'm done eating. Call me when you've got it all."

Ted didn't want to leave Corona without coming up with more information about Miss Miller. She could be dead and buried or alive and kicking a few blocks away.

One slice turned into two. He made notes on a napkin and calculations on his smartphone. By focusing on the numbers, he was able to tune out some of the Mexican rap music coming out of the overhead speakers.

Though he'd seen only the bare bones of the court docs, Ted knew that Barbara Miller had lost three buildings. According to ACRIS, the city's online real estate records, she owned nine others. Even if all twelve buildings were standard three-story walk-ups, the combined rents would have added up to a nice piece of change. In Manhattan, most midsize landlords had been driven out of the business by a crushing combination of competition, government taxation and regulation, and massive amounts of capital, both foreign and domestic. But in the outer boroughs, it was still possible, though becoming harder every year, for a business like Miller's to survive. And be quite profitable.

He estimated taxes, water bills, management costs, and insurance. He already knew—again from ACRIS—that six of the properties were not mortgaged, so it was a safe assumption that the others were no different. As long as her maintenance costs were under control, Barbara Miller was netting well over a million dollars a year.

Manny was right. It made no sense. People ran into all kinds of troubles in their lives—rich people as well as poor and those struggling in the middle—and Ted thought that he had heard all of their stories. But this case was unlike any other. Miss Miller was old, granted, and therefore liable to have been hospitalized, developed dementia, or died. But the management company should have taken care of paying the bills and collecting rents. That was both what they were paid for and how they got paid. They would have to be his next call. He'd need to give it some thought first. They weren't going to easily open up for him.

As soon as he heard from Lester.

Ted finished the second slice and flipped through an abandoned copy of *El Diario* while he waited. Spanish had been the dominant language of the streets when Ted was growing up, but he'd never conquered the accent. He understood a little of what he heard, if the idioms were familiar, but he had trouble framing sentences more complex than those needed for ordering a meal. But he could read it well enough—given both time and a picture above a story to lend some context. The news didn't read any better in Spanish.

LIBRE, PERO SIN HOGAR

Six men, arrested and then released by Immigration, had returned home to find their apartments emptied, their belongings gone, and the buildings boarded up and awaiting demolition. The feds—ICE and Homeland Security—had raided two buildings in Queens a month before, netting two men ostensibly wanted in Peru for terrorist activities and four alleged undocumented aliens. That was background. The current story was that all six people had been released as evidence mounted that they were all legal immigrants—the Peruvians had been in the States for decades and both were citizens. But while they had been in custody, their apartments had been emptied and the buildings sold to a development company. Ted wasn't surprised to see that it was LBC—Reisner. When contacted, the recent landlord of the buildings had claimed to have no responsibility, though he'd offered the men $1,000 as a "hardship donation." Buried in the last paragraph was a quote from an ICE spokesman, apologizing for the unfortunate situation and claiming that they could not reveal the sources that had led to the raid.

The story danced admirably on the knife-edge of hinting that LBC had orchestrated the deal, duping both the feds and the citizens. The implication was probably not actionable, or the editors would never have let it through, but the point was clear to anyone with a skeptical frame of mind. Most New Yorkers fit that description.

It was past time to have heard from Lester. If he'd struck out, Ted needed to follow up on the bits and pieces he had. He was about to punch the buttons to call him when the cell phone buzzed in his hand.

Cheryl. He gritted his teeth and answered. "Molloy."

"I'm payin' you, and I expect updates. Did I tell you that? Every day I want to hear what you're doing."

"Cheryl. Good to hear from you."

"Don't give me that. Where are you?" She paused in her attack for a nanosecond. "And what the hell are you listening to?"

"I'm working, Cheryl. In fact, I can't talk long. I'm expecting to hear from one of my investigators on a good lead."

"Do you know who shot my Richie?"

"No. I don't know. I told you, let the damn cops handle that. That's what they do. Meanwhile, I am following up on that surplus-money case."

"This thing Richie and you were doin' together?"

Ted decided not to argue the point. "Yeah. That thing."

"Yeah? And?"

"And I've discovered some interesting anomalies."

"Say what?"

"Some weird stuff."

"I know what anomalies are, asshole. I want to know what you've found."

"I'm waiting on a callback. Could we talk about this later?"

"Give me a taste."

"I have no way of knowing if somebody else is working this one, but the money is real. I need to find a lady named Barbara Miller. She's in her nineties and owns a few buildings. If I can cut a deal with her, we're set."

"That doesn't sound complicated. Or weird."

"There are other people involved. I don't want to go into it."

"Is that what's taking you so long?"

"Do you know how many Barbara Millers there are in Queens?"

"You just need one, don't you?"

"I'd like to find the right Barbara Miller, if it's okay with you." Ted's phone beeped with an incoming call. "I've got to go. This might be the call I've been waiting for."

"I want to know who killed Richie. Meet me at the Korean barbecue place on Northern Boulevard at eight o'clock. I've got a business meeting, but I should be done by then."

Ted's inclination was to avoid all unnecessary contact with this woman—he didn't trust her. But it occurred to him that he had questions about Richie that only she could answer, and he needed to see her face when he asked. If she was going to lie to him, he would at least make it a little more difficult for her. And he could fit in a quick meeting and still make the game before first pitch. "How about before your meeting? I've got Mets tickets."

"Fine. Six o'clock."

How many Korean BBQ joints were there on Northern Boulevard? They outnumbered the Dunkin' Donuts ten to one. "Wait! What's the name of the place? Where on Northern?"

"I don't know—I don't speak Korean. A hundred and fiftysomething block. Near Murray. You'll see it."

And she was gone.

14

TED CHECKED THE SCREEN. The number looked familiar. He hit the FLASH button. "Lester? Talk to me."

"What's a Lester?" an angry female voice asked.

"Jackie?" It slipped out of his mouth before he had time to think. "Sorry. Jacqueline." No wonder the number looked familiar. Jill had given it to him the night before.

When Jacqueline Clavette was pissed off, her voice developed the volume and tones of a coffee grinder. "What do you want, Molloy?"

"I didn't expect to hear from you." She had been next on Ted's to-call list.

"Cut it out. Jill told me you forced her to give you my private number, so I thought I'd save you the trouble of dialing." The ability to recognize sarcasm is said to be an early indicator of intelligence. Ted had no trouble identifying it. Every word was soaked in scorn.

Of course Jill had told Jackie that she had given Ted the private number. He should have expected that. Jill was fun and bright and beautiful, but she was not brave. Avoiding confrontation was her greatest strength—and weakness. But he'd known that about her long before they'd married. He didn't resent it; it was simply her way.

"I'm sorry, Jacqueline. I sometimes forget that, though Jill is surrounded by lawyers, she is not one herself. I pushed her too hard. Don't take it out on her, all right?"

"I don't know why she keeps up with you, but if you don't leave her alone, I will take action."

Ted had heard this before from Jackie on more than one

occasion. He gave the threat the acknowledgment it deserved. He ignored it.

Ms. Clavette wasn't ready to let it go, though. "This is harassment. She is my wife now."

And has been for some years now, Ted thought, but he kept silent.

JILL HAD BEEN NEITHER a virgin nor exclusively heterosexual before she met Ted, and she had never pretended otherwise. The surprise, for both of them, was belatedly discovering that her sexual attraction to women was neither a fad nor a phase but a defining characteristic. She made no choice. But both she and Ted had accepted who she was and moved on.

Her family had not been so accepting. They blamed Ted through the divorce for, as her Aunt Grace repeatedly put it to anyone who would listen, "doing something to our girl." Through this barrage of blame, Jill kept her head down, and for a while she and Ted rarely spoke. She had used all of her bravery capital coming out to the family; she had none to spare for resurrecting Ted's profile in their eyes.

He had already made the move from appellate litigation to commercial real estate transactions, where he once again excelled. It was not the kind of work he had ever planned for himself, but the money, power, and prestige plastered over all moral qualms. In the aftermath of the mortgage crisis, the division was gutted. Ted wasn't let go—the firm devised a subtler method of moving him out the door. They offered him something he couldn't accept. A dead-end job. He walked.

Two years later, after he'd bounced through two other firms on a downward career trajectory, Jill called him one night.

Ted was watching the Mets get shellacked on the road by the Braves.

"Hey," she said.

Pain—real physical pain—shot up into his sinuses, and

his eyes began to tear. He lost the ability to form words and merely grunted, "Hey."

Neither of them spoke again for an eternity.

"Ted?" she whispered.

"Give me a sec, okay? I left the kettle on." He hadn't. He put the phone down, went in the bathroom, and splashed cold water on his face. He dried it off and looked at himself in the mirror. He could do this.

Ted picked up the phone. "How're you holding up?"

"I should have called before."

He wasn't going to argue with that.

"So, what's up?" He tried to sound casual but only managed cold.

She let it slide. "I had a fight with my mother."

That was monumental news. "Good for you. What was her problem?"

"The monsignor is running an LGBT prayer group. She wanted me to join."

"Does that mean she's finally going to accept that you like girls?"

"Not exactly. They're supposed to pray themselves straight. How are you?"

"How am I? Big question. Ups and downs. Ups first. Your grandfather helped me out. He persuaded Cromarty, Gaines to take me on as counsel."

"I know. Father was very upset with him."

"Yeah, well, I made a hash of that, too. I lasted eighteen months."

"Oh, no. Why'd they let you go?"

"No. I left. Esrig, Keane offered me a partnership."

"Oh."

The indictments of Esrig and Keane for running a pyramid scheme disguised as a law firm were still in the news.

"The feds shut the firm down last week." And the current

rumor was they would soon be coming after all partners and select staff. Ted believed that he had nothing to fear, but he had hired a lawyer just in case.

"Oh. I'm sorry."

Was he surprised that she hadn't known? Hadn't heard? Possible? Unlikely? He filed it mentally under Unknowable. "Thanks" was all he said.

"So what have you been up to?" She was trying to keep it light; her conversation was bordering on inane. She was frightened.

He wanted to say something stinging, something hurtful. But she'd see through it. He didn't want to hurt her. He just wanted her to know that he was in pain.

"Are you seeing anyone?" she asked.

He realized that she had something to tell him and that she wasn't quite ready to spill it. She was seeing someone, he surmised. He let her take her time. He was in no hurry to hear about it.

"You don't want to hear stories of my naked wrestling bouts with all the hordes of sexy women who can't resist unemployed lawyers living in Maspeth, Queens," he said.

"Ooh. Maybe I do."

It was a joke. A small one. Neither of them laughed, but it was a start. A moment of letting the curtain part. Maybe there were emotions they could still share.

"It would have been good to hear your voice every now and then."

There was a very long pause before she whispered, "Yes."

He had hoped for more, but that single word was enough. "I'll let you go. Call sometime, if you get the urge. I'd love to hear from you. See how you're doing."

She didn't reply.

Words are so easily misunderstood, but silences can speak so clearly.

"Bye, Jill." His thumb hovered over the red button. He didn't want to hang up, and he didn't want to hear any more.

"Wait!"

He took a deep breath. "I'm here." Whatever was coming was better than nothing at all.

"I'm sorry." The words were spoken so softly he might have imagined them. "I'm sorry," she said again, louder yet choked.

"Me too. You deserved something better. I hope you find it."

"Not about us. I'm sorry I didn't call. I'm a coward. But I'm getting better."

"Oh. Yes." He had expected a hurtful revelation and had been presented with something that touched a much deeper pain.

"What will you do now?" she asked.

The question was too massive to tackle. There wasn't a law firm in the tristate that would touch him. There'd been a need for real estate lawyers when the market was ballooning, but since the crash they were all cashing in their IRAs and living on a diet of hope and futility. "I'll find something."

"You're a good man."

He didn't know what she meant by that, but it felt good to hear her say it.

"Have you been to any games lately?" she asked.

He took a long time before answering. What was she really asking? Did it matter? "They're two wins from clinching the wild card. If they get a streak, they might not need it."

"Will you take me sometime?"

Ted could hear what it cost her to ask, but he was too choked up to reply.

"Sorry. I shouldn't have asked," she said.

"No. No. It's okay. I'd love to take you to a game."

"I've missed you."

He thought he heard a tiny sob. "I know. Me too."

"You're sure?"

"Pick a day," he said.

"Tomorrow."

He laughed. "They're in Atlanta. How's next Tuesday?"

AND NOW HERE WAS Ted in need of the cooperation of Jill's new love. Well, he might be able to get by without Jacqueline Clavette. But a few answers from her would clear up a number of issues about the Miller properties. He swallowed and tried to sound as if he were smiling.

"I'm sorry if I caused you two any aggravation. And if she tells me she doesn't ever want to go to a Mets game with me as long as she lives, I will respect her wishes, though I may not believe her."

"I could get canned for talking to you."

"So far, all you've done is yell at me. I think the firm would approve."

"Do not contact me. Understand? Not on my private line. Not at the firm."

The woman's one great failing as a lawyer, and the reason she had never been prodded into the role of negotiator, was that she tended to set absolute boundaries. Compromise was a dirty word. Ted thought it worked for her more often than not—she was good at her job—but it kept her from being effective on a larger stage.

He had no leverage, either emotional or rational, but he had to make one more attempt to get her cooperation. "If you answer one question."

"I'm hanging up now," she said.

"Just one. Where's Barbara Miller? How can I find her?"

"Who?"

"Come on, Counsellor. She's a client. Barbara Miller. Little old lady in Corona. Owned a bunch of three stories."

"I'm not going to share client information with you."

"You have just confirmed that you know her, so cut me a break. I only want to talk to her. I met some friends of hers." Acquaintances really, but he thought the slight exaggeration was warranted. "They want to know that she's all right. They're worried about her. She disappeared, they say."

"What are you up to, Molloy? Don't stir up trouble. The firm went easy on you. I can promise you they will not be so friendly next time around."

What was she talking about? The firm had blown him off—along with six other lawyers and a score of paralegals, secretaries, and other support staff. That was being easy on him?

Somewhere deep in his psyche there were still remains of the cocky attaché-case-bearing gunslinger fighting for the little guy, the lawyer he had once dreamed of becoming. His own opportunism had had more to do with destroying that youth than the actions of a vengeful family law firm had. Though he still resented the firm's treatment of him, his regrets were all his own. But he now existed in the liberated state of one with nothing left to lose.

"Thanks for the warning, Jackie. I'll give it all the attention it deserves."

15

THE PHONE RANG AGAIN an instant later.

"You okay?" Lester asked.

"I'm still getting over my last two calls. It seems I have a knack for pissing off strong-willed women."

"Don't we all. Can you get a car to take us to Seaside?"

Seaside was most likely an hour from Corona no matter how you cut it. Traffic on Woodhaven made all the difference. "You've got something good?"

"Barbara Miller."

Ted found a gypsy cab depositing a fare at the hotel down the street and persuaded the Yemeni behind the wheel to expand his universe by driving all the way to the beach. The man—who introduced himself by first citing his birth country, then announcing that he had only recently arrived in the States but loved America already, and finally giving all four of his names, the one he used most often being Mohammed—indicated with shakes of the head and double shrugs that he had never been to the South Shore before and today was not a good day for a first attempt. A fifty up front closed the deal.

Ted sat back and tried not to anticipate. Lester might have hit the jackpot, or they might arrive in Seaside only to find a blank-faced woman in the grips of dementia. Ted was taking no bets.

The car lurched and scooted around a Snapple delivery truck. Ted realized that his recently reluctant driver was flying down Woodhaven, weaving like a kid on a skateboard.

"Stop when you get to Atlantic," he said, gripping the door handle white-knuckled. "We need to pick up my partner."

The driver waved a hand that should have been holding the steering wheel. "Okay. Okay. No problem."

No problem. The single most-used phrase by immigrants, cashiers, reservation clerks, baristas, and almost everyone else in the service industry. No problems anywhere.

"And don't get me killed getting there," Ted added.

"Inshallah." Mohammed looked over his shoulder without any alteration in speed.

"Amen," Ted said, wishing that he had the same faith in divine guidance.

He heard the word "partner" echoing inside his head. Without planning or forethought, he had described Lester as a partner. Not an employee. He barely knew the man. Who knew where this business of trusting people might lead?

Trust. A quaint concept Ted remembered from an idealistic youth, a concept that engendered in his adult self a sneering cynicism.

Lester was direct. Ted liked that. The man was taking the work seriously. But his past was a blank—and he drank. Ted had nothing against a man who took a drink or two, but a man who *needed to* was an entirely different matter. His father had been such a man, and the best thing he had ever done for Ted was to leave.

The cab whipped over to the right at Ninety-First Avenue, crossing two lanes of heavy traffic without causing any immediate destruction, and continued barreling south in the service lane, avoiding the overpass. Ted took a slow breath when the car came to rest a moment later, blocking a fire hydrant outside of a divey-looking strip club.

"Where you friend?" Mohammed asked.

Lester wasn't there.

"Give him a minute. We got here a little quicker than I expected," Ted said.

Mohammed let his impatience show by turning up the

radio. Brian Lehrer was taking calls from listeners who favored the LBC development in Queens.

LBC again, Ted thought. The media was in a self-regenerating loop and would remain there until, by some sleight of hand that would ever escape him, the subject changed, and the cameras and microphones about-faced and stampeded in a new direction.

The featured guest was Queens councilman Kevin (Ki-nam) Pak, whose district did not encompass the project, though he was undoubtedly on the pro side. Therefore, the conversations between Pak and the callers were a bit tepid. Lehrer was frustrated—everyone was making nice. No drama. Pak had probably agreed to come on the show only if he didn't have to argue with protestors on the air.

"And we now have McKenzie from Ridgewood," Lehrer said. "McKenzie? Are you there?"

"Hi, Brian. I always enjoy your show."

"Thank you. Are you calling to thank Councilman Pak for his support of this project?"

"I wanted to ask Mr. Pak one question . . ."

Ted knew that woman's voice. The protestor from the courthouse. There couldn't be two. Like silk and good whiskey. *A voice like that ought to be licensed.*

"I want to know how much LBC paid him under the table to switch—"

They cut her off.

"Please, people," Lehrer said. "We know there are a lot of you out there who have strong feelings about this development, and you will get your turn to air those feelings. Tomorrow. Today we want to hear from those of you who support . . ."

Ted tuned out the rest of it. He had to admire the woman for going straight for the throat. But he made a mental note not to get between her and her target.

"I think that your friend," Mohammed said.

A Q24 bus was gliding across the intersection in front of them, momentum carrying it through a fully realized red light. Lester was standing at the rear door wearing a big grin and waving. A minute later he was clambering into the back seat. He was holding a pastry box.

"Let's go," he said and gave the driver an address.

"How did you find her?" Ted asked.

"You'd have got there," Lester answered. "I got the management company info off the tax rolls. I called them up."

"And they just gave you her address?"

"Not exactly. I told the girl on the phone that I was delivering a birthday cake from the tenants' association." He held up the box. "She was very nice. Gave up the address right away."

"That's it?"

"I can be very persuasive."

It was not how Ted would have handled the situation, but as the frontal assault on Jackie Clavette had been a total failure, he had to admire Lester's approach. "Nice work, and if anyone ever asks me, I never heard that story."

And for the briefest moment, he thought again that finding this resourceful assistant had been much too easy.

16

THE NEXT HURRICANE TO hit Seaside was going to sweep the Imperiale out to sea. If you placed your aged loved ones in that assisted-living facility, you were secretly hoping for a good-sized storm surge.

Lester led the way. He signed the register at the front desk and announced, "We are here to see Barbara Miller. This is her grandnephew Eberhard Wilmot from San Diego. He has recently arrived in town and discovered that she is a resident here."

The receptionist was a college-aged girl with Korean features and slightly protruding eyes. She took in Lester's rumpled suit and stained tie. "And you are?"

"Mr. Wilmot's factotum. We would like to see her immediately. Mr. Wilmot is concerned that she is not being treated as a lady of her means and station deserves."

Ted couldn't remember ever hearing anyone using the word "factotum" in conversation before. Apparently, neither could the receptionist, who seemed to be impressed with Lester's performance. She tapped at her computer.

"Miss Miller is listed as having no known relatives," she said.

"Well, that is an obvious mistake," Lester said. He had center stage and all the best lines. "Her nephew is standing right here."

That seemed to satisfy what little curiosity the girl could summon. "She's playing bingo. Down that hallway, the game room is on your left."

Surprised at this easy victory and relieved that he had not been asked to provide ID for Eberhard Wilmot, Ted hustled down the hall. "How am I supposed to remember an alias like Everhard Pillpot?"

"That's the point," Lester said. "No one will remember."

"What were you going to do if she didn't buy it?" Ted asked.

"Improvise." Lester's face was a mask of inscrutability.

"You're scaring me, Lester."

"Who breaks into nursing homes? Through the front door? Somebody shows up to visit at a place like this, the staff will lay out a path of rose petals for them." He made a show of examining their surroundings. "Nice digs."

The furnishings in the lobby were all a touch ornate but not well-made. At first glance, the place looked both grand and inviting, but the eye quickly picked up the chips in veneer, the worn fabric. Ted thought management must have picked up the furnishings used—and cheap.

However, his only frame of reference was the nursing home where his mother had lived her last few years while he was finishing college. Medicaid had picked up the tab. This place was a palace in comparison, though Ted was sure that hidden behind the pleasant furnishings and the Febreze-scented air was the same loneliness and despair.

The game room had a half-dozen round tables, a smattering of unmatched chairs, and plenty of room for the twenty or more wheelchairs and their occupants. On the long wall facing the players was a big flat-screen television showing a vibrant checkerboard arrangement of black numerals, some highlighted in red, others in yellow. Most of the faces were intent on checking the board against game cards. Along the far wall was a single line of wheelchairs alternating with folding chairs. All of the residents in the wheelchairs were fast asleep, curled forward, heads hanging down. The other seats were taken by aides, who were all busy playing bingo.

"B seven. B seven." The number caller was a fleshy twenty-something brunette in a baby-blue pantsuit. The outfit made her look about thirty years older. Ted imagined that this was the desired effect.

"Bingo," a dull voice murmured.

A sense of relief washed across the room. The grueling bout of concentration was over. Another would begin soon, but for the moment the contestants could relax.

The emcee meandered over and checked the old woman's card. A moment later, in a voice devoid of any celebratory emotion, the girl announced, "We have a winner."

This was the signal for two young black women in dark grey scrubs to dash about the room collecting nickels and handing out fresh cards to the clients and the aides. The clients were uniformly white, mostly women, and all well-dressed. The aides were all dark skinned, a mix of men and women, and they spoke in accents rooted in developing nations around the globe.

Ted took advantage of this lull in the inaction to sidle up to the emcee. "Excuse me. Could you direct me to my great-aunt? Barbara Miller?"

She stared him down like a professional. In the split second before she spoke, he saw past her boredom. This was not the job she had dreamed of a year ago as she completed her BS in social work, but nevertheless, she was going to take it seriously. Times were tough. Jobs scarce. The country was on a full-out assault upon health-care costs, and labor was an expense. He felt for her. "You don't recognize your own aunt?" she said.

His sympathy lifted and his vision cleared. A bossy bureaucrat stood before him.

Lester intervened, speaking in a confidential whisper. "Mr. Filbert grew up on the West Coast. There was a rift in the family. They haven't seen each other in thirty years or more." He sounded like a funeral director discussing prices of coffin linings. Concerned, discreet, sincere, but embarrassed at the necessity.

Ted was worried that in order to uphold Lester's narrative he might have to fall weeping on the old woman's breast. As soon as he knew who she was.

"Barbara? Barbara, you have a visitor," the young woman said to a sleeping woman in a wheelchair. Then, turning to the aide beside Miller, she said, "Anora? Miss Miller has a visitor."

Anora was a round-faced woman with an island accent. Ted guessed Trinidad. She was thrilled that her charge had company. She said something else after expressing that, but he missed everything but the pronoun "she."

"I understand," Ted said. "We were never close."

That non sequitur earned him a microfrown of confusion and another round of rapid-fire, heavily accented English. He looked to Lester for help, but judging by the way his suddenly quiescent partner was intently studying a bingo card, he had cut Ted loose.

Barbara Miller had a pinched face with papery thin skin. The bones of her skull were her dominant feature, around deep-set eyes and sunken cheeks. She was long past looking old; she'd graduated to ancient.

Anora shook her arm gently and murmured. Miller's eyes popped open and bored into Ted's. "Who are you?"

"Is there somewhere we can talk?" Ted asked.

For a moment Ted caught suspicion behind those glaring eyes. But she was also intrigued. Bored beyond all reason, ready for an adventure.

"Take me to the library," she ordered.

Lester and Ted followed as Anora wheeled the crone out of the great room and down the hall. The library wasn't an ideal forum for private conversation. A wide archway was all that separated it from the main lobby, but as there was no one else there, Ted thought it was as good as they were going to get. Three walls were covered from floor to ceiling with mahogany shelves holding thousands of bestsellers. Someone had a budget for books and kept the room stocked. Ted wondered if anyone but the staff ever read them.

"How are you, Miss Miller?" Lester pulled over a chair and sat next to her.

Ted sat facing them. Anora took a couch on the far side of the room.

"My name is Lester, and this is my friend Ted. How are you doing?"

"Do I know you?" Miller asked.

"We've never met."

"I didn't think so. Who's this Ted? I heard what you told Little Miss Smiley Face back there, but that's horse hockey. I don't have any family out west. Or anywhere else."

Ted thought she was sharp enough—and tough enough—to weather another ninety-three years. "My name's Ted Molloy."

"Never heard of you."

"Would you like some cake, Miss Miller?" Lester asked, holding up the pastry box.

"What kind?"

"Yellow," he said. "With mocha-walnut frosting."

"Buttercream?"

"Yes, ma'am."

"How'd you know?"

"I didn't. It's my favorite."

"You I like."

Anora must have been following every word, because at that point she jumped up and scurried out of the room. She was back in seconds with paper plates, plastic forks, and a long serrated bread knife.

"I'd offer you coffee," Miller said, "but the crap they serve here doesn't deserve the name."

Lester cut the cake. Miller watched him closely. "That's from Lulu's," she said. Her expression was deliberately neutral.

"Yes?" Lester asked, for the moment unsure of how to read her comment.

She sniffed. "I've always preferred Andre's."

"I'll remember for next time."

"Give me a small piece," Miller said.

"I thought it was your favorite."

"It is, but my stomach doesn't let me enjoy a lot of anything. Small servings or else I'm on the damn pot all night. Don't get old."

Lester patted the back of her hand and passed her a wedge. "Getting old isn't for sissies."

The woman made a sound like a throat-clearing cough— her version of a laugh. "Damn right."

"Miss Miller," Anora said in a cautioning tone.

"Excuse me, dear," Miller said, smiling thinly. "Sometimes I forget you're there." She turned to Ted. "Or at least I want to."

If Anora was offended by this verbal slap, she kept it to herself, smiling politely as one might in the presence of a toothless tyrant.

They each took a bite of cake, and for a moment the silence was broken only by the sounds of forks on plates.

"Good cake," Miller said. "What do you want?"

Ted could tell he had zero chance of getting anything over on this woman, and he was becoming impatient with Lester's extended schmoozathon. He laid it out straight:

"You lost a few buildings to foreclosure this year. There's now a big chunk of surplus money sitting waiting to be claimed. I can get it for you. We split whatever I get. There's enough for you to move someplace that's got decent coffee."

Lester's eyes widened. He probably thought he'd been getting somewhere with his butter and sugar, but Ted knew better. Miller was as sharp as any squinty-eyed New York landlord he had ever come across.

She'd thrust her jaw forward, but she'd let Ted finish his pitch. "That's a load of manure," she said when he was done.

"I don't think so," Ted said.

"Then you've got the wrong Barbara Miller."

She was so adamant that for a moment Ted considered that she might be right. Could Lester have made a mistake?

"You own property in Corona," Ted said.

"And Jackson Heights," she said. "All over. It's been in the family for generations."

"We can show you the foreclosure file. Some of it, anyway. The buildings went for taxes and water. Two years unpaid."

"And I'm telling you that's impossible. I've got a management company that runs all my buildings. I've worked with them for thirty years. They wouldn't let that happen." She was angry and the words were starting to tumble and slur.

Across the room, Anora began to shake her head and make "Stop" motions with both hands.

"The last time I sold a building was 2007, because I thought the market was getting toppy. I was goddamned right," Miller said. The *t* in "toppy" projected a fleck of saliva. Ted watched it soar across the intervening space and come up short, landing a foot or so in front of him.

He was beginning to regret the whole encounter. He tried another, less confrontational tack. "How long have you been here, Miss Miller?"

"Oh, don't try your tricks on me, young man," she said. "You're a sharpie. I can tell. Asking direct questions like that and expecting me to shout out an answer. That's not conversation. We're having conversation." She was no longer spitting mad, but her face was bright red. She wasn't giving an inch.

Anora murmured, "Three, almost four years."

Miller drew herself up and glared at Anora hard enough to raise welts. "I don't like you interrupting all the time. I've mentioned that before, I think." Miller looked at Ted thoughtfully for a moment before saying, "I've been here three, almost four years."

Ted felt his resolve dissipating. Barbara Miller was a tough old bird and was covering up well, but the signs were clear. Early-onset dementia had taken both his mother and grandmother; he knew the signs and all the tricks the women had used to cover their errors, confusion, and emotional outbursts. And though the progression of the disease had been erratic, with plenty of good days mixed in with the bad, the end result had never been in doubt.

Even if he could get Barbara Miller to sign an agreement, it would not stand up to a challenge in court.

In a futile attempt to convince Ted that her memory was much better than it appeared, she began telling him all the things that she did remember. What remained unclear, however, was whether these events had actually happened.

"That's when the girl brought me here. Social said I couldn't live on my own anymore. I don't know why they said that. I kept a clean house, took my pills on schedule, and ate regular. I ate better than I do here. The food used to be better here, but they've been cutting corners. I think they're not getting deliveries, so they have to make do. It's the companies. The companies are in trouble. They don't advertise anymore. They have to advertise."

He tried to sift through the barrage for specific facts. A pattern was starting to form, and the picture was ugly. "Who called social? Your doctor? A visiting nurse? Home companion? Someone must have brought them in." He shot a look at Lester, who frowned.

"No," Miller said. "They showed up one day. Two women. Not very nice. Asked too many damn questions, so I told them off."

"But they came back?" Ted asked.

"With the girl. She can tell you. She knows the whole

story. Where is she? Where's my girl?" She was becoming agitated again and beat her hand on the armrest of her wheelchair. From the cracked and worn look of it, she often did so.

"She's right here, ma'am," Lester said.

"Not her," Miller spat. "This one's useless. She changes my diapers. I want the girl. The girl with all my papers."

Ted wanted to shake it out of her. Who was the damned girl? "Tell me about her, Miss Miller. The girl. With the papers. Legal papers? Was she a lawyer?"

"She was very young. And blonde."

At ninety-three everyone under seventy-five must seem young.

"Am I very young?" he asked.

"No," Miller said. "But you're close. If you were a doctor, you would be. Are you a doctor?"

Ted was losing her. Pushing too hard. Direct questions threatened her. Frightened her. He looked to Lester for help.

"Have you finished your cake?" Lester asked.

She looked at her plate. She had taken only a few bites. "Oooh. No more for me. I still have plenty." She carved a large bite with the edge of her fork and carefully brought it up to her mouth. No sooner was she chewing it than she began speaking again. "She was very pretty. And tall. For a woman, I mean."

Ted gave Anora a questioning look. She nodded and said something that he thought he understood. "She was a lawyer," he said. "Right?" Anora flashed him a tight smile. They were communicating. Ted wanted two minutes alone with the aide.

Ted knew of a tall blonde woman lawyer whose name was on the case file. Jackie. The only part of the description that Ted would have disputed was "very pretty." But he allowed that his opinion on that subject might be skewed.

"I'm sorry, Miss Miller. We didn't mean to trouble you. We'll be going. Can Anora show us out?" He stood. Lester gave him a questioning look and rose slowly.

"The girl," Miller said. "You find that girl."

Ted stopped. He didn't want to rattle her again, but if one or two more questions might get at the full story, he was going to try. "I'll need something to go on," he said. "Do you know her name?"

"Questions. All you have are questions. I don't have all the answers." She was adrift again.

"Was the girl's name Jackie?" A last forlorn hope.

Miller's distress evaporated. She set her plate thoughtfully on Lester's empty chair and leaned back, eyes closed. "No," she finally said.

Ted silently cursed his own stupidity. "Jacqueline? Jacqueline Clavette?"

The woman repeated the pantomime of thinking hard. "She had very good diction."

Ted looked to Anora for help. She shrugged.

"She had you sign some papers." He was close and could feel it.

"Hundreds," Miller said. She was back. Clear. The lapses in her memory were no longer threatening.

Paper always leaves a trail. "I'm going to pursue this, Miss Miller." Another thought occurred to him. "I'm going to have Lester stop by again tomorrow with another paper for you to sign."

She looked at Lester. "Are you bringing cake?"

He smiled. "If you like."

"Go to Andre's this time," she said.

17

ANORA FOLLOWED THEM OUT to the lobby. "You're no nephew," she said, making it a challenge.

Ted understood the words perfectly.

"No, you are right." He was being reminded that he had first approached her employer under a pretense. Now he needed to build trust.

"You wan' sometin'," she said.

"I do," he said. "I'm not doing anything out of my love of fellow man—or woman. But I'm going to help her. Someone worked her over for a lot of money. She's going to get a chunk of it back."

"I can help you."

"Say that again," Ted said.

"She'll not sign, not if I tell her no."

A shakedown. Ted had to admire her forthright approach. No sidling into it, just a straight-up holdup. "I assume you want something in return. How much? I'll have Lester bring it tomorrow."

She shook her head. "I wan' a green card."

Well, at least she wasn't a *cheap* blackmailer. "I wouldn't know how to begin to get you a green card."

"You are a lawyer."

The accent and cadences of her speech were no longer indecipherable. "Not exactly. I could go to jail for practicing law. And I know nothing about immigration law. Zilch." Actually, he reflected, he knew two things about immigration law: it was both complicated and capricious, and it got more so every year.

"You know lawyers."

Ted's landlord, Mr. Ortiz, was a storefront abogado. Ted

could ask him to look into it, but he had strong doubts that anything would come of it. "I don't know the right kind of lawyers," he said.

"Then she won't sign."

"We can make this happen," Lester said. Ted raised both eyebrows. Lester ignored him. "Not a problem. You prep Miss Miller and let us take care of the rest."

Anora, focused on Lester, had missed Ted's reaction, but now she turned to him. "Dat woman, the one she talked aboot—she is not a good person."

"Do you know her name?" Ted asked. "Anything else you can tell me about her?"

"She say she's a lawyer. I know that."

"I could really use a name. Please think."

Shaking her head, she replied, "She very bossy."

A dead end. Anora wasn't going to be much help with anything else. Ted wanted to get Lester out of there before he made any more unlikely promises.

"Thanks for your help," Ted said. "I'll have Lester come by tomorrow."

They headed for the front door.

"Bye now," the bug-eyed girl at the desk called out. "Oh, wait. Mr. Willard. You need to sign out." She waved a pen.

"It's Fillmore," Lester said, signing out for both of them. "Eduard Fillmore of San Pedro."

Mohammed was waiting, engine running, at the curb. Ted stopped Lester before they got to the car. "I hope you have a plan for helping Anora get a green card. I don't have much, but I do have my word, and I'm not too comfortable with people making impossible pledges in my name. Are we clear?"

Lester looked him in the eye. "We'll figure it out. But without that signature, you and I have nothing at all."

"If she gets us that signature, we are going to help that woman get her green card. Understood?"

"I never said anything different," Lester answered.

"I want you on it as soon as you get that signature."

Lester nodded. "Can do."

Ted opened the car door and gestured for Lester to get in first.

"And one other thing," Lester said.

"What's that?" Ted asked.

"She's wrong. Miller, I mean. You go to Andre's for pastry. Lulu's for cake."

18

MOHAMMED PERSUADED THEM THAT the fastest route to Jamaica was the Van Wyck. It wasn't.

"It never is," Lester said.

"Where can I drop you? I've got to get up to Flushing for a meeting," Ted said.

"Hillside. You can cut over and take Queens Boulevard. You're on to something with this Miller and her lawyer. I saw it in your face back there."

"It's the lawyer. She's the connection."

"You know her?" Lester asked. "This Jackie Somebody? Where did that come from?"

"Jacqueline Clavette. An old acquaintance. From a past life." Ted didn't want to say more until he was sure of his facts.

"And?" Lester wasn't going to let it go.

"Her name was on the original file that Richie showed me." Ted was positive that he'd seen it in that brief moment almost a week earlier, but he had not registered any other pertinent information—like whom she was representing. "And she was at the courthouse yesterday. I saw her just before we found that butchered file."

"Sounds like a stretch," Lester said.

Ted silently agreed. Was he trying to tie her to this case out of spite? Could it be that simple? Bitter, angry man accuses old rival of high crimes. "Tomorrow we've got the auctions—to meet these Corona Partners people. As soon as we're done, I want you back to Miller with a one-page agreement that I'll draw up tonight." There wasn't time to run it by his trusty landlord/lawyer/tax advisor, Israel. "Get a notary to go with you. Have Anora witness it, too, if the notary agrees. If Miller seems competent to the notary, we can get it by a judge. If not, we lose. But if we do nothing, we lose, so it's worth the trip."

A yellow cab cut in front of them, filling a break in traffic the size of a Midtown parking space. Mohammed leaned on his horn, screamed something in Arabic in a way that sounded like he meant it, and flipped the cabbie a middle finger. Ted approved of this cultural assimilation.

"What's the document?" Lester asked. "Power of attorney?"

"No. That would be too easy to challenge. It's a simple agreement to allow me to pursue her interests in the abandoned funds."

For the briefest moment, the traffic looked ready to surge. Mohammed hit the gas and a second later slammed on the brake. Ted rocked forward and bounced back. Lester braced himself with his feet against the seat in front of him.

"Okeydokey?" Mohammed called over his shoulder.

"Fine and dandy," Ted said. "You're doing a great job, my friend. Just get us there."

Mohammed grinned at him in the mirror, hit the gas, and swerved into the left lane, gaining three car lengths on the yellow cab.

"Mohammed," Ted called to the back of the driver's head, "how do I get hold of you if I ever need a ride?"

"No problem," he said, producing a business card with a magician's flourish.

Ted tucked it into his wallet and turned to Lester. "Once you have the signed document, I want you to run it to the courthouse." If he gave it to Mr. Ortiz, it would sit on his desk until Monday.

"But suppose this other lawyer—the 'girl'—has already filed," Lester said.

"I don't think she has. Richie would have found it. Talk to the judge's clerk, and try to get a read, but I think we may have an edge here."

"But if the 'girl' has a signed agreement, won't that predate yours? As soon as she does file, she'll blow your paper out of the water."

"New York is a race jurisdiction state."

"That doesn't mean what it sounds like, right?"

"Race—like footrace. First to file gets precedence."

"Ah. But the 'girl' must know that. Why hasn't she filed already?"

"That's a very good question, Lester. It goes to intent. Suppose that keeping a secret was of greater importance than picking up an extra few bucks."

"A few bucks? We're talking a million-two."

"Which makes it a very big secret, don't you think?"

19

CHERYL RUBIANO WAS SITTING alone at a table for six at the Korean BBQ. She was sipping her way through a large club soda. Ted sat next to her and ordered an OB Lager.

"Are we expecting a crowd?" he asked, indicating the empty seats.

Cheryl's hair had recently been styled and lacquered into a tall cone. The chorus to "Love Shack" ran through his head. She was wearing full war paint, from foundation to blush to liner. "I have a business dinner. We have half an hour before any of them arrive."

"That works for me," he said. "I've got a ball game that starts in an hour."

It was early and the occupied tables all held families—extended families. Grandparents, infants, toddlers, pre- and current teens, smiling wives, and grim-faced husbands kept up an indecipherable background chorus, to the arrhythmic beat of clinking plates and water glasses. Waiters, most of whom looked old enough to be grandfathers themselves, were already harassed and overworked, and the place was still half-empty.

Cheryl called for *banchan* and then waved the ancient waiter away. "So. Report."

There was a lot that Ted wasn't ready to share, a lot that he didn't know but suspected. "Before I start I have a question for you. That file you gave me. It was only cover pages. Richie had copies of the full court records. When I saw him last, that file was an inch thick."

"What? You think I'm holding out on you?"

"No." Though he thought it at least possible. "You said he gave you that file. Did he often do that?"

"Never. He carried everything in that black backpack."

"So, why? Why this file?"

"He told me to take the file to you and you'd know what to do. He called it his life insurance policy."

The waiter returned and placed three small bowls on the table. Cucumber kimchi, marinated lotus root, and dried squid.

Ted had never been a fan of kimchi, and cucumber gave him heartburn. He tried the lotus. "And the originals? I mean, his copies. The full records."

"No idea. They must be in the backpack."

The lotus root was sweet enough to make his teeth hurt and so salty that he had to wash it down with half the beer. "The backpack is missing, I imagine."

"It's not in my apartment, if that's what you mean."

"And the cops never mentioned it?"

"Not to me. Now, let's hear it. Who killed Richie?"

The change was abrupt. Not only the subject but also the tone. There was emotion in her voice. Ted was thrown for a moment. He continued cautiously. "I don't know. If his death is connected to that file, I will find the connection. I have located the owner of those properties and think I can cut a deal."

"This is about the money?" Now she sounded bored.

He didn't answer immediately. He took a slug of beer and eyed the dried squid. "I'm trying to keep up here, Mrs. Rubiano. It'll be easier for me if you simply tell me what you want me to do."

"Richie wanted me to have that money, and—don't get me wrong—it would be very nice. When you get it, I will make it worth your while. But I am paying you to find out who killed him."

"Say the word and I will give you your thousand dollars back and go my way." He took a bit of shredded squid and popped it in his mouth. A hint of salt. A nice crunch. He took another.

"No. I want you to find who killed him."

"Then let me do it my way. Look, if this was some random thing—a mugging, let's say, or one of his old marks taking revenge—I'm not going to find them. The cops might. They might not. But the chances of me coming up with a name are two ticks below nil."

She opened her mouth to lay into him, but he didn't give her the chance.

"However, if he was killed because he found out something about this surplus money, then I am already halfway there. There's a cover-up going on. Right now I think someone tricked an old lady into letting those properties go. That someone might have had a very good reason for keeping Richie away from the truth."

"You said this case was . . . what? A lotto ticket? A super long shot? I think you were just trying to get rid of me. But suppose you *was* telling the truth? Right? Then why would anybody kill that man?"

"I'm still looking into it. Richie believed in it. Maybe someone else did, too. I've found that a lot of people thought he was on to something."

She looked away and focused on a family of six at a nearby table. Ted couldn't see the attraction. "So maybe he told the wrong person," she said.

"Look, I need to find his backpack, if I can. I tried to get the originals of the files at the courthouse, but someone sliced out the pages with a razor. They're hiding something. And the only way to get to the bottom of this is to see the copies Richie made."

Without facing him she asked, "Where is this property?"

He told her, referencing the LBC tower. "Without those plots, the whole Reisner project would have ground to a halt."

Her gaze remained fixed, but something cold and hard washed over her features.

"Are you with me?" he asked. "You know the place I'm talking about, don't you?"

Her eyes swung back to him slowly, but her mind was elsewhere. "Bring me a name." Her flat delivery was chilling.

The fire hadn't abated. It was there but cloaked. Ted felt the ground shift beneath him. Was he being played? She had been married to a con man and came from a family of grifters. Was this some sudden zombie act, or was this the real Cheryl, all the darts, jabs, demands, and orders merely distractions?

"And the property?" Ted asked. "The money? I swear there's a connection."

"Forget about the money. Get me the name of the guy who killed Richie."

"I'll do what I can. That's all. But I'm telling you, the police will do a better job at this."

Ted wanted to continue to argue the point, but she had stopped listening. Cheryl's eyes were focused over his shoulder. Ted turned to look. A party of five Asian men in dark suits had entered the restaurant and were standing by the hostess podium.

"My business meeting," Cheryl said. "Right on time. Call me tomorrow. Keep me posted." The zombie was gone, hidden behind the efficient businesswoman.

He took a last swallow of beer and wound his way through the now-packed restaurant. The hostess gestured toward Cheryl, and the men headed her way. Their path converged with his, and Ted almost bumped into the leading man, who zigged when Ted expected a zag.

"Excuse me," the man said with a politician's big smile. Queens City Council Member Kevin Pak.

TED LOVED WATCHING METS baseball in May. In the spring there was always hope. Late in the season—the last weeks of August—there might also be hope. But that hope was always tinged with the anxiety of impending implosion. The curse of the Mets. They were there to break hearts.

He marked the years with the fortunes of this team, the way that ancient peoples might have remembered the Year of the Late Snowfall or the Year of the Long Drought. He had turned five the second time they won the World Series, beating the Boston Red Sox. He had broken an arm riding a skateboard when he was ten; he remembered hammering the cast on the seat back in front of him while watching David Cone strike out three batters with nine pitches. He made dean's list every semester in college save the first, having spent three weeks watching the playoffs, only to have the team lose the Subway Series in five soul-crushing games.

Then there were the Willie Randolph Years. The first two were all about rebuilding and renewing hope. The team kept that hope alive until one could almost believe the curse didn't exist and that baseball rewarded hard work, talent, heart, and good coaching. It did not. When they inevitably collapsed in the last three weeks of the third season, Ted was working long, late hours making his mark at HFB, and surreptitiously checking his iPhone during game times, right up until the last brutal loss. The owners—and the press—blamed Randolph. The fans knew better. This was what the Mets did—they broke hearts.

But now it was May, a warm night, and he had a ticket. Jill was unavailable; he had a spare. He bought two beers and two of Nathan's finest and used the empty seat beside him for a makeshift dinner table.

It was a long first inning. St. Louis managed to load the bases with only one out but couldn't get a man home. The Amazins drove the count on the Cardinals' pitcher up to twenty-eight but never got a man to second base. The next five innings held more disappointment and not much else. Ted nursed the second beer until it was too flat to drink. He decided to beat the seventh inning rush and went to find a Bronx Pale Ale and a third Nathan's.

When he got back, the Amazins were loping onto the field, and the scoreboard still read 0–0. As he set about finishing his dinner, a shadow fell over him. He looked up and found a huge hulk of a man standing in the aisle. The man ignored Ted and took the spare seat next to him.

Late in the game fans often came down to fill in the empty seats closer to the field. If there was plenty of room, security tended to look the other way unless someone made a strong objection. What was odd was that there were multitudes of available seats in much better locations all over the stadium. And the fact that in this sea of total strangers, Ted recognized this man.

This was Cheryl's giant. And this was no accidental meeting. In all likelihood, this was also the man whom Jill had caught spying on them the night before. Ted had never been stalked before and was surprised to find that his initial reaction was amusement rather than anxiety or fear. He decided that the best way to play this game was to wait. Eventually, the hulk would deliver his message or otherwise announce his purpose.

Though well-dressed in a blue blazer, button-down shirt, and grey flannel slacks, he was not attractive. The guy had a head like a basketball if anyone had ever wanted to carve such a thing out of granite. Tiny ears and mouth, hairless except for a pair of handleless push brooms that were stuck over each beady eye, and as grim looking as the Gowanus Canal. Where one would usually expect to find a neck, there was merely a tattooed indentation. The rest of him was in proportion: a trunk like a double-door refrigerator and upper arms like bowling balls. Ted doubted that the man could go bowling; those fingers would never fit in the holes. On the other hand, with hands that big, why would he need to use the holes?

Ted smiled and tried for eye contact, having once read that such a tactic connotes trust and openness, leading to positive communication. The guy might not have read the same article.

They watched in silence as the Cardinals went down hitless. Ted could not read the guy at all. It was like sitting next to a black hole. Ted was, therefore, surprised when the man leaned into him as everyone was standing during the stretch.

The guy spoke softly in a high-pitched whisper. *Steroids.* "I want you to do something for me."

Ted was sure he had heard correctly. He stalled. "Sorry. What was that?"

"You heard me. You're Eddie Molloy."

"Ted Molloy. We have a mutual acquaintance, I believe."

"You're working on a thing for Cheryl," the giant said. "You should hurry up and make it right."

The man shifted his stance, and Ted, looking up at him, was momentarily blinded by the floodlights above, which reminded him of his first sighting of this gargantuan thug through the window at Gallagher's. "Isn't this where you're supposed to tell me you want me to find your Velma?"

The guy's eyes almost crossed as he tried to make sense of that. "Who's Velma? I don't get it." It hadn't worked. He looked confused and might not have liked feeling that way.

"Robert Mitchum? Charlotte Rampling? *Farewell, My Lovely*? No? How about Dick Powell, 1944?" Confusion was doing a cross-fade to anger. "I gather you don't watch Turner

Classic Movies." How had this troll found his way to Ted's spare seat? Who knew Ted was coming to the game? Lester. And Cheryl. Ted knew which way he'd bet on that hand. He had mentioned it to her at the restaurant.

Ted was enjoying himself. Feigning innocence, he asked, "Have you been following me?"

The guy swung a hand in front of his face as if he were pushing aside spiderwebs. "So what's the holdup on getting Cheryl her money?"

"Take Me Out to the Ball Game" segued into "Lazy Mary."

"You two should get your priorities straight. I saw her a couple of hours ago, and she told me to drop the money thing." Something made him stop there and not mention her insistence on finding Richie's killer.

"That's not right. She wouldn't do that," the man said. The high-pitched rasp of his voice was more evident the longer he spoke, as though he might have been out of practice.

"I'll call her tomorrow and straighten it out. Okay, friend?" Ted thought about leaving, but he would have to squeeze by this giant. It wasn't going to work.

"What do you know you're not saying?" the guy prodded.

"I'm trying to be polite about this. I don't know you, and it would be unethical for me to share information regarding a client without that client's express permission." The Cardinals took the field, and the fans around them began to take their seats.

"You got some set to be talking about ethics."

"Yo! Siddown, big guy." The voice came from two rows behind. Ted realized that most people in the section were already seated. The relief pitcher was warming up. Ted sat.

The big guy did not. He turned and faced the man who'd yelled. "Would you like to rephrase that, asshole?"

The fan was sitting with friends. He was a regular. Season ticket holder. If something got started, there was a good chance the troll would be fighting half the section. "Yeah. I meant to say, 'Sit the *fuck* down, big guy.'"

The chant started. Four Mets fans were pointing at the big guy and yelling, "Asshole!" in unison. It spread quickly. By the fifth "Asshole," there were two dozen others who had joined in.

A blaze of rage erupted on the man's face, but it turned to stone immediately. He bent down, his bulk looming over Ted, obscuring the field, fans, and everything but that massive face. "You take care of Cheryl. She is owed big-time. Half a mil, Eddie. She's waiting. Get it. If not, you'll never see me coming."

"Asshole! Asshole!" The whole section had joined in, everyone pointing and jeering.

Ted raised his hands in surrender but said nothing. If this guy did come chasing after him, he was sure he'd feel the ground shaking.

The big man pushed his way to the aisle and stomped up the steps, followed by a chorus of boos. Ted stayed where he was.

-21-

TED COULDN'T SHAKE THE feeling that his life had been invaded. This man, or other persons unknown, had gone to a lot of trouble—possibly even followed him on previous occasions—to impress on him the idea that he should be frightened. Well, it had worked.

That night, he couldn't sleep. The giant's voice continued to whisper, like a cold wind through a cracked window. Ted's brain, both exhausted and energized, would not stop. Old movies didn't help. Ted needed the reassurance that there was some structure in the universe, some standard of continuity, something he could rely on. He needed a *Law & Order* all-night marathon.

"Objection. Leading the witness. You should have called that one, McCoy. You're slipping," he said, providing his own legal commentary.

It was coming up on one in the morning. He was to meet Lester at the courthouse in a few hours for the foreclosure auctions. Showing up red-eyed and dopey wasn't going to cut it.

The jury came in with a guilty verdict. Surprise. McCoy won. McCoy may have been a semicloseted liberal, but the show's true bias was always evident. The credits rolled at super speed, and the next episode began.

A pair of young lovers walked a lonely street in the West Village. They laughed together. Kissed. There was the sound of a moan from behind a dumpster. The girl screamed. Ted hit the MUTE button. He had watched the same episode the week before.

Ted reached for his cell phone. "Hey, Siri. Call Jill."

The phone rang four times, and he was surprised when it was Jill who answered and not her voice mail.

"You're up," he said.

"You too."

"What are you watching?"

"Something with Olivia de Havilland. I came in in the middle. It's good. I think. You?"

"My hero."

"Jack McCoy. You must have had a hard day."

"Is Jackie back?" Part of him wanted to blurt out all of his growing suspicions. *Hey, Jill, I think your wife is scamming some old lady out of her property. And helping those jerks build that ugly skyscraper in Corona.* He filed the urge under Old Resentments with all the other poisons. They were more likely to kill him than to lead to any greater understanding of what was really going on.

"You know she doesn't like that name." Jill didn't put any energy behind it. "She's pissed at me." If there was any part of her that felt sad or troubled, she didn't let it show.

"And me," Ted said, though he could not remember a time when Jacqueline Clavette had not been angry with him. She had resented his early success when they both worked for the family firm, she resented his prehistory with her wife, and she resented his friendship with Jill now.

"I'm sorry," Jill said, surprising him.

"No, my fault entirely. I shouldn't have put you in the middle." He let her have a moment for that to soak in. "Hey. Do you remember that guy you thought was following us the other night? The big guy at the game."

"What?"

"A big, ugly, bald-headed guy. You tried to point him out to me."

"I did?"

He could hear the television on her end. *The Dark*

Mirror. Late forties. De Havilland played twins. "You don't remember?"

"Is it important?" She must have heard some urgency in his voice, because her voice became more animated, more engaged.

It was late. "It's all right. Forget it."

"What are you doing up?"

"I couldn't sleep. I have some things on my mind." If he continued with this case, he was going to have to tell her at some point. And he was going to continue.

"How was the game?"

"You didn't watch?"

"I cooked."

"You didn't miss much." What would he tell her? That a double-door refrigerator in a suit had shown up and made threats? Or that he suspected Jackie was a candidate for disbarment, if not prison?

He couldn't tell her. Not tonight. Maybe he was wrong. Being wrong would be good.

"Jacqueline's away again next Thursday," she said.

"Mets are on the road. Pittsburgh and then out west."

"I'll check the schedule. We'll find a night." Her voice softened with concern. "Get some sleep. You sound . . ."

"Stressed?"

"Worried."

"I'm good. Good night, Jill."

And as his thumb came down on the big red dot, Ted thought he heard her whisper, "Love you."

22

THE GROUP OF PROTESTORS in front of the courthouse had grown. There were now more than two dozen men and women holding signs, chanting slogans, and buttonholing uninterested passersby. Ted wouldn't have minded seeing the redhead who'd accosted him a couple days before—under other circumstances. As it was, he backtracked and took the long way around the block.

He met Lester on the courthouse steps. His brown suit was pressed, and he was wearing a new white shirt. He was sipping coffee from a Kennedy Fried Chicken cup.

"You're looking good," Ted said. "I haven't missed anything, have I?"

"No, team Corona's still inside. You clean up real good yourself."

Grey chalk stripe from Kozinn. Custom shirt and shoes. Remnants of an earlier version of Ted Molloy. "Old habits. If you dress like a million . . ."

"Only this is Sutphin Boulevard," Lester said.

Maybe the Mimi Fong tie was a touch over the top, but Jill had given it to him, and it was his favorite. Lester had a point. Auction bidders were filing in, mostly men but some women, in everything from donated coats to tracksuits and high-tops to silk sports jackets. The lawyers all wore the identical uniform of shiny blue suit, white shirt, red tie, and scuffed black oxfords. The women wore pumps.

"I want these guys to know we are serious people," Ted said. "Money. Power. Influence."

Lester nodded. "Yeah, well, you're all that and more. The Corona boys were near the front of the line. Two guys. I got somebody to point them out to me, introduced myself, and told them you want to chat when they're done. I told them you're a big buyer. An investor. It got their interest."

"I'll try to play the part."

"They've got three properties to bid on. They were almost first to go into the courtroom. If we're lucky, they'll be out soon."

"Can we go in and talk to them?"

Lester shook his head, and Ted thought of an old work-horse. "I told you. If you want to get inside for the auctions, you have to show up before nine—and bring certified checks."

Ted raised hands in mock surrender. "I know. I'm impatient, that's all."

"The court also takes cash," Lester said with a grin.

"That's interesting." Ted thought for a moment. "Somebody could launder money that way."

"Yeah? How would that work?"

"You put down cash at the auction, right?" He warmed to the subject. It was the kind of crime he could almost admire. Simple. Effective. Victimless. "You pay full price. There's a deed, but there's no need to report the transaction to any government body except the county clerk. Then, when you sell it, you get paid by check—which you can deposit anywhere. As long as you pay capital gains on the sale, who's going to care? It's only illegal if your *intent* is to launder money."

"You have a criminal mind," Lester said. "I would not be surprised to learn that Corona Partners uses cash rather than certified checks."

"Oh?"

"Wait till you meet these guys."

The first wave of lunch seekers had left the building before Lester nudged him. "Here they come."

Corona Partners was represented by two hard-looking men in their early thirties, clean-shaven, one with cropped hair, the other bald. Both wore tight designer jeans, white silk T-shirts, and thigh-length black leather jackets. The one with hair had the unreadable face of a poker champion. The other was taller and had the flattened nose and scarred eyebrows of a boxer. They both looked like hired muscle. Ted thought he might have overreached. They probably had methods of negotiation that he lacked.

The two were looking for Lester in the crowd. He hailed them with a raised hand. The taller one carried an oversized legal briefcase with a thick wire leash that ran up his sleeve.

Lester gave them a big fake grin. "Thanks for agreeing to see us. My boss has a few questions for you guys, if you don't mind. This is Ted Molloy."

The two heads swung, and they both examined Ted, as though committing his features to memory.

"You are cop?" the stone-faced one said. The accent could have been Russian. Eastern European, certainly.

Ted tried a laugh. It sounded like a cough. "Do I look like a cop?"

The man let his eyes inventory Ted's clothing: suit, shirt, shoes, and tie. "You look like cop on the take."

So much for dressing to impress. "I used to practice law."

"Cop. Lawyer. Same, same. All crooked."

Ted had suffered through his share of bad lawyer jokes and a few good ones. But being called crooked by the poster child for the Russian mob was a new low. He shook it off. "Can I buy you a coffee? Lunch? A drink? Or we can chat right here."

"What we chat?"

And there it was. Ted took a deep breath and dove in. "I might be interested in buying, if you're selling."

"We buy and sell. All the time."

The role of high roller did not sit well on Ted's shoulders.

He felt naked in front of these two. He decided to take his chances with a direct approach. "Your firm flipped some properties the other side of Flushing Meadows Park. I'm trying to get a handle on what went on. Corona Partners doesn't usually get involved in deals this big."

"What deal?"

"I've got the block and lot or the address. Which do you want? This was a group of properties that came up for auction as a package."

"Why do you care about this? They are sold. We don't own these."

The guy knew exactly what properties Ted was asking about. "I want to buy in that neighborhood. I'm looking into this transaction."

"You should forget this one."

"That's what I thought at first, but now I'm not so sure."

Leaning in to Ted, the man spoke in an exaggerated whisper, as though bestowing a great confidence. "No. Be sure. Forget this one."

"Records show that LBC bought the properties, but you guys were not the sellers. So county records must not be updated yet. Does Corona Partners also do business under another name?"

"Hey, Ted. You no listen. You are too busy making questions."

The sounds of traffic, the protestors, and the gabble of voices from the constant flow of lawyers and petitioners had receded, as though the Russians traveled in a soundproof bubble. Each word spoken inside the bubble was magnified and possessed a clarity that was almost painful. Outside the bubble did not exist.

Ted persevered. "The seller is listed as One-Hundred-Fourteenth-Street LLC, which really tells me nothing. You see what I'm saying?" He was practically stumbling over his words in his haste to get his questions out. "So, can you give me any leads on who you sold to?"

The other Russian closed in on Ted. Even with one arm encumbered by the briefcase, he looked like he would have little trouble creating a lot of damage.

"Persistence without wisdom is pointless. Foolish. I do not think you are a foolish man, Ted. Why act the fool?" His accent was as strong as his partner's, but his command of English was much greater. The sense of menace was a push.

Ted's hands and face tingled with adrenaline—or soaring blood pressure. The double threat from these two thugs had ionized the air around them. But he also felt the constraint of being in such a public place. Nothing bad could happen on the courthouse grounds, steps from police officers, surrounded by witnesses. He could not see how this false sense of security would ultimately betray him, so he blundered on blindly. "If you can't answer me, then tell me who can. I know I'm annoying—it's that lawyer thing kicking in. I can't help myself. Just give me a name and a phone number, and I'll go away."

The same man answered. "I am trying to help you, Ted. When I tell you to forget about this, I am your friend."

"A name?" Ted said. "That's all I'm asking."

The first man stepped between them, his face inches from Ted's. "A rodent ask me that last week. I think he not so smart, like you. I tell him same thing. Don't ask again. Be smart, Ted. Goodbye."

The two men sauntered away down the steps. The bubble burst, sounds returned, and Ted felt light-headed and shaky, like a man who'd stepped off a curb and had a bus miss him by inches. He turned to Lester, whose main contribution after introductions had been to stay out of the way. "These guys are buddies of yours?"

"I never said that. I said I recognized the name Corona.

I went inside and asked some people on the line, and they pointed me to those two goons. I could say I'm sorry, but I'm not. You wanted to talk with them. Now you've done that."

"And what do we have to show for it?" Ted asked.

"We know that some nasty-ass mothers want you to stop looking into this."

23

TED FELT HIS BODY begin to relax, but his mind was still buzzing with conflicting thoughts and possibilities. He gestured for Lester to walk with him, and the two men crossed the plaza and turned down Sutphin, skirting the edge of the ragtag group of protestors.

"Any ideas? What next?" Lester asked.

"We need Barbara Miller's signature." He stopped walking to search his pockets for the document.

"Hey! Wise guy. Yeah, you. Hold up."

There was that voice again. A bit strident this time. It was the woman from the protest group, the one he had heard on the radio. He would have known that voice anywhere. And he knew that she was talking to him. At that moment Ted did not want to talk to her or anyone else. He began walking again.

"You know that girl?" Lester asked.

"I want to talk to you," she called.

Ted looked over his shoulder. The red hair streamed out around a face flushed with indignation.

"She's one of the protestors," he said, lengthening his stride. The light at the corner was changing. Either they made a crazy dash for it through midday traffic, or they subjected themselves to a speech on good citizenship. Even if the message was to be delivered in a voice guaranteed to raise hormone levels in a male corpse, Ted still leaned toward running.

"Maybe we should split up," Lester said. The woman had broken into a trot and was covering ground.

"She's only after me," Ted said.

"That's what I'm talking about," Lester said.

The absurdity of two grown men in suits being pursued by a single unarmed—and very attractive—young woman, steps from the courthouse, hit Ted. "You go," he said to Lester, handing over the typed agreement. "Get to Seaside and get Miller's signature. Find me at Gallagher's when you're done."

Lester made a gesture like tipping his cap and hustled away down the street. Ted waited for the woman.

"Don't run," he called. "Please. I'm here."

She planted herself in front of him, hands on hips. "Why are you ducking me?"

"We haven't been formally introduced," Ted said, giving her a blast of his most charming smile, a holdover from better days. He was prepared to endure her lecture, but he wanted it to be on his terms.

She opened her mouth and closed it again. Perhaps he had overwhelmed her.

"Ted Molloy." He held out a hand. She ignored it. She had yet to smile.

She found her voice again. "I want to know why you were talking to those two Russian mobsters. You do know they're mobsters, right?"

Then again, maybe he had read the situation all wrong. He retrieved the flagging hand and used it to point to her feet. "Your socks are cute." She was wearing a button-down blouse and khakis with a pair of backless Merrells. Her socks were mismatched. "Port and starboard?" One red, one green.

She looked down. "Oh, darn." Her eyes met his, and she cocked her head to one side, challenging him, daring him to make further comment. "I've got another pair like these. They're my clown socks." She had pale blue eyes and near-translucent skin. Ted imagined she wore hats and 55 SPF all summer to avoid getting freckles. He wanted to tell her not to worry—she'd look great in anything, including freckles. He couldn't remember why he had been in such a hurry the other day.

"Okay," he said, "but you're a happy clown." How old was she? It was hard to tell. Younger than him by a decade, at least. She carried herself with a confidence that added a few years. Twenty-nine, he decided. Exactly a decade. She was too young for him. And too intense. But she was a beauty. And there was that voice.

She frowned for an instant, possibly distressed that he was refusing to take her seriously. But instead of cutting him dead, she looked into his face. Then she surprised him by granting both the smile and an extended hand. "Kenzie Zielinski. I'm a community organizer."

"'McKenzie from Ridgewood'?" He took the hand and was pleased by her strong grip. "You were on NPR yesterday. I knew I recognized that voice."

She smiled again. Ted thought it a very good smile.

"You heard me? Yeah, Kenzie or McKenzie, I answer to both. I can't believe they cut me off. Kevin Pak is such a crook. They're all crooks." She laughed and threw up her hands in a gesture indicating acceptance of inevitability. "It's a thankless job, I know. Why would you be a city councilman if you couldn't skim a little, right?"

"I hadn't given it much thought."

"Typical. You see? That's exactly what I'm up against. People won't recognize a threat until it's too late to do anything about it. Now answer me. What were you doing with the Brighton Beach Banking Association back there? You don't look their type."

"I suppose I should be flattered," he said. So far, the charm assault had been a bust. On the other hand, she wasn't preaching or lecturing. They were talking. Talking was good.

She looked him over. "You're not a regular here."

"I used to be. I've been breaking in a new research assistant."

"Lester. Yeah. Everybody knows Lester."

Did he detect a hint of dislike or disapproval? "That doesn't sound like an endorsement."

"He's all right. I want to know where you stand on the Spike."

"The tower? I think it's both ugly and going to happen no matter what."

A flicker of a scowl. "You're half-right. I hear you're looking into the history on some of those properties."

Ted shouldn't have been surprised. The courthouse was a petri dish for rumor. She could have learned about him from any number of sources. Lester may have been overzealous in his research, or Little Richie indiscreet.

"Who's been sharing my secrets?" he asked.

"Oh, come on. People tell me things. It's called trust. If I give them up, then pretty soon nobody tells me nothing."

Ted knew about trust. It rarely paid a dividend. "My interest in the project is very limited."

"You're not an LBC guy." She gave him another look over. "Or a lawyer. Your shoes are shiny, and your suit isn't."

Without reason, he felt flattered. "Are you a lawyer?"

"Organizer. I told you."

"So you did. Is that a real job?"

"I'm not going to let up, you know. You're going to tell me what you're doing."

Ted realized that they were both enjoying the game. The same attitude from a man might have been annoying or worse. But as long as they were talking, this good-looking woman was focused entirely on him. What was there not to like about that? He made a decision.

"Sharing trade secrets doesn't help pay my beer bill, but for you I might make an exception," he said. "Are you willing to trade?"

She tilted her head and squinted one eye. "I've been working to stop this damned project for two years. They have a big head start on me, but I've learned a lot."

She wasn't going to give up what she knew without getting good value. He respected that. "So, it's worth having a conversation. Are you free for lunch tomorrow?"

"Okay," she agreed immediately. "But we split the tab."

That meant choosing a place that a community organizer could afford. "Vietnamese all right with you?"

24

TED OVERDOSED ON GALLLAGHER'S iced tea that afternoon, earning himself a caffeine headache, but he reduced the stack of paperwork that had been building all week and returned all of the important phone calls. Lester managed to get the notarized agreement from Barbara Miller and filed it with the appropriate clerk before the courthouse closed for the weekend.

"Quitting time, Lili," Ted called out.

"Coming up." Lili was finishing her final prep for the first wave of happy hour devotees. Nearby shift changes set the pace. The nurses from the hospital up on Broadway stopped in for a white wine or vodka and tonic and a chance to meet up with the firemen from Engine 287, who showed up for a Guinness or a Bud and a chance to chat up a nurse. Paulie McGirk had hit his limit, but Tito, the Hungarian waiter who worked at Keens Steakhouse, had taken Paulie's place, prepping himself for work with a brandy or two—"gasoline," he called it. Later on, the retail clerks from Target and the Queens Center mall would arrive wanting cosmos and Long Island iced tea. Ted liked to be long gone by then.

"Here ya ah," she said, plunking down a pint of SingleCut lager and following it with his weekly tab. He peeled off two of Cheryl's Benjamins and told Lili to keep the change.

The beer was light and hoppy. A good beer for spring, with a promise of summer. He had earned it. There was nothing more he could do about the Barbara Miller case until a judge looked at the file. He was free to enjoy the weekend, and lunch with a beautiful woman on Saturday.

The bar was already beginning to get loud, packed with firemen who all looked to be six foot three, broad shouldered, and handsome. One of them put money in the jukebox on the wall, and an old Allman Brothers tune began to play. A pair of nurses burst out in high-pitched laughter as another of New York's bravest completed the punch line to a joke Ted had heard told a dozen times on Friday nights. He would have bet the nurses had heard it before, too. He finished the beer and stood. It was time to move on. The Mets were on the road, and if he hustled, he could put in an hour at the gym before game time.

The front door swung open again, and another pair of tall men walked in and looked around. The happy hour lights were dim, and it took Ted a moment to recognize one of them as Detective Duran. Ted sat back down. The detective saw him anyway. He tapped his partner on the arm and pointed. Neither man was smiling.

"How you doing, Mr. Molloy?" Duran said. "This is my partner, Chuck Kasabian."

"I was just leaving," Ted said.

Duran ignored Ted's dubious attempt at escape. "Do you have a minute?"

It wasn't really a question. "Sit down," Ted said. "Can I get you something? Lili makes a wicked Shirley Temple."

Kasabian could have passed for a fireman in a suit, if such a thing existed. He was tall and fit, with a face like one of the old Marlboro men from the days when rugged cowpokes smoked cigarettes while herding cattle against a background of Wyoming sky. Before they all got fitted for nasal oxygen tubes. He squinted at Ted and said, "What do you call a busload of lawyers going over a cliff?"

"I don't practice law," Ted said.

"A good start," Kasabian said.

"You need a snare drum if you're going to keep telling jokes as old as that. Ask me if I know any detective jokes."

"Don't be a wiseass, Molloy."

"I do know some, but I'd probably have to explain them to you."

Kasabian didn't crack a smile. "Do you own a gun, Molloy?"

"Without a permit? That would be against the law, Detective."

Duran had told Ted that if he had to come back, he wasn't coming alone. And now Ted was facing the bad cop. He spoke to the good cop. "Am I now a target of that investigation we mentioned?"

"You need to clear up some issues, and then we'll get out of your hair," Duran answered.

"Oddly enough, I am not comforted," Ted said.

"If we're going to be wasting our time," Kasabian said, "I'd rather do it at the precinct. Let's take him in."

"Mr. Molloy has no reason not to cooperate with us," Duran replied.

Ted took a small measure of comfort from that double negative. Duran was still playing good cop. "Why are you here?" Ted asked.

"Murder," Duran said.

Kasabian was impatient. "You had dinner with the wife of the deceased last night. Was that a romantic meeting?"

They were keeping close tabs on Cheryl—or him. "We went over this." Ted glared at Duran.

Duran was unimpressed. He'd been glared at before. "Come on, Ted. Let's do it again, for Chuck," he said. "He missed your story first time around."

Ted bit back a sigh. Stonewalling the cops only worked when you were in the power seat. He had nothing. They'd want to hear the story three or four times, looking for the tiniest inconsistencies, before they'd quit. He wasn't going to make it to the gym, and if he wanted to get home in time for the first pitch, he had better get started. Putting off the confrontation until he had counsel was pointless. And he might learn something from the questions they asked.

"Mrs. Rubiano is a very strange woman," he began. "She believes that I can somehow find out who killed her husband. She actually tried to hire me to do this." The remaining hundred-dollar bills in his pocket suddenly felt like lead plates. "I am also working on recovering some abandoned funds—that's what I do. Her husband started on the case after I said I wasn't interested. At first she was very insistent that I go after this money, but as of last night, she told me to drop it. Flat out, no discussion. She is a forceful and resourceful woman, if somewhat inconsistent in her moods and desires."

"He's lying. I don't buy a word of it," Kasabian said.

Ted recognized this for the gambit that it was. The detective wasn't challenging the facts; he wanted to provoke a response. Kasabian probably had a good side to him. Nice to his kids. Only beat his wife when she deserved it.

"I wouldn't in your shoes," Ted said with an insincere smile. "But there's more. Later on last night I was approached at the Mets game by a steroidal man who made vague but believable threats indicating that if I did not get this money for Mrs. Rubiano, I would be forced to endure his presence again."

"Did this guy have a name?" Duran asked.

"We didn't exchange business cards," Ted answered.

"Tell us about this abandoned-funds thing again," Duran said.

This was safe ground, and he now had enough information to make a story out of it. Ted recited his standard pitch about how he went about doing the research, making a deal, and petitioning the court. Then he described some of the oddities of this particular case, omitting any mention of Miller's mental condition.

"So you've got the missing pages from the court file, the fact that someone basically stole those buildings from Miss Miller, and the involvement of those Russian hoods. I think there's something very suspicious about the whole thing." Ted felt smug and didn't mind if it showed a little.

"Hoods?" Kasabian said.

"What?" Ted said.

"You said 'hoods.' Not 'gangbangers,' 'thugs,' 'punks,' or even 'mobsters.' You said 'hoods.'"

"Guilty. I watch too many old movies."

"And you've got an active imagination, I would guess." Kasabian's sneer said that he didn't have much appreciation for imagination.

"I want to hear about this guy who talked to you at the ball game," Duran said. "Describe him and tell me exactly what he said."

"I don't remember the exact words," Ted said. The "ass-hole" chant was all that came to mind. "But when I told him that Cheryl wanted me to drop the money thing, he didn't believe it."

Kasabian almost rolled his eyes. "So, she's Cheryl now?"

Ted tried to ignore him and mostly succeeded. "He's tall, broad, thick through the waist like a weight lifter, not a body-builder. Shaved head. Some tats on his neck, but I couldn't tell you what they were. I'm convinced he's the same guy who was hanging around with Mrs. Rubiano earlier this week. I mentioned him to you then."

"There's a lot of guys like that around," Duran said. "Anything else?"

"He ties a Windsor knot with a button-down shirt," Ted said, ticked that Duran hadn't shown any interest in the troll.

"What are you? The fashion critic?" Duran asked with a smile. Kasabian laughed without one.

"Sister Alberta Marie would have smacked me on the head

with a ruler for not tying a four-in-hand." He was beginning to have fun tweaking these two.

Duran nodded as though he recognized a fellow Catholic-school sufferer. "The guy wears a tie to a baseball game?"

"He was definitely overdressed for the bleachers." Ted was feeling much too comfortable, he realized.

Kasabian was watching him, waiting for a misstep. "Have you got plans to see Mrs. Rubiano again?"

"Have you got any other ideas as to who killed Richie? Or why? Or do you think if you bust my chops enough, I'll confess just to shut you up?" Ted was fed up. He had cooperated—maybe not to the fullest extent but far beyond what any competent criminal defense attorney would have allowed.

A swell of raucous laughter rolled from the bar, drowning any chance of communication. As the roar subsided, Kasabian sat back and shot a glance at his partner.

"My partner thinks you're telling the truth," Kasabian said. "I don't. I think Mr. Rubiano was a punk, only one step up from people like you. But it's my job to find out who did him. And I think it's you. I don't know whether the wife is involved or not, but I'm going to find out."

It felt good to have the issue stated so bluntly. There was no further need to be polite. Or to stick around. "Then we're done, aren't we? Unless you're going to arrest me. No? I didn't think so." Ted turned to Duran. "This is the last time we talk without my lawyer."

Duran didn't like it. Ted didn't care.

· 2 5 ·

TED HAD A MOUTH full of Listerine when the downstairs door buzzed. He was already running late. He spat and hustled.

"Who's there?" He spoke into the device with no expectation of anything resembling communication. As expected, the answer from the street door was unintelligible, though the tone was authoritative and insistent. Not the cops. Not the Russian mob. Though he had not been confronted by a Jehovah's Witness, process server, or magazine subscription salesperson in years, Ted was reluctant to let his guard down.

He checked his phone. His Uber was eight minutes out. "Speak up. Who the hell are you?" he yelled.

Through the crackle and distortion, he made out the faint words "Con Fitzmaurice."

Jill's grandfather. His Honor Cornelius Fitzmaurice.

Ted buzzed him in and opened the door.

AT THE REHEARSAL DINNER twelve years earlier, Ted and the Judge had found themselves alone together for a moment. Maybe it had been planned that way.

The dinner was winding down. It had been of necessity a small affair—ushers, bridesmaids, family, and assorted plus-ones. Ted had manfully picked up the tab, despite the pain to his bank account. Jill's mother had ungraciously agreed to limit the count to fifty, and with only minor emotional bruising, they had made it. Ted was the sole representative of the Molloy clan. His mother had been gone before he'd finished law school. Ted was the last survivor of a line distinguished by the absence of their mark on history.

The ushers were a mixed lot of Jill's brothers and Ted's

friends, the best man, Carter Harken, a gentle soul who had rejected an offer from Whyte & Pace to join a tech start-up in London as lead counsel. Despite knowing next to nothing about the Internet, international law, or stock offerings, he was already worth mid eight figures—but had never learned to hold his liquor. He'd been shit-faced before the salads were cleared. No matter. Judging by the frowns from the Fitzmaurices, they had been anticipating something like this. They were in mufti; the formal wear would not be brought out until the next day. The Judge, in a rare show of good cheer, was sporting a paisley bow tie with his blue suit and spit-shined wing tips.

"You surprised me, Teddy. I never saw you for the kind of sycophant who married solely to advance your career." It was a joke. The Judge signaled this by smiling for a split second after delivering the line.

Ted had learned not to fear the Judge's humor. The wounds could sting but rarely required stitches. They were each holding flagons of cognac, aged for half a century in French caves. The Judge treated it like the house wine. Ted would have preferred a beer. He generally avoided spirits and was all too aware that a bottle of this stuff cost as much as a month's rent. Most of Jill's family lived as if they were blind to cost. They did not despise money—they worked hard at acquiring it—but they spent it freely.

"I love your granddaughter, sir. She loves me. It's that simple."

The old man chuckled, honestly amused at the sincerity. "Simple? Teddy, I have failed you. Nothing is simple."

"No. I know that. The Jesuits beat that into me my freshman year of high school."

"And you believe that the two of you will be happy together?"

The Judge was digging. The only defense was a strict

adherence to an appearance of openness. Sometimes it worked. "I hope that I can make Jill happy. I think I can."

"Jill. My favorite. You know that? Of course you do. I make no secret of it. She'll upset the applecart someday or severely disappoint me." He looked away as he said this so that Ted could not read his eyes.

"Sir?" He decided that the Judge had already downed more than a few of these after-dinner treats—and more than a few pre- and during-libations as well. But drunk or sober, he was equally devious.

"I wish you both the best, Teddy. And I hope to hell you know what you're getting yourself in for. Forgive me. I'm sure you do. I think the world of both of you, but never forget that I'm the damned patriarch of this clan. You are marrying Jill, but you will need to earn a place in the clan. Nothing personal. It's our way."

In the end, Ted had failed to find his place.

THE JUDGE WAS NOW retired from the bench and looked a generation older than Ted remembered. He'd read that the governor had offered a two-year exemption from the mandatory retirement age but Con had turned him down to "spend more time with his family." Knowing the Judge's distaste for any family member other than Jill, Ted had written an entirely different scenario in his mind, one in which the stench of backroom favors, promises, and sellouts had hung about the old man like a malodorous fog. The Judge had left when he still had the chance of having a courthouse named after him in some upstate county rather than being pilloried by some muckraking young reporter who had not yet learned that dealmaking and corruption were the yin and yang of life in Albany.

"May I come in?" the old man asked.

Ted realized that he'd been staring.

"Is Jill all right?" he said, not able to imagine another reason for this apparition being on his doorstep.

"I should have called. Forgive an old man; I was afraid that you might avoid meeting with me." He peered over Ted's shoulder at the meager expanse of his living quarters.

"On the contrary. Curiosity would have won out over anger and resentment. Come in. I can spare you a few minutes. But I warn you, I have to leave soon." Formal, nonconfrontational, but with limits. His ground, his rules.

"I could drop you somewhere. We could chat on the way."

They were negotiating turf—home advantage—Ted realized. As humble as the squalor of his abode was, he did not want to have a conversation with this formidable figure in the padded luxury of the back of a chauffeured Mercedes. There were neighborhoods in Queens where a vehicle like that could be stripped for parts while waiting for the light to change. Neither did Ted want the Judge to know enough of his personal business to see where Ted was going or whom he might meet there.

"Maybe next time," he said. He wanted to know why the Judge had come but would not give him the satisfaction of having to be asked.

The Judge hesitated. "I hope I don't make you late," he said finally, and stepped over the threshold. "Once you hear what I have to say, you may have some questions."

First round to Ted. The discussion would be held across his IKEA table.

The Judge took a chair and angled it so that he was sitting with his back to the wall, facing the room. Ted took the chair opposite and angled it the same way, forcing the older man to uncomfortably turn his head to speak.

"I can offer you water or seltzer. There might be a beer." Despite his time as a part of the Fitzmaurice clan, Ted had never developed the family appreciation for brown-colored spirits. And his budget would not have supported cognacs distilled before he was born.

"Nothing, thank you. How have you been?"

"I get by."

The Judge had helped Ted land his next job after he was given the boot but had warned him that was as much as he could do. Ted blamed only himself for making a dog's breakfast of that opportunity. As far as he was concerned, they were even. Neither owed a favor or expected one.

"Yes," the Judge said. "I knew you were resourceful."

Ted fought the urge to check the Uber clock. The Judge would like him to be distracted.

"I know that you and Jill have kept in touch," the Judge said. The lightness of his delivery was a warning in itself.

This had to be a feint. His Honor hadn't come all the way out to bucolic Maspeth to chat about family.

"We're friends," Ted said.

He nodded. "Has it ever crossed your mind that what happened between you two was, in a way, inevitable?"

"Are we talking about sexual orientation? Or family interference? They think I turned Jill off from men."

"I thought you were aware of her preferences. Before the marriage, I mean."

"You knew?" Ted had been taken off guard and had revealed an iota of his ignorance. The old bull had succeeded. The lunch Ted had been anticipating for twenty-four hours was forgotten. He wanted to stay home and fight.

"Oh, yes. Jill has always talked to me. Confided in me. It was painful. I wanted to believe that the two of you could find a better solution."

"You could have helped."

"I thought I did."

Ted shook his head. "Only when it cost you nothing. You got me an interview. Thank you. But you did nothing, said nothing, to the family when it counted. One word from you would have meant a lot."

"My duty was to the family. I don't agree with all they do, but I can only lead where I know I will be followed. Family politics are as complex as any other kind. More so, in fact. And don't be so sure that interview cost me nothing. All favors have a price. That's the world I live in."

"Is that how you explain it to yourself?" Ted wanted to smash the Judge's patrician reserve—and maybe his nose, too. He pulled himself back from that abyss. "And why are you here?"

"What exactly is your complaint? You landed on your feet."

True. He wasn't homeless, hungry, or destitute. But neither was he living the life he had imagined when he first worked for the Judge, fifteen years before. "They hated me and made every day that I stayed around after the divorce pure torture. When they offered to keep me on—it was in a way that would ensure I would be even more miserable." He stopped. Rehashing the past was a weak man's play. He was allowing himself to be baited like a lawyer with his first case.

The Judge's eyes lit up. The advantage had swung to him and he knew it. "What do you expect from them? A family is a pack. To wrong one is to wrong all."

THE WHOLE CONVERSATION SO far had been jousting for position. The point would be revealed only when the Judge held the high ground. Ted knew he was being manipulated but could not resist. "And they hounded her after the annulment. They couldn't live with an amicable divorce. They had to push on Jill until she stopped speaking to me."

"In the end, Jill went along with their wishes," the Judge said. "That was the price they demanded. She paid it, until she didn't have to any longer."

"That's a cold-blooded perspective," Ted said.

"You think? I would imagine perspective is all, isn't it?"

Ted was done. He knew the one chink in the old warrior's armor—Jill—and Ted would not attack there, no matter the provocation. Screw it. He had a lunch date. He made an elaborate show of checking the time on his phone.

"Why are you here?" Ted asked.

"I'm taking too much of your time. Again, my car is at your service."

Ted's phone pinged. A text. Uber. "I have a ride. They'll be outside in four minutes."

"Then I had better get on with it, hadn't I?"

All the fuss had been preamble. The ancient history had all been distraction.

"Make it quick," Ted said.

There were two red pencils in a coffee cup on the table. The Judge took them out, examined the points, and replaced them, aligning them in precise parallel. He smiled grimly when done. "I was sent here today with a request. From Jill. She would not presume to ask you herself, but believe me—I do speak for her."

"She doesn't need you for that. Jill knows that she can ask me anything."

"It has to do with Jacqueline."

Ted acknowledged that he could be difficult on that subject. But there was no need for Jill to have sent the old man.

"I've got no fight with Jackie," Ted said. "We don't get along, but I wish her no harm."

"Ah, Teddy. You never were a good liar."

"Time to go." Ted stood.

"You can tell me whatever you like, but don't lie to yourself." The Judge remained seated.

"My ride is here."

The Judge held up his index finger. One minute. "You're

working on a surplus-money case. I'd like you to withdraw your filing."

Damn. Ted should have known. All that smoke about family had been there to keep him from thinking. And it had worked. So who was really behind the Judge's visit? Not Jill. Who in this mare's nest of players did the old man represent?

"Not a chance," he said.

"Jill is afraid that if you prevail, Jacqueline will take a fall."

Another realization hit. The Judge knew that Jill was Ted's chink, too. "Is that what you told her?"

"It's true—Jacqueline may have been overly aggressive in pursuit of an outcome and will now suffer some embarrassment for her actions. And it will be embarrassing for a great number of other people. Powerful people who would rather owe you a favor than punish you after the fact."

"Who? Give me names." *And let's get this game over with.*

"It's not that simple. Tell me what you want, and I will get it delivered."

"I told you what I want. Names."

"You want the money? The million or so, whatever it is? It's yours."

Ted held back a laugh. How far would they go? "How about five mil? Why not ten?"

"How about you get to practice law again?"

He was a cunning bastard. With a phone call or two, Cornelius Fitzmaurice could reopen those gates for Ted. He wanted so much to say yes. And so he didn't. "And Miss Miller? It's her money. And she's owed a lot more."

"She's being well provided for. What does she need anyway? A better wheelchair? *Two* scoops of vanilla on her dessert? She's in one of the best assisted-living homes in Queens, for which she pays nothing. She's got twenty-four-hour care. The best doctors. How much longer has she got? Months? A year?"

The old man was miles ahead of him. Of course, he had come prepared, but who had prepped him? Where had he come by this detailed knowledge? How much more did he know that was still hidden from Ted? Ted chose the all-encompassing question: "How do you know so much about this?"

The Judge smiled as though from on high. "People talk to me. That's how these things get done. You know that."

Ted's phone pinged again. The car was waiting. There was no reason to stay any longer; the Judge had delivered his message and would offer no more information of use. Ted stood and walked to the door. "It's time for you to leave."

"Think about it, Teddy. I'd like to help."

Ted opened the door and made a show of getting out his keys.

"You will have some important people beholden to you. People who don't forget. This isn't just some local pissing match. It goes to Albany. To the top."

Ted was shocked—not only at the revelation itself, but also at the fact that the Judge had presented it so casually. But Ted also understood that this was as much threat as inducement. He let none of this show in his face but jiggled the keys. He needed to give this some thought. And he needed to get away before the Judge saw that he may have scored a hit.

The Judge sighed and rose to his feet. He stopped in the doorway, blocking it. "Do it for Jill."

They both knew that Ted would not let her be harmed. But would that protection extend to the family? No. To Jackie? Jacqueline. Ted wasn't so sure. He needed to shake the old man. A thought flashed through his mind, and he gave it voice before he had the chance to temper it. "Answer me one question. Why did Richie have to die?"

"Who?" For the first time, the old man appeared to be genuinely confused. Maybe he was a great poker player.

Ted pushed further. "Who saw him as a threat? Christ, you could have bought him off for pennies on the dollar."

"I don't know what you're talking about."

Was he lying?

Nothing Ted could say or do would crack that Fitzmaurice carapace. There was nothing more to be gained by talking with him.

"Leave," Ted said. "You couldn't tell the truth to save a life."

"Teddy. Hate me if you must, but understand this. There will come a time—and we are swiftly approaching that time—when I will no longer be able to control events. Do you understand what I'm saying? Think about this. Take the offer. Cut a deal. It's the only wise move."

26

"**I COULD MAKE A** meal of this," Kenzie said over an appetizer of chicken wings with taro fries.

"It's not too late to change your order," Ted said.

"Yes it is. Besides, I really want the *bun cha*. I'm hungry."

He laughed. "It wasn't the words 'pork belly' that got you?" She had taken some care in prepping herself for what was ostensibly only a business lunch. Her hair was tamed into a swoop that cascaded over one shoulder. She had on a white silk blouse with the barest hint of pink in it, black slacks cut in a way that made her long legs seem even longer, and sandals—no socks, matched or otherwise. She had also dabbed on a touch of makeup.

"Why were you such a jerk the other day?" she said, pausing with a taro fry suspended between them.

"It's a way of entertaining myself. I was in a hurry and didn't want to take the time to hear your whole pitch."

"Well, that's certainly direct."

"Why did you pick me out?" he asked.

"I told you. I heard about you."

The courthouse regulars prized their insider knowledge of who was up to what and why, and they traded information with the avidity of poolside matrons at a country club.

"So you know all about me." He took a long swallow of beer. Kenzie's Google profile was sparse. A framework was implied by six or seven newsworthy incidents covered by local—and left-leaning—news organs. A collegiate athlete with the same name produced more hits.

"What? I'm having lunch with somebody famous? Sorry.

I don't follow celebrity news. Are you dating a Kardashian or something?"

"You googled me," he said. It was half question, half statement.

"Well, duh. Let me see. You're smart. Divorced. You wrestled in college. You look good in uniform."

He looked like a dork in that photo, but he was proud of his achievements. "Four-year full scholarship."

"You used to practice law. And your ex is gay. And remarried. Does that cover it? Are you famous for something else?"

"I was famous once in high school. I got arrested on a field trip to Washington, DC—for jaywalking. Jaywalking and being a jerk. The charge should have been 'Contempt of Cop.'" Having grown up in New York City, Ted had never imagined that other cities might enforce such draconian laws. The policeman hadn't seen the humor in the situation.

"I've been arrested," she said. "Three times. Never famously, but the *Post* quoted me once."

"Arrested? For protesting?"

"I'm an activist, remember? They arrest us, take us in, then they let us go without charging us. It's a game we all play. If I didn't get arrested every once in a while, people would think I didn't know how to do my job." She was hogging the taro fries and he let her.

"Who pays your salary?"

"George Soros, who else?"

He could hear that it was a joke she had used many times before. He laughed anyway.

"I suppose I should be more ladylike and take little bites, but these are really good." She took another fry. "Mmm. Heaven. Why do you want to know who pays me? Conservatives ask me that. You're not a conservative; I can tell by the way you part your hair."

"How do conservatives part their hair?"

She waved away the question. "We get by on contributions and favors. I aspire to minimum wage. My office is a big closet in a small church. I'm going to turn thirty in a couple of years, and I live in an apartment in my parents' basement two blocks from my dad's shop. When I move out, they'll rent it and take a cruise."

"Meanwhile, they've got your back."

"Mom's a school librarian. I think she gets what I do."

"And your father?"

"A repairman. He fixes everything from lamps to computers—anything that plugs into the wall. He wears a pocket protector in his shirt and carries about a hundred keys on his belt. He worries about me all the time."

"A fixer—a rare talent these days," Ted said.

"So now you know everything about me."

"Everything?" he asked.

"What do you want to know?"

"Do you like baseball?"

"Boring. Slow death." She speared the last fry.

The pang was less devastating than he would have thought. That it was not a total deal killer was a revelation. Maybe he was finally growing up.

Kenzie blithely continued as though they were discussing sports in general and not one of his obsessions. "Football is less boring but barbaric. I don't know why it's legal. Hockey is like gladiators on ice. Basketball is good, but it's hard to be a fan in New York. I'm still getting over the Knicks trading Patrick Ewing."

"What were you then? Ten? Eleven?"

"It was traumatic."

"How about the Nets?"

"You're kidding."

"The Liberty?"

"Is this like some kind of a test? Like if I say I like women's basketball, I'm gay or a feminazi or something?"

Jill had often teased Ted that his ability to recognize the sexual orientation of women was subpar, but he held no doubts about this woman. "No, but I'm not going to invite you to go to a game with me if you don't like women's basketball."

"I thought we were meeting to exchange information."

"We are. But maybe there could be more exchanges in our future."

"Let's see how this goes first."

She hadn't said no, and he had not had to remove his foot from his mouth. The arrival of their lunch entrées gave him a chance to regroup. Ted had the pho *bo*. It was good, and he thought it would be a complement to the *bun cha* if Kenzie wanted to try it. She did.

"That's great," she said.

"Want to swap?"

"Not a chance."

They both dug in. Moans of gustatory enthusiasm ensued. Ted flagged a waiter and asked for two more 333s. An ice-cold beer with the beef and broth was heaven. If they never got around to discussing surplus money, crooked politicians, or Russian mobsters, he would be a happy man. He managed to smother his disappointment when Kenzie finally asked, "So. The Russians?"

He took a moment to organize his thoughts. Best to start with the basics.

"Do you know what it is that I do?" he asked. "How I make my money?"

"Something with foreclosures. Basically, you're a carrion feeder. Am I right? Maybe not a vulture, but . . ."

"Thank you. I prefer to think of myself as a rogue lion. Hunting without benefit of belonging to a pride but strong, wily, and powerful."

"Or a coyote—slinking along, playing mean tricks, and getting by on a diet of mice and kittens."

"Okay." He knew that she was teasing, but he wanted her good opinion, and if that meant explaining himself, so be it. "But a noble coyote with ethics. There are hundreds of reasons why people walk away from a piece of property, leaving money on the table. I'm merely trying to reunite those people with what is rightfully theirs. Clients are generally very happy to get a little of their money back."

"This time it's not little, though. That's the rumor at any rate."

"I don't normally get involved in cases like this one. It's too big, too complicated, and there are already too many lawyers involved. For the same reason, I avoid anything to do with divorce. But as everyone I meet has told me to stay away from this one, I have become interested. So, I keep digging." And he would continue, despite the Judge's warning.

An overly efficient busboy whisked all the dishes off the table. Ted would have appreciated another minute or two to gaze at the remains. He asked for a glass of seltzer, and Kenzie ordered a coffee before continuing. She was dogged.

"What do the Russians have to do with what you're working on?"

This would be more speculation than hard fact, but Ted felt he could open up to her. "I think they're fronting for LBC. They sell to cutouts . . ." He paused as he saw a question flicker behind her eyes. "Cutouts. Corporations or LLCs that exist only to hide the people who really benefit from a deal." She nodded in understanding, and he continued. "The bad guys can make payoffs that are tough to track. I don't have all the pieces or connections. But Corona Partners—the Russians—bought properties at auction that LBC now owns. That is not a coincidence."

"No. It's not."

Ted had made a conjecture based on a smattering of

evidence and a skeptical view of human nature. Kenzie spoke with greater authority.

"I've got photos of the Russians meeting with LBC execs, a couple of politicians, even a judge. But I don't have a paper trail." She smiled, quite pleased with her information and his surprise.

"Where were they meeting?"

"Some tired old steak house in Great Neck. It's a block outside the city limits, so I guess they thought no one would see them there. Always on a Tuesday. I hate playing the cynic, but these idiots are both arrogant and dumb—a winning combination."

"Who shows up?" Ted asked. Finally, pieces were falling into place. Now he needed specifics. "What's his name? The guy who's always on television."

"Reisner. Ronald Reisner. Chairman of the board of LBC. No, he's too smart. He sends his people. Sometimes a lawyer, sometimes one of his stooges. He's got a very small group of execs that he trusts. Having one of them deliver a payoff or a bribe is his way of testing their loyalty."

"Are the Russians there?" Ted asked.

"Not always. I don't really get their part in this. Why would Reisner need muscle if he's got judges and city councilmembers in his pocket?"

"You're talking about Kevin Pak?"

"He's one of many," she said.

"They're not only muscle," Ted said. "The Russians have money they need to launder." It was a good question, though. Why would Reisner want to partner with gangsters? The Russians were not known to be silent partners. "Maybe he doesn't have a choice," Ted mused. "Does he need their money? Is he tapped out with his lenders?"

"You'd think that would be major news. *Big Banks Slam Door on Billionaire Developer*. The *Post* would love it."

They were beyond the realm of known facts. "Or the Russians might be controlling the politicians."

"Maybe," she said, though she sounded unconvinced. "You know why it's called Sutphin Boulevard?"

Ted was about to take a sip of the bubbly water, but he placed the glass on the table. "I'm going to assume you are making a point."

"Run with me," she said.

"All right." There was not a less boulevard-like street imaginable. It was a two-lane road that should have been called Cow Path Lane. "I think it was named for a minor robber baron from the eighteen hundreds."

"John Sutphin. Banker, real estate tycoon, and politician."

"With those three careers, I would think the best you could say was that at least he wasn't a pedophile. Was he?"

"He was actually a really good guy. He was an honest banker who encouraged his poorest customers to save rather than borrow. He also provided free housing for about a hundred indigent families. And he was county clerk for a couple of decades without a hint of scandal. Now, I'm sure he cut some deals during his time, but he never forgot who he was really working for. The voters, not the developers. Not the rich. He donated all the property for the courthouses and offices."

"A guy like that wouldn't have a chance at getting elected these days," Ted said.

"It wasn't always like it is today, and it doesn't have to stay this way."

Ted made a point of remaining apolitical—partly out of skepticism, partly out of cynicism. But he had a soft spot for optimists. Especially the good-looking female variety.

"What do you need from me?" he asked.

"Can you document everything you told me? I've got a guy at the *Times* who will listen, but he's going to want hard evidence." Her eyes were bright, and she had the poised posture of a setter waiting to be released after a covey of quail. She was beautiful.

Ted shook his head. "I tracked the purchases and sales, but there are missing transactions, and files have been vandalized."

"And when's the last time that happened?" She raised an eyebrow. "They'll sit on the deeds until they think we've all forgotten about it, then they'll dump all the records into the system at once."

"It happens all the time. So? Who's going to complain?"

"Besides some community organizer?" She flashed a rueful smile.

Ted found her intensity and intelligence intoxicating. He was falling in lust. "Other than destroying files, which I can't prove, what they're doing is not illegal. Shady, yes."

"They had to get variances," she said. "They had to get air rights. Every property owner in Queens knows you don't sell your air rights unless you're getting top dollar."

Ted silently debated going further. All that they had talked about so far could be labeled general background information. There could be no repercussions. No specific people had been mentioned other than Ron Reisner and Councilman Pak, and they were both highly public figures.

"I'm sorry if this sounds mysterious or melodramatic, but I need you to tell me you won't share what I'm about to tell you with anyone else," Ted said.

"I haven't been sworn to secrecy since middle school. Okay. Cross my heart and hope to die." She flashed him a challenging smile.

"A powerful oath," Ted said. "My client is a woman. An old woman named Barbara Miller. She owns some buildings in various neighborhoods in Queens. She used to own three more that sat on property that LBC needs to build that tower."

"I should know about her. We talked to two dozen land-lords. How did we miss her?"

"You came along too late." Kenzie had a tiny mole on her neck—a beauty mark. He wanted to kiss it. "They got to her first. She is now in an assisted-living residence in Seaside."

"Is she competent?" she asked.

"I talked to her. She's easily frightened, but you get her on a sunny day, and she'll be fine. And tough as an old shoe."

"You like her."

"I do." She wanted to know if the coyote had a heart. It may have been beaten and battered, but it was functional.

"So this one is personal," she said.

"I suppose it is. But I've been threatened if I continue and also if I drop it. I've been pushed around before. I don't like it."

"Okay. So what's next?"

"Dinner?" he said, hoping that his willingness to share had earned him a second meeting, possibly a date.

Though she smiled encouragingly, her words stopped him. "Don't rush me. I don't respond well."

He had a line of retreat prepared. "I meant dinner at a has-been steak house out past the city line. Where I can go and watch these crooks in action."

A hint of disappointment flickered in her eyes. A romantic dinner might still be in their future. "Tuesday night. They're at the same table every week."

"Tuesday. I'll have to wait until then," Ted said.

She cocked her head to one side as though a thought had only then occurred to her.

"Yes?" he asked.

"How about breakfast tomorrow? There's someone I want you to meet."

27

"TED?"

The body responded to the ringing of the phone. His hand reached out and grabbed the device; his thumb did the rest. All this was done with muscle memory. His brain was not yet engaged. "Uh-huh."

"What are you doing?"

Sleeping? Past tense. "Jill?" His voice croaked. Allergies? No, beer.

"Hi."

Ted checked the time. "Jesus. It's four-something. Are you okay?"

"I'm watching *Laura*," she said.

He tried to focus. Who the hell was Laura? "But you're not hurt? You're safe?"

"I'm fine, silly. I'm watching a movie. Well, I'm not fine, but I am safe. Okay?"

What day was it? He remembered that he had gone to bed on Saturday night after an eleven-inning heartbreaker on the road, during which he had finished off a fresh six-pack of Brooklyn Defender IPA, one of Brooklyn Brewery's higher-alcohol brews, and two cans of Bud Light that had been sitting in the refrigerator for so long that he could not remember how they got there. As he had not yet seen the sun, he guessed it was early Sunday morning.

"*Laura*? Yeah, yeah. Didn't we see that together?" They were talking about a movie. He felt like a genius for having made the connection. Then he realized that Jill had just told him that it was a movie.

"Gene Tierney," she said.

"Yes. Got it."

"She had a very sad life."

At 4:19 in the morning, with or without a hangover, it was difficult for Ted to summon much sympathy for a long-dead Hollywood star. "What time is it where you are?" he asked.

"Uh." A pause while she pondered this meaty question. "Four-nineteen."

"Same here," he said.

"I can't sleep, Teddy."

Ted was suddenly wide awake. On guard. He knew Jill and what she sounded like when she was suffering through one of her mild anxiety attacks. Years before, he might have held her and made up funny stories and promised her that one day they would run away to Tasmania and live off the sales of their organic, carb-free mango chutney. And she would have laughed. Not tonight.

"Talk it out. This is not about Jackie, is it?" Ted drew the line at marriage counseling.

"Grandfather was here."

"Yeah. Here too. He said you sent him."

"Why?"

"You didn't?"

"He scared me," she said.

"He would never hurt you."

"That's not it. He's afraid for Jacqueline. And for you," she said.

"Me? Not likely." The Judge had said that it was Jill who was concerned for Jackie, but he'd also said she might suffer embarrassment. Who was the dissembler?

"No. He is." Her faith in the old man was unshakable— and maddening. "What did he say to you?"

"It didn't go as well as he hoped," Ted said. "He's not worried *for* me; he's worried *about* me. He thinks I'm doing something that will hurt the family. Or the firm."

"Are you?"

"Am I what?" He did not want to go down that road with her.

"Doing something that would hurt Jacqueline?"

Both Jill and the Judge were worried. Ted was sure now that his hunch was right. Jackie wasn't merely the lawyer of record on those case files. She was deeply involved. "Jackie needs to do what's right. If she does, she'll be fine." And if she didn't, he would see she wasn't the only one to be taken down.

"What does that mean?"

"She'll know," he said.

"You are doing something. Why? Why hurt her?"

"I don't want to hurt anyone." That wasn't quite true. He wanted to crush Jackie, the firm, and every member of the Fitzmaurice clan—except Jill. And he wanted to be able to live with himself afterward. He didn't think both were possible. "Tell Jacqueline to talk with me. Not yell at me. Talk. Converse."

"For once, just do what I ask without making me beg."

Something was off. Jill's panic had been replaced with this strident demand and its laughable premise. Begging had never been any part of who they were. He could sense strings being pulled. Had her grandfather put her up to this? Or was it Jackie standing over her? Or was he being paranoid? Or perceptive? "Have her call me."

"She won't," she said.

"Then don't take it out on me."

"You used to be nice. Be nice."

-28-

IN A SNIPPET OF a dream just before waking, Ted saw a wave of dark red hair splayed across the pillow next to him. He opened his eyes in full expectation of McKenzie Zielinski lying beside him, asleep and satisfied. The reality—that he was alone and hungover—engulfed him and followed him as he staggered to the bathroom and then to the kitchen. He made a pot of strong coffee and drank it with three tablets of ibuprofen.

His thoughts were dark and full of doubt. Though he looked forward to seeing Kenzie in an hour, Jill's phone call hung around his neck like a noose.

What was he playing at? Was he idly poking a stick into a hornet's nest? What did he owe to Jill? To Richie? To Cheryl? To anyone? What would he say to Jill if his suspicions about Jackie were revealed to be true? Jackie would take a great fall. She would be lucky to stay out of jail.

And there was the Judge. A manipulative puppet master, admittedly, but one who had treated Ted fairly in the past and who might, despite the threats and attempted bribes, be giving wise advice. Or were all these doubts the product of too much stress and too much beer the night before?

Whom could he trust to help him answer all these questions?

The coffee and ibuprofen did their work. He called for an Uber and set out.

ROOSEVELT AVENUE ON A clear Sunday morning in May was a testament to the American immigrant dream. Families were streaming out of the Spanish-language church in the middle of the block. Many of the fathers were in suits, though Ted didn't see a single tie. The mothers wore dresses, low heels, and hats. The little boys all had collared white shirts, and the girls sported flouncy dresses with petticoats. The scene, adjusted for the darker skin tones, could have been a subject for an early Rockwell magazine cover.

Somewhere nearby, older children lurked, already wrestling with modern realities like drugs, gangs, and the dearth of opportunities for all but the fortunate. Somewhere nearby was a homeless alcoholic, sleeping behind a dumpster and dreaming of a highland village in Central America that he should never have left. New York rewards the strong and the lucky. Everyone else gets by or gets devoured. It has always been that way.

Ted, hidden in shadow beneath the overhead subway tracks, watched the pageant play out from the opposite side of the street. Farther down the avenue was the coffee shop with a six-foot hand-painted sign reading DESAYUNOS ALL DAY. Judging by the line out front, it was doing a brisk business. He was not early or late. He thought about standing out in the direct sunlight where he would be more visible but decided his hangover took precedence.

"Hey! What are you doing over there?" Kenzie, hair as red as he remembered it being in his dream, stood in the doorway of the coffee shop. She waved him over. "Come on. I've got a booth."

The noise hit him first. Everyone seemed to be talking at once. An infant squalled; squabbling siblings were told to behave by shrill female voices. Harried waitresses with pencils poking from their hair took orders, refilled coffee, and hustled black-clad busboys into clearing dishes. Everywhere was the sound of cutlery connecting with plates.

The atmosphere hit next. Hot, humid, and laden with scents of cooking pork; boiling oil; grilled, toasted, and fried breads of every description; and over it all, peppers. Peppers in a dozen varieties. Ted's eyes watered, but his senses finally woke. The hangover receded and made way for an appetite. Suddenly he was ravenous.

"Are you okay? You look like the canary that swallowed the cat." Kenzie was full of energy and good spirits, as though she had slept well and been up for hours.

"This is the best I've felt all morning. Where's your mystery man?"

"He'll be along. Let's get you some coffee." She waved for the waitress and with further hand signals indicated they needed two cups—pronto.

"I don't drink often enough to get good at it," he confessed. "I had a few beers watching a ball game." And a late-night phone call and too many things on his mind.

A busboy set two cups before them and turned to go.

"And water," Ted said.

The young man looked at him with perfect incomprehension.

"*Agua. Dos, por favor,*" Kenzie said, earning a huge smile from the busboy before he ran off. "This friend of mine who's coming—he's like the saint of Corona. You'll like him. And"— she paused for dramatic effect—"he knows everybody and where all the bodies are buried. You'll see."

Ted was rallying. Sitting across from this woman certainly helped. "If you say this guy is okay, then I believe it."

A family of five went out the door, and as the last of the crew, a preteen boy in a suit too big and too grown-up for him, squeezed around a big-hipped waitress and dashed out, a familiar face peeked in.

Despite the heat, the Preacher was wearing the same dark overcoat. He stepped through the door, and Ted could see that the duct-taped boat shoes had been replaced with a new pair of high-top black sneakers. Ted's contribution had gone to a good cause.

"Here's somebody I know," Ted said.

Kenzie looked over her shoulder, not entirely registering

what Ted had said. "Oh, he's here." She threw a big wave in the Preacher's direction.

"This is your guy?" Ted asked.

"Yeah," she said. "You'll see. He's very cool."

The Preacher had seen her wave and was approaching with a warm but amused expression. Ted stood to greet him. They shook hands.

"Isn't this a workday for you?" Ted asked.

"My pulpit is the subway turnstile. My church, the street. As a freelance messenger of the Lord, I am out here minding my flock six days a week. Sundays, I rest and let others spread the Word."

"Can I buy you breakfast?" Ted said.

Kenzie recovered quickly from her initial surprise. She slid over and the Preacher sat next to her. "So, one of you better tell me how you two got to be such buddies."

"We met for the first time this week," the Preacher said.

"And he helped me find Barbara Miller," Ted added.

A Latina waitress who could have stood in for a Botero model came to the table with menus and a third cup of coffee. "Ah, Padre, it has been too long."

"*Hola, Princesa. Estos son mis amigos.*"

"Welcome. Welcome," she said, handing menus to Kenzie and Ted.

"I think a plate of carbs, protein, and grease has a chance of making me whole again," Ted said.

"And a dash or two of hot sauce," Kenzie added.

Ted looked over the menu while Kenzie ordered two eggs over easy and rye toast well done, butter on the side. Ted realized there were too many choices in front of him and the idiosyncratic spelling ("bagel and cram cheese") was distracting him. The Preacher ordered a "Spanish omelete." Ted closed the menu and handed it back. "I'll have what he's having."

"Was I of any help?" the Preacher asked. "Did you find the missing Barbara Miller?"

"Yes, thank you," Ted said. "She's all right. In fact, she is in a very safe facility. She didn't choose to be there, but the people there are taking good care of her."

"A nursing home?"

"A good step up from that," Ted said.

"But you're not pleased."

"They stole real property from her, but she'll never miss it. They also stole her freedom, which in my book is a greater crime, though I believe she's better off where she is now."

"Who is 'they'?"

"The tower," Kenzie said. "It's all connected."

Ted found himself talking before he knew what he wanted to say. All the pent-up anxiety and all the doubts spewed out of him. "I've got a set of facts, things I know to be true. Then I've got a bunch of things that I've been told. Some of them might be facts. It all fits together and makes a picture, but I have no idea if that picture is real. Or whether I am seeing all or only a part of the larger canvas. I can't trust anyone's motivations, as there's a fair amount of money involved. And I realized last night that I can't even trust my own motivations."

The Preacher said nothing. Kenzie's raised eyebrows spoke volumes.

"I'm not making much sense, am I?" Ted asked.

"Nope," Kenzie said. "I think you need sustenance."

The plates had arrived, the omelets wrapped in warm flour tortillas with sides of *papas* so red with ground pepper that Ted's eyes watered and his nose began to itch just from looking at them. The Preacher grabbed the bottle of red sauce. "You go easy with this, or you'll be on the crapper the rest of the day, hear?" He poured a healthy slug over the eggs and began to eat.

Ted took his advice and let two drops hit the edge of the plate. He brushed the tortilla in that general direction and took a bite. His sinuses opened up, his nostrils ran, and tears flowed down his cheeks. He loved it.

Kenzie gave him a sympathetic smile. "How are you doing?"

"Eat some of them taters," the Preacher said. "The starch will help put out the fire."

"You're kidding," Ted said. "They're covered in chili powder."

"Yeah, but that's a slow burn. Try it."

Ted hiccupped. His throat felt as if he'd been breathing flames.

"Eat 'em," the Preacher said.

Ted did. The Preacher was right. The potatoes were spicy but warm, not searing. The combination was delicious.

"Better," Ted said. "I may yet live." With each bite the world became a kinder, gentler place.

The anxiety of the last few days faded. The paranoia of the predawn call settled into a feeling of mild unease. He needed allies. The Preacher had trusted him; it was time to reciprocate.

Kenzie finished her eggs, spread butter on her toast, and then scraped off most of it. "When you're up to it, tell my friend the whole story. I'll help out where I can."

The café was packed and filled with the babble of three or four different languages. Ted looked around. Three young bearded Sikhs in turbans. A tall, thin man with tribal scars on his cheeks sitting with his family, his wife and daughter in brightly colored head scarves—all three of them in white shirts buttoned to the neck, while the preteen son slumped in low-cut baggy black jeans and a Knicks jersey. A long table of brown-skinned men, women, and children, all with the distinctively Mayan facial features, none of them taller than four foot ten, all talking at once. The café offered the privacy of the bazaar, their conversation overwhelmed by the cacophony around them. Ted could speak freely without fear that anything he said might be overheard and repeated.

He began with the cops coming to question him—twice—about the death of Richie, murdered almost a week before, and finished with his conversation that morning with Jill. He hit all the high points but didn't dwell on details. Ted didn't excuse himself or apologize, nor did he attempt to play the hero for cutting a deal with Barbara Miller.

"Her property was key," Kenzie said. "Without those plots, Reisner was stuck."

Ted nodded and plunged on. "Kenzie cares about stopping the tower. I know you're firmly in that camp. But I'm juggling a lot of other issues. If I keep pursuing this, I will hurt someone who cares about me. We may be divorced, but she is my closest friend. Her family will be devastated, and if I'm right her spouse will likely go to jail. On top of that, the local power elite will want my scalp, the biggest real estate developer this side of Manhattan will try to bury me with bullshit legal filings, and then there's the Russians."

The Preacher understood. "Nowhere is safe with those people. You cross them Russians once, and you'll pay for it every day until you die."

"On the other hand, if I pull the filing, I can walk away with my career restored and a fair amount of green in my pocket. Miss Miller won't get her buildings back—or her money—but she's ninety-whatever and being well taken care of. Mrs. Rubiano won't get any money either, but I believe she's as crooked as any of them." There would still be the not-so-small matter of Cheryl's mysterious giant, but Ted kept that to himself.

"And the tower goes up," Kenzie said. She had a good poker face, but there was steel in her voice.

"That's not my fight," Ted said.

"It should be," she said.

Ted didn't let her surety detour him. He forged ahead. "Friday afternoon, my guy filed papers with the court on behalf of Miller. Assuming the usual level of efficiency one finds at the courthouse, the clerk didn't even look at them. There's a good chance I can undo everything tomorrow. Pull the filing and forget the whole damn mess. I've got other cases I can work on that won't ruin people's lives."

Kenzie was still simmering. "That tower will affect every person in this part of Queens. All these people here"—she swept her arm to include the whole diner—"will be squeezed out. A community will die. Don't tell me that won't ruin lives."

"The man is opening his heart." The Preacher spoke softly, without anger or recrimination. "He is seeking our help."

Kenzie stared down at the table. "I hear you," she said after a long silence. She looked Ted in the eyes. "What are you going to do?"

"I don't know," Ted said.

She jerked her head in a decisive gesture. "I need some air. I'm going for a walk. Let me know when you get your head on straight."

The Preacher moved aside and let her out. Ted watched her leave, hoping she would look back. She didn't.

"Well, I fucked that up royally," Ted said.

The Preacher nodded sadly in agreement. "You see that pretty waitress, you let her know I could use a refill." He nodded at his empty cup.

The dining room was, if it was possible, even busier than when they had arrived. "We may have a bit of a wait."

"She likes you, you know?" The Preacher leaned back, crossing his arms and giving Ted a look of deep appraisal. "These kinds of questions are easy for her. What's hard for her is to understand your conflict. She thinks you have to think like her, or she can't respect you. She's wrong."

"I find that I very much want her respect."

"No doubt."

The busboy swung by with the coffee carafe and gave them both refills. They sat in silence while the Preacher doctored his mug with cream and two sugars. Ted sipped his coffee black.

"And the police? Will they still think you killed your partner?" the Preacher asked after taking a long sip.

"Not my partner, please. I'm sorry Richie's dead, and I hope they find who did it, but the guy was never a partner. Or a friend. But no, I'm not worried. There's no case against me, and there won't be for the simple reason, I didn't do it."

"But you made promises."

"Yes. I did," Ted said.

"And honoring those promises is important to you."

"Yes."

"I don't give advice," the Preacher said, his voice indicating that he might if asked.

Ted shook his head. "It's my problem. My decision. Whatever I end up doing is entirely on me."

The Preacher smiled his approval. "I'll put two questions to you: What do you regret right now? And what will you regret a year from now?"

Ted didn't have to think long or hard about the first question. The answer was Cheryl. He needed to see her and extricate himself from whatever game she was playing. Give her the money back and sever any further communication.

The second question was the tough one.

THE FILE WOULD HAVE to sit in the judge's inbox until the next morning. There was nothing Ted could do to change that. Meanwhile, he had to tender his resignation with Cheryl and give her back the thousand dollars. It was time for a sit-down. Ted didn't know whether or not he owed her an explanation for walking away from the affair, but she owed him some straight answers.

Richie had lived in Sunnyside, but Ted had never bothered to ask the address. He wanted Cheryl surprised and on the defensive, so he couldn't call first and ask. New York State voter rolls made it too easy. Though there was no listing for a Richard, it took Ted about a minute on his smartphone to come up with an address for Cheryl Rubiano. He was on his way.

Sunnyside was squeezed between the new skyscrapers in Long Island City and the vast expanses of the Calvary Cemetery. It was a tall town for Queens, packed with apartment buildings and industrial space rather than single-family homes. Cheryl had a fifth-floor apartment near Greenpoint Avenue.

A coffee shop on the corner, diagonally across from the entrance of her building, gave Ted a vantage point from which to watch and prepare for this ordeal. The morning rush was long over, so for a five-dollar tip, the waitress let him sip coffee by the window.

Cheryl had her secrets. Their first meeting had been an odd mix of high emotion and irrational demands that had left him both confused and dismissive. He had gone along with her mostly as a way of getting rid of her. The second session had been entirely different. She had been pharaonic in giving him orders—right up to the moment when he had revealed to her the properties involved in the case. Suddenly she had wanted him to drop the pursuit of the money and focus only on the murder of her husband. Had she finally realized that the case Richie had chosen to pursue could be tied to La Bella Casa, Reisner, and Pak? There had been no tears for Richie, only a seething anger that Ted had felt was the most real emotion he had yet seen in her. This made her meeting with Councilman Pak and entourage doubly suspicious.

And then there was the giant. How could something that big remain a mystery?

The street was an ever-changing circus as the late morning merged into early afternoon. Hipsters with man buns and tattoos mixed with men in djellabas, women in hijabs, and Asians of both sexes in khakis and polo shirts. Teenagers of all skin colors wore ball caps or jerseys proclaiming allegiance to one or another New York sports team. A troop of spandex-clothed bicyclists cruised by to brave Queens Boulevard on their way to points east. Despite the varied cultures on parade, there was a communal feel to the display. These were all kindred folks going about their Sunday chores, observances, or recreations.

Except for the giant.

The monster from the Mets game came out the front door of Cheryl's building dressed in a three-piece ivory-colored suit and bloodred tie, strode past the coffee shop, and continued up Greenpoint. Ted swung away from the window, afraid that the man might see him. He could see the glint of the giant's pale shaved head floating above the fray for the next few moments. The guy moved quickly, as if he had an appointment to keep.

There might be a perfectly reasonable explanation for why the man who had threatened Ted was coincidentally leaving

Cheryl's building on an early Sunday afternoon. They were friends. He lived in the building. He had visited the widow to offer condolences. None of those explanations were compelling.

More questions. Ted was owed answers. If Cheryl could not provide them, he would have no residual guilt about pulling the file and taking a pass on the whole mess. Cheryl didn't know it, but the decision was all hers.

The first hurdle to be vaulted was the locked front door. In every old movie Ted watched, the good guy buzzes all of the apartments at once, and someone always lets him in. That might have worked in Manhattan, with hordes of restaurant delivery guys working twenty-four seven, but in Queens that would never happen. First, because it was hard to find an intercom system that worked in a building more than twenty years old. And second, because New Yorkers have all seen those movies.

But there's always a way.

A bent-backed woman draped all in black from babushka to boots was hauling a loaded grocery cart up the four steps. This was his opportunity.

"May I?" Ted said, easily lifting her burden and gesturing for her to proceed. She gave him a long suspicious appraisal. Something in Ted's face must have registered as worthy of her trust—if only for a moment. She gestured for him to follow, and he hoisted the full cart up the stairs while she fished out keys and opened the door.

Ted stepped forward and followed her into the building. She stopped, whirled around, and began vigorously shooing him out in a language with a lot more consonants than vowels. He held up his hands to show he meant no harm, but she began to screech. Ted couldn't understand a word of it, but the message was clear. She kept up the attack until he was outside on the stoop again, at which point she stopped, rustled through the deep folds of black cloth around her, and handed him a prayer card. Then she slammed the door closed. With him outside.

St. Matthias the Apostle. Patron saint of drunks. The replacement for Judas, the first apostle to be chosen by lottery. His feast day was coming up. The prayer was a knockoff of the AA prayer about fixing things and serenity. Ted stuck the card in his pocket.

At that moment, the door punched him in the back, and he staggered, almost going down. A teenage boy in typical street uniform of hoodie, ball cap, and oversized jeans pushed past Ted and jogged out to the street.

He was gone before Ted had a chance to protest. He grabbed the closing door before the latch caught. He was in.

"WHO IS THAT?"

Ted knocked loud and often, keeping the other hand over the peephole so his face would remain hidden for as long as possible. Either Cheryl Rubiano had been fast asleep, or she had a tremendous ability to ignore routine cacophony

"We need to talk," he said, and rapped again. The door across the hall opened a crack and immediately slammed shut. "Come on, you're bothering everybody on the floor."

"I don't want to talk to you," she said.

So she recognized his voice. He removed his hand from the peephole. He was now free to knock with both fists. Bam. Bam. Bam. It was a good door for banging on. Resonant. Tympanic.

"Stop that or I call the cops."

"And I'll tell them I work for you," he said.

"You're fired."

"I came here to quit. All I want is some answers. I'll give you your money back."

No answer. Was she thinking it over, or had she gone for a gun?

"What the hell do you want to know?" she said. He was wearing her down.

"I think we'd both be more comfortable discussing this inside rather than through the door," Ted said, slathering on a calm, reasoned, confidential manner.

Five seconds ticked by. Plenty of time to make a decision. He raised a fist, prepared to bang on the door once more, and heard the top lock click. The door swung open.

"Come in here." She was dressed for bed. The smell of gin seeping out of her pores was so strong Ted was concerned about a contact high. He didn't think he reeked of stale beer. Of course, he'd showered, shaved, and fortified himself with strong coffee and hot sauce. Cheryl needed another twelve hours, detox, and a makeover.

She led the way down a short hallway to the living room. The sunlight was bright. Her nightgown was thin. Translucent. She wasn't wearing underwear. A butterfly tattoo swayed with each step.

The decor was modern but not sterile. An L-shaped couch faced a glass and chrome coffee table. Two low swivel chairs completed the seating. A bookcase displayed a collection of porcelain dolls, some of which looked quite old. It was hard to imagine Richie relaxing in this room. There was no sign that he had ever been there. Not a picture, a memento, or even a dropped sock.

Cheryl lowered herself onto the couch. "Make yourself useful. Put up some coffee." She might have let Ted in, but she had not surrendered. She was in charge.

There was a Keurig on the counter with a stainless carousel of pods. Espresso and dark roast predominated, but there were a few forlorn containers of mocha almond. He found mugs and made two espressos, letting his sit while hers brewed.

"How do you take yours?" he called.

No answer. He stuck his head out. Cheryl was splayed on the couch, fast asleep.

He drank his coffee, then gave himself a complete tour of the premises. *It can't be snooping if you're invited in*, he thought. The king-size bed was a mess, a blanket trailing on the floor and the top sheet free floating. Two people performing an athletic pas de deux might have left such a trail. Or one tormented drunk with a guilty conscience.

The damned dolls all seemed to be watching as he passed through the living room on his way to search the bathroom. Cheryl was still out.

The medicine cabinet revealed a man's razor, shaving gel, and a gift set of Armani deodorant and eau de toilette—Giò—which Ted was sure had never been used by Richie Rubiano. He had always exuded a more natural aroma. But a man had been here—and often enough to leave grooming supplies.

Ted heard Cheryl snort and gasp. He closed the cabinet and returned to the living room. She had pulled herself upright but looked only half-awake. Ted sat down facing her and waited until her eyes focused.

"Ah, Jesus," she said. "Are you still here?"

"Feeling any better?" he asked. He avoided making eye contact with any of the porcelain heads behind her.

"Where's that coffee?" she whined.

The mug was on the table in front of her. Ted let her find it on her own. She took a sip of the tepid brown liquid and winced. But she drank it.

"How can you fuck up coffee from a Keurig machine, for the love of Pete? Did I fire you?"

"Yes. And I want to ask you about that. But I have a couple of other questions first."

"I don't want you screwing around any of this, you hear? Forget about those properties. The old lady. All of it. I told you that."

"You told me to find Richie's killer. I think they're connected." He wasn't interested in convincing her—or himself. He wanted a reaction.

When it came, it wasn't what he expected. Cheryl withdrew into what appeared to be a dark place. She seemed to deflate, her aggressive attitude gone. "It's too late," she said in a whisper so faint he almost asked her to repeat it. "Drop it."

"I've got police harassing me. I want out." He didn't feel it was necessary to explain that his ex-wife and her grandfather were also strong motivating impetuses. "I'll be happy to refund your money."

She waved a hand dismissively. "Money," she said with a sneer.

Ted didn't buy it. What could move this woman more than money? The answer came to him even as the question formed in his mind. *Fear.*

"You were on fire when you first came to see me," he said. "Now you're ashes. What changed?"

She looked at him with real pity in her bloodshot eyes. "You're a nice guy. But you think you're smart. And you are. Just not smart enough. Walk away, Eddie."

"As soon as I get some answers," he said.

The demand roused her ever so slightly. "I don't have to tell you anything I don't want to."

"We'll start with an easy one. I think you work for Councilman Kevin Pak. What do you do for him?"

"What? Is this supposed to be some big secret? I'm his admin. One of two, actually."

"Okay, but what do you do?"

"I'm senior admin, though we don't do titles," she said.

He didn't say anything. Sometimes silence creates a better question than repetition.

"Outreach. Fundraising. Business leaders need his support.

They have to go through me to talk to him. A campaign contribution always helps."

That kind of transactional democracy, which Ted took for granted, would have been called corruption in a foreign government. "Pay to play," he said.

"Who cares? Why do you want to know?" She took a long slug of the cold coffee.

"I think your councilman is involved with Reisner and LBC and . . ."

He never got to the last part of his accusation, *the Russian mob*. Cheryl was laughing too hard.

"I would hope to hell he is," she said. "It may not be his district, but his vote cost them good money. They wouldn't have got to first base on that project without his okay."

"I've heard the Russian mob is financing that tower."

She laughed again, though this time there was a brittle edge to the laughter. It was a stall. She was preparing a lie. "All the big banks were fighting for a piece of that deal. Why would LBC need dirty money? Why are we talking about this?"

He didn't trust her, but he had to keep her talking. "LBC uses a Russian real estate investment company to hide their interest in buying up the property they need. And I'm convinced that they're laundering cash for Russian gangsters."

"I doubt that very much. Those guys are too smart to leave a million bucks on the table." She stood and swayed into the kitchen. "I'm making some decent coffee."

He couldn't read her. Was she hiding something? Covering for someone?

He heard the sounds of her changing the pod in the coffee machine, followed by the click and hiss of it brewing. He was about to call out to her when it hit him—she was playing him, letting him stew alone while she regrouped. Ted was ready for her.

Cheryl's face appeared in the doorway. Her expression and

body language were textbook bored. But her eyes showed something else. "Tell me what you think you know."

Ted tossed out a wild card: "Who's the giant?"

"What?"

The question had rattled her.

"The big guy?" Ted said. "Sharp dresser? He's got a voice like Alvin and the Chipmunks. He stalked me. Threatened me."

"I don't know who you're talking about."

Ted remembered the detective's warning about her. Cheryl had grown up in a family of grifters. Lying would be a skill she'd been taught since birth. But she was frightened, and the mask had slipped.

"I saw him leaving the building," he said. He tried a feint. "His razor is in your bathroom."

"He's a friend," she said in a tone meant to end the discussion.

"It's good to have friends," he said. "Does this one have a name?"

"Why do you care?"

"Because I don't think he wants me to quit. He was very insistent that I collect that money for you."

Her eyes burned at him. "I said drop it."

Ted tried a different tack. "So why did you fire me? What are you afraid of now?"

"Who says I'm afraid?" She was back in full form, ready for a fight.

"And now you no longer care about Richie's killer."

"I didn't say I don't care. I told you to back off."

"Do you care? Really? Why do I not believe you?"

He had touched a nerve. "I loved him. Once."

"There doesn't seem to be any evidence of it around here. You've scrubbed every sign he ever lived here. How long has he been gone? A week?"

"Almost a year," she said.

The dolls' eyes all seemed to swivel in his direction. They'd known all along. They were enjoying this moment.

"He left me. Is that what you need to hear?"

Was that another lie? Her pain came through loud and clear, but Ted couldn't trust even that. The assault he had prepared was blown apart.

"I'm sorry," he said. "I had no idea. What happened?"

"None of your damned business. He left. Cleared out. He was living in some guy's basement in Hollis."

"Was this before or after the giant moved in?"

"Don't call him that," she said. "And he doesn't live here."

"What? He just stops by to shave every once in a while?"

"Whatever you think you know, you don't know the half of it."

She lied so easily. Everything she had ever said was suspect. It was time to take what sanity he had left and get out of there.

"Thank you," he said. "You helped me make a tough decision. I'm done."

The dolls all seemed to be glowering at him. How could he be so heartless, so cruel?

"You should leave," Cheryl said.

Ted stood. The risk in staying longer was that he might reveal more of what he knew without learning any more than that Cheryl was prepared to lie—about everything.

TED CURSED HIMSELF AS he rode down in the elevator—Cheryl's cash was still in his pocket. Somehow, he had missed his moment to dash it down in front of her and storm out. He wasn't going back.

He was glad to be done with the case, and yet he had unanswered questions. He was convinced Cheryl knew—or suspected—much more than she had admitted. Her demeanor had first changed at the restaurant when he told her that Richie's case was tied to the LBC tower. She had not known it before. And as soon as she did, she warned Ted off that path of investigation. Now she was warning him off trying to find Richie's killer. What had changed?

There was a fire hydrant in front of Cheryl's building. A flat-grey Ford Taurus with black steel wheels was squatting in the space, engine running. Two large men sat in the front seat. They could not have better advertised themselves as cops if they'd had a cruiser with siren and flashing lights. Duran and his partner. What was the man's name? Casava-something?

"C'mere, Molloy," the partner called. "How's the widow? Still in mourning? You been consoling?"

The interview had left Ted depressed—confused and angry. He didn't like the feeling.

"My friends call me Ted. You can call me Mr. Molloy, Chuck."

The cop swung open the car door and jumped up onto the sidewalk, rolling his shoulders, prepared to teach Ted some manners. "Detective Kasabian, Molloy."

Ted spoke around him to Duran, who was behind the wheel. "Hey, I'm trying to get to Pesso's in Bayside for gelato. You guys want to give me a lift?"

"Didn't your old man ever tell you nobody likes a wiseass?" Kasabian said.

The cop was bigger than Ted but not by much. He carried his weight too far forward, leaning into the balls of his feet as he tried to appear threatening. Ted hadn't wrestled since college, but he thought the cop would be a sucker for a double leg takedown.

"My father kept all his good advice to himself," Ted said. "I've tried to live by that same code."

"What did the widow tell you?" Duran asked. He didn't seem interested in his partner's macho performance.

"I'm fired," Ted said. "She didn't want to talk to me. Go ahead; you give it a shot. Maybe you'll do better. Here's a tip: ask her about the giant."

- 3 0 -

FIRST ORDER OF BUSINESS on Monday morning was to tell Lester the play was over. Ted owed it to him. The man had pulled rabbits out of hats, forded impassable rivers, climbed towering mountains, and bought Barbara Miller cake.

Ted checked the records room first. Lester had some research to do on two surplus-money deals he had unearthed. There was no sign of him. He wasn't on the main floor either. Ted immediately thought of the aroma of vodka and breath mint that Lester carried with him the first day.

There was only so much time Ted was prepared to expend on being considerate of the feelings of an employee who seemed to have decided to blow off the morning shift. Hangovers were for weekends. Everything changed on Monday morning. Ted gave up the search and moved on to the next order of business.

The file was in the hands of the judge's clerk. Ted had never met the man. Clerks could be touchily protective of their charges. It could take years to develop a relationship. Courthouse regulars made it a point to schmooze these gatekeepers. Ted was going in blind.

It was rush hour for the elevators. He wriggled forward, but he was an amateur, a part-timer. The regulars were unafraid to use knee-high briefcases as weapons of persuasion. Teamwork might have been effective, but it was not in evidence. This crowd couldn't maintain simple good manners. Ted naively assumed that if he remained upright, the flow of humanity would eventually bring him to an elevator door. Not so.

A door opened and the current shifted, catching him off-balance. A heavy shoe clipped his ankle and he stumbled.

He found his footing and swung around to face the offender. A strong hand gripped his arm, and he felt a three-fingered jab in a kidney. His back went into a spasm, and he thought he might fall to the floor. This was no accident; he had been attacked. Another pair of hands grabbed his other arm.

The frenzied crowd thinned momentarily, and Ted finally got a glimpse of his assailants. Ivan the Terrible and his pal— the Russian salt and pepper set. Ted tried to pull away, but they frog-marched him through the crowd.

Ted yelled. "Get your—" was as far as he got. The rest of his sentence was swallowed in a gasp of pain when those fingers jabbed again. He was surrounded by police, lawyers, and various officers of the court, yet he was as vulnerable as a baby.

They thrust him up against the wall opposite the elevators. Not one person, anywhere in the lobby, was looking in his direction; everyone else was staring at the lights over the elevator bank, handicapping which car would be next to arrive empty. The poker-faced man held Ted upright easily while the guy with the boxer's nose stepped in close, giving himself enough room to swing a fist. It was a short jab—a hook to an inch south of the solar plexus. Ted brought both knees up to protect his stomach. It worked for a nanosecond. The boxer closed in, brushed Ted's legs aside, and threw another punch, putting his full weight behind it. Ted folded like a damp dishcloth. He thought he was going to die.

The first man spoke in Ted's ear. "You make mistake, Eddie. I give you good advice, but you don't take it. You file papers and now people are very upset. Many people." He slapped Ted's face. Not hard enough to bruise, but he had Ted's full attention. "Are you scared now? Good. That is good. You should be."

"No, no," Ted whined. "You don't understand." He hated the sound of his voice, wheedling and near-hysterical.

"Be a smart guy," the man said. "Smart guys learn from others' mistakes."

He let go of Ted, who slid down the wall holding his guts in place.

They stepped into the crowd and were gone.

31

HE HAD TO FIND Lester. He had to get to the judge's clerk. The first move, however, was the most difficult. He had to stand.

Was there such a thing as a glass stomach? It seemed he had one. In ten years of wrestling, he'd never had to take a punch. He didn't ever want to take another. Something felt broken. He pressed his back against the wall and slid upright. He didn't vomit. That was a victory.

"Are you feeling unwell, sir?"

Ted looked up into the cold eyes of a heavyset man in uniform. The words were right, but the tone was a hair this side of threatening. Ted focused on the words on the shoulder badge. NEW YORK COURTS. The bailiff was trying to determine whether or not he was a threat. At that moment Ted could not have threatened a kitten.

"Two men assaulted me," he whispered through gritted teeth.

"Excuse me, sir?"

The bailiff either hadn't heard or hadn't understood the words. It did seem incredible to Ted that someone had struck him with such violence in the midst of a crowd and there were no witnesses crying out. The perpetrators had melted away like wraiths.

Ted gave up. "I'm fine, thank you. Low blood sugar."

"I understand," the bailiff said. His tone had softened. "Would you like to rest for a minute?" He gestured toward a wooden bench down the corridor.

"No. Thank you. I need to get upstairs. I'll be okay."

"Let me give you a hand." He cleared a path through

the throng blocking the elevator—suits made way for the uniform—and made sure Ted got on board. "What floor?"

Ted didn't like having to take the man's help but accepted that he needed it. "I'm good," he said when he was safely in the car. He stabbed a random button while trying to remember where he had told Lester to take the damn filing.

The Russians knew about the filing. The realization had no sooner hit him than he remembered that they also knew his name. More specifically, they had called him "Eddie." Fear and pain had kept him from registering the real threat. These people knew a lot about him. If Cheryl was somehow involved—and who else called him Eddie?—the Russians would know his address, hangouts, and daily routine, such as it was. They could find him anytime they felt the need to jam somebody in the kidneys, or in the gonads, or upside the head.

Ted didn't typically get migraines, but something very like one descended on him at that point. The pain was instantaneous and blinding. A massive vise was pressing on his temples. His scalp crawled as if spiders were weaving webs there. His peripheral vision shrank so that the space in front of him—a crowded elevator—appeared through a pixelated tunnel, like a kaleidoscope. He needed air. The doors had opened and were closing again.

"Getting off." Judging by the snap of heads in his direction, he might have spoken somewhat more loudly than necessary.

A man held the doors. People made way—not reluctantly as before, but scurrying out of the way of the pasty-faced man. Ted stumbled through the crowd. Once clear he rested his forehead against the government-green wall. It felt cool. Ted thought he might survive—if he could somehow get the pace of his heartbeat down to an easy jog.

How had he let himself become involved in this asinine fool's quest? What in hell had he been thinking? He was no superhero. No champion. He had violated his own set of commandments and had no one to blame but himself. Ted had to stop the madness. He had to find the judge's office and talk to the clerk.

"I'VE ALREADY STAMPED IT RECEIVED." The clerk was practically rubbing his hands together with glee. If, in fact, "he" was the correct pronoun. So round as to be gender-neutral, the clerk had close-cropped grey hair, unadorned fingernails, and no sign of either having shaved or having an Adam's apple. Despite the abrupt change in the weather that had produced an early heat wave, Ted's happy tormentor was wearing a flannel shirt buttoned to the neck, well-worn corduroy trousers, and powder-blue boat shoes.

"But it is still in your possession. You can release it." Ted knew that he was asking for an exception. Only the person who had submitted a document could authorize its removal.

"You should know that I can't do that."

A minor rebuke. He would have been disappointed if the clerk hadn't found some way of making him feel small. "I understand. But I am the one who signed the document. Lester McKinley works for me. I authorized him to submit a filing on my behalf. Now I would like it back." The request seemed an uncomplicated one—to a sane individual whose life was not governed by mysterious and capricious rules of procedure.

"Then you should direct Lester to come here and take care of this business himself. I've worked with Lester for years. He knows how things are done."

Where *was* Lester? Ted was teetering on that uncomfortable fulcrum of concern and annoyance. "What happens if I can't find him?"

"I guess you'd have a problem."

The clerk was enjoying themself way too much. Ted remembered that the Russians had known about the filing.

Who had Ted told? Kenzie and the Preacher. Neither could have, or would have, passed along that information. Yet the Judge had known almost immediately. The only other two individuals who knew that a motion had been filed were Lester and this clerk. For a heartbeat or two, Ted allowed himself the bitter luxury of assuming that the missing Lester had been the one to tip off the Russians, the Judge, or both. But the smile on the clerk's face told a different story.

Ted felt failure washing over him. "Lester doesn't seem to be around this morning."

The clerk looked up at a wall clock identical to every wall clock in every bureaucrat's office Ted had ever seen. "I can give you until noon. That's when I put all new filings in the judge's inbox."

He had fewer than three hours to produce the only man capable of keeping the Cossacks from making good on their threat.

32

THE INFORMAL ARRANGEMENTS THAT Ted maintained with those few who had worked for him had their drawbacks. Other than a cell phone number, he had no way of contacting Lester—and his phone went straight to voice mail. Ted left a message that he hoped conveyed the seriousness of the situation.

The pain in his gut flared into a wince-inducing stab only when he took a deep breath. The bathroom mirror revealed a deep purple mark with tendrils snaking faintly across his belly. Was there internal bleeding? How would he know? An inch or two higher and he might have had a ruptured liver—if there was such a thing—or a busted sternum. A couple of inches lower and the Molloy genetic trail would have reached a sudden and tragic end.

He rode the elevator down to the lobby, his mind jumping between ideas for locating Lester. Kenzie knew who he was. Would any of her protestors be of help? Lester had once mentioned a sister. Could Ted locate her? Damn. This was inconvenience squared. What would he do if the case file ended up in front of a judge? The Russians would not like that. Ted would have to hire a lawyer to *lose* a case.

The crowds downstairs had dissipated—morning deadlines were over—and he walked out past security and down the steps. He scanned the loiterers out front for the two Russians, half expecting to see them glaring back at him. There was no sign of them.

The plaza held a tall sculpture that vaguely resembled a twentieth-century subway token. Around it were a series of knee-high concrete mushrooms—each representing one of the original towns of the borough—that served as less-than-comfortable seats, resting points for weary litigants. Lester Young McKinley was sitting on Howard Beach.

"Thank god, I found you," Ted said. "Jesus! What happened to you?"

Lester looked up. Large sunglasses—the kind you see on Floridian retirees—did not entirely hide the stitches and bruises on his face. His right hand was encased in fiberglass and suspended in a blue sling. He looked very small.

"Morning," he said. The word slurred, but it wasn't from vodka. Ted could see wires holding his teeth in place. "Sorry I'm late. I'm feeling a little under the weather this morning."

-33-

TED HAD ALL THE right information but had come to the wrong conclusion. Fear will do that. He could admit that he was afraid of so much—physical pain, Jill's disapproval, the power of her grandfather and his cronies, and, not least, failure. He had surrendered at the first blow struck—or before. But seeing Lester, a pawn on this battlefield, reminded him of something—someone he used to be.

Once upon a time, Ted had been a young man from an undistinguished background, his father an absent alcoholic and his mother a striver who had lost all pretensions. Ted had studied long and hard and finished law school at the top of his class, proud to be chosen to begin his career at the feet of an eminent judge. Someday, he thought, he would champion the poor, the unlucky, the pushed aside, thumbing his nose at those in power, the corrupt, the uncaring. That guy had become lost along the way. Power, money, and prestige had turned his head. And when they were taken away, he was back to where he had begun.

Lester was no threat to anyone. The sole reason he'd been given a beating was to send a message—to Ted.

"You want to tell me about it?" Ted said, taking a seat next to him.

"Russians." He swallowed saliva before continuing. "Two. They broke in the front door and came straight to my room."

"They knew where to find you." Ted wouldn't have known where to find him. Lester had once mentioned an SRO in Hollis but not an address. They'd followed him or put a lot of effort and energy into running him down.

Which meant they had resources and were willing to use them.

Lester nodded, saving his words.

"Was it the same two? The ones we saw right here?"

Lester shook his head. "Never seen 'em before."

"What did they want? Did they say anything?"

"Nothing."

"When?" Ted asked, unconsciously copying Lester's terse style.

Lester took a moment to answer. "Yesterday afternoon."

While Ted was sleeping off his hangover. "Thank god somebody got you to a hospital."

He nodded again. "Neighbor. Drives a cab. Took me to Great Neck."

"What the hell? Why'd you go all the way to Nassau County?"

"You ever been to an ER in an outer borough? People die there."

"This guy must be part angel," Ted said.

"Son of a bitch wanted me to pay double the meter when we got there. I told him to go ffffuck himself."

"Sounds right," Ted said. "What did they look like? Can you describe them at all?"

Lester answered with a dismissive shrug. "We didn't take a long time getting acquainted. I had my feet up and might have been dozing off. They came in, took care of their business, and got out."

"Yes, they're quick. I ran into the two guys from Friday just now."

Lester's expression shifted to exaggerated disbelief.

Ted's bruises didn't show. "They went easy on me."

"I'd say so." *Shay sho.*

Ted looked for the Russians again. If they were all in a forties B movie, this would have been the cue for the bad guys to reappear. There weren't many people around at all. The line of protestors that morning was sparse. Mondays. There was no sign of Kenzie. He found he very much wanted to see her.

"What are we going to do?" Lester asked.

"I came here this morning prepared to ditch the whole thing. Pull the file. Screw it, I thought, there's easier ways of making a buck. What do I care if that tower gets built or if some developer bought off a politician or two? I'm sorry Richie's dead, but I have to watch out for myself and the people I care about."

"Understandable," Lester said.

"But I don't want to do that now." Both the Judge and the Russian mob wanted him to pull that file; therefore, he would do the opposite. "Fuck 'em if they can't take a joke."

"Well put."

"I don't know how, but I want to fuck them up."

"I like it," Lester said.

"Got a plan?" Ted asked.

"No, but I wouldn't mind a little get back. Besides, I made promises."

"To Barbara Miller?"

"And Anora. She wants that green card," he said.

They both stood. "Okay," Ted said, "but she's got to wait in line. We have other priorities."

"Agreed. You got any ideas?"

"Not yet, but it's early. Let's get some coffee."

"I NEED TO TALK to him, Jill." The cell phone was both conduit and barrier. Ted wanted to reach through it and shake her.

Gallagher's was his fortress. He was in his usual spot, the back booth by the window, with a partial view of the street. The front door and the whole tavern were wide open in front of him. The bartender had the desk sergeant at the 110th Precinct on speed dial. Russian mobsters were not welcome.

The noon deadline had passed. Ted had been trying to connect with the Judge for hours. Calling Jill was his Hail Mary pass.

"Call his office," she said.

"I tried that." When Ted had told the secretary he wanted to speak to Con Fitzmaurice, she had said he was in luck because the Judge had "just walked in." But when she came back on the line a minute later, he had not yet arrived. Ted gave her credit for trying to sound convincing. "He's not taking my calls."

"I don't want to be involved in anything like this, Ted."

"Like what? Just give him my message, and tell him I'm ready to talk. He's going to want to hear what I have to say."

"Will this help Jacqueline?"

Jackie deserved everything coming her way, but Ted wasn't going to lie to Jill. If she thought he was lying, he would lose her—and he wasn't ready for that. Besides, Ted needed her.

"She's in trouble," he said. "I don't think that's any secret. If I don't talk to the Judge, she will take the fall."

He'd left out a few details, but everything he'd said was true.

"I'll call you back." She hung up.

Ted let out a long-held breath.

"Did she go for it?"

Lester's face came into focus. Ted pushed away his coffee.

It had grown cold and had been bitter to start with. "She's calling him. We wait. You want a drink? I could use a shot of something."

"I might need a pain pill later on. I'd better not start drinking."

"I admire your restraint, but I want a jitters killer. What should I get?"

"You're not a whiskey drinker," Lester said.

His father drank scotch. The smell of it gave him a head-ache. "I stick to beer. Usually."

"These aren't usual times. Vodka. There's no sense in wasting good bourbon if you don't have the taste for it. Vodka'll get the job done. See if they keep a bottle on ice. It'll go down a lot easier."

The lunch crowd had come and gone. Ted saluted Paulie McGirk in the mirror as he passed. Paulie's eyes were open, but Ted wasn't sure there were any functioning nerve cells behind those bloodred orbs.

Lili's eyebrows shot up when he asked her for the shot, but she pulled a blue-labeled bottle of Smirnoff out of the ice and poured a hefty slug.

"You celebrate something?" she asked.

"Not exactly," he said and returned to the booth.

He braced for the burn, but the cold liquid went down like silken ice. A warm glow spread out from his belly, reaching fingers, lips, and cheeks moments later.

"Oh, shit," Ted said. "It works."

"One billion satisfied customers," Lester said.

"You want anything to eat?" Ted asked. He'd been too jittery to think about food before.

"Like maybe a smoothie?" Lester flashed a metal-crusted grin.

"Right. Sorry."

Ted's cell phone rang. Jill.

"What did he say?" he asked.

"I don't feel good about this," she said.

"Will he call me?"

"No. He said he won't talk on the phone." She sounded small and frightened.

Her paranoia must have been contagious—or the Judge already had a strong case of his own. "Okay. Thanks for trying."

"But he'll meet you."

That was interesting, but now Ted's own paranoia fluttered in his chest. All he said was "Ah."

"What?" The single word exploded in his ear.

"Did he mention a place? A time?" Ted sensed a trap. Hired thugs wouldn't grab him inside the Century Club, but there would be no way to avoid them if they wanted to take him on the street. A neutral location, on the other hand, might mean that Ted could actually trust the old bastard.

"*Keller v. Zuckerman/Scotto LLC.* One o'clock tomorrow. He said you'd know what that meant."

A complicated case that had dragged through the system for years. A pair of shady lawyers had bought buildings in East New York and converted them to affordable-housing units, using government grants. Once these two sharks filled the apartments with Section 8 tenants, they had leveraged the buildings with loans from banks and private lenders, borrowing more than the properties could have ever drawn at auction. Then the mortgage crisis swept through Brooklyn, and Zuckerman/Scotto LLC stopped paying. For anything.

Everybody sued, but the courts were swamped, and foreclosures took forever. Misters Zuckerman and Scotto managed to collect three years' rent from their tenants without paying a dime for taxes, interest, insurance, maintenance, or heating fuel. Zuckerman, despite a vigorous defense by Hasting, Fitzmaurice, and Barson, eventually went to jail and was, no doubt, still there.

Scotto wasn't so lucky. On his way home to Staten Island one night, a delivery van sideswiped him on the Verrazano Bridge. When Scotto got out of his car to exchange insurance information with the van driver, two men burst out of the side door, grabbed the lawyer, and boosted him over the rail. Two hundred twenty-eight feet later, he hit the water on an incoming tide. His body was recovered near a pier at the end of Bay Ridge Ave.

It was Ted's first real-life lesson in the difference between justice and the law.

Ted understood the Judge's code. Lionel Keller, a tenant who had merely wanted his heat turned on, had lived in a Zuckerman/Scotto-owned three-building enclave on Dumont Avenue. HFB LLC had been forced to step down as counsel to the commercial real estate company while pursuing Zuckerman's criminal appeals. Ted, having been lead counsel to that company, followed the progress of the various suits. Mr. Keller sought to recoup rent after living in his apartment for three years with no heat and intermittent water service. He was represented pro bono by a top-tier law firm that took his case all the way to Albany and the New York State Court of Appeals. Keller lost. Judge Fitzmaurice cast the deciding vote.

That was Ted's second lesson.

He had no idea what had become of the unfortunate Mr. Keller, but the buildings were still there. It had been a rough neighborhood back then and probably still was. There was a good chance that Ted and the Judge would be the only white faces in sight. Loitering Russian mobsters would have nowhere to lurk. It meant that Ted could trust the Judge—possibly.

All Lester and Ted had to do was stay alive until one o'clock the next day.

THEY NEEDED BOTH TRANSPORTATION and anonymity. A phone call, a ten-minute wait, and Mohammed pulled up in front of Gallagher's. Lester and Ted hustled across the sidewalk and jumped into the car.

"How's it goin', boss?" Mohammed said.

"Your English is really coming along," Ted said.

"Not English. American," Mohammed answered. "Where to?"

"American," Ted agreed. "For starters, how about you drive? Random. Anywhere. I want to see if anyone is following us."

"Now you're speaking."

"Talking," Ted said. "Now you're talking."

Lester rolled his eyes.

"How are you holding up?" Ted asked him.

"Doin' just fine for the moment, but I'm going to take one of these pain pills in a while, and then I'm going to want to sleep."

Ted kept watch out the rear window as Mohammed made a series of right turns, accelerating and braking in a fashion that earned him more than a few angry salutes from other drivers. He had a knack for squeezing through gaps in traffic. Lester closed his eyes and mumbled to himself. The only time Ted felt his heart stop was when they cut off a Q18 bus as it pulled away from the curb. Mohammed gunned it, only to discover a woman with a baby stroller in the crosswalk on the other side. He swerved and the car bounced over the curb, missing woman, stroller, bus, and the dark-eyed girl selling single roses on the corner.

"Do you see anyone following us?" Lester asked.

"No. I think we're okay," Ted said.

"Then you can tell our man up front to go easy on the women and children," Lester said.

"And us."

"For a moment there, I forgot that I was in pain."

"Mohammed. Take us to Ridgewood."

"I'm down with Ridgewood," Mohammed said. "You got an address?"

"Not yet," Ted said. "Head down Forest Avenue until I tell you different."

"Where we going?" Lester asked.

"We need a place to hole up for the night," Ted said. "McKenzie Zielinski. The protest lady. No one will connect us, so they won't be looking for us there. She's got friends. I'm hoping they can hide us."

"You got a number for her?"

"No."

"You took her to lunch and couldn't get a phone number?" Lester formed a thumb and forefinger into an L.

"It was a business lunch," Ted said.

"How about an address?"

"No."

"Oh. Good to see you've got this all planned out."

"Her last name is Zielinski. How many can there be in Ridgewood?"

"In Ridgewood? Legions?"

QUICK FIX REPAIR WAS located in a storefront on Fresh Pond Road, next door to a deli that advertised STUFFED CABBAGE— SATURDAY ONLY in large block letters across the front window.

Ted told Lester to wait in the car with Mohammed. Lester had put the sunglasses back on, but they hid only the bruises around his eyes. He looked like one step up from roadkill.

A muted buzzer went off as Ted pushed open the door to a shallow waiting room. A counter separated the client space from the work and storage area. Shelves held desktop PCs, laptops, a few antique lamps, and an assortment of ancient power tools. Everything was labeled with customer information and a dollar amount, presumably the cost of the repair. One hundred twenty-five dollars seemed a fair price for getting an HP reliably streaming *Game of Thrones* again, but Ted doubted that anyone was coming to pay the eighty-dollar ransom on a variable drill unless they had some deep emotional attachment to it.

"Be right there," a voice called from behind a curtained doorway.

A sign over the counter read CRACKED SCREENS FIXED WHILE YOU WAIT—ALL CELL PHONE REPAIRS MUST BE PAID FOR IN ADVANCE. FREE ESTIMATE.

"No rush," Ted said. There were two plastic chairs against the wall. He took one and looked out the window. Mohammed's car was idling in front of a fire hydrant across the street. Lester was slouched in the back.

The curtain was swept away, and a man in his midfifties in a short-sleeved white shirt and rimless spectacles emerged from the back room. He had the tall, gaunt frame of Abraham Lincoln and a protruding Adam's apple as sharp as an ax blade. His shirt pocket held a plastic protector bursting with plastic pens, tiny screwdrivers, and a metal flashlight the size of a cigarette.

"How can I help you?" he said.

"I'm looking for a Mr. Zielinski," Ted said, though he was sure that he was looking at him.

"I'm Peter Zielinski." He was curious, not threatened. A man with a clear conscience.

"I'm a friend of McKenzie's. Ted Molloy."

If he recognized Ted's name, he gave no sign. "Is she in jail again?"

"No. I don't think so."

"'Cause you look like a lawyer. And it wouldn't be the first time."

"I need to get in touch with her. Can you get her a message?"

"She's not answering her phone?" His voice rose in pitch. Ted was scaring him.

"I haven't tried her phone for the very simple reason that I don't have her number."

Now Ted had confused him. "I thought you said—"

"We met last week. I'm old school, I guess. I don't ask for a lady's number. I wait until she offers it." It was a weak excuse and sounded like one.

The man was now on full alert. "And how did you find me?"

"She told me you had a repair business. There aren't many."

He nodded rapidly a few times. Stalling. Processing. "So, leave me your card. If I hear from her, I'll tell her you came by."

The card would go in the trash the moment Ted walked out the door. He was losing.

"Could you give her a call? Give her my name. She'll talk to me."

"No. I don't think so. You leave your card."

Ted had pushed too hard, too fast, and now he'd hit a dead end. Lawyers talk for a living. Thinking, arguing, persuading—these were his tools, his talents. When they failed him, he had no plan B. Grabbing the man and shaking him until he gave up his daughter's number wasn't going to work. He dropped a card on the counter but kept his expectations to himself.

That buzzer sounded again as the door opened.

"Is this the guy?" Lester asked. "The father?"

He had removed the sunglasses. One eye was so bloodshot it looked as if he should have been weeping blood.

"I'm with him, Mr. Z.," Lester said. "You see all this?" He held up the cast and indicated his bruised face with the other hand. "Some very nasty people are upset with us." He was doing much better at speaking around and through the metal in his mouth, but Ted could tell it was costing him to do so. "She may be next. I'm not asking you to trust us, but she ought to be warned."

"What in hell are you people involved with?" Zielinski said. He was scared. Lester had gotten to him.

Lester ignored the question and turned to Ted. "Did you give the man your cell phone number?"

"I did," Ted said.

"Then let's go. We should keep moving."

He was right. Ted started for the door.

Lester spoke to the man again. "Ted and Lester. Tell her. It's the right thing to do."

Lester followed Ted out to the street.

"You make a convincing case," Ted said.

"Let's hope," Lester answered.

36

IT DIDN'T TAKE LONG. Kenzie barreled around the corner and down the thoroughfare. People on the sidewalk stepped out of her way. She was heading for her father's store.

"Hold up," Ted called, extricating himself from Mohammed's chariot.

She saw him and came wading through the light traffic, fists clenched.

Ted's relief at seeing her unhurt didn't last long. The anger on her face was formidable. He wasn't sure what he'd done to deserve it, but there was no doubt in his mind that her wrath was aimed at him. "Can we talk?" he said. "Give me one minute. Thirty seconds."

She kept coming. The punch came from low to high. She didn't have her weight behind it, but her long limb transmitted a ton of force. He let her hit him, trying to relax and flow with it. Her fist landed on the side of his head, above the ear and well back from the temple. It hurt, but he stayed upright.

"You son of a bitch!" she yelled into his face.

"Are you done assaulting me?" Ted said. "Can we talk now?"

"How dare you come and frighten my family? Who the hell do you think you are?" Her hand had to be hurting, but she shook it once and formed a fist again.

Ted held up both hands in defense. "You got your one shot. Now you've got to hear me out."

She swung again. He blocked it.

"Ow," she cried. "That hurt."

"Hey, lady," a voice called from a Canada Dry delivery truck. "Get outa the street."

She flipped the driver off but moved exactly one step closer to the curb. The truck eased by.

"Tough broad," the driver called to Ted. The man was grinning.

Ted pretended he wasn't there. Half-assed misogynist male bonding wasn't going to help the situation. "I'm sorry. I didn't mean to scare your father, but we had to find you. Take a look at Lester, will you?"

Lester had stayed in the car. Ted stepped aside as Kenzie looked in. Lester was pitiful, shrunken, damaged, and barely capable of keeping his head upright.

"Oh, no," she said. "Oh, my God. Who did this?"

"Russians," Lester whispered in a pained rasp, playing the moment as if it were his final scene.

"Holy hell," she said. "Those fucking creeps. I hope the cops bounce them on the sidewalk a few times before bringing them in."

"We haven't told the police," Ted said.

"What?" she said. "Why the hell not?"

"Kenzie, listen to me. We don't know who else they're after. They roughed me up, too. Nothing like Lester, but they got me in the courthouse. Cops all around us. Nobody saw a thing. But I don't think those guys would have cared. They're very scary."

"And you're here to warn me? Why would they be after me?"

"I'm not saying they are. I don't know. But they're after us because we've been looking under rocks connected to the Spike. If they're not looking for you now, they may be later."

"I'm no threat to them," she said, but she didn't sound certain. "But you are. We've got to hide you two while we figure out our next step." She noticed Mohammed for the first time and raised her eyebrows in an unspoken question.

"This is Mohammed. He's new in town. We're expanding his horizons."

"It is pleasant to meet you," the driver said, not meeting her eyes.

Kenzie stepped close to Ted. "Can you trust him?"

"I think a fifty-dollar bill would buy everything he knows, but someone's got to know to ask him," Ted said. "I think we're okay."

"Can Lester walk?"

Ted looked down at him. Lester was milking his moment. "With encouragement."

Kenzie stepped between them, facing Ted and close enough to give them a moment's privacy. "Does this mean you've resolved those ethical concerns you were so worried about?"

Ted met her eyes. "No problem."

37

THEY SPENT THE AFTERNOON huddled in Kenzie's tiny office at the church. Lester, because of his wounds, got the comfy chair. Kenzie took an ancient secretary chair behind the desk, and Ted paced or perched on the cold radiator. They hashed and rehashed plans for the next day and the meeting with the Judge.

"I need him to say something—anything—incriminating with Lester close enough to get it recorded," Ted said. "He expects me to be begging him for help. It will make him less cautious."

"What makes you so sure he'll let his guard down?" Kenzie asked.

"Jill. That's his focus. If Jackie takes a fall for defrauding Miss Miller, he believes Jill will be devastated. He will do anything to protect her. Including talking to me."

"Jackie's the spouse, right?"

"My ex-wife's wife, yes."

"She's also counsel for Barbara Miller on the buildings the old lady lost," Lester said.

Kenzie looked at Ted with raised eyebrows.

He nodded. "It gets complicated. It looks like Jackie— Jacqueline Clavette—did a piss-poor job of protecting her client's interests."

"And maybe she's behind the surplus-money angle," Lester said.

"This is all speculation," Ted said. "Without the full file, I can't say for certain that Jackie screwed up. Intentionally or not."

"He's a lawyer," Lester said. "I'm not. Jackie did it. Guilty."

"Either way, she's key," Kenzie said.

"But here's my question," Ted said. "If she is the one who put it over on Miller, *and* she's the one who managed to hide a million plus bucks in surplus money . . ." He paused.

"No 'if' about it," Lester said.

"Then why aren't the Russians beating *her* up?" Ted asked.

Lester grunted, which Ted took for support. Outside an ambulance went by at speed, the siren's Doppler effect peaking in an instant and the sound immediately fading into the background of what passed for normal in the city. The three of them, all deep in thought, took no notice.

Kenzie spoke first. "I see three possibilities. One, she's working for the Russians. The surplus money will end up in their pockets. She'll find some way to deliver it."

"Based on character alone, I'd have to rate that unlikely," Ted said.

"I agree," she said, "but not based on her character. Theirs. Those guys wouldn't trust a woman."

Lester nodded his agreement.

"On the other hand," Ted said, "those guys seem to be incredibly well-informed about our interests. Suppose that's her role."

"Hold that thought," Kenzie said. "Two, she's playing her own game. Somehow she's keeping the Russians at bay with promises, lies, or distraction."

"Dangerous," Ted said.

Lester nodded again. "Those guys would break your arms for trying to cheat them out of the change on a cup of coffee."

"Which brings me to number three," Kenzie said. "She's protected. There's some Mr. Big pulling strings. Someone who can tell the Russians to back off. Someone who knows about the money and just doesn't care because he's focused on the bigger payoff."

"Reisner," Lester said.

"Or some higher-up at Corona Partners," Ted said. "Or

a politician or banker with pull. Someone senior who they'd all listen to."

Or someone who cared more about Jackie's well-being than about the money.

They discussed the setup for the next day until Lester's discomfort became obvious. He was in pain. He reluctantly took a pill, and they sat silently until he fell asleep.

"Why is he doing this?" Kenzie asked when Lester's breathing indicated he was deep in dreamland.

Ted wanted an answer to that question also. "I'll ask him that someday."

"They messed him up."

"Why him? Why not me? Is that what you're asking?"

"No, but that's another good question."

"I don't know," he said.

"You dragged him into this."

"Not exactly. Is it my fault he got beat up? Do I feel responsible? Is that your point?"

"No. I'm concerned that you might be feeling that way . . ."

It came down to trust. Ted had had suspicions when Lester first appeared. They had not entirely gone away. Now the two of them were bonded by the Russians' assaults, and the questions had become moot.

"If I thought he needed an apology, I'd give it to him. We're good."

She nodded once; she understood.

"I need a walk." Kenzie said. "I'll go nuts sitting here."

"Go," Ted said. "I'm still in hiding until tomorrow." And he found he was exhausted. He cradled his arms on the desk and rested his head. "Wake me when you're back."

"I'll find us some dinner," she said.

He was asleep before Kenzie made it out the door.

Dinner was takeout from the Polish deli down the block. Lester managed a bowl of mushroom soup and an order of mashed potatoes. Kenzie and Ted finished off a platter of pierogi. A black-eyed old woman who muttered angrily to herself delivered blankets but didn't stay long. The priest kept his distance. Ted and Lester were potentially toxic.

"You'll have to sleep on pews, but you'll be safe here," Kenzie said.

"Do you snore?" Lester asked.

"My ex never mentioned it," Ted said.

"Well, I'll tell you tomorrow," Lester said.

"I'm afraid to ask."

"If I snore?" Lester asked. "Only when I'm asleep."

TED'S NAP HAD UPSET his internal clock. It was the middle of the night and he couldn't sleep. Lester seemed to have no such problem. The pain pills must have helped. Lester's admission that he snored was confirmed. In triplicate.

Too much hung on their success the next day. Ted knew the best thing he could do was relax and rest. He would need all his faculties to outwit the Judge. Ted somehow needed to get him to implicate himself or one of the other actors in this convoluted drama. It wasn't going to be easy. Another beer might have helped Ted to think—or sleep—but he'd finished his one long ago. Water wasn't having much effect other than to give him an urge to revisit the toilet.

The bathroom was a closet-sized room with a single small window a few inches above eye level. Ted was not a short man. He had to look up at a sharp angle to see out.

The view wasn't much, but at that moment it was magic. A full moon hovered above the church steeple, bathing the ancient slate roof in mercury. Ted couldn't move. Moments when he took the time to look up at a New York night sky were as rare as good luck. There was never much to see.

He washed his hands in the bowl-sized basin and crept back to the dark church sanctuary. He found his pew and sat, adjusting the thin blanket as best he could in the vain hope of creating comfort. Something had changed. There was a strange stillness in the air.

Lester was no longer snoring.

"You mind if I ask you something?" Lester spoke quietly, his voice almost dreamy from the medication.

"You breathing?" Ted said. "For a second there, I wasn't so sure."

"What the hell are you doing here?"

"Come again?" Ted said.

"You don't need this. You went to school. Law school. You got to play with the big dogs. Hell, man, the only thing I've ever done was serve two years working in an army warehouse in Stuttgart, where I wrenched my back. Never worked a straight job again. But you had it made. Why? What happened? Who'd you piss off?"

Ted was sure it was written—somewhere. Thou Shalt Not Divorce Thy Boss's Daughter.

THEY HAD NOT SPOKEN to each other in months, but he was not surprised to see her name appear on his phone. Jill would have heard. Someone in that family of sharks would have been delighted to deliver the news.

"Security took my notebook, laptop, work phone. They wouldn't let me touch anything on my desk. I was out the door, on the street, by eight-twenty." Ted pried the top off the second bottle of Bass ale and took a long swallow.

Jill sounded less concerned than perplexed. "Didn't they offer you a different job? You're too good for them to let you walk."

"They did offer me something." It was a cut in pay. He would have had to surrender his junior partnership and accept a counselor position—in a dead-end department with no hope of advancement, opportunity, or challenge. It was less an offer of employment than a test to see how low he was willing to stoop. He'd walked instead. "It was not what I want. As a matter of fact, I would rather tend bar if I had to." That was a stretch. As he rarely drank anything stronger than the occasional beer, he wouldn't know the difference between a martini and a Manhattan.

"What are you saying? You could still be working there."

"It was not a real offer, Jill. The job was a dead end. Worse."

"What? Not up to your standards? You're unemployed, Ted."

"If you were to design a job that I would truly hate just to screw with me, this was worse. Trust me, Jill. I would have gone postal in no time."

When she spoke again, she was less adamant and argumentative. "Why would they do that? I don't understand. You're a good lawyer. Can't they always find room for a really good lawyer?"

"Actually, no. But someone thought long and hard before offering me something that I would never in a million years accept."

"But why? I don't get it?"

"Revenge. They could have cut me loose, and I would have walked away with a fat severance package and a year's health insurance. As it is, I've got about three months' savings and my IRA."

"That's not fair," she said.

"There's no such thing." He had always believed that. For all his drive and hard work, the world owed him nothing. But he'd been targeted. Screwed.

"I'm going to speak to my father," she said.

The thought of his ex-wife begging her daddy, a man whom Ted had never liked, respected, or felt any kinship with, to intercede for him was nauseating. He was a lawyer and desperately wanted the opportunity to practice again, but he was also a poor kid from the streets of Queens who'd made it out, and his pride was what had always carried him.

"Please don't," he said. "I'll land on my feet. If I'm going to ask for help, I'll do it myself, and it won't be through your father." Ted was already thinking of bypassing the father and asking for her grandfather's help instead. Ted had earned the Judge's assistance in the past, and there was no shame in seeking it now.

"No, Ted. It's not right. I told him I wanted you taken care of. He said he would see to it."

Ted's stomach did a somersault. "Wait. What are you saying? You knew?"

"Well, I knew they were going to be making some cuts. Everyone did."

"Everyone" meant everyone in the family. Jill's worldview could be very limited in some ways.

"And you made him promise to offer me a different job?" Ted said. "To keep me on?"

"Of course," she said.

Of course, Ted thought.

NINE YEARS LATER THE memories still pained.

Lester cleared his throat. "You still with me? I thought you checked out for a minute."

Ted shook his head in a forlorn attempt to dispel the ghosts. "Bad choices, Lester. I don't blame anybody but myself." Which wasn't entirely true, but Ted wished it were. "I kept making bad choices until the bottom fell out. In the end, I settled for a bad deal rather than take my chances fighting an injustice."

"You're not the first. The deck is always stacked."

"I wish I could say I'd make better—stronger—choices next time around. But I really don't know." Ted found his bottle of water and took a long slug. "Now it's my turn."

"What's that?"

"The day we met. You were waiting for me. Meeting you—hiring you—was no accident. You made it happen." The question was implicit.

"Truth?" Lester asked.

Ted laughed softly. "We're talking after midnight, sitting in a church, and it's a full moon. What do you think?"

"Truth is never as pretty as you think it's going to be."

"I'm listening," Ted said. In the faint light from the sanctuary lamp, Lester's bruises faded, and years were stripped away. He appeared younger, healthier, and a touch sadder. The rollback of time removed a layer of forbearance, revealing a man who had not yet learned to hide his disappointments.

Lester sat up and took a deep breath. "Richie Rubiano was a dope. Everybody knew he was working on something worth a million bucks. I didn't know what it was about or how this shit worked, but I wanted some of it. I've got nothing else. An ex-wife and two kids who wouldn't know me if they had to step over me lying on the sidewalk and a room in a flop that's only mine as long as I can pay a week in advance. So I put myself in front of you, figuring you were my best shot at getting a piece of that."

"You wanted a cut?"

"Truth, right? A cut? At a minimum. If I thought I could have conned you out of all of it, I was ready to go down that road. Hell, you worked with Richie. I figured you must be a scammer yourself, and that meant fair game."

Ted let a beat go by, waiting for Lester to continue. When he didn't, Ted asked, "What changed your mind?"

"Who says I changed my mind?" Lester gave the question a touch of bravado.

Ted smiled at him. "You're here."

Lester looked away, taking his time to frame an answer. "It was the old lady. Miller. You were straight with her. She's prime for a good con. They already got to her once. You could have spun her a story and taken her for everything she's got left. Only you didn't. I realized that despite the strange way you have of making a living, you're not a crook." Having finished his speech, Lester lay back on the long pew and closed his eyes. Moments later he said, "Of course, if you were to offer me a percentage, I wouldn't say no."

39

THEY FOUND LESTER A baggy suit at the parish thrift store, disagreeing briefly on whether blue or brown was more convincing. Lester won with the argument with the point that stains would show up better on the brown. Ted didn't haggle, paying too much and earning disapproving looks from both Kenzie and the church volunteer at the checkout.

Kenzie claimed the job of distressing the clothes based on her as-yet-unrevealed artistic talents. She attacked with ketchup, coffee, and the contents of a vacuum cleaner bag. She balked at urine, but Lester persevered, though insisting, reasonably, that only his own be used. Ted withheld an opinion. Verisimilitude in costuming was out of his jurisdiction. And he wasn't going to be the one posing as a wino.

Mohammed dropped Lester off two blocks from the address, leaving him to shuffle the rest of the way in his bedroom slippers, carrying an ass-pocket flask of Relska Vodka. He was in place by eleven o'clock. Two hours early, but they agreed he needed the time to fade into the background.

Kenzie stayed hidden in Mohammed's car with her camera and telephoto lens. It was coming up to noon, but the wide streets were nearly bare. The pathways between the projects on the other side of the boulevard, however, were crowded with young black men wearing white Stanley Kowalski shirts and black jeans and young black women minding toddlers. Ted did not see one person look at him, but he could feel that they all knew he was there and did not like it. A white man in a suit was an affront or possibly a threat. Ted recognized all the societal reasons why this hostility existed and empathized. But on this day the malice was focused on him. He imagined the towering structures as buttes in some John Ford western, smoke signals rising and alerting one and all of his presence.

He crossed the street, avoiding any chance of confrontation. This was their neighborhood, and he was the intruder. Moving on was all he could do to return normalcy to their world.

The advantage to Ted and his coconspirators was that Russian mobsters would be even more apparent and less welcome.

Ted kept walking. Once out of the shadow of those tall buildings, he was able to concentrate on the meeting ahead. Lester would have identified the best place for a private conversation held in public view and settled in there.

East New York had clawed its way back from the worst times, but the terminal disease of inescapable poverty hung about. There were no abandoned or burned-out cars, though once there had been plenty, as the remains of stolen, stripped vehicles had been left, wheelless, seatless, and engineless on side streets, windshields plastered with parking tickets. Many of the boarded-up buildings had been taken down or revitalized with paint, plaster, and panes of new glass. But the pall of hopelessness was evident in the iron bars on first floor windows and steel grating around every bodega. These people were not going to be shopping in LBC's giant mall—they'd be lucky to get jobs there sweeping the floor.

Lester was splayed across a concrete bench in the shade of a struggling gingko tree. His eyes were closed, and his mouth was slack, but he registered Ted's approach with a snort and a whisper. "He's late."

Ted checked his watch. One o'clock, on the nose. "Not yet," he whispered. He stepped away and waited next to a street sign. NO PARKING, 12PM–2PM, TUES & THURS.

"This doesn't feel right," Lester said.

Ted sat down next to him. "Ten minutes."

40

THE SQUAD CAR CAME slowly down the block. There was no other traffic and no one on the street other than Lester and Ted. Lester—dirty, disheveled, smelling of booze and urine, with his sling hidden beneath his jacket—appeared to be sleeping on the bench. The cops ignored him. Ted was the anomaly. The car stopped in front of him.

"Are you lost, sir?" The young cop who spoke, a light-skinned black man, was riding shotgun.

"No." Ted didn't think the question warranted further explanation.

"Do you have business around here?" The cop had an attitude. The politeness was overdone. He wasn't there to help.

Ted tried smiling. "I'm waiting for someone."

The two cops conferred for a moment. The sunlight, reflecting off the windshield, created a shimmering blind. Ted couldn't see the driver. He wished they would keep rolling on down the street. If the Judge saw them, he would cancel the meet.

The young cop opened his door and sauntered over. The driver got out and stood behind the car. He was older, white, fifties. Grey brush cut. Probably had had the same haircut since he left the army. He squinted against the sun, watching Ted intently.

"Can I see some ID?" the young cop asked.

Ted stood slowly. "I'm reaching for my wallet," he said before placing his hand behind his back and lifting the slim billfold from his right hip. "Is there a problem?"

"I thought I smelled marijuana," the cop said. "Did I smell marijuana?"

Ted had seen this shakedown often enough on the streets,

though he had always ignored it. It was an indignity inflicted mostly on young black or brown men—though to be fair he had also seen kids with white or yellow skin treated the same way. Race-based profiling was difficult to maintain in a borough that boasted citizens of almost every ethnic persuasion on the planet. The possible aroma of burning weed was enough of an excuse to demonstrate the power of the beat cop. But Ted wasn't young or in any other way an obvious choice for rousting.

"I don't smell anything, Officer," Ted said.

"Would you turn out your pockets, sir?"

He wasn't armed or carrying drugs. He didn't even have any loose change. But the pockets on his grey flannel slacks were tacked in place. They did not turn out.

"I'm afraid they don't work that way. I'll empty my jacket pockets, but . . ." He shrugged.

"Place all the items on the bench and then step away," the cop said.

"What's this about?" Ted asked, though he quickly complied. "I'm simply waiting for a friend." His wallet, his phone, a pen, a small tin of Altoid mints. Then his fingers found the envelope with the remaining $800 of Cheryl's money. That much cash in this neighborhood was going to generate suspicion. He paused for a moment before placing it on the bench.

Lester snorted in his sleep. The cop gave him a quick glance and then ignored him. Ted stepped back and the cop picked up the wallet.

"Edward Molloy," he read aloud. "What's your address, Mr. Molloy?"

Ted rattled it off. "That's really my wallet and ID." Keeping his voice level and free of any attitude, he continued. "I can tell you my Amex number if you want."

The cop ignored this. He reached for the tin of mints. "Is there anything in here?"

"Yes," Ted said. "Mints."

The cop shook the container before handing it to Ted. "Would you open it, sir?"

Ted snapped it open and risked a look up and down the street. No sign of the Judge or a car that might be his.

"Is your friend running late?" the cop asked with the barest hint of disbelief in the existence of this party.

Ted ignored the innuendo. "Is there anything else, Officer?" Why had this cop chosen Ted? What unimaginable profile could he possibly fit?

The cop glanced at the tin and then down at the items on the bench. "Would you open that envelope?"

Ted froze for a split second.

"Sir? Do we have a problem?"

"No, Officer." Ted felt as if he were falling down a steep precipice—in slow motion. He picked up the envelope and opened it.

The cop looked inside. "Would you mind stepping over to the car? I want my partner to see this."

Lester snorted again. It sounded less like a snore. More like a strangled laugh. Ted found none of this funny.

The older cop thumbed the bills in the envelope. He looked up. The squint had nothing to do with the bright sunlight. It was a sign to the world that after twenty-some years of seeing it all, hearing it all, and maybe even smelling it all, he had lost his sense of wonder. He wasn't buying any of it.

"You see, Mr. Molloy, while it is quite unusual for us to find a perfectly innocent man, well-dressed and carrying a large amount of cash in large denominations, sitting on a bench in this neighborhood, we do occasionally come across not-so-innocent men of a similar description who are here for the purpose of purchasing illegal drugs," the older cop said. "Would you be one of those people, Mr. Molloy?"

Ted heard Lester give a hacking cough.

Ted knew enough to say nothing. They could roust him, maybe even take him to the precinct. But there were no grounds for an arrest. Why would they want to spend their afternoon doing the necessary paperwork only to have to release him the moment his lawyer arrived? And the bigger question was why they were giving him trouble at all. He could easily have a legitimate reason to be there.

"I haven't done anything. I'd like to go. May I have my possessions?" Out of the corner of his eye, Ted saw Lester pull himself erect and stagger away.

The squint narrowed slightly. "Why don't we do this at the precinct? Is that all right with you, Mr. Molloy?"

"Am I under arrest?" Ted asked.

"Not at this time."

"Then I'd rather not," he said with a smile.

"I'm going to insist, Mr. Molloy." The smile hadn't worked on the first cop either.

"I have an appointment," Ted said, though he was no longer sure that this was true.

"I think it was canceled. Meanwhile, I don't believe that you are safe in this neighborhood, especially carrying this much cash. Pick up your things, and we'll give you a ride to the station."

And the realization struck. Lester must have figured it out long before, but he'd had the advantage of being an observer, not the mark. Ted had been played.

"He sent you, didn't he?" Ted said.

The older cop slowly shook his head. "I don't know who you're talking about."

They weren't leaving without him.

"Can you at least play the siren?" Ted asked. "I've always wanted to ride in a cop car with the siren wailing."

Ted let the young cop guide him into the back seat.

41

THEY LEFT TED ON a metal folding chair inside the entrance. A policeman seated behind a thick Plexiglas window buzzed the two patrolmen through a door, and they disappeared into the inner sanctum of the precinct.

Ted took out his cell phone, half expecting the desk cop to stop him, but the man ignored him.

"Kenzie? Did you pick up Lester?"

"He's with me."

"Take him to the church, and let him get cleaned up."

"How are you? What are they doing to you?"

"Nothing now. They left me sitting here. No one said a thing."

"What happened? Where's the Judge?"

Ted gave a sour laugh. "It is a demonstration in power—and a game. Judge Fitzmaurice never had any intention of meeting me there."

"Just for a laugh at your expense?"

"No. He knows I haven't rescinded that motion and he's pissed. He told me what he wanted on Saturday. It's Tuesday and I'm not falling in line."

"What do we do?"

"I'll give you a call when I know something. I have a feeling it's going to be a while."

Ted entertained himself by checking the upcoming rotation for the Mets' road trip. When he had wrung all the juice out of that distraction, he checked the time. He'd been waiting for all of five minutes. It felt like an hour.

Thirty minutes later, no one had come in or gone out the door since he'd arrived. The desk cop had a pencil in his hand

and was staring intently down at something in front of him. A crossword puzzle? Sudoku?

Ted stood and walked over. The cop saw him coming and slid to the side whatever it was he had been doing.

"Can I help you?" he asked. Ted saw the nameplate over his badge. MENENDEZ. He had a Clark Gable mustache, so perfectly groomed he must have trimmed it that morning.

Ted swung his head to the side, trying to appear casual. He saw what the cop had been reading. *Civil Procedure, 7th Edition.* Law school. First year. "Well, Officer Menendez, I'd like to know what's up."

"How's that?" He seemed genuinely confused by the question.

"Well, those two officers left me sitting here."

"Who would that be?"

Ted described the pair.

"What's your interest in them?"

"They picked me up and drove me here. They told me to take a seat. I haven't seen them since."

"I couldn't say. But they're out on patrol. If you would like to wait, they'll be back by four. That's end of their shift."

"Shit," Ted said. It slipped out without thought. He'd been played again.

"If it's an emergency—"

Ted cut him off. "No. Thank you. It's fine. Really. Fine." He spun around and headed for the exit.

"Sir?" the cop called after him. "Your ID?" He held up a brown envelope.

Ted walked back and took it from him. He checked inside. His driver's license. The envelope with Cheryl's money. He counted it. All there. He looked up at Officer Menendez, who was making no effort to hide his smirk. "Thank you again. I'll be sure to let everyone know how hospitable you've all been."

"Have a good day."

But Ted was out the door, his fingers already punching in Kenzie's number on his phone. "These sons of bitches left me sitting on a goddamn folding chair and went out the back door."

"So they're not holding you?"

"No. Damn it."

"You'll have to explain why that's a bad thing."

"Damn. How's Lester?"

"Sleeping it off. He did some self-medication with that bottle of vodka."

"Damn."

"He'll be fine. He needs the rest. I left him wrapped in blankets."

"You have the car and driver?"

"Mohammed? We're headed your way now."

Ted was standing on the curb outside the entrance. The street was lined with automobiles parked half-on, half-off the sidewalk. Police cruisers, government issue, stripped down models, and personal vehicles took up all the space in front of the spiked iron fence. Pedestrians would have to worm their way through or walk in the street. Wheelchairs, baby strollers, and shopping carts had no chance of getting through. If the point was to prevent terrorists from being able to place a car bomb directly in front of the precinct, it was an effective barrier, at the expense of community inconvenience and disfavor. Ted thought the explanation was much simpler—the cops parked there because they could get away with it.

"There's a deli on the corner," he said. "I'll be waiting out front."

"Eight minutes," she said.

It took less.

Mohammed looked a little wild-eyed. "Are we in the hood?" he asked as Ted hopped in the back.

"Are you nervous?" Ted asked. Considering that the man's home country was practically in a perpetual state of war, Ted was unprepared for this shyness.

Mohammed muttered something that sounded like prayers.

"I think all this cloak-and-dagger action has pushed Mohammed out of his comfort zone," Kenzie said. "We may want to give him the night off." She appeared to be calm and in control.

Ted thought they could all use some down time, but it wasn't in the cards. "We need to regroup and come up with another plan," he said.

"What do you really think happened with the Judge?" Kenzie asked.

"He survived Albany politics for fifty years," Ted said. "He's developed an infallible threat-alert system. If he could patent it, he could make billions licensing it to the military."

"He set you up?"

"Beautifully. I'm sure of it."

She laughed gently.

"And that's funny because . . . ?"

"Lester played us the recording of you and those cops."

Ted grimaced. "I'm sure that in another decade or two, I will also find it amusing."

She laughed harder. It was a good sound. He found he was smiling.

"That's better," she said. "They're up on points, but I'm used to losing. The difference is that I don't quit when they're ahead."

Ted had to laugh. "So what's next?"

"Steaks. It's Tuesday night. Let's see who shows up at Reisner's table this week."

42

TED TRIED—AND FAILED—TO IMAGINE in which decade the facade of the restaurant would have been fashionable. There was a wagon wheel over the entrance and a vehicle on the roof that could have been a badly aged simulacrum of a buckboard. But the western motif didn't hold up, as the front walls were covered with a faux stone patina, reminiscent of a poor man's castle.

"I've never been here before," Ted said. "Is it this cheesy inside, too?"

"I wouldn't know," Kenzie said. "It's my first time, too."

The Uber had dropped them on the far side of the broad boulevard, a short ways past the city line. A mild misting rain had set in, and Kenzie ran to the covered doorway of a used auto dealer showroom. Ted joined her and struggled to open an umbrella.

She was wearing a long-sleeved black dress with a scoop deep enough to reveal that there was no bra underneath. Her distinctive red hair was hidden under a straight black wig that hung to the middle of her back. She had ladled on the eyeliner. The shadows on her pale skin gave her an eerie, but intriguing, look.

"I'm on a date with Morticia Addams," he said. "I wish I looked half as dashing as Raul Julia." Ted had not bothered with a disguise, as he did not expect to run into anyone who might recognize him.

"You need a fedora," Kenzie said. "You could pass for one of those private eyes in the old movies."

"Philip Marlowe," he said, doing his best Bogart impersonation. "I'm the shamus."

She raised both eyebrows and shook her head, indicating

incomprehension. Ted was crushed. First she didn't like baseball, and now this. "Bogart," he said. "*The Big Sleep.*"

"That's a movie? It must be before my time."

He pulled his battered ego upright. "Who's supposed to show at this meeting? Will Reisner come?"

"The father? No. The head of the LBC empire can't be bothered with small fry. We may see the son. He'll bring a bagman. A lawyer or one of the midlevel managers."

"And whomever they're paying off," he said.

"This is where it happens. City councilmen, county executives from all over the tristate, planning and zoning board members. Maybe a judge or two. We'll just have to see what gets thrown up on the beach tonight."

Traffic was light on the boulevard that long after rush hour, but the few cars made up for the light volume with excessive speed. The rain hissed under their tires as they passed. Ted silently cursed the Uber driver for not making the U-turn and depositing them in front of the door.

"Ready to make a dash?" he said. "The light's about to change."

"I can't get these shoes wet."

"Shall I carry you?"

"No. I'll fly across on my broomstick."

The light was a block away. It turned red. They waited until a delivery truck rumbled by, brakes squealing as it approached the intersection, and then they ran.

"I SPECIFICALLY ASKED FOR that table over there," Kenzie said, exhibiting a pout that would have melted the heart of any man.

The maître d' shrugged. He had no heart.

"There's no one sitting there," she said. "It's an obvious mistake."

"Reserved," he said.

"By me," she said.

He shrugged again. The action perfectly communicated the thought: he didn't give a rat's ass what they wanted, or what they had requested, or even if they walked out in high dudgeon. On a tired Tuesday night, he still had a line of people waiting for a canceled reservation. Ted considered tipping him a dollar for the pure pleasure of pissing him off but decided he would rather remain forgettable.

"Just send a waiter over." He held Kenzie's chair for her.

"We're not going to be able to hear a thing," she said.

Kenzie's sources had told her that the LBC people had a long-standing Tuesday night reservation for the large round table in the corner of the middle dining room. The fireplace and a wainscoted wall provided privacy on two sides. An aisle cut off the big table from all but one deuce. She had asked for that two-top, claiming it was where her husband had proposed, and been assured by the woman on the phone that she could have it. If the request had made it into the reservation book—which Ted doubted—the maître d' had ignored it.

"It's so noisy in here we wouldn't have heard much anyway," Ted said. "At least from here we can stare without being obvious."

The table they'd been given was across the room, tucked behind two four-tops that were already occupied. They wouldn't be invisible, but they were partially shielded.

Ted looked around the room. The chairs were all oversized, as were most of the clientele. Neither the Wild West nor the Camelot decorating scheme of the exterior had made it to this dining room, which seemed to be modeled on Adirondack Arts and Crafts meets Prague Art Deco. A lot of money had been spent to produce this effect, and Ted couldn't help but feel that the expense had been unwise. But something else was bothering him, and it took a minute for him to identify the problem.

"In Queens you don't usually get this white a crowd," he said.

"We're outside the city line," she said. "This is the burbs."

Ted glanced around again as the maître d' escorted a woman toward the big table in the corner. "Ah, no." He scooched his chair around so that his back was to the room.

"What?" Kenzie asked. She grasped the table to keep it from rocking.

"Big hair? Lemon yellow? Just came in?"

Kenzie laughed. "An old flame?"

"No. That's Cheryl."

"*That's* Cheryl?"

"Yes. Why?"

"Well, you didn't mention that she's a very attractive woman—in the Kardashian mold."

"I didn't think it was relevant."

"And that's a nice outfit. It's a shame they didn't have it in her size."

"If she's here, that means Pak is coming." Ted wanted to hide under the table. He should have been prepared for this contingency. A fedora. A fake mustache. A face mask.

"She's looking over here."

A waiter with the build of a beer keg lumbered up to the table. "Did anyone get your drink orders?" He wore a butcher's apron the size of a tablecloth. For a table for eight. His bulk blocked them from view. Ted breathed a little easier.

Kenzie gave the guy the kind of smile that says, *You're late, incompetent, and lazy, but I'm not holding it against you.* "A Bombay martini. In and out. Up. Two olives. And I think you better get him one, too."

"No," Ted said, keeping his face buried in his chest. "Water."

"Bottled? Sparkling?" the waiter asked.

"However it comes out of the tap will be fine."

The waiter shrugged. It was a good imitation of the shrug the maître d' had performed and delivered a similar message. He strolled away in no apparent hurry.

"What's she doing?" Ted asked.

"Texting. Two more just showed up. There's a really fat guy in a grey suit. I don't know him. Sixty plus. Bald. Very ugly. He's trailing a hottie in a Herve Leger off-the-shoulder bandage dress that looks sprayed on. She's barely old enough to vote."

"You know the designer?"

"I know both the designer and the dress. But I don't have enough junk in the trunk for it. Or cash in the wallet."

Ted wanted to come up with a comment on her curves that wouldn't get him in trouble. Something along the lines of not having noticed a lack of trunk space, but classier. The moment passed. Kenzie saved him with her next announcement.

"Here comes Pak. They're all shaking hands and taking seats. The hottie seems to be wondering why she's there. She may be medicated."

"I can tell you don't like her," he said.

"I'm reporting what I see."

"How does the Harvey Whoever look on her?"

"She's got the back for it."

"You notice that I haven't tried to crane my head around to catch a glimpse."

"You deserve a medal. Actually, you could take a look. Cheryl's facing the other way. See if you know the old guy."

Ted casually looked around the room, turning slowly. Councilman Pak and the other man were standing a few steps from the table, their heads together. The guy's head was like a polished bowling ball abandoned on the north pole of a small planet. Kenzie's description was spot on. Councilman Pak was selling something hard, but nobody was buying. Their discussion was restrained but tense. Neither man appeared to be happy.

"Negative," Ted said.

"He looks like he's got money."

"How's that?"

"Why else would she be with him?" Kenzie said.

"I can't argue with that logic."

"And here's the star of the show," Kenzie said. "Baby Reisner. The heir apparent."

Ted turned a bit farther and reeled back. "No!" A fortysomething couple was crossing the dining room. The man had black hair slicked back à la Gordon Gekko. His chin preceded him by an arrogant inch or two, so that he seemed to be looking down at people. Two steps behind him strode a woman in the law firm uniform of blue suit and white silk blouse. Her honey-blonde hair was expensively cut in a short-cropped shag, and though she wore almost no makeup, she didn't need it. She had a body that would always draw looks but held herself in a manner that telegraphed, *If you're not talking business, don't bother.* It was Jackie.

Ted ducked his head and swore quietly. How had an estate lawyer gotten herself pulled into this kind of maelstrom? Did she even know what was going on here? Of course she did. Jackie was not only smart; she was shrewd.

"Really?" Kenzie said. "Does he know you?"

"Not him. Her. That's the lawyer."

"I guessed that. She's carrying a briefcase."

"She knows me," Ted said. "It's Jackie."

"That's intriguing," Kenzie said. "One of the bad guys."

"And if she sees me, we're done."

"She never even looked in this direction." Kenzie was watching the group across the room.

Ted was rethinking his decision to turn down the martini. "I can't get up and leave, can I?"

"I think that would be a very bad choice."

A different waiter arrived with Kenzie's martini. "Are you ready to order?" he said.

"I asked for water," Ted said, moving the chair again to ensure he couldn't be seen. He was still reeling. There could no longer be any doubt—Jackie had deliberately defrauded Barbara Miller in order to provide those properties to LBC. It was not coincidence that had placed her here with the young Reisner. She was a major coconspirator.

"We could use menus," Kenzie said.

The waiter shrugged. Ted thought this must have been part of their training for the job. "Sorry," the waiter said, though he managed to convey that he wasn't in the slightest. "You want to see the wine list?"

"Yes," Ted said. "It'll give us something to read while we wait."

Kenzie took a sip of her martini. "Too much vermouth."

"Send it back."

"No, I'll never get another."

A thirtysomething Latino in a white tunic plunked down two glasses and a pitcher of water. Ted smiled his thanks. The man filled the two glasses and produced menus from under his arm.

"What's your recommendation?" Kenzie asked him. "Porterhouse or the rib eye?"

"*No sé,*" the man said, before racing away.

"I guess he's not our waiter either," she said.

"What's going on?" Ted asked.

"Now, that's interesting. Your friend Cheryl is sitting next to the lawyer. Jackie."

"Cheryl is not my friend. Neither is Jackie. Jacqueline."

"Jacqueline. Okay." She took another sip. It seemed to go down easier than the first. "So, the three men are talking. Laughing. The old guy is telling a story now. The hottie is wondering why nobody is looking at her."

Ted risked another look. Cheryl and Jackie were chatting together like old friends. This was not their first meeting, or second, or third. Ted tried to fit this new information into what he already knew but felt his foundation shifting and tilting. He turned away before he got caught staring.

Kenzie continued to report. "And now the asshole maître d' is stopping by to pay his respects. It's all positively medieval. Prince Reisner is giving him the two-handed shake. And. Wait for it. Yes! Reisner flashes a bankroll the size of Jackie's briefcase, peels off a bill, and tucks it in the guy's breast pocket."

"You're enjoying hating this place," Ted said.

"Did you ever eat at that Bahá'í place near the courthouse?"

"I don't know it."

"The food's simple. Nutritious. Tastes good but nothing fancy. But the women who work there are about the nicest folks you'd ever want to know. They're nice to everybody."

"I think I'd hate it. What's going on over there now?"

"A tray of drinks. The waiter and the old guy are talking. He's ordering for the table."

"Watch the women. Jackie and Cheryl. That's where the action will be."

"Okay," she said, sounding dubious. "Why?"

"The men will talk. That's all. But if money changes hands, it will be the women who do it."

"How do you know?"

"It's the only reason they're here. This way both Reisner and Pak can testify under oath that they had nothing to do with cash payments for favors."

"I'm going to record them," she said.

Ted's immediate reaction to this escalation of their surveillance was mild panic. This wasn't part of the plan. They could too easily be caught. He held his breath and watched Kenzie manipulate her menu as a shield for her phone.

"That's going to work right up until the waiter takes our order," he said.

"So I've got a while—oh, damn."

"What?"

"They're heading for the ladies' room." Kenzie stood.

"Wait. You can't follow them into the bathroom and tape them in there."

"I can goddamn well try." She was gone.

Ted was stuck, afraid to look behind him without Kenzie to scout first. He calmed himself and tried to think through the ramifications of what he had just now learned. Cheryl had come to him with two requests—to find Richie's killer and to follow the case of the surplus money. Then at some point she had lost interest. In both questions.

He had no trouble fixing the exact moment when she had lost all interest in the money. It was when he had made her realize that the Miller properties were tied up in the LBC project. Now that he'd seen her here, this made perfect sense.

But later she had pulled him off Richie's case—fired him. Something had changed.

She must have received new information. Had she found out who killed Richie and stopped caring? Or was she afraid? Of whom? Of what?

And who would have provided that information? Jackie? Ted didn't think so. He could easily imagine her furthering her career by abetting a conspiracy of wealthy power brokers. He was convinced she had defrauded Barbara Miller. But an accessory to murder? Not likely. If she knew anything about Richie's death, she would have run to a safe harbor—the Judge or the cops. She was weak, venal, ambitious, and cruel. But she wasn't evil. Or stupid.

Each question led to two more. His head began to pound.

"Will the lady be returning?" The beer-keg waiter was standing there with an expression of constrained impatience.

Ted wanted to get rid of him. He needed to think. "Tell you what," he said. "Bring us two shrimp cocktails, steak for two medium rare, creamed spinach, and hashed browns."

"The porterhouse?" the waiter asked.

He wanted the man gone. "Yes, yes." But now he also wanted a beer. "What craft beers do you have?"

"Heineken?"

Ted was an admitted beer snob, but he could be flexible when faced with ignorance or prejudice. "That'll be fine."

The man drifted away and left Ted with his unanswered questions and a headache. Kenzie had been gone long enough. He couldn't risk going to check on her; he might be seen and recognized. Two minutes more. And then what? Two more minutes? He caught movement out of the corner of his eye. Jackie and Cheryl were returning to their table. He kept his face averted.

"Damn. Damn. Damn," Kenzie announced as she threw herself into the chair facing him.

"They didn't make you, did they?"

"No, nothing like that." She spoke quickly, spewing words across the table. "But I saw the handoff. Those two bitches have no shame."

"Slow down. Just tell me what you saw."

She slugged down the remainder of the martini and spiked the glass on the table. The laws of physics must have been temporarily suspended. It didn't break. "When I walked in, they were standing at the sink. They looked at me but didn't react. I walked to a stall, and as I passed them, Cheryl made a show of reglossing her lips, and the other one made herself busy washing her hands. I sat on the toilet and watched through the crack around the door. You don't get to see a whole lot that way. I wasn't going to get a picture. But Jackie took a big envelope—it was folded over the long way—out of her purse and handed it to Cheryl like it was the most natural thing in the world. Like they do this all the time. It disappeared into that ten-gallon tote she carries. They didn't try to hide it. I don't think they cared whether anyone saw them or not."

"So, basically, we've got nothing. It was an envelope. It could have held newspaper clippings or recipes. We have no proof of any bribery."

"Can we order?" she said with a tight, forced sigh. "I'm suddenly very hungry. And I want another drink."

He could hear the defensiveness in her voice, but he really would have liked to have a video of what she'd seen. "A video might have helped."

"You make it sound like I screwed it up."

She was reading things all wrong. He was disappointed but not with her. "What? No. I'm pissed we've wasted our time—again—on another crazy idea."

"Fine. How would you have handled it?"

"I'm not saying I would have done any better. It was . . ." He couldn't think of what it was, but it wasn't good.

"What? It was . . . what?"

"Shrimp cocktail?" The waiter set his offerings down before them.

"You ordered?" Kenzie did not need to add the words "without me."

"Can I get you anything else?" the waiter asked.

"Yes. I want the rib eye." She enunciated each word with the precision of a pistol shot. "Black and blue. And another martini. And this time tell the bartender to just wave the vermouth bottle over the shaker. Any questions?"

"Does the gentleman still want the porterhouse for two?"

Ted shook his head, as much to clear his brain as to indicate a negative response. "I'll have what she's having."

"Certainly, sir." The waiter wasn't happy about it.

The hell with him, Ted thought, though he managed to smile mirthlessly until the man left. He looked to Kenzie only to find she was staring angry laser bolts at him. He tried not to cringe.

"Do we have a problem?" she asked.

"I thought I was helping. Who knows when we might have seen a waiter again?"

"Oh, forget about that. Do we have a problem about me not getting you the pictures you wanted?"

"Absolutely not. We'll have to find some other way of catching them."

Kenzie attacked a large shrimp with the ferocity of a pit bull. A very attractive pit bull, despite the Morticia disguise.

"What?" she said, looking up and catching his gaze.

"I'm sorry," he said. "Was I staring?"

She graced him with a quizzical look before returning to the shrimp. "I suppose we could follow Cheryl. At some point she's going to pass that envelope along to her boss."

"Councilperson Pak. A man of the people."

"Yes," she said. "As long as those people can afford to provide him with envelopes full of cash."

Ted found himself staring at her again. She was easy to look at, but that alone didn't explain the attraction. She had a passion that was missing in his life. It must have been there once, but he'd given it up for ambition. A bad swap.

He was also a bit in awe of her ability to be so direct. She didn't need to take control and give orders; she merely stated where she stood and allowed him to do the same. It could be disconcerting at first, but he was becoming comfortable with it. With her.

Kenzie polished off the last shrimp and looked up again. For a moment she looked into his face and smiled. Then her gaze shifted and her eyes widened. "Whoa. They're leaving."

Ted risked another quick look over his shoulder. The whole group was standing and shaking hands. Jackie picked up her briefcase and walked away from the table. Ted ducked his head and turned to Kenzie.

"Are they all leaving?"

"Reisner and Pak are sitting down again. Cheryl ordered another drink. The ugly guy and the hottie are . . . Jesus Christ, they're coming this way."

Ted watched Kenzie's eyes. He could almost see the reflection of the odd couple approaching.

"I know this face," the man said. He was hovering behind Ted. "But not the hair. You are a pretty girl. With red hair, you would look like a model." The air of menace oozed off the man, though his voice was gentle. The accent was British, but beneath lay a rougher, more guttural sound. He stepped forward into Ted's field of vision. "You, I don't know."

Kenzie was frozen. Angry but frozen.

Ted stood slowly. "In my country it's considered rude to chat up a man's date without introducing yourself first."

For what felt like minutes, the man examined Ted with flat black eyes. There was no feeling behind them, only cold depth. The man smiled with half his mouth. The smile was scarier than the stare. He tipped his head. "It is the same in my country. Good night." He turned to leave.

Kenzie unfroze. "I don't know you. Should I?" Her voice cut through the hubbub of dinner conversation at the nearby tables. A few diners shot her quick glances but looked away again when they read the ugly man's angry face.

"You don't know me?" He took a step toward them, daring one or the other to take the challenge. "You know nothing," he sneered.

Ted held up both hands in a placating gesture, but he did not retreat. "Can we take it down a notch? You're out of line."

But Kenzie pushed past him. "I may not know you, but I know who you are. Trust me, I will see that the world knows who's bribing politicians, pushing us aside, and destroying our communities. I'll make you famous. If you aren't afraid of me, you're a fool. I'm coming for you." She finished with an index finger point to his chest.

Ted always thought this was a bad move. A crazy person might grab the finger and do nasty things to it.

This guy ignored it and leaned in, using his height and bulk to intimidate. He was back in control and spoke softly, kindly, almost apologetically. "A man should choose his battles carefully. Life is both precious and fragile." He walked away calmly but stopped at the entrance to the dining room and looked back at them. He took out a cell phone and spoke for a moment. Ted met his eyes across the long room but couldn't read anything in them. Finally, the man left. The hottie followed like the pilot fish keeping up with the shark.

"ARE YOU OKAY?" TED asked.

"Well, I'd like my steak," Kenzie said, attempting a laugh that failed to rise above a cough. She dropped into her seat and looked around for the waiter with a forced air of distraction.

"He didn't scare you?"

"He did. So? I'm on the street in front of the courthouse three or four days a week. I have an office in the rectory of the church three blocks from my apartment. I walk there every day. If someone wants to hurt me, they have plenty of opportunities. And my *job* is pissing off powerful people."

"They've already come for Lester and for me. I don't think you're immune."

"You've made your point," she said. "But if I choose not to be afraid, I . . ."

"Your steaks." The beer-keg waiter dropped the plates and backed away without serving the sides of potatoes or spinach.

She attacked her steak with knife and fork and popped a

bite into her mouth. Neither of them spoke for a few minutes as she concentrated. The second martini arrived, and she swallowed half of it. Ted sipped the beer.

"You were talking about choice," Ted ventured.

"I know it's scary," she said. "I feel it. But what am I going to do? People do scary shit all the time. I don't jump out of airplanes, run into burning buildings, or ski down mountains at eighty miles an hour. Some people do. I stand up to powerful people. Sometimes I get arrested. More often I get pushed aside. But what I hate the most is when they ignore me."

"Well, I don't know who that guy was, but he is *not* ignoring you."

"Exactly. I win."

"I don't want to see you hurt," he said.

"And in an earlier century, that thought might have been very sweet."

"They put Lester in the hospital."

"My call, Ted." She emphasized her words by jabbing her fork in his direction. "My call."

"I think they killed Richie Rubiano."

"And I don't want you to order for me. Understood?"

"I think we're talking a huge difference in magnitude here."

"Actually, we're not. I like you, Ted. I think we have some chemistry. I'd like to see how we are together. I'm intrigued."

"You are?" Ted had never felt more out of his depth. He'd been sure he had been hitting all the wrong notes.

"Just don't try and be my daddy. Please?"

"Are you saying you'd like to . . ." He slid to a halt, unsure how to finish the question.

"Maybe," she said with a grin.

"Then I will squash all chivalric notions."

"Get the check." She dropped her fork onto the plate and

swigged the remains of her drink. She waved a hand for a waiter. None were in sight.

Ted fished out a credit card and flashed it at a passing busboy.

"*No crédito,*" the kid said, not breaking stride.

"They're leaving," Kenzie said. "I want to follow Pak. Have you got cash?"

Ted felt as if he'd hitched himself to a whirlwind. He pulled out the envelope with Cheryl's supply of hundred-dollar bills and threw two of them on the table.

"Hurry," she said. "Catch up with me out front. I'll grab us a cab." Kenzie stood and strode through the dining room, following the disappearing figures of Cheryl and her boss.

Ted ran through the math, computing the smallest acceptable tip. Two bills wouldn't cover the meal. Three would constitute an enormous tip for world's worst service. But Kenzie was out the door, and he couldn't wait for change. With an "Aw, shit" that resounded loud enough to turn heads, he dropped a third bill and raced to follow.

43

THE BAR WAS PACKED with large, loud people waiting for their reservations to be honored. Ted saw Kenzie disappear through the archway at the far end of the room. He maneuvered through the crowd after her, held back by his own size and a disinclination to use brute force. By the time he got free, she was out the front door.

"Was everything all right, sir?" The tuxedoed maître d' was Ted's last hurdle. Armed only with a greasy smile, the man was partially blocking the way. Ted sidestepped him and dashed out onto the street.

There was no sign of Kenzie, nor of Cheryl, Pak, or Reisner. Reisner would have had a car waiting. Possibly Pak, too. Where was Kenzie? The rain was no longer a steady mist. It was approaching a deluge, and he'd left the damned umbrella inside. He wasn't going back.

He surrendered his sanctuary in the doorway and quick-stepped out into the rain.

The lights from the dealership across the road cast jagged shadows sliced through with stark shafts of brilliance on the wet pavement. Fluorescent puddles with multicolored neon reflections created an effect somewhere between psychedelia and cubism. And far down the sidewalk, a thin and bedraggled figure lurched on unsteady heels, heading for the Queens border. It was Kenzie.

"McKenzie!" Ted yelled. "There's got to be a better plan than this," he muttered. "I'm coming," he called. The pelting rain had already soaked through his suit jacket. "Ah, hell," he said and ran after her.

A big intersection loomed ahead. Across the boulevard,

store signs beckoned in English, Korean, and Spanish. Blue-white light from above rearranged the scene from cubism to hyperrealism. Kenzie rushed the crosswalk as the pedestrian light ticked down the last four seconds. A horn blasted as she failed to make the curb before the light changed. Off in the distance, Ted saw a black limousine being swallowed by the flood of traffic entering from Little Neck Parkway.

"This is not working," he thought aloud. They needed to have a discussion about strategy and chain of command.

He leaped off the curb and landed ankle deep in cold rainwater. His foot squelched with each running step, but he was catching up. He called again and saw her stop. She waved him on impatiently, then turned to the oncoming traffic and held up a hand for a cab.

Any yellow cabs in Queens were heading for the airport or Manhattan. They weren't going to stop for a sodden woman with mascara running down her cheeks. Ted waved and called again, but she was staring into the oncoming lights and did not respond. He kept running.

Kenzie was speaking to him, one hand cupped next to her mouth, projecting words that failed to carry over the noise of the traffic and the rain. He read urgency but also a sense of the absurdity of it all—her bedraggled Don Quixote to his rain-soaked Sancho Panza racing on foot to keep up with a low-level politician rapidly escaping in the dry comfort of a limousine.

Afterward he remembered quite clearly the sound of the approaching automobile. It was a distinctive sound—deep, throaty, and revved much too high. But if it had stood out so blatantly, why hadn't he reacted quicker?

Kenzie's expression changed in an instant to one of pure horror. Sometime in their thousands of years of evolutionary survival, his people had developed the fast-track neural response to immediate danger. He did not consciously connect the sound of the approaching automobile with the look on Kenzie's face, but his body reacted anyway: tuck the chin, roll on the shoulder, push down with both hands, spring upright.

The movement, drilled in to him by wrestling coaches decades earlier and forgotten by all but muscle memory, saved his life.

The car was a blur as it flew past him, so close that he staggered backward two steps before finding his balance.

He didn't know cars. Didn't all sedans look alike these days? Later that night, the detectives said it was a BMW 6 Series. Ted didn't know what that meant. Like most native New Yorkers, his automobile knowledge began and ended with the difference between taxis and everything else. Jill had owned an old Saab, which he had sometimes driven on weekends, but if he had ever had to leave it parked in a crowded outdoor lot, he never would have been able to find it again.

Kenzie had had a beat more time in which to react. Unfortunately, she had wasted it in frozen fear. At the last possible second, she threw her body to the right, making a lopsided swimmer's racing dive onto the pavement. Though it saved her life, it wasn't enough.

The car's tires bounced up over the curb. She scrambled on hands and knees out of the direct path and almost made it. The right front fender clipped her ankle, spinning her body like a toy on a string. A street sign that declared NO PARKING HERE TO CORNER stopped her. Then the car was gone, swerving across lanes and out of sight.

Through the cacophony of the racing engine, squealing tires, car horns, and his own scream of "Nooo!" Ted was sure he heard Kenzie's head smack against the pavement. He ran to her and dropped to his knees. She was moaning loudly. That was good. She was alive. Her eyes were open but unseeing. Blood was seeping out from beneath the wig. Rain pelted her face and those open eyes, but she made no move to cover herself. She was both wide awake and unconscious. Ted put one hand over her face and with the other dug into his pocket for his cell phone.

THE JURISDICTIONAL ISSUES SLOWED the early hours of the investigation. Nobody wanted it. The incident referred to as a carjacking by Nassau County Police took place at the steak house in their jurisdiction. The attempted vehicular homicide, as it was identified by New York's finest, had clearly been in Queens. With Lester's words regarding outer-borough hospitals in mind, Ted demanded that Kenzie be taken to a Nassau County hospital, further complicating matters. One of Cheryl's hundred-dollar bills slipped to the EMTs resolved the issue of where to take her. The two NYPD detectives argued that the victim was no longer in their jurisdiction. The Nassau cops countered that the more serious crime had occurred on the other side of the county line. Ted wanted to leave and check on Kenzie.

Cops from both sides questioned what witnesses they could find.

The heavyset waiter reported that the couple had been arguing at the table and had left without finishing their meal. The hostess, who had barely acknowledged Ted when they arrived, remembered the woman running out alone. The maître d' thought the man had been wild-eyed and aggressive. The valet parking attendant had seen the man chasing the woman and yelling at her. No, he didn't know what the man had been saying, but he'd sounded angry. Or frightened maybe. And, no again, the attendant couldn't remember a thing about the two guys who stole the car, despite having handed one of them the keys to the BMW while standing under the full glare of the overhead light above the entrance. Ted, still nursing bruises from his previous encounter and now with new scrapes and dents, understood the man's selective memory and forgave it. Bad things happened to people who remembered too much.

Ted didn't say much. Beyond a perfect faith in his intuition, he didn't have a lot to offer. Remarkably little that could have been called "fact." The central piece of information that he might have provided—that Kenzie had been chasing a city councilman who had been driving away in a limousine—sounded too preposterous to be believed. Unless, of course, you knew McKenzie from Ridgewood, the fearless and sometimes impulsive community organizer.

Orders finally came down from some higher level, New York lost the toss, and the Nassau cops melted into the night. Ted rode to the hospital with two unhappy detectives. Their moods didn't improve when they arrived.

"Mr. Molloy?" The nurse approached Ted, ignoring the two hulking men bracketing him. "The patient is asking for you. Will you come this way?"

"This man is a suspect. We're going to want to talk to her first," one of the detectives said, latching on to Ted's arm.

"Am I under arrest?" Ted pointedly asked the other cop.

"No," he said. "You're a witness."

Ted shrugged off the first detective's grip.

"A person of interest," the first one countered.

Ted looked to the RN for adjudication.

"You'll get your turn," the nurse said to the first detective. She spoke with absolute authority.

The cop considered his options. He had none. They were on her turf. "All right. You can have him. But for five minutes only."

The nurse gave him a withering look before turning to Ted. "This way, please." She led him past the security and triage desks and into the heart of the ER. Ted was braced for the usual chaos and clutter of a New York emergency room. He was stunned to find an orderly, clean, and modern facility that gave off a quiet, controlled hum of coordinated efficiency. It was like stepping into a futuristic movie version of an ER.

Kenzie was in a glass-walled room on the far side of the area. The door slid open automatically as Ted and the nurse approached. "I'll hold them off for at least ten minutes," she said. "If you need anything, press the button on the cord. If it's an emergency, hit that red button on the wall."

Kenzie smiled as he entered. Ted was hit by her transformation from a tough woman into a vulnerable girl. She'd somehow shrunk four inches and dropped forty pounds. They'd washed the mascara off her face, and a gauze wrap had replaced the wig, but there were brown splotches of dried blood matting her hair, and her right ankle was immobilized in a Velcroed splint. Blood pressure and pulse monitors beeped quietly. She looked pale and a little tired. He wanted to wrap his arms around her and stroke her face with his fingers and tell her how frightened he had been and how relieved he felt at that moment. But he didn't. He let her lead.

"It seemed like a good idea at the time," she said.

"Were you seriously trying to hail a cab within city limits in the rain?"

"I thought they'd have to wait for their car to be brought round. I stepped outside the door, and they were already pulling away. How are you?"

"Bumped and bruised," Ted answered. "My suit's a goner. I'm okay." He'd taken worse falls but not in more than a decade and a half. "What have they said about you?"

"I'm lucky. They keep saying that."

"Anything more specific?"

"Will you tell my folks?"

After his last session with her father, Ted would rather have gargled razor blades.

She read his reaction and his feeble attempt at hiding it. "I'm kidding. I already spoke to them. My mom is on her way."

"I would have, you know." He hoped he sounded convincing.

"Yeah," she said with a light laugh. She wasn't buying it. "So I'll be wearing a boot for the next couple of weeks. It's a fracture, not a sprain. It's supposed to heal quicker with no lasting effects. Except fifty years from now I'll get arthritis there and be able to predict changes in the weather by how much pain I'm having. I'll be sure to blame it on you."

"How's the head?" he asked.

"This old thing?" She pointed to the gauze bandage. "I just wear it to generate sympathy. Is it working?"

"I was there, Kenzie. I heard you hit the ground."

"Yeah. They want to keep me overnight for observation. They did a scan. I'm waiting to hear."

"Are you in pain?" he asked.

"See? Sympathy. It's working." She pointed to the bandage again.

She was hurting. He could see it in the strain around her eyes, in the paleness of her skin. But she wasn't going to admit to it.

"Why did you take off without me?" he asked.

"I was sure you'd catch up. If I'd found a cab, we'd be staking out Pak's office right now. Or getting pictures of Cheryl delivering the payoff. We're going to get those bastards."

"From what I've been able to figure out from listening to the cops argue about it, two well-dressed guys in ski masks walked up to the parking lot, flashed guns, and drove off in the first car they saw."

"That's crazy," she said sounding as though it wasn't crazy at all. "Nobody's telling me nothing. Keep talking."

"Well, after trying to run you down—and almost succeeding—they left the car in a diner parking lot out by Alley Pond. Nobody has come forward with an ID or even a decent description." Ted didn't need either. He knew who had done it.

"They weren't after me. They were trying to hit you," she said. "If you hadn't jumped, they would have hit you and knocked you into next week."

"Maybe," he said after a too-long pause. It occurred to him that he had now twice taken a lesser beating. Were these messages? Was his proximity to Lester and Kenzie putting them in greater danger? No, he decided, this wasn't about him. The threat had been immediate, targeted, and directly in response to her standing up to the man in the restaurant. "No, I think the fat man sent them. To get you."

"Right. Like I'm a big threat to any of them. They don't need to kill me; they can just ignore me."

"I want the cops to keep watch on you."

"I'm not going anywhere," she said. "Doctor's orders."

"You know what I mean."

"You need protection more than I do. And you need a place to stay. A hideout. Talk to my friend the Preacher. He'll know someone who can help."

"Already on my agenda." He was less afraid for himself than for her. He needed to think, to plan. And he couldn't do either while he worried about her.

"You know, you have pissed off all the right people. I'm proud of you. If I could move, I'd give you a kiss."

"Don't move," Ted said. "Let me." He bent over and lightly kissed her on the lips. He liked kissing her. "I had this wild fantasy that we were dashing out of the restaurant to go have mad, passionate sex."

"That's sweet. Give me another kiss."

He did, less gently this time. She returned it.

"And don't think you're getting off that easy, bud."

"Is that a promise?" he asked.

"I'll collect on that when I'm out of here."

45

LOUD VOICES FROM THE corridor interrupted them. The police must have worked up the courage to face down the head nurse and were forging into the inner sanctum.

"They're not going to let me stay," Ted said. "I'll call in the morning."

"Or I'll call you."

He leaned over for another kiss but stopped before their lips met as the door swooshed open.

"Well, you do get around." The voice was unpleasantly familiar.

Ted looked up. Detective Duran and his less agreeable number two. Kasabian. Ted was proud of himself for finally remembering the other cop's name.

"Detectives," Ted greeted them.

Duran stepped into the room. "Sorry to break this up, Ms. Zielinski. There are some detectives out here who want to speak with you. And I need to talk with this guy."

"I was just leaving," Ted said.

Duran tried out a grim smile. "Then we can walk out together."

"I'll talk to you in the morning," Ted said to Kenzie.

The other two detectives pushed their way into the room. Their barely contained hostility took up all the extra space. Ted led Duran and partner out of the ER.

The waiting room was near empty. An exhausted-looking older man cradled a sleeping woman in his arms in the far corner. Two young men, faces etched with deep worry lines, stared down at the grey carpet. A few hard couches lined the walls, and uncomfortable-looking chrome and thin-cushioned chairs faced them, creating not truly intimate spaces. Flat-screen televisions hung in every corner, delivering nonstop local news, with traffic and weather currently being displayed on green maps of Long Island. It was raining. Traffic was light.

"Do I need to call a lawyer?" Ted asked, throwing himself into one of the grey chairs, forcing the two detectives to take the even less inviting couch in front of him.

"Why would you need a lawyer?" Kasabian asked.

Ted sat forward, leaning in as though imparting some secret information. "Because it's coming up on midnight after a pretty shitty day, and I've just left a friend in the ER, and some dickhead cop thinks this is a good time for me to answer his trick questions."

"Easy." Duran gestured for his partner to stay seated. Kasabian complied, but he wasn't happy about it. "Those guys"—Duran waved, indicating the other two detectives— "see you as a possible perp. They ran you through the system, and I got a message. I believe you're only a witness, but if you fuck with me or my partner . . . No, if you so much as make another wiseass remark, I will toss you to my colleagues and good fucking riddance. Any questions?"

Ted knew he needed help. He and Kenzie were thrashing around and getting thrashed in return. They had no evidence of anything. But he had to keep Kenzie safe. Could he trust them? Or had they already been compromised like the two in the squad car from earlier in the day? Something in their approach, however, reassured him. They didn't trust him and didn't try to hide it. So while they were not on his side, they weren't trying to game him. Now, could he trade his patched-together tale in exchange for Kenzie's security? Would they believe him? And if they did, would they honor an agreement? He had no choice but to try.

"Can you get my friend someone to guarantee her

safety?" Ted asked. "Twenty-four-hour protection while she's here?"

"Not without hearing a very good story," Duran said. "Maybe she was collateral damage in a car heist that went wrong."

"Those guys were after her," Ted said. "It was a hit. Not an accident."

Duran smiled. "I'm still listening."

And there it was. If he told them about the fat man, he'd have to share it all. Explain why he and Kenzie were there at dinner. Put all of their suppositions out in the open and hope that they didn't sound like some paranoid's rant. But he needed their help to keep her safe. The alternative was to leave Kenzie and hope the Russians didn't come back. And that was no alternative at all.

"Bear with me," he said. "Some of what I've got, I can back up with a paper trail, but a lot of it is speculation. You guys need evidence, and I don't have it. Yet."

"Tell me your story," Duran said.

Ted didn't tell them all of it. Most of it. But he held off on pointing the finger at Jackie Clavette, identifying her only as "a lawyer." The first time he got to a point in the telling where he might have used her name, he skipped right over it without a thought. But by the time he described the scene in the steak house, he was acting with full deliberation. He knew why he was doing it. Not to protect Jackie or the firm. He was looking out for Jill.

"I dialed 911 and tried to keep the rain off her face." Ted wanted water. His mouth was dry from exhaustion, stress, and too much talking. "Give me a minute before you start asking questions, okay?" He went to the men's room, used the urinal, washed his hands, and lapped some water from the tap. When he straightened up, he found Detective Kasabian standing at his side.

"I buy your story, but you're not giving us all of it," Kasabian said. "If there's something you want to share in private, now's the time."

Ted wasn't prepared for this. Had Kasabian switched roles, bad cop turned good buddy? Was this a new game they were playing? Or was this cop on the level? There was no reason to trust him. But if opening up a touch helped to close the deal, it was worth the gamble.

"What does Duran say?"

Kasabian took his time answering. Ted thought the detective was having his own difficulties with trust. "He's in with your girlfriend telling those other two detectives that this is now our case. He believes you, if that's what you're asking. Like me, he'd love to take down a city councilman and a big-shot developer."

Ted recognized that he had been handed an important piece of information. Which meant that he was expected to reciprocate and offer some of his own.

"I know the lawyer," he said. "But I won't give up the name until I'm positive about her guilt." He could see that the detective wanted to push it—force the issue and get the name. Ted forced himself to relax and waited for the other's next move.

Kasabian finally nodded. "Okay for now. Maybe we find out on our own. If we don't, though, I will want that name." He handed Ted his card. "I want to hear from you. Anything you find out, you call. Don't make me come find you. Meanwhile, I'll get a couple of uniforms to keep an eye on the girl. What about you?"

"Me? As in police protection?" Ted hadn't considered asking.

"I don't know that I can make it happen, but I'll try," Kasabian said. "Of course, if you were to give me the name of this lawyer . . ."

Ted wondered how far he was willing to go to keep

Jackie's name out of it. "I'm mobile. Ms. Zielinski is not. I can do without. She can't." First, he needed to talk to Jill. If she'd take his call. In the long-ago world of the day before, Ted would have trusted her with his life. But the world had changed.

46

MOHAMMED SHOWED UP EARLY. Ted and Lester had pushed their luck and spent another uncomfortable night sleeping on pews at the church. Lester was already grumpy, sipping lukewarm coffee through a straw and eating mashed bananas from a squeezable foil pouch.

"It says here they're organic. I believe 'em."

"Why's that?" Ted asked.

"'Cause it tastes like dirt," Lester said.

"Take it with you. Time to go." Last night's late call to Jill had gone straight to voice mail. Not surprising, given the hour, but Ted wouldn't feel easy until he heard her voice.

"You hired the man for the day. What's the hurry?"

Ted wanted to swing by his apartment for a change of clothes. He also needed to check his mail—despite the distractions of this case, he had a business to run. Then he wanted to find the Preacher and a more comfortable place to hole up. More comfortable and safer. But his main priority was to get to the hospital to check on Kenzie.

"Come on. Mohammed's waiting." Ted stuffed his toothbrush and disposable razor into a jacket pocket.

"That's what you pay him for," Lester muttered as he pulled himself upright. He jammed the almost-empty foil packet into the fully empty paper coffee cup. "He's probably eating real food and slept on a bed last night, not an oak church bench."

"You're feeling better," Ted said.

"I'm aching everywhere."

"How's the teeth?"

"Taking hold; thanks for asking."

"You're talking a lot more and slurring a lot less."

"I suppose you think you're being kind to notice." He held the door for Ted.

The monster rains had ceased sometime in the night, and the sun had been up for two hours, drying the streets and sidewalks. It was going to be hot later on—the sun was already strong—but for the moment one could believe in things like new beginnings. Ted rarely allowed himself to feel that way, even when the weather presented the opportunity.

"Back to my apartment, Mohammed," he said. "Take a right at Flushing Avenue and I'll tell you where to turn."

"I'm on it, boss." He pulled away from the curb with a neck-snapping lurch.

"Safety first," Lester mumbled.

Flushing ran into Grand Avenue which was a challenge to Mohammed's love of speed. Traffic to and from the expressway slowed them to an excruciating crawl. The five-minute drive took twenty. Mohammed tapped out frenetic rhythms on the steering wheel while Lester glowered in the back seat, feeding his foul mood. Ted tried to make plans—or at least to organize his thoughts—but his concern for Kenzie overwhelmed all else.

Israel Ortiz—Ted's landlord, accountant, and lawyer and the emperor of the first-floor emporium—was at his desk in the far corner of the store, surrounded by displays of candles, Bibles, framed pictures of a Latino-looking Jesus, and dolls representing Shango, Oshun, and Obatala figures, though they all looked identical to Ted. Just inside the door Israel's secretary, Phateena, looked up as Ted entered and made a noise halfway between a squeak and a squeal.

"Israel," she cried. "He's here." She stood and quickly walked out of the room, her rubber sandals making slapping sounds as she retreated.

Israel looked green—seasick.

"What's up, Israel?" Ted didn't move. He felt that the wrong signal, the wrong word, could shatter the tension in the air.

Israel stood slowly, giving himself plenty of time to think of a tactful way to present his case.

Ted had seen the act before and didn't buy into it. "Just tell me what the hell happened."

"There was a man looking for you," Israel answered.

"You say that like it's a bad thing."

"A big man. He frightened Phateena."

"And you, too, it appears."

Israel nodded.

"Did he say what he wanted?"

"You know this man?" Israel asked.

Ted had a bad feeling that they'd met before—and not that long ago. "Not big. Frigging huge. Squeaky voice? Like Axl Rose on helium. Am I right?"

"He went in upstairs."

Israel meant he had let the giant into Ted's apartment. Breaking in through the metal door and frame would have left an expensive mess. Israel had handed over the keys.

"Did he take anything?" Other than his laptop, Ted owned nothing of any value. His paper files were all backed up in the cloud. Setting up a new computer would be a nuisance, nothing more. Nevertheless, he felt sick to his stomach.

"I don't know," Israel said, but from the tone of his voice, Ted could hear there was more coming.

"Yeah?" he said.

"He did some damage," Israel said.

What could the guy have done? Smashed Ted's IKEA furniture? His ten-year-old flat screen? Ted could replace it with a new model with twice the features at half the cost. "Well, I'm sorry you and Phateena were upset. But I'll take care of it. I doubt he'll come around again." There was no point in releasing his anger and frustration on two people who were already terrified. "Did you report it?"

"The police are upstairs now."

Israel must have been well and truly frightened. In normal circumstances, the only reason to report an apartment break-in was to get a case number to provide the insurance company. Ted didn't have insurance. The sum total of his possessions wouldn't qualify for the deductible on a policy.

"I'll go talk to them. Then I'm going to pick up some spare shirts and get out of here. I'll be away for a while. Maybe a week or so." Ted had no idea how long he would need to stay out of the Russians' crosshairs, but more than a few days sounded like a lot.

"Ted, I am sorry." Israel looked more embarrassed than apologetic.

"No, don't sweat it, Israel. It's the big city. Shit happens and people are nuts, but I'm going to take care of it. This was in no way your fault."

"No. I am sorry that I have to say this, but you have to move. Right away. I can't have that man here."

Ted let it sink in. He could argue, but what was the point? If the giant wanted to find him, he would always look here first—as would the Russians if they wanted to slap him around again. He would never be safe here.

"I'll continue to get my mail here," Ted said.

This took Israel by surprise. "Why? I mean, if you're gone—"

Ted cut him off. "You want me out? We could be in Housing Court for months, and you might not win. I'll pay you to hold my mail. Ten bucks a week."

"I don't know."

"Yeah, you do. And I'll bet you still want me as a client."

Israel's surprised expression was all Ted needed. The fees

Israel had been paid for basically no work at all added up over time. "Take the deal, Israel. You owe me for two weeks' rent plus my deposit. Cut me a check. I'll pick it up the next time I come by for the mail."

"Phateena won't like it. She's frightened."

"So are you. So am I. So what?"

THE SMELL HIT TED as soon as he started up the stairs. Burnt plastic. He was surprised the aroma hadn't permeated Israel's office—yet. He held his breath and charged up to the landing. A uniformed patrolman holding one of Ted's kitchen towels over his mouth and nose blocked the door.

"Hold up," the cop said.

"This is my apartment," Ted said, sidling around him.

The cop dropped the towel and took Ted's arm. He had a grip like a blacksmith. "You wait." He was convincing. Ted waited. "Detective," the patrolman called. "I got a guy here who says he's the tenant."

Ted got a look around the cop. A second patrolman stood by the kitchen window silently begging the air shaft to grant him a breath of fresh air. Beyond him, two suits, both with wet towels covering their faces, were examining the damage to the rest of the apartment. One was tall, broad shouldered, and black. The other was his partner. Duran and Kasabian.

"Come in, Mr. Molloy," Detective Duran said. "We were just talking about you."

Two detectives for an apartment break-in was unheard of in the outer boroughs. Even in Manhattan you'd have to be living on Park or Fifth Avenue to be granted that kind of attention. "What are you guys doing here?" Ted asked.

"When your name pops up in connection with a crime, I take an interest," Duran said. "And what's it been? Eight hours? Ten? Can you blame me? Trouble seems to follow you around."

Ted looked into the kitchen. The oven door hung open, but the heat had not yet fully dissipated. The particular aroma of melted plastic was explained. The remains of his laptop had melted into a blackened goo that had oozed and dripped through the racks with odd bits of metal shining through like tiny misshapen marshmallows in last week's chocolate pudding.

"It's not like I go looking for it," Ted said. The furniture was all broken. Most of it would have surrendered to a good kick from a three-hundred-pound steroidal madman. "Do you know who did this?"

"God's honest truth, we think we do," Duran said. "But what gets me is that I think you know, too."

"I told you to ask Cheryl about the giant."

Kasabian crowded Ted, standing too close and leaning in. "You know what my ex told me before she left? She said I had gone from discerning to skeptic to cynic. She couldn't live with that. And she couldn't understand why. I told her it was the job. Everybody lies to me. And when they're not lying, they're not telling me the truth, which amounts to the same thing."

"I didn't lie to you," Ted said. "I told you to check him out."

"Forgive a confirmed cynic, Mr. Molloy, but you failed to mention that this person was known to you or that he might have reason to toss your home and destroy your possessions."

"I don't even know his name."

Duran flashed a sad smile at him. "I wish I could believe that. Really, I do." He even sounded sincere.

Ted took the moment to retreat to the relatively open space of the main room. It was a mistake; he could see much more of the damage from there. "He threatened me. He wanted me to get Cheryl Rubiano that surplus money. Somehow, he followed me to a ball game. He's a nutjob."

"Your landlord gave us a very good description," Duran

said. "Including the visible tats. The man is well known in legal circles. He's been arrested fourteen times. He has never been to jail. He's never been tried. Witnesses recant or disappear. He's that kind of a guy."

"Who is he?" Ted asked.

"You make it sound like you don't know."

"I thought he was weird. A little scary."

"Stavros Nikitopoulos—also known as Nicky Greco, Nick Stavros, or just 'the big Greek guy.' He makes his living intimidating people as protection for con men. If the mark wises up and comes after the grifters, he finds he's facing our boy Nick. That tends to dissuade said mark from taking any direct action."

"And there's the connection," Ted said. "She and Richie might have been out of that business, but they'd all know each other. Ask her. She told me they're friends, but there are a toothbrush and razor in her bathroom in his size."

"Thank you," Duran said. "That's something I didn't know. See how easy it was?" He and his partner shared a look. A question was asked and answered without a word being spoken.

Kasabian took over. "Look at you. Telling the truth. Let's see you do it again. Ready? Who's the lady lawyer?"

Ted shook his head. "Say a name and maybe I'll tell you whether you're right or not."

"Look around, Molloy." Kasabian gestured at the destruction surrounding them. "This is no time for playing games."

The apartment was totaled. Ted's tiny closet had been emptied, and every article of clothing he owned was in the tub and liberally sprayed with bleach. His Mimi Fong tie, nearly unrecognizable, lay on the top of the pile. The empty bottle peeked guiltily around the shower curtain.

"I've said all I'm going to say. And now I have to be somewhere. Call me when you've got the case number." He walked out and allowed himself to stomp down the stairs. Anger felt good. It reinforced his determination. Leaving everything behind was easier than he would have imagined.

The advantage of having a minimalist life was that starting over would be a lot less painful this time.

47

"**EVER HEAR OF A** guy named Nick Stavros?" Ted asked Lester after filling him in.

"Should I?" Lester asked.

"Maybe Nicky Greco?" Ted wasn't ready to attempt the pronunciation of Nikitopoulos.

"Sounds Greek." Lester was only half listening.

"Forget I asked."

Lester shook his head. "Why would the Russians farm out a job like that? Intimidation is what they do best." He held up the cast. "Exhibit 1-A."

"Yeah, but it's not working, is it? We didn't back off."

FROM THE LONG ISLAND Expressway, the segue out of Queens into Nassau was a gradual progression. Concrete and neon gave way to green trees and the occasional expanse of manicured lawn. The hospital was a gleaming temple surrounded by what could have passed for a bucolic suburban university. The effect was meant to be reassuring but was lost on Ted.

"I don't know how long I'll be," he told Lester. "For all I know, they've sent her home already. I couldn't get her on the phone."

"Did I tell you to call the nurses' station?" Lester asked.

"Did I tell you I couldn't get a straight answer out of anybody?" Lester's foul mood was wearing on Ted. "Did you run out of those pain pills?"

"I can't stand taking them. They make me feel stupid."

Ted would gladly have taken stupid if it came with pleasant. "Are you in pain now?"

"And they obstruct my natural body functions."

"Your what?"

"I can't take a crap."

Ted took a breath. "Okay, so that's a problem. What do you need? Prune juice? Raisin Bran?"

"Well, with a little touch of vodka, I can control the pain and let my innards take care of themselves."

Of course. "I'm going to need you functioning, Lester."

"That's my point."

Ted hesitated for only a moment. There were more pressing issues. "Don't make me regret this."

Lester scowled. "I'm not looking for favors."

Ted thought a mood adjustment might do wonders. To Mohammed he said, "See if you can find him a liquor store nearby."

Mohammed's eyes widened a bit, but he didn't complain.

Ted watched them pull into traffic. He was already kicking himself for giving in so quickly, but he needed to check on Kenzie. As he turned for the door, his phone rang.

It was Jill, finally returning his call. He answered with a brusque "We have to talk."

"What happened yesterday? Grandfather said you never showed up."

The old man might have adored his granddaughter, but that did not preclude him from lying to her. "Can we meet up?" What he had to say would be marginally easier in person.

A car pulled up and disgorged a distraught woman and a teenager. The boy's arm was wrapped in a white towel turning a bright pink in the center. *Skateboard accident,* Ted thought.

"I'm worried about you," Jill said. "What's going on?"

Ted stepped off the sidewalk to make way. "It seems I've thrust a stick into the hornet's nest."

"I told you—"

"Please, don't. This is about Jackie. She is about to find herself in big trouble."

"And you did this?" There was a hint of hysteria in her voice.

Ted bit off an angry response. There was enough blame to go around. He was willing to take his share, but at that moment it wasn't terribly important. "I am doing my best to keep her name out of it. But it's not enough. Please, let's sit down and talk. I'll bring a friend who can explain this. Jackie needs your help. And mine."

"I don't know what you're doing, but you're only making things worse. She's a good person."

"Jill, please listen to me. Or if you can't, at least get her to call me."

"She won't talk to you, Ted. And if she knew that I was, she would be thoroughly pissed at me."

"Ask her this then. Where was she last night?"

"What? Stop."

"I saw her, Jill. She was making a payoff to a councilman. She's tied into a whole slew of very bad people. They put my friend in the hospital. This isn't going away on its own."

"I don't believe you," she said after a long pause.

Ted found that he was neither surprised nor hurt by this revelation. But if he wanted to salvage anything of his friendship with her, he had to persevere. "Fine. Don't believe it. But if you love her, tell her what I said. I'm not the enemy, Jill. I want to help."

The line was dead.

48

THE HOSPITAL SECURITY GUARD outside the ER looked up from his iPhone as Ted approached. Ted gave him a nod and marched onward in the hope that the man would go back to his Candy Crush.

"Can I help you, sir?" the guard asked. He was a minimum-wage mercenary in a polyester uniform. Ted hoped the NYPD was putting up a more aggressive defense inside.

Ted could see the young skateboarder and his mother in a glass-walled office up ahead. They were being interviewed by a severe-looking nurse.

"No, thanks." Ted gestured vaguely in their direction, imitating a man impatient to catch up with family.

The guard shook his head. "Just a moment, sir." This time he hit the last word with enough force to slow Ted's progress.

Damn. Ted tried a different maneuver: let the guy think he was a medical professional. "I'm checking on a patient."

The guard put down his phone. A bad sign. "Are you a doctor?"

Brazen it out. "McKenzie Zielinski. Concussion. Fractured tibia. She was brought in last night." Ted knew he was saying too much. Doctors never explained. The tibia *was* a leg bone, wasn't it?

The man stood. The game was over. "You'll need a pass." He pointed down the hall to the reception desk at the main entrance. "Someone there can help you."

Reception was staffed by a blue-haired woman wearing pearls and an open white smock. Rhinestone glasses hung from a silver chain around her neck. Two more security guards were there to back her up, but neither gave Ted a look.

They were both engaged in examining something compelling on a computer monitor.

"I'm here to see a patient. McKenzie Zielinski." He spelled it. "She's probably still in the ER."

She tapped on her keyboard for a moment. Her smile changed to a pursed-lip moue. "She's not in the ER."

"Was she released?" He'd missed her. How was he going to maneuver around her parents to get to see her?

"It seems she's been moved to the ICU. Are you family?"

"ICU" sent Ted into a tailspin. A fractured ankle didn't land you in intensive care, so it must have been the head wound. He felt a cold sweat form on the back of his neck.

"I'm her fiancé," he said. He couldn't risk being turned away.

The woman answered a phone and without a greeting said, "Hold, please." She looked up at Ted as though he had only then appeared. "Yes?"

"I need a pass for the ICU," he said with as much forbearance as he could muster.

She tapped some more. A small device on the counter began to chatter, and a visitor pass chugged out of the printer. "Second floor."

The two uniformed guards had never looked up.

The elevator traveled between floors with the speed of a sloth on painkillers. Ted would have taken the stairs, but he didn't know where they were. When the doors finally parted, he was through them and down the corridor in a flash.

He swiped his pass at an electronic lock, and the door swung open onto another corridor. This one was quiet, with muted lighting. The walls were all glass so that every occupied bed could be seen from the nurses' station. Ted stopped there.

"McKenzie Zielinski?" he said.

There were six people working at computer monitors behind the counter. Not one person looked up.

"Room four."

Ted didn't stop to figure out who had responded. "Thanks," he said over his shoulder.

He stopped at the door of room 4 and stared. Kenzie was hooked up to even more monitors. A breathing mask covered much of her face, and a saline drip had also been added. The long bruise on the side of her head and face had cast multicolored tendrils across her forehead and cheek. But she appeared peaceful.

"You can go in," a voice said from behind him. He turned. A nurse in blue scrubs was standing there. The suggestion had the feel of an order.

"What the hell happened?" Ted said. "When I left her in the ER last night, she was hurting but she was okay."

"I'll see if a doctor will talk with you."

"Is she asleep?" Ted knew she wasn't, but he had to ask.

"She's in an induced coma." The nurse must have decided that his distress needed immediate attention. She spoke quietly. "There was some bleeding in the brain, which caused swelling."

Ted felt light-headed. His blood pressure must have spiked—or dived. He wanted to sit.

"The swelling results in elevated pressure," the nurse said. She sounded tremendously offhand to Ted. "She's sedated. The fluids will disperse, and the swelling will go down. Then we will take her off the heavy meds, and she should be fine."

"Or?"

"This happens with head injuries sometimes. And this is pretty standard treatment. Are you family?" The question was rote; her eyes were already moving on.

He was losing her, but he needed answers. "Fiancé. Is there a chance she won't wake up?"

"I've got other patients." She looked down the hallway as though hordes of ill and injured were awaiting her ministrations.

"What about permanent brain damage?"

"Go sit with her. The doctor will have to answer any other questions."

This time Ted had the good sense to back off a touch. "Thanks. Will she know I'm here?"

Ted could see her take a moment to decide whether or not to continue the conversation. Compassion briefly won out over procedure. "We think she can hear and is processing at some level, so, yes, speak to her—quietly." She drew herself up and reasserted her dominion. "And don't bring up any stressful or emotional BS. I'll know and I'll kick your butt out of here." She turned to leave.

"Wait. Didn't the police have a guard on her?"

The nurse shook her head.

"They said they would," Ted said, pushing it. It was important.

She half shrugged with a sad smile.

Ted took one of the two chairs next to the bed. It was hard, unyielding plastic. A place to perch only. No one over the age of eight would have been comfortable sitting there for any length of time.

He was angry. The detectives had blown him off. But anger would do nothing to solve the problem. He needed to think.

The blood pressure cuff on her arm expanded, paused, and, with a ping, subsided. The ventilator whooshed quietly. He heard the soft murmur of conversations from the adjoining rooms. Talk, the nurse had instructed him. *What does one say to a woman in a coma?*

"Hi. It's Ted. Ted Molloy. We had dinner last night."

Kenzie continued to breathe regularly.

"We kissed," he said.

Her eyes did not fly open. She did not sit up and smile at him. But she did keep breathing. Or was the machine doing it all for her?

He took a deep breath and tried to shake off the anger and anxiety. "The rain stopped. It's a beautiful day out. I'd like to take you for a walk in the park." He sounded like an idiot. "Maybe I could bring a book and read to you."

Pressure. Bleeding in the brain. So maybe they had given her blood thinners. Wouldn't that work? What was he thinking? How would he know what treatment was right? *Just talk. Tell her something positive.*

"I'm waiting to talk to the doctor, but the nurse was very encouraging. She said you're going to be fine." It wasn't a lie; he'd simply left out the qualifier, "should." "And you look good. Except for that bruise, you look healthy. Strong. And beautiful."

A gurney passed by the doorway, propelled by a stout Latino in green scrubs. A tall, pencil-thin woman in white coat followed. The doctor? Would he be able to get some of his questions answered? The wheeled patient and entourage continued down the corridor and out of sight.

"I know if I tried apologizing, you'd sit up and tell me off. You make your own decisions. Take your own chances. But if you do sit up, I won't care if you're putting me in my place. I feel bad for dragging you into this. I'm sorry."

She did not sit up. She exhaled and the machine made a chuckling sound, which he took as encouragement.

"So, you know. I liked kissing you."

He was terrified and doubly terrified of allowing it to show.

"I don't think I've ever known anyone quite like you. No, let me rephrase. I've never met anyone like you before. You are unique. Powerful, funny, smart."

She looked so at peace.

"Sorry. I sound like a commercial for McKenzie Zielinski." She exhaled.

"Great. Now you're laughing at me. You should be. I'm pathetic. Maybe I'll sing something. Do you like the Pogues?"

Inhaled.

"They're an acquired taste, I guess."

If he stopped talking, he was going to start crying, and that was simply not going to happen.

"It's just as well. I'm not much of a singer."

Words weren't coming easily. Emotions were.

"Do you have any clue how hard this is? You should try it sometime. Ah, hell. You'd probably be brilliant."

But the longer he kept up this admitted nonsense, the better he felt. She could hear him. She was going to survive. Kenzie would come out of this and smile at him again.

"Look, since I'm doing such a shit job of talking about nothing, why don't I talk about something real? And if it upsets you, then you say so and I'll stop. Deal?"

A citrus-tinged chemical aroma blew in through the open door—some kind of antiseptic or cleanser. The odor overwhelmed the other stray smells that his senses had barely registered. Rather than hiding them, however, the cleaner forced them to his attention. Both fresh and soiled bedding, various unidentifiable medicinal smells, coffee too long in the pot, a touch of hope, hints of despair. Ted tuned them all out.

"Fine. Cheryl's boyfriend tossed my apartment last night. I wasn't there, of course. Lester and I spent another night in the church. Anyway, I'm now in the market for a new apartment and furnishings."

Her chest rose and fell. The machine whooshed. He noticed, for the first time, the hint of a blue vein in her cheek. Had her pallor revealed it, or did she keep it hidden with a dusting of makeup? He felt like he knew her better having discovered this minor secret.

"You okay? I'm not upsetting you, am I? At first I was sick over it. And scared. Now I'm just pissed off. Like you said, it's time to go get these SOBs."

Whoosh.

"Not SOBs. Bastards. That's what you said. Bastards."

He paused.

"So how do I do that? Suggestions? The floor is yours."

Silence, broken by a soft sob from the corridor. A bent woman in raincoat and rubber boots—a visitor who must have arrived during the deluge the night before—passed down the hall and out the electric-gated door.

"Yeah. I draw a blank, too."

And a thought came to him.

"Where's your phone?"

49

KENZIE'S BELONGINGS WERE IN a flimsy wardrobe: the slinky black dress, ripped and ruined by bloodstains. The spiked heels, which she wouldn't be wearing anytime in the near future. The wig had been stuffed soaking wet into a plastic bag, which was clouded up with condensation. And on the top shelf, shoved to one side, was her purse, a glass-beaded black clutch with a brass clasp. It looked old, like something she might have found it in a vintage clothing store.

Ted sat down again. "I'm going to look in your purse. Normally I would never do that, but these aren't normal times."

She didn't object.

Lipstick. Keys. A slim metal credit card holder with a Visa and a folded, crisp twenty-dollar bill. And her cell phone.

"See? Success."

He noticed a zippered pocket. There was something inside. He debated for only a moment. He opened it and found two foil-wrapped condoms.

"Wow." He zipped the pocket closed. The implications of this discovery were both pleasing and disconcerting. Kenzie had come to dinner prepared, her decision already made or at least more than half-made. Should he feel flattered? He did. Did he also feel a step behind the beat in their mating dance? He did, but maybe it didn't matter. There was also the possibility that the mere existence of the condoms in her purse had nothing to do with him. He took the phone and replaced everything else.

"I will never admit to having seen these," he whispered.

He woke the phone. "I'm going to need your thumb." He gently took her right hand and pressed her thumb to

the screen. Nothing happened. "Not your thumb? Okay."
He switched to her index finger. The screen flashed. He
was in.

"And this is something else I would never do. Except I
am doing it. I'm not intentionally violating your privacy. I'm
looking for a way to get those bastards."

He opened the camera function. The most recent photo
file opened with another touch. It was a video. *The* video.
He tapped it.

The picture was clear enough, though the distance and
perspective were not perfect. Cheryl could be identified only
occasionally in profile. Jackie never, as the back of her head
was to the camera the whole time. The others were easier to
make out: the fat man, Pak, and Kid Reisner. The camera
lingered on each one. It passed over the model—Ted gener-
ously granted her that description—in a blur.

"This is dynamite, Kenzie. I'm sending the video to my
phone," he told her as he found his own number in her phone's
contacts. "I'll share it with that detective as soon as I get the
chance."

He checked his phone. The video had come through.
He pushed her phone down into the purse and opened the
wardrobe.

Kenzie's voice hissed at him in a hoarse whisper. "What
are you doing?"

He whirled around, fighting to control the explosion of
emotions that were all firing at once. Guilt—her purse was
in his hand. Elation that she was awake and aware. Confusion—Kenzie's eyes were still shut.

A woman was standing at the door. Kenzie's mother—there
could be no doubt. She was a stunning redhead with the
same light blue eyes, though in her case they peeked out from
behind gold-framed glasses. She had either danced nightly in
the Fountain of Youth or given birth in her early teens. She

could have passed for an older sister. And there was the voice. Breathy, husky, and deep.

"I'm Ted Molloy," he said, knowing that would mean nothing to this woman, but he had to say something while he thought of a way out of this predicament. He was holding the damn purse.

The clincher for identification of the woman was the attitude. "I didn't ask who you were. I asked what the hell you're doing."

"I was worried," Ted said.

"Yes?"

Ted thought this would have been a perfect time for Kenzie to wake up and explain everything to her mother.

"I was with her last night," he said. "I wanted to see that none of her things had gone missing."

Apparently he had blurted out the magic words. "You were there? Did you see who did this?" The woman softened visibly. Her voice was no longer commanding but pleading.

"I saw it happen, but, no, I couldn't see the driver. It was dark, raining. And it happened so fast. You're Mrs. Zielinski?" If Mrs. Zielinski was there, then Mr. Z, as Lester called him, was probably not far. Ted needed to be gone before the man arrived.

She smoothed Kenzie's hair. It hadn't needed smoothing. "I am. Dolores Zielinski. Dee." She almost reached out a hand to shake but stopped herself. "What did you find? Was anything missing?"

Ted handed the purse to her. "I don't know. Her wallet and phone are there." Too late, he thought of the zipper pocket. "I don't think she was carrying much cash. I'd guess it's all there." He began to edge past her toward the door.

"Ted Molloy?" she asked, obviously trying to remember if she'd heard his name before.

"Yes. Kenzie and I met recently."

"So you were on a date?" She had managed to shift her stance so that she was subtly blocking his exit. It was well executed, too well to have been unconscious.

If she was as perceptive as her daughter, he could not risk lying to her.

"Yes and no." He was not comfortable with this line of questioning. The condoms in the purse would give one message and a tale of bribery and fraud an entirely different one. It was time to change direction. "When you arrived was there a policeman here?"

"Yes. Why?"

"When I left here last night, I asked that they keep an eye on her."

"Why would you do that? The detective told me this was an accident. A car theft." Ted was stunned but he struggled to recover. He could not let her see his surprise. "Was this someone from NYPD? Detective Duran? Or Kasabian?"

"I don't think so."

"Duran's a big black man. Long face. Square jaw. Kasabian looks like the old Marlboro man—"

She cut him off. "No. No. They were nothing like that. Could they have been local? I mean from here. Nassau County. They were here this morning."

"What did they say?"

"Not much, I'm afraid. They talked to me for a minute or two, told the uniformed policeman he could go, and they left."

A string of curses ran through Ted's mind, but he managed to stop them before they erupted out of his mouth.

"Is everything all right?" she asked. "I didn't think to ask them to stay."

Ted did not want to frighten her. He'd talk to Duran or Kasabian as soon as he could get away from her. They'd had a deal. "I'm sure it's fine. They wouldn't have left if there was a problem."

Ted watched her rearrange her features to appear fully convinced. It was an impressive attempt. A less skeptical man might have believed it. "Where did you two meet?" she said, making polite conversation. "According to my daughter, her life begins and ends with her work."

He tried a laugh to reassure her and dispel any suspicions. He failed. The laugh was false, and Mrs. Zielinski was sharp. "She stopped me on the street. In front of the courthouse."

"Hmm?" It was a perfect response. She gave nothing away and at the same time invited more. How did a librarian develop lawyers' skills? Ted didn't fall for it. He had more pressing issues. He needed to talk to the detectives.

"I should be going," he said. "I'd rather we had met under other circumstances."

She brushed by him and placed the purse in the wardrobe. "Will you be back?"

Ted heard footsteps approaching down the hall. Mr. Z? Trapped. He'd waited too long.

"I'll try and stop by this evening." He ducked out the door. A tall, spindly man in doctor's coat passed him, moving quickly down the corridor. Ted released an anxious breath and headed for the elevators.

50

MOHAMMED HAD THE CAR idling at the curb. Ted joined Lester in the back seat, and they headed toward the LIE. Lester had a bulging plastic bag in his lap.

"How's the lady?" he asked.

"Not good," Ted said. "What's in the bag?"

Lester flashed him a view of the contents. Ted guessed there were two dozen or more airline-sized vodka bottles.

"What's this?" Ted said.

"Controlled dosage," Lester said. "Is she going to be okay?"

"I don't know. The nurse thinks so. They've got her in an induced coma."

"That doesn't sound good."

"No," Ted agreed, though reluctant to admit to a negative thought. "It doesn't. How many of those have you had?"

"One an hour should work."

"So you've had one so far," Ted said.

Lester held up two empties. "The key to dealing with pain is to stay in front of it. Did you get to talk to a doctor?"

"No. Her mother showed up, and I thought that was a strong indication that I should be somewhere else."

"What's the mother like?" Lester asked.

"She's too young for you."

"You say that, but you've never seen me dance."

"I need to speak to Detective Duran. There's no guard on her. The mother said they pulled the uniforms early this morning. I talked to the hospital security guys on the way out but they're useless. Empty uniforms."

"Will Duran listen to you? I've got a bad feeling."

Ted nodded agreement. He did not like this situation at all. "I did manage one thing."

"What's that?"

"I was able to get the video Kenzie shot at the restaurant last night. I've got Councilman Pak, Cheryl, Little Reisner, all of them. Once Duran sees it, he'll have to take this seriously."

"Meanwhile, we need some place to hole up where we won't wake up being clubbed."

"I have an idea about that." Ted looked at Mohammed, who appeared frazzled and in need of a break. "How're you holding up?"

"Rock and roll," he replied.

"Mohammed thinks we're high maintenance," Lester muttered.

"He's got a point," Ted said. "Take us to Corona. I'm looking for a guy who might help us."

"IF IT'S COMFORT YOU'RE looking for, I won't be much help."
The Preacher eyed Lester warily. The sling, the stitches, and the
bruises on his face added up to a troublesome package. Ted
noticed that he was also a bit red-eyed, which could have been
the vodka or, almost as likely, the effect of having slept only
sparingly on a hard pew for the past two nights.

Ted had found their man delivering his message to a
smirking group of Hispanic teenagers outside a Dominican
deli. The Preacher made a brief show of annoyance at being
interrupted, but it was obvious to all concerned that the gang
of youths—both male and female—were much more interested in one another than anything the grey-bearded man in
the ankle-length overcoat might have to say.

"I don't need turndown service and a chocolate on the
pillow," Ted said. "I need anonymity. A mattress and a shower
would be nice. And a roof."

"I'll take a pillow," Lester said.

"McKenzie thought you could help," Ted said.

If there had been any reluctance on the Preacher's part,
it crumbled at the mention of Ms. Zielinski. "Come along,
then," the Preacher said. "Manny Singh may have something
for you."

THE ENTREPRENEURIAL MR. SINGH led them up a flight of rickety
stairs that seemed to have been tacked on to the rear wall of
his market as an afterthought. They passed a featureless door
marked FIRE EXIT ONLY on the second floor and continued up
to the top.

The aromas of cardamom, garlic, and mint enveloped

them. Caramelized onion and slow-cooked lamb provided a bassline. Something sweet—warm honey, perhaps—drifted in as counterpoint. Ted's mouth watered.

"There is no key," Manny said. "But you will not need one. You will see." Ted and Lester followed him into a dark hallway. "Please to keep your voices down. Most of my tenants work nights and are sleeping now. They are mostly cooks, waiters, sous-chefs. In Manhattan."

They passed a room with sagging couches grouped around a silent television. A soccer game was in progress, but no one was watching. Heavy rugs hung from the walls and covered the two windows, allowing only a thin ray of sunlight to hit the floor.

"This is the community room," Singh said. "Anyone can use it. No food in here, please." He continued toward the rear of the apartment, passing a spotless bathroom on one side and a large and similarly spotless kitchen on the other. An ankle-height night-light was the only illumination in the hall, and it took Ted a moment to see that they were facing two doors.

"I don't know who is here right now, but there are a few beds available. Take your pick." Singh cracked open the door to the right.

The bedroom was lit with more night-lights. Four two-tiered bunk beds filled the walls. There was a low coffee table in the center of the room surrounded by brocaded pillows. Most of the beds were hidden behind hanging blankets suspended from the bed frame above or from curtain rods on the ceiling. Light snoring could be heard from behind one of the blankets.

"The rules are simple. Respect your neighbors. They are almost all Afghan, but you will find them very accepting and welcoming. No women allowed. No drugs. Tobacco and alcohol are allowed, but drunkenness is not." He looked sharply at Lester, who nodded in reply. "You pay weekly. In advance."

Ted took out two more of the hundred-dollar bills. The envelope was getting thin. "Is there any place to stow our things? I mean if we go out for a while."

Singh smiled with barely concealed disdain. "No one will steal from you here. Leave your things on your bunk. They will be there when you return."

Ted laid his jacket on a top bunk. Lester took a lower bunk on the other side of the room.

"What do you think?" Ted said, keeping his voice low.

"I wouldn't mind having a lock on the door," Lester said. "But somebody would have to be stark raving mad to bust in on a dozen or so guys who handle knives for a living."

52

LESTER SWALLOWED ANOTHER MINI bottle of medicinal Smirnoff and crawled into his bunk. Ted went out to the community room. He had calls to make.

The first was to the NYPD detectives. Ted wanted to know why Kenzie had been left with no protection—and what the NYPD was prepared to do about it. He took out Kasabian's card and dialed.

The moment he heard the detective's voice, Ted started talking. "What the hell is going on? Why did you pull protection on Ms. Zielinski?"

"Who's speaking?"

"You know who this is, Detective. Ted Molloy, and you screwed me, and you left McKenzie Zielinski lying there for those assholes to come in and finish what they started last night."

"Hello again, Mr. Molloy. I did not pull protection on your friend. I don't make those decisions."

Ted didn't want lessons in police bureaucracy. "Suppose for the moment that you are not jerking me off again. I'll bite. What happened?"

"As of oh-nine-thirty, the NYPD is no longer pursuing a case involving Ms. Zielinski."

"Why the hell not?"

"Orders from on high. Nassau County has jurisdiction now."

"What? Why? Fuck it. Let me talk to Duran—"

The detective cut him off. "I'll let him know you called. Meanwhile, I will tell you this: we made our argument for keeping the case and were told in bold capital letters to back off."

Ted tried to swallow his anger; it wasn't helping his case. He tried persistence. "She needs protection."

"Are you listening? Providing protection for a crime victim outside NYPD jurisdiction is not standard procedure around here."

He made it personal. "What are you going to do for her?"

"Nassau County Police believe their investigation will show this was an accident resulting from a carjacking gone wrong."

The hell with being reasonable. "That's bullshit."

"It's their case."

"What about the bribes? The fraud on Barbara Miller? Reisner and Pak and the fat guy?"

"We have no evidence of any crime."

"Are you fucking kidding me? Shit. I can't talk to you. Get me Duran."

"We are working the murder of Richard Rubiano, but we have other active investigations, and his case is now over a week old. As a close associate with motive, you are considered a possible suspect and will be until we find closure."

"What about the big Greek? Nicky."

"Being sought as a person of interest. We are investigating multiple scenarios."

"McKenzie Zielinski was attacked because she got involved in this. If anything happens to her, it's on you."

"I don't know what to tell you, Molloy. But it's not my case."

53

RELEASING ANGER AND FRUSTRATION on Detective Kasabian was an indulgence. Ted had enjoyed it, but he was left with more problems than solutions. Short of calling in a bomb threat, he had no idea of how to protect Kenzie while she lay all but dead to the world.

He found himself retracing his steps down the staircase to the street. The whole structure seemed to groan with each step, echoing his encroaching despair. He was running out of options, and when none were left, where would he be? He was losing, and he hated it.

Back in middle school he had joined the wrestling team only because the coach had told him he could be good at it. Eventually, he came to realize that this was the coach's standard way of recruiting players. Everyone, regardless of any innate talents, got the same pitch. But Ted had stuck it out. He lost often the first two years, but in high school he began to win. In his junior year, he lost one match—to a wiry Hispanic kid from the South Bronx who knocked him out of contention for statewide competition. The following November, he pinned the same kid in eight seconds. He had learned something about himself: he did not like to lose.

And despite the disappointments he had faced in his career and his marriage, he still didn't like it.

This was a fight he had not sought. The moment when Richie Rubiano dumped the file on the table at Gallagher's was clear in his memory. But somehow, the case had found him, and the stakes had never before in his life been any higher. Like it or not, it was his to lose.

At the bottom of the stairs, he turned down the alley and

walked out to Roosevelt Avenue. The sidewalks were busy, which gave him a comfortable feeling. There was anonymity in crowds. He felt the tension in his shoulders. He must have been carrying it for days.

Across the street the chain-link fence around the proposed construction site was a grinning, arrogant barrier forcing pedestrians to skirt the obstruction by stepping out into the roadway midblock. It was easy to see why Kenzie hated it.

He strode across, looking for signs of progress within the stockade. No one was there. All the windows of the buildings inside the fence that faced the street had been covered with sheets of plywood, and the graffiti taggers had been busy marking them. SHORTY LIVES ran along the windowless top floor of one building, making Ted stop for a moment to contemplate how anyone could have reached that point armed with a half-dozen different cans of spray paint. It was an homage to Shorty 140, one of Queens' most prolific street artists, who had been arrested eventually, but not before hitting every overpass on the LIE, as well as hundreds, if not thousands, of other sites throughout the borough.

"That boy made himself famous. For some of these young guns, a little street cred is all they're ever going to get."

The Preacher was standing over Ted's left shoulder. He could have sworn the man hadn't been there a second earlier.

"He's no boy, Preacher. He's as old as I am. And," Ted said, nodding at the building, "he's still famous."

"Foolishness. Vandals."

"Maybe. Or a protest? Sad, futile, powerless, but noble."

"And your dilemma? When we spoke the other day, you had a decision to make."

Ted took his time composing a reply. "I admit I'm confused ..." A subway train passed overhead, and for a long minute, the two men waited patiently for the noise to abate. Ted began again, "I admit I'm confused, but the decision is made. I don't know whether I made it or had it handed to me, but *I* seem to keep forging along."

"The battle against evil takes the righteous through many a dark path. Keep the faith and the light will find you."

"That's a comfort."

"You're not a religious man."

"Some days I think my life would be a lot less complicated if I were."

"To be afraid is to be human. To do what's right despite your fear is divine." The Preacher left Ted staring at the fence.

54

LESTER WAS UP WHEN Ted returned, lounging on the low, broken sofas in the community room watching golf with two young men. To Ted's eye, they could have been brothers. Both were dark-eyed, handsome men with black hair and near-identical mustaches. They were dressed in pressed khaki trousers and matching pistachio-colored polo shirts. They greeted him with brief nods.

"Glad you're back. Say hello to our roommates, Khalil and Khalil. Gentlemen, this is Ted." Lester waggled a finger at his own shirt. "They're fans."

Fans? Ted didn't see the connection.

The two young Afghans flashed brilliant white smiles that disappeared in an instant. Ted nodded in reply.

"Khalil told me something interesting," Lester said. "He's halfway through a nursing degree in the city. Ask him about medically induced comas. And you might want to sit down first."

Ted sat.

"I am sorry about your friend," the young man said. He looked at Ted as he spoke, but his eyes immediately flashed back to the television screen, where a man wearing the same outfit of khakis and pistachio-colored polo shirt was setting up for a putt. "One moment." They all watched in rapt silence as the golfer took aim and swung gently. The ball rolled into the hole. The adoring crowd clapped politely. The two fans on the couch shared a high five. Khalil's eyes came back to Ted. "Is she responsive?"

"No," Ted said. "Not that I could see. The nurse said she could hear, though."

Khalil blinked once, swallowing this bit of information. "What I have explained to Mr. Lester is that the swelling could be quite serious. It restricts blood flow to the brain. There is a risk of permanent damage if the brain is starved of oxygen for too long. When did they induce her?"

"Induce" sounded like a way of making an invitation with an "or else" at the end. "Sometime last night. Early this morning? I'm not sure."

"They will be monitoring her brain waves. Is she breathing on her own?"

"She's wearing a mask. It sounds like it's pumping air."

Khalil blinked again. "If in three days there is no improvement, they will remove the breathing apparatus."

Three days. Ted refused to accept it. "The swelling may already be coming down," he said with more hope than conviction.

"There is often some measurable immediate relief. By itself, it is meaningless."

"Jesus!" The matter-of-fact presentation of this news made it all the more shocking. Why hadn't the nurse mentioned this? Need to know. He wasn't family. He thought of Kenzie's mother, counting the hours until her daughter woke or never woke again.

"There's more," Lester said.

"What?" Ted asked, though he felt that he had heard too much already.

"If she comes out of the coma—" Khalil began.

"When," Ted said. "Can we stick with the idea of 'when' she comes out of the coma?"

Khalil continued as if Ted hadn't interrupted. "Her mental and physical functions could be affected."

Memory? Speech? Cognitive? Would she be able to walk? To take care of herself? A wave of despair washed over Ted.

"This is possible," Khalil went on. "I cannot say how

likely. I do not have enough information." Another golfer was on the green and readying his putt. This one wore a lavender polo. Khalil's eyes were straining toward the screen. "I am sorry about your friend."

Ted wanted to break something. Or someone. He wanted someone else to hurt as badly as he did. It almost didn't matter whom. But he would find the people responsible for this. He reined in his rage. "Yes. Thank you, Khalil. I needed to know."

"Are you going to be okay?" Lester asked.

No. He was not going to be okay. Not until Kenzie came out of the coma, walking, talking, and 100 percent herself in every way. Then he might start on the road to being okay. But for the moment, he was able to function.

"Let's go sit out on the stairs and let these gentlemen get back to watching their game," Ted said. "There're things we need to talk about."

Lester pulled himself out of the deep couch and followed him outside.

55

"I'M SORRY. I THOUGHT you had to know."

There was a produce truck parked in the alley below. The driver and his assistant were off-loading into the back of Manny's store, carrying on a loud conversation in a language that could have been Chinese or Vietnamese. Or Hmong, for all Ted knew. They didn't appear to be arguing, but the voices were strident. Ted tried tuning them out. It wasn't easy.

"I should have realized it myself," Ted said. "I'm not thinking. I'm hoping." He was also angry—and guilty. He was reacting and not in control.

"Besides people trying to kill you—and me—and that pretty lady ending up in the hospital, and your apartment turned upside down, I can't imagine why you're feeling low."

An explosion of yelling came from below. The truckers were done unloading.

"Let me see how many of those vodka bottles you have left," Ted said.

Lester opened the bag. It was almost full. "One of us has to be able to think straight," he said.

Ted related all that had transpired over the past few hours, interrupted once by the produce truck starting up, emitting deafening diesel farts of blue smoke. The frustrating talk with Detective Duran's partner elicited a snort of disgust from Lester.

"You're going to want to show that video to someone. Aside from a few real estate filings, which may or may not be fraudulent, that's the only hard evidence you've got of any kind of conspiracy."

Ted nodded absently. "First thing I've got to do is figure

out how to get some armed guards for Kenzie—without upsetting her parents."

"Khalil got me to thinking about that," Lester said. "Follow me for a bit. As long as the lady is in a coma, they don't have to worry about her. It's only when she comes out of it that she can start talking about what she remembers. Until then, they've got a free pass."

"On the other hand, she's unable to defend herself or escape. They could easily find her."

"They don't let just anybody into ICU, am I right? Someone on staff would notice a stranger strolling around even if he wasn't a Russian hit man. She's safe."

"Maybe." Lester made a good point, but Ted wasn't convinced. Access to the ICU was restricted, but he had sailed in with ease. On the other hand, she was definitely not capable of giving information or identifying her attackers at the moment. Her condition protected her even more than the presence of armed guards would. "It's good that one of us is thinking straight. I was ready to call in the cavalry. Air strikes. Drone attacks. Weapons of mass destruction."

"Let's save all that until we really need it."

56

TED LEFT LESTER WATCHING golf with the two Afghans and went back outside to make his next call. He was ready.

"Detective Duran, please. And, no, I don't want to speak to his partner."

Duran picked up a minute later. Ted's luck had changed.

"I've got nothing to add," Duran said. "Detective Kasabian filled me in on your earlier call."

"Your partner is an obstructionist."

"Don't throw four-syllable words at me, Molloy. I went to public school."

"There's a case here. A good case. Let me help you break it."

"We've been warned off." Duran sounded a touch less absolute about it than his partner. "What does Nassau County have to say?"

"You know, I haven't talked to them."

"Well, maybe you should."

"They think this is a carjacking," Ted said in exasperation.

"And maybe they're right."

"They're not. If you give me five minutes, I'll show you why."

Duran paused before answering. Despite his reservations, he was intrigued. "What have you got?"

"Meet with me."

"I'm a busy guy." Now he sounded bored. Was he losing interest or playing hard to get?

Ted laid down his sole trump card. "I have a video. All the players are in it. You'll see. Come to the place we first met. See what I've got, and you decide if it's worth anything."

"I've been instructed to focus my efforts elsewhere."

Ted held back his frustration and forged ahead. Formality would have to pass for forbearance. "I have information relevant to your ongoing investigation into the death of Richard Rubiano."

"We no longer believe the cases are related."

Ted couldn't get a read on Duran. Was this truth or was this more obstruction coming down the chain of command? "Give me five minutes, and I'll prove you wrong."

"Don't bullshit me."

"Can you afford to ignore me?"

"You are becoming a pain in the ass. My partner isn't going to buy into this; I'll tell you that."

"Don't bring him," Ted shot back. "I can be there in twenty minutes. In half an hour, you're rid of me, or you're a hero. Come on, take a chance."

NURSES AND FIREMEN WERE two deep at the bar at Gallagher's, spilling into all the booths on that side of the room. Ted waggled two fingers at Lili, and she passed him a pair of Brooklyn IPAs while simultaneously pouring shots of Jameson for a cluster of off-duty firemen. Ted retreated to his usual booth, only to find it occupied by four nurses drinking martinis. They were engaged in a heated debate on the relative merits of *Girls* versus *Broad City*. Seeing Ted hovering near the table, one of the women tried, flirtatiously, to elicit his opinion but lost interest when he admitted that he had never seen either show. Ted moved on.

An apparently empty booth nearer the door beckoned. Ted plunked himself down, glad for the packed house and the noise. Despite the attack at the courthouse, he felt safer in a crowd. And the alcohol-induced hilarity would drown out his conversation with the detective.

But the moment he settled in, resident barfly Paulie McGirk sat up, rising like a drunken Lazarus from the bench on the other side of the booth. He grinned sleepily at Ted.

"'S that beer for me?"

"No," Ted said. There wasn't another free booth available, or he would have moved.

"I thought you'd say that," Paulie whined.

"Tell you what," Ted offered. "I'll buy you a beer if you let me have this booth."

Paulie did not have to weigh the decision for very long. "That's a good deal," he said.

Ted waved at Lili and, when he got her eye, pointed one finger at Paulie. "Lili's got your beer."

"You're a good man, Johnny. I'll remember your generosity." The last word was squeezed into three syllables and ended with a small spray of spittle.

Ted seriously doubted he would.

He could see only part of the street from this vantage point, so he kept his attention split between the door and the view. He didn't have to wait long. Detective Duran came through the door alone, as promised. Ted let him scan the room before raising one of the IPAs in welcome. Duran eased his way through the melee, squinting against the onslaught of a particularly loud peal of high-pitched female laughter.

"How's your friend?" he said, once settled across from Ted.

"Still in the induced coma. They're focusing on bringing the swelling down. Who pulled the guards?"

"Very high up. That's all I was told."

"Who could do that?"

"Nobody in the department made that call. This came from outside. Someone with connections."

A councilman? A major real estate developer? Or a retired judge? Ted felt his anger rising up again.

"I seriously doubt I can help you," Duran was saying. "But show me what you've got."

Ted stuffed his anger beneath the surface. It could wait. He handed the phone to the detective. "Watch."

Duran played the video through three times before raising his eyes to Ted. "You know all these people?"

"No. I know who they are, though. Some of them. There's Cheryl, of course. Pak I've seen before. I'm told that's Reisner's kid. It would be easy enough to get verification."

"Too bad you couldn't get the father on tape," the detective said. "The head of the biggest real estate development firm in the city would be a nice addition."

"I'm told the son only speaks when his father okays it in advance."

Duran was nodding impatiently. "Do you have facial recognition on this phone?"

"Why would I?" Ted asked.

"My daughter's sixteen. I use it every time I meet one of her boyfriends." He tapped the keys on Ted's phone, forwarding the video to his own. When he heard the incoming chirp, he opened an app and let the phone search for matching faces. A minute or two he later he grinned and handed Ted the phone. "Is this your guy?"

It was a younger and thinner version of the fat man from the restaurant. He still had hair, but it was thinning. He had already developed the same pose of smug arrogance. The picture was followed by paragraphs of miniscule type.

"That's him," Ted said, straining and failing to read the copy.

"This is why I'm here, isn't it?" Duran asked. He swiped the screen again and began to read.

"I don't know who he is, but I'd bet an arm that he made the call that resulted in my friend lying in a coma."

"It says here your man is a banker."

"Says where?"

"*Euromoney*. From"—Duran scrolled down the story—"six

years ago. It's an article on sons of Russian oligarchs. His name is Sokol Orlov. Born in Moscow. Studied at Cambridge. London School of Economics." He looked up. "I read someplace Mick Jagger went there." He continued reading. "Three years at Blandon, whatever that is."

"Private bank," Ted said. "Olde with an *e*. The joke goes they lent the Dutch the beads to buy Manhattan. What else does *Euromoney* have to say?"

"Sokol eventually saw the light and went to work for his father. Diversification. Special projects. But he stayed in New York to oversee their 'growing real estate portfolio.'"

"Where does the money come from?"

Duran quickly scanned the rest of the short article. "Says here the old man is the largest manufacturer of 'edible chemicals in Russia.' Preservatives, flavorings, colorings. He's the flavor-crystal king."

"Mesquite-flavored barbecue potato chips?" Ted asked.

"Stoli Razberi."

"Anything else there?" Ted gestured toward the phone.

"That's it. Sokol is younger than he looks, by the way. A lot. He's forty-one."

"Evil adds years."

"That's what I tell them after I'm done reading them their rights," Duran said.

"So the reporter doesn't mention that this guy is guilty of extortion, loan-sharking, money laundering, murder for hire, and general mayhem?"

"Puff piece."

"So, was the trip worth five minutes of your time? Can you do anything with that video?"

Duran sighed. "Mr. Molloy, I would love to run with this. The very thought of linking a corrupt city councilman with a Russian money-laundering scheme makes me rock hard. Never mind the fact that the widow of a recent murder victim is enjoying their company. But without some corroboration from an actual witness, I have nowhere to go with this. The LT will toss me out of her office."

"I was there. I watched Kenzie make that video."

"You are a person of interest in the Rubiano case."

"I've been downgraded? Kasabian said I was still a suspect."

Duran's face closed up. "We are examining another theory that may or may not preclude your involvement."

Ted let it go. The cases were one, he was sure. He and Lester didn't have all the connections, but they were close. "Tell me what you need. I'll find some way to make it happen." Ted tried to sound confident.

Duran softened a tad. "Give me someone who will talk to me. A witness."

Ted ran through a mental checklist. Cheryl wouldn't talk to the cops unless he could prove without a doubt that she was complicit and facing hard time—and maybe not even then. Jackie was protected by client confidentiality. Then he hit on it. There was one possible witness—she was also a victim.

"I've got someone," Ted said. "The old lady. Barbara Miller. She'll talk to you."

"That's a hard sell. Didn't you tell me she's got Alzheimer's?"

"Dementia, at any rate," Ted admitted. "But you catch her at the right moment, and she's as sharp as either of us."

"If she isn't crystal clear on the main points, I won't talk to her. I can't afford to make a mistake."

Ted didn't like it, but he understood. "I'll see her tomorrow and let you know."

"Heeeere's Johnny!" Paulie McGirk was back, swaying to a slow rhythm distinctly out of pace with the Allman Brother's "Whipping Post," which was blaring from the jukebox. He stood at the end of the table, his face scrunched in concentration. "Did I forget to tell you something?"

"I'm in a meeting, Paulie," Ted said. "Let's chat some other time."

"Did those two guys find you, then?" Paulie asked.

"What two guys?" Ted asked, though he had a strong feeling he already knew.

"I don't know," Paulie said, unhappy to disappoint, so unable to maintain eye contact. "They didn't leave a card. They came in today, asked if you'd been in, then they left."

Duran was following this conversation intently. "Describe them," he said.

"Who's this?" Paulie asked in an exaggerated stage whisper.

Ted thought that identifying Duran as an NYPD detective would make Paulie clam up and disappear. As much as Ted wanted to get rid of the brain-addled bar sponge, he wanted to hear about these two guys. "He's a new friend, Paulie. Very interested in keeping me safe."

"Then he should keep you away from those two guys," Paulie said.

"What did they look like?" Ted asked.

Paulie stood, mouth agape, for long seconds. Direct questions on matters of fact often sent him into this kind of trance.

Ted tried another approach. "They were tough guys? Scary?"

"I wasn't scared."

Whether this was drunkard's bravado or alcoholic depression, it was probably true.

Ted tried softening his approach. "I meant they were scary dudes. Most people would be scared of them."

"Without a doubt," Paulie agreed. "They had shark eyes. Know what I mean? Like they would have been happy to kill you, but maybe later when they weren't so busy."

Ted knew exactly what he meant.

Duran tried again to get a less subjective description. "Was one of them taller than the other? Fatter? Thinner? Both the same?"

"One of 'em had a shaved head and a face like a boxer." Paulie flattened his nose with his index finger so it resembled the nose of a fighter who'd taken too many punches to the face. "And they had funny accents."

Paulie lived in a part of the world where even the minority who grew up speaking American did so with an easily identified and often ridiculed accent. Ted let himself smile. Just a touch.

"Anything else you can add?" Duran asked.

"That's the story."

"Thanks, Paulie," Ted said. "I'm going to tell Lili to put one—and one only—beer a day for you on my tab all this week."

"Thanks, Johnny. You're all white."

Ted chose to have misheard. "And you're all right, too, Paulie. Let me know if they come around again. Don't talk to them if you can help it, but if they ask, you haven't seen me."

"You can depend on me, Johnny." Yawing erratically, Paulie shuffled toward the bar.

Duran snorted a laugh. "You do travel in elite circles. First Nicky Greco and now Popov and Jackoff, the Russian tag team."

"So?" Ted said, facing Duran. "Can we agree that there are evil forces out there meaning to do me and my friends some serious harm?" He was being hunted. His apartment had been torn to shreds; two people hospitalized, one in a coma. Bribery, fraud, assault, and worse. What more did Duran need?

"Get me that witness," Duran said.

THE WEATHER HAD TURNED overnight, and a mini squall buffeted the car as they raced down Cross Bay Boulevard. Jamaica Bay was covered in whitecaps, and the rain didn't so much fall as explode from one horizon to the other, hitting the window on Lester's side like shrapnel. Lester flinched constantly. He looked rested and clear-eyed, though his mood matched the weather. Mohammed's driving didn't help.

Lester kept one hand gripped on the door handle in case he needed to bail out. "This trip is like fishing for eels. They're a bitch to catch, and once you've landed one, you wish you hadn't."

"Duran needs a witness," Ted said. "We have to find out if Barbara Miller is capable of making a coherent statement on her own behalf."

"If you'd care to make a wager on our success—"

Ted cut Lester off. "I know it's a long shot, but we don't have a lot of options."

"Amen to that." The car slammed through a pothole. The bag on Lester's lap clinked, and he hugged it to his chest. He had skipped his dose of liquid medication that morning but had brought the bag with him.

"Are you always this nervous a passenger?" Ted asked, enjoying a little the other man's discomfort.

"This guy learned to drive dodging terrorists in Beirut."

"Beirut's in Lebanon. Mohammed's from Yemen."

"That's two places I'll never go."

THE SAME YOUNG WOMAN guarded the front desk at the assisted-living facility. If she remembered Ted or Lester from their visit a week earlier, she gave no clue.

"Please sign in," she said, pushing a three-ring binder across the desk. "Who are you here to see?"

Ted was glad to see Lester shake off his bad mood and turn on the charm he had shown the last time they were there. He no longer wore the metal brace on his teeth, claiming a miraculous recovery—though Ted wouldn't believe it until he saw the man chow down a steak and corn on the cob—but his arm was still in the sling, and the plastic cast showed. He was on the mend, but it was a forlorn look.

"You may not remember us from last week," he began. "We are here to visit with Miss Barbara Miller. She is the aunt of her only nephew"—here he gestured grandly as he created yet another forgettable alias for Ted—"Ethan Phillips."

The woman looked at them blankly through thick glasses. "Barbara Miller?" she said, in a suspicious tone.

Ted felt the first stirrings of impending disaster. Lester plowed on.

"Yes." He held up a white box with red lettering: ANDRE'S HUNGARIAN BAKERY. "We brought her a little treat."

"One moment," she said before picking up the phone and turning away. She whispered with muted intensity for a minute before speaking to Lester again. "Would you take a seat? The director will be right out."

Lester smiled confidently at Ted and led the way to a high backless couch on which they perched like petitioners at the manor house. Ted thought they were screwed.

A tall pinch-faced woman wearing sensible shoes, a heavy grey skirt that reached to midcalf, and what could have been a man's dress shirt buttoned to the neck strode across the lobby. She introduced herself in a monotone voice at triple speed, adding her title, education, credentials, length of service, and a brief résumé. It was a performance that would have qualified her to announce the disclaimers for a pharmaceutical ad. Ted missed her name but got the gist of the speech. This woman was in charge here. "Who are you people?" she finished. "And why are you here? Do not dissemble, as I know that Miss Miller has no family."

Ted looked to Lester—it was time for improvisation—only to find Lester staring at him with a blank, unreadable face.

Ted took the last resort of a failed lawyer; he told the truth and threw himself on the mercy of the court. "My name is Ted Molloy. I am not her nephew. I am a limited business partner with Miss Miller. If you like, I can show you our signed agreement. I need to speak with her."

She didn't react to his admission of attempted trickery. Instead, she cocked her head to one side and appeared to be deep in thought. "Miss Miller is no longer a resident here. She left yesterday afternoon." The woman spoke much more slowly, incorporating the event into her worldview.

Ted found he wasn't surprised at all. He was still a step or two behind the opposition. "Who authorized her move?"

She drew herself up. He had maligned her personal integrity. "It was all quite regular. The gentlemen from the ambulette company came with a signed court order." The words came faster this time.

He stopped himself from grinding his teeth. "Who gave the authorization?" A judge, obviously, but Ted wanted to see the name on the form. "May I get a copy?"

"That is not possible. Patient records are inviolate." She was back at full throttle, consonants leapfrogging over vowels, syllables indicated rather than realized.

Lester rolled his eyes.

"Tell me this, then," Ted said, slowing his own speech in hopes that doing so might have some effect on her. "Isn't this all a bit unusual? Don't you usually get notice well in advance?"

"One moment," she said and turned and walked into an office, almost immediately reappearing with another woman.

She rattled off an introduction, and this time Ted caught the essential information. This was the staff social worker, Mrs. Starkey. Or Stocky. Or possibly Sparkey or Spaaki.

She was a harried, frizzy-haired woman whom Ted guessed to be in her early sixties, and judging by the dark bags under her eyes and her well-gnawed lower lip, she was counting the days to retirement. The director left her in charge and strode back to the office.

"Barbara Miller was transferred to a full-service nursing facility out of state. The paperwork was all in order, but nevertheless, I would not have authorized the move if I did not think it was in my client's best interest. Obviously." She was firm but pleasant, and she spoke at a normal pace.

"Of course not," Ted said. As long as she was talking, he thought he could take a direct approach. "Where did they take her?"

He'd misjudged her. "What was your association with Miss Miller?"

"I've already explained—" Ted began.

"Not to me," she said, laying out the rules of engagement.

"Business partners. I'm concerned for her. We have competitors who would not refrain from trickery, or worse, to gain an advantage."

"Nonsense. Barbara Miller could not be your business partner, because she has been judged to be incompetent to handle her affairs."

"As of when?" This could invalidate the claim to the surplus money, leaving Ted with no legal standing. And no leverage.

"This week. I suggest you take your concerns to the county court."

After Miller had signed the agreement. Ted stood. He was angry and frustrated, and patience wasn't accomplishing a thing. "I need to find her. If someone here doesn't become a lot more cooperative in the next few seconds, I am going to call the police. You could be an accomplice to kidnapping."

Again, he had misjudged her. Rather than wilt at the threat of police, she put her back to the wall and stood her ground. "We have nothing more to discuss."

"No," he said, meeting her eye. "You need to give me some answers."

Lester stood and took Ted's arm. "I think we all need to step back and take a deep breath."

"I don't know what any of you are up to, but rest assured I am going to find out." The woman, eyes locked with Ted's, barely registered Lester's presence.

"I've got a feeling we're all really on the same side here," Lester said. Ted let him take the wheel. "Am I right? We are all concerned for the welfare of Miss Barbara Miller. Can we keep that in mind and try to talk nice to each other?"

The woman gave Ted one final defiant look before turning a softer face to Lester. "I am confident that she is in good hands."

"Would you at least share the name of the ambulette company?" Lester asked.

Ted could see her mulling over the ethical issues involved in releasing this bit of inconsequential information. It took her a minute, but she came down on the right side. "I don't see how that would violate confidentiality. Let me check with the director." She scurried to the office.

"How did you do that?" Ted asked.

"I have no idea," Lester said. "But it won't be that easy getting the ambulance people to open up."

Whoever was orchestrating the defense was a magnificent chess player, anticipating Ted's thoughts and plans. He was beginning to feel hopeless. Which was the point, of course.

The director reappeared. "I am uncomfortable offering any further information. If you would like to leave a business card, I will call the ambulette service and ask them to contact you directly. That is the best that I can do."

Ted could tell when he was beaten. The woman wasn't going to budge. He thanked her and gave her his card.

But Lester wasn't done. "One more thing, if you don't mind. Could we talk with Miss Miller's aide for a minute? I think her name is Anora. She was a big help, and I need to thank her."

"She's been reassigned to another patient and is working right now," the director said.

She was probably watching her new charge play bingo. Or they were both nodding out in the lounge in front of CNN.

Lester worked his magic again. "We won't keep her long."

THEY WAITED FOR ANORA in the library, where they had met the last time. There was no one else there. Ted imagined that in another decade or two, rooms like this—devoted to providing a comfortable space to store and peruse hardbound copies of brightly colored dreams—would have disappeared, replaced by reclining couches with virtual reality headsets. Aging baby boomers could be laid out in rows, fed a soy and vegetable soup combined with tranquilizers and stool softeners, and monitored occasionally for continued heartbeat and respiration. He hoped that when he got to that point, they'd have some old noir movies programmed.

But if he wanted to stay alive now, he needed to keep focused. These depressing thoughts came from his growing fear that the forces against them were going to prevail, in which case his best bet would be to emigrate to Tasmania or Uruguay—he'd heard the beaches were great.

Lester sat quietly with the pastry box from Andre's on his lap.

Anora sidled into the room, and Ted could see she was frightened. No. She was terrified. She seemed to have shrunk inches in every dimension. Her eyes had the thousand-yard stare of the doomed. He let Lester take the lead.

"Come and sit with me. You look like you've had a rough couple of days. We've all been there. You're safe with us." Lester spoke in a gentle voice.

She took a seat across the room and gazed intently at the floor.

"Okay, sit all the way over there. I'm adaptable." He pulled his chair a few inches closer to her. "There. That's better."

She flashed a sideways look at him.

"I guess you were there when they came for Miss Miller."

No response.

"Was it the lawyer who brought the papers? The same one? The woman?"

She gave a tiny shake of her head.

"No," Lester said soothingly. "This time it was a man. Two, maybe."

A slight nod turned into a shudder.

"Yeah. We've met those guys, too."

Another flashing glance.

"Don't worry. They won't be back. They like to scare people, that's all."

Ted found himself lulled by the quiet compassion and sincerity in Lester's voice. He wanted to believe it, too.

"They threatened you, didn't they?" Lester said.

A shrug.

"Said they'd know if you talked to anyone. Did you recognize them? Have they been here before?"

Another quick shake of the head.

Lester carried his chair across the room and sat next to her. He patted the back of her hand. She tightened but did not flinch. "They won't be back. They may have said it, but it won't happen. Did they tell you where they're taking her?"

Another shake of the head—but this time an uncertain one.

"No, they wouldn't tell you. But maybe you heard them talking?"

She froze.

Lester made no change in his tone or pace. "I mean they wouldn't even care if you heard. They probably acted like you weren't even there. But you're smart enough to keep your ears open and the brain working, aren't you? You couldn't stop them, but you might be able to help us find her again."

She looked up at Ted. "You said I would have a green card."

Lester shot a sharp look at him.

"Yes," Ted said. "We promised. But we all want to know that Miss Miller is safe and being cared for. That's first order of business."

"She did not want to go." She chose to direct this to Lester.

Lester nodded, signaling understanding and comforting. It was working. She looked better. Less afraid. "What did you hear?"

"I don't know. The ugly one. He said something, speaking German, I think."

"Maybe Russian?" Lester asked.

"Yes," she said. "I don't know."

"The social worker lady, what's her name, says they took her to another nursing home."

She shrugged. She didn't know. "Old people do not like change. She was frightened."

Lester smiled encouragingly. "None of us do, but you're right. The old ones take it harder."

"I want to help her. I'm sorry."

"You've been a big help already. There's nothing to be sorry about."

Ted stood. Anora had nothing to offer. It was time to move on and try another avenue, though he wasn't sure what that would be. "I haven't forgotten my promise. It may take a little time, but I will do everything I can to make it happen."

She didn't believe him. He could see it in her eyes, but he wasn't going to convince her by repeating it. Especially since he had no idea how he was going to manage it.

Lester shook her hand. "We'll see you again, Anora." He joined Ted at the door.

"Would the name of the ambulance company help?" she asked.

THEY STOOD ON THE front steps waiting for Mohammed to bring the car around. The boardwalk blocked any view of the ocean, but the scent of salt air was refreshing, sweeping away the odors of age, loneliness, and quiet despair. Despite the bleak news, Ted found his thoughts and mood were already lighter.

Lester wasn't as sanguine. "She's dead, isn't she?"

Ted had already considered the question. "They need her. If our filing leads to a hearing, the judge will demand we produce her in court or show evidence of why we can't. If she's dead, that throws the whole case into probate—which means more delays and the possibility that some third cousin twice removed shows up."

"She might simply disappear."

"Same problem, only the delays would be worse. No, they've got her on ice somewhere."

"I'd say the odds of getting any usable information out of the ambulette company are only slightly better than me getting a scratch-off Win for Life."

"We're going to find her, Lester."

"Or we could spend the next month calling all the elder-care facilities in the tristate region asking if they took in an old lady yesterday. How many do you think there are? Five hundred? A thousand?"

"If we get stuck, we start by calling the top-tier nursing homes first. And then we're going to nail their asses," Ted said.

Lester did not look at him. He stared out at the wind-swept boardwalk. "You believe that? Or are you just wishing it was so?"

"I don't know, but right now it feels pretty good."

"With or without the police?" Lester said, not turning his head.

"I don't know that either. Does it matter?"

Lester finally faced Ted. "When do we get Anora her green card? She's earned it."

Ted grimaced. "I made a promise. I may not yet have a plan, but I am aware I made a promise, and I mean to keep it."

Mohammed came into view, his car slaloming through the half-filled parking lot. Lester frowned. "You ever go to Coney Island when you were a kid? Play on those bumper cars?"

"He's not that bad," Ted said.

"That's not a ringing endorsement."

They walked to the curb. Lester stopped and faced Ted again. "There's still a lot we don't know."

"That's a reasonable synopsis of our situation."

They nodded at each other, both acknowledging how far they yet had to travel—and the costs they might have to pay.

Lester looked away first. "And then there's the immediate question," he said.

"What's that?"

Lester held up the pastry box. "What the hell am I going to do with this cake?"

59

TED LEFT LESTER AT the Afghan dormitory with instructions to call and get whatever he could from Cross County Ambulette Transportation Services. Mohammed made the midmorning trip to the hospital in record time while Ted hid behind the *Daily News*, deliberately not watching their erratic progress. When traffic slowed, Mohammed sometimes created a fourth lane on the highway, squeezing between other vehicles like a daredevil motorcyclist.

Ron Reisner was in the news again, though not on the front page. The sod on the soccer fields, laid a month earlier, had all turned brown and died. Reisner's legal team said that the great man had no comment. The accompanying picture must have been provided by the publicity department for LBC as it showed Reisner in a one-armed buddy hug with the current governor, together showing more smiling white teeth than the C-list red carpet at the SAG Awards. Ted had to admit, the man did not look like someone who bribed public officials; was alleged to have defrauded subcontractors, tenants, and investors; and was also quite likely a party to attempted murder for hire.

Passing through the electronic door, which swept open *Star Trek* fashion at his approach, Ted felt a rush of conflicting emotions. The events of the long night two days previous rushed back at him. His mind had been busy whitewashing fears, a survival mechanism carried over from years of rewriting memories of an abusive alcoholic father. If you don't think about the really bad things, it's like they didn't happen. Almost like.

"Are you all right?" the silver-haired volunteer at the front desk stage-whispered to him as he stood in the entryway, not sure of what he expected to find when he made it to the ICU. Was Kenzie there? If they had moved her, was that a good sign? Suppose she wasn't responding to treatment; would they take her off life support? Had they already? He should have called first. Was bad news easier to take when it came over the phone?

The flip side of the whitewasher. The morbid gloomsayer. Now he was thinking of death.

"Sir?" She sounded concerned for him but conveyed in that single syllable that he was behaving strangely.

"Fine." He nearly strangled on the word. He took a deep breath before continuing. "Is McKenzie Zielinski still in ICU?"

Pleased at having something to do, she smiled and tapped away at the computer before her. "Yes, indeed," she said brightly. Printing out a pass, she gave him detailed, and unnecessary, instructions on how to find the elevator. The sign over her head read ELEVATOR in eight-inch letters followed by a red arrow.

It wasn't until he was riding in the car, each floor announced with an electronic chime at a dirgelike tempo, that another fear, lesser but immediate, bubbled up in the cauldron of his mind.

The chances of running into Kenzie's father at her bedside were rapidly approaching 100 percent. Their first meeting had been a disaster. The man might see him this time and scream for security guards.

The elevator arrived at his destination before Ted had decided on the appropriate opening words.

He slid the pass through the reader at the windowless double doors marked by both a discreet black-on-grey three-letter sign—ICU—and a detailed bullet-pointed warning, printed in a mini font and obviously written by highly paid outside counsel, that cautioned visitors and staff as to what was allowed and forbidden beyond this point. Ted noted that alcoholic beverages made the forbidden list. He could have used a shot of Lester's vodka right about then.

Stepping into the ICU was entering a different world. The overhead lighting was dimmed so that the brightly lit nurse's station looked like a stage set with actors in place awaiting the entrance of the star. Sound was muffled, even more so than elsewhere in the hospital. People did not speak; they murmured or whispered. The only jarring noises were the monitors beeping sharply in counterpoint to the gauzy breathiness of ventilators. The warring scents of medicines, industrial and personal cleansers, and various forms of human waste created a miasma that assaulted the sinuses the moment the doors opened. Ted thought that while you worked there, you must lose all sense of smell, like fast-food workers who could smell only stale grease when they arrived at home.

He waded through this alien land, unconsciously holding his breath in anticipation of bad news. He found it.

The tableau he came upon when he reached her room was devastating. Mrs. Zielinski sat in a chair, her head bowed, murmuring—a prayer?—and holding a ball of tissues. Her husband stood behind her with one hand on her shoulder, his gaze on the peaceful face of his daughter. The ventilator was gone.

Kenzie's hair, though cropped in places, was otherwise long and flowing. Someone—her mother?—had combed it, and it fanned out across the pillow. Kenzie's pale arms were bent, her hands crossed at her chest. She was beautiful and as still as a portrait.

A stab of emotional pain hit Ted in the gut, and for a moment he felt dizzy. He was too late. She was gone. The universe was asking too much of him right then. He needed time to resolve all the thoughts and feelings that were crashing in on him. Time. He had none.

Kenzie's father, possibly sensing Ted's presence, turned his head. He gave a sad smile and spoke. "Come in. Please. I'm glad you're here."

Mrs. Z looked up at Ted and beamed a smile. "She's improving."

In the next few minutes, the two parents filled him in on the morning's developments. The swelling was gone. Though Kenzie had not yet come out of the coma, her vital signs were all good. Brain activity appeared normal. Subdued but normal. They would know more when she woke up. This miracle could happen at any moment. Ted was reeling, attempting to take it all in at once. Impossible. One fact stood out: Kenzie was alive.

"Or it could take longer," Mr. Zielinski said in a half-hearted attempt at tempering his wife's expectations.

She squeezed his hand and went on speaking to Ted. "The doctor was very encouraging."

"And he also said it could be another day or two," Mr. Zielinski said. "Her brain needs to heal, the nurse told us."

The stark warnings of the student nurse, Khalil—the three-day horizon, measured in brain wave activity, ending in death, life as a vegetable, or some horror in between—ran through Ted's mind for what must have been the hundredth time. This time, however, the thoughts broke out of the maddening loop and were gone. Ted could see that the IV was still connected to her arm and the pulse monitor on her right index finger was clasped in place.

A thousand questions burned to be first out of his mouth. "Does she? Is she?" He quashed an urge to yell in exultation. Her continued safety was his first concern. "Will they keep her here? Or do they move her to another ward?"

"No one's said anything about moving her," the mother

said, revealing in her lack of surety that neither she nor her husband had yet considered this question.

Ted thought this a good time to make amends for his last conversation with Mr. Zielinski—and to suggest that their relief at Kenzie's improvement must not sway them from continued vigilance. "Mr. Zielinski, I didn't handle myself very well the first time we met. I tried to bully you—to frighten you."

"You were trying to warn me," Mr. Zielinski said.

"That's kind. And maybe more forgiving than I deserve."

"My wife told me about your visit yesterday. You managed to get her on your side. Let's leave our misunderstandings in the past."

Ted wasn't finished. He needed them both to help keep Kenzie safe. "The danger was real. And that hasn't changed. The police are doing next to nothing. We need to be here for her until she's strong enough to fight her own battles."

"We're ready to listen," Mrs. Zielinski said. Her husband nodded in agreement.

"Then let's make a plan," Ted said.

60

CROSS COUNTY AMBULETTE TRANSPORTATION Services had ceased operating as such two years earlier, according to Lester. Ted had called him while waiting out front at the hospital for Mohammed to return.

"The assets, including four vehicles, were purchased by Auburndale Transport and Limousine, which provides similar services but which is not, surprisingly, located in or anywhere near Auburndale, but in Brighton Beach." Lester paused, expecting a response. "Moscow on the Atlantic, as it is otherwise known."

"Keep talking," Ted said.

"I called them. The lady on the phone spoke with a Russian accent. We didn't get very far."

"What did she say? Anything?"

"She said, 'Nyet.' She said that a lot," Lester said.

"How could she resist your charms?"

"I did learn that they're licensed in New York, Jersey, and Connecticut, which tells us that Barbara Miller is probably not in Boston."

"Or Philadelphia," Ted said.

"What's next?"

"I'm going into the city to stir things up a bit—without getting beat up. It's time I got my ex to face up to a few things. I'll be back later this afternoon."

He had another call to make. To his best man.

"Ted?" Carter said. "My man. It's not my birthday and it's not Christmas, so why is my old friend calling me? Getting married again?"

"Not anytime soon, Carter. What about you?"

"Getting married? Not on your life. I just heard from Petey. Fusco? Getting divorced. I was his best man, too. That makes me three for three. So, what can I do for you? Hey, come to London sometime. It's always raining, the beer's warm, and when you ask for ice in your drink, you get one cube. Otherwise, I love it."

"How about we meet up somewhere warm where the drinks are frozen and the sun shines? I need some information. About a guy."

"Sure, if I can. Who's it?"

"A Russian. Sokol Orlov. Worked at Blandon."

"Oh, yeah. In one word, bad news."

"Why am I not surprised? Do tell."

MOHAMMED HAD FOUND A place to grab an early lunch. Though he'd finished it before returning to pick up Ted, the aroma lingered. Ted had skipped breakfast and was overwhelmed by the cornucopia of scents in the car. Lamb, stewed tomatoes, onions, and a laundry list of spices, some of which he recognized and others, exotic or subtle, which wafted by unnamed.

"What is that I'm smelling?" he groaned.

"*Saltah.*"

"Okay, so that's what it's called. What's in it?"

"Lamb and . . . I don't know what you call it here. Weeds."

The food was gone; only the maddening smell remained. "I want to go to Manhattan."

"Oh, good. I have a brother who went to Manhattan once."

"I HAVE TO CALL up, Mr. Molloy." The doorman recognized him, though it had been a decade since Ted had last passed through this marbled lobby.

"I understand, Osvaldo." Ted would have preferred to appear at Jill's door unannounced. "How's your boy?"

Osvaldo's younger son had obtained a full-ride basketball scholarship to Georgetown. But that had been many years ago.

"He's clerking for a federal judge; thanks for asking. Let me ring Miss Fitzmaurice." Though twice married and in her midthirties, Jill would always be addressed as Miss.

Ted felt uncomfortably at home, as though he could pick up his mail, check for packages, and head directly to the elevators, hitting the button for the sixth floor. Of course he could do none of those things without permission.

"He's got an offer from some big firm," Osvaldo continued while he waited for Jill to answer the phone. "But he wants to work in the DA's office. Hello, Miss Fitzmaurice. I have Mr. Molloy here looking to come up."

There was a long pause as he listened.

"I don't know, miss. Shall I ask him?" He smiled awkwardly at Ted. "She wants to know what you want." He held the receiver up so that Jill could hear his response directly.

"World peace and a solution to climate change," Ted said. "Oh, yes, and about five minutes of her time. Maybe ten. I came all the way from Great Neck."

Osvaldo listened to her response. "Yes, miss." This time his grin was grim. "She says to send you up. And if you're not back down here in fifteen minutes, I'm supposed to call the cops."

"Thank you," Ted said. "And give your son my congratulations. The law is a calling, and I hope it treats him well."

He stepped into the elevator, and before pushing the button, he checked the time. Would Osvaldo really call the police? He would. Fifteen minutes and counting.

There were two apartments per floor, all identically laid out. Jill was waiting at the door to 6A when the elevator doors slid open.

"This had better be good," she said. "We can talk in the living room."

It was no longer his home, and the memories clashed with the changes. The artwork in the entryway, previously three Lichtenstein pop-art prints that they had chosen together, had been replaced by dark line-drawing portraits of unsmiling women. Ted guessed that one was Virginia Woolf, but he could not have said exactly why he thought so. The once-white walls were a soft grey, and the Persian rugs they had purchased through multiple daylong, agonizing sessions at ABC Carpet were gone. They now walked on grey wall-to-wall carpeting a shade or two darker than the walls. The furniture, which had been sprawling, off-white, and built for comfort, was now all black leather with gleaming stainless-steel accents. None of this fit with the Jill he had married. She might have gone along with the changes to expunge any faint remembrances of their past, but the replacements had to have been pushed on her. The sole touch of color was a two-foot-tall glass sculpture on a pedestal in the far corner—a vaguely vaginal shape with streaks of lime green and fuchsia running through it. And spots or dots—black and white specks that gave it visual texture. *Jill had would not have picked that piece*, he thought. It was a gift from Jackie. He hated it.

"A business dinner with clients," she began without explanation or context. "One of whom is a member of the Reisner family. You've heard of them."

Ted understood right away. Their last conversation. He had told Jill to ask Jackie where she had been the night before. "She didn't mention any of the other players?"

"Should she have?"

"There was a city councilman and a banker for the Russian mob."

"I would be in no way surprised that my wife meets with politicians. She was in Albany last week. The firm is giving her new opportunities."

"I repeat—Russian mob."

"You called this person a banker. She met with a politician, a banker, and a real estate developer. That's her job. Once upon a time, you would have been at that table."

Ted couldn't deny it. "She passed a bribe to the councilman's assistant." He'd never been asked to do anything like that. He wanted to think he would have refused.

"I don't believe it," she said. "It was a campaign contribution."

"You're saying it was legit?"

A pair of pigeons landed on the window ledge and began cooing at each other in full throat.

"Oh, God," Jill said, stomping to the window and banging on it with her fist. "Get a room, you two." She turned to Ted. "They make me nuts."

The birds separated and marched to opposite ends of the ledge, muttering unhappily.

"'The course of true love never did run smooth,'" Ted said. "Dick Powell."

"William Shakespeare," she snapped.

"Him too."

The cooing started up again. While Jill had her back to the window, the two feathered lovers had returned to stage center.

"Shit!" Jill unlocked the casement window and tried to turn the ancient crank. The handle didn't move. "Here. You do it." She stepped away and stared at Ted until he rose.

"Okay, but this doesn't count toward my fifteen minutes."

The windows had been installed long before Jill had taken up residence. The mechanism froze up regularly and had to be coaxed into operation. Ted tried the crank. It didn't move. The bigger pigeon—easily identified as the male by his self-adulating poses—strutted the length of the ledge. The female stared at Ted.

"It's going to need some . . . lubrication," Ted said.

Jill didn't respond.

"Really," he said. "Is there any 3-in-One in the house?"

"I wouldn't know."

"How about cooking oil?"

"Olive oil?" she asked, turning and heading for the kitchen.

The male bird tried to mount the female, but with a twitch and a shuffle step right, she unseated him, never taking her eyes off Ted.

"What would you do if I wasn't here?" Ted called to her.

"Wait for Jacqueline to come home!" she yelled.

He waited until she returned with the olive oil. "I think she's in trouble, Jill. Serious trouble. Jail-time trouble."

"Not possible." She handed him two paper towels with the bottle of oil.

"No? Because she's too honest? She's ambitious."

"That's not a crime."

Ted concentrated on the window while he considered his next words. He let a few drops of the oil ooze out onto the mechanism. They promptly ran off the sides and splattered on the sill. He mopped them up with a paper towel and tried again. The female pigeon was engrossed in his project. The male bobbed and cooed, more exaggerated in movement and volume.

Opening remarks. Frame the story for the jury. Lessons learned and never forgotten. He took a deep breath and began.

"Jacqueline Clavette scammed a woman named Barbara Miller out of her property."

"Isn't that what you do?" Jill said. "Scam people out of what's rightfully owed them?"

"The difference is that when someone does a deal with me, they know the split up front, and they can take it or leave it. Your wife robbed an old lady. She was aided in this by one or more judges. She did this so that Ron Reisner and his corporation, LBC, could purchase those lots and build a one-hundred-story mixed-use tower. Reisner wanted those properties so badly that he was willing to overpay by more than one million dollars. Miller wouldn't sell at any price. Are you getting all this?"

He tried turning the handle. With a reluctant groan, it moved a quarter of an inch. The birds flew off. *Progress.*

"Ms. Clavette served LBC's interests in other ways. She helped carry cash to politicians. LBC needed approvals, exemptions, and variances to allow the construction of a high-rise of that size, commanding so much airspace. Local, municipal, and state-level elected officials were involved. All of them needed to be greased. I would guess that when she went to Albany last week, she took an extra suitcase." He looked over his shoulder at Jill. She was listening, but she wasn't giving anything away.

"Conspiracy, fraud, and bribery," he continued. "In the end the crime of conspiracy may be the most egregious. Because with something this big, with so much money being thrown at it, there is going to be some poor hungry soul who sees an opportunity to scoop up a bit of loose cash. Someone basically dishonest but mostly harmless. Someone like Richard Rubiano."

If Jill had ever heard the name before, she covered it well. She didn't blink. He turned back to the window and tried the crank again.

"And the big players can't have that. You let one lonely loser get away with that kind of action, and the whole house of cards could come down. They had to shut him up. Permanently. Oh, and did I mention? The Russian mob is involved."

The handle turned and the window opened.

"I'm talking about murder," he said.

Jill didn't respond.

Ted closed the window, leaving a bit of play in the handle. "There you go. It'll be easier next time."

Jill's face was a blank, but he could see something was

going on behind her eyes. Maybe he was finally getting to her. Getting her to listen.

"I don't think your Jacqueline has any idea about people getting murdered—or roughed up or run down by cars. It's not her style. She tells herself—and maybe you—that she's facilitating campaign contributions. Pay for play. Small change. Nobody cares. And the old lady? She's safer in the home. If she lives to be a hundred and ten, she can't spend all she's got. Jackie did her a favor."

"You should go now," Jill said, speaking in a near whisper.

Ted checked his watch. "Almost. I've got two minutes to go. I can't make this stop, Jill. It's way too late. The police are circling, and when they move, everyone involved will go down as accessory to murder and kidnapping. The fraud, bribery, and white-collar crimes will be gravy. If Jackie talks to me, I will do what I can for her. Not because I care what happens to Ms. Clavette but because I care a lot about what happens to you."

"You stupid, arrogant prick," she began quietly, almost conversationally. "You are talking about the woman I love, and you calmly call her a murderer and think I'm going to take your side. To get the firm to hire you again? Is that it? Get out."

"I came here to help you."

"Get out."

"There's a paper trail." Less than a minute left but he bet that Osvaldo would wait a few minutes before calling, and the police response would take another five minutes or so. He kept going. "There are witnesses. The cops are going to find Barbara Miller, and then it will be all over for Jackie."

"Leave. Now."

"The million in surplus money? Was that her little nest egg? A little something that she put aside for the two of you? Payment for all the dirt she had to wade through?"

"She earned every goddamn penny."

An admission.

And a revelation. "You've known all along, haven't you?" He didn't wait for her denial. "Hate me if you have to, but please tell her to go to the cops. It's her only chance at this point."

"You are all so stupid," Jill said.

"I see it. The firm was never going to give Jacqueline Clavette a shot, no matter who she was married to—so she took it. She made it happen." Another thought hit him. "And she kept records. Every meeting. Didn't she? She was ready to take them all down if they tried to ditch her. Your father, Reisner, that fat Russian, the damn governor, if she had to. She was smarter than all of them."

Or so she thought. "Oh, shit." Ted was nearly struck dumb. "Do they know?"

"The police will be on their way," she said.

"She can't let them know, Jill. They'll kill her if they figure it out."

She moved past him and opened the door.

He stopped in the doorway. "Tell her. They've killed once. They've tried to kill a second time."

She swung the door hard, forcing him to step back. He heard the lock click into place.

61

TED HIT THE BUTTON for the basement and begged the cosmos for a tiny bit of luck. The cosmos came through. The elevator continued past the first floor without stopping.

Jill possessed a tribal loyalty that came with a specified set of ethics. Family was all. Jackie was included in this pact—as long as she was no threat to the inner circle. He should have expected Jill to respond exactly as she had.

As he stepped off the elevator, tubes of fluorescent lights automatically sputtered to life as he stepped out into the laundry room. A single red bulb over a door on the far side of the room marked the exit to the back alley. He hit the push bar, and the metal door flew open, accompanied by a buzzing noise. A muted alarm, loud enough to notify the staff but discreet enough that no tenant would be disturbed.

He was in back of the building, facing the basement door of the adjoining building. Empty trash cans lined both sides of the alley. To his left was a tall fence, topped with razor wire. To his right, a concrete ramp led up to a metal gate and the side street. He ran.

The gate, of course, was locked, and it fit too well in its frame for him to squeeze over or under. He was trapped.

He rejected the thought of hiding in a garbage can. The odds of getting away with it were infinitesimal, and the thought of being found there was unbearable. He walked to the door and waited for the forces of law and order.

A moment later the metal door banged open again, and Osvaldo showed his head. "You there, Mr. Molloy?" He let the door swing to behind him. "I had to call. Sorry about that."

"Where are they?"

"I sent them up to Miss Fitzmaurice's apartment. Come with me. I'll let you out." He took a nest of keys from his belt and led Ted to the gate. "On your way, sir."

Ted thanked him. "And best of luck to your son." He fought the urge to run and instead walked confidently out onto the street with the air of one who belonged on the Upper East Side of Manhattan. Not one but two police cruisers stood in front of the entrance to Jill's building. Ted walked in the other direction, expecting an authoritative voice to hail him at any second. A familiar car sat idling at the curb, partially blocking a fire hydrant.

"Hey, boss," Mohammed said. "We go back to Queens now?"

62

MRS. ZIELINSKI PLAYED SCRABBLE like a gladiator. There could be only one winner, and that player could be crowned only when everyone else was dead. Ted was down to six unusable tiles when she placed an *X* in front of an unguarded *I* and announced that this was a letter in the Greek alphabet. Ted challenged. She told him that it was also the proper title for the fourteenth star in a given constellation. Ted accepted defeat with as much grace as his demolished ego allowed, proud of his sole double-score word—"MALARKEY," which had linked the *M* in her "EMPATHY" with the "KEY" he had inserted on his previous turn. When it was over, her score was in the mid six hundreds, while his had barely made it out of double digits.

He checked his watch. *Ten till midnight.* The nurses were preparing for the shift change. He'd been there since eight, Kenzie's mother since four. Her father was returning at 4 A.M., and Lester was due at noon. In staggered shifts, they had her covered twenty-four hours a day.

"Not enough time for a rematch," Ted said.

She laughed, quite pleased with her win. "Not that you want one."

"No," he admitted. "I can handle losing, but it's more difficult when the final result is obvious so early in the game."

She slid the tiles into the case. "Will you be all right?" She was not referring to his bruised ego.

"Me? You have my word. And I will call if there's any change. You two need some rest."

Kenzie was no longer sedated, but the doctors wanted her to awaken on her own. The swelling was down, the emergency over. Now it was a matter of waiting. And hoping.

"Do you have something to read?" Mrs. Zielinski asked. "Can I get you anything before I go?"

Ted had to smile. Being mothered was an unusual sensation and not unpleasant. "I'm fine. There's a *Law & Order* marathon that goes until six A.M., and there's coffee at the nurses' station." *And a security guard on the floor all night,* he thought.

Giving him one last brave smile, Mrs. Z gathered her things and left Ted alone with her daughter.

Kenzie was breathing on her own, and most of the monitors had been removed. The blood pressure machine made sounds periodically as the armband inflated. Greevey and Logan investigated a Wall Street banker. Ted watched until the alert on Kenzie's saline drip went off. The bag was empty. A moment later a serious-faced nurse bustled in and changed it.

"She's doing fine. You might want to order her breakfast," she said, placing a menu on the bed table. "She'll be hungry."

Prediction or prognosis? Either way he was encouraged.

Ted looked at the menu. Pancakes or scrambled eggs. Powdered, institutionalized, and barely qualifying as food. Maybe he'd run out and get her a bagel.

The nurse stopped at the door and whispered to him, "Get her the pancakes. The eggs are awful."

Ben Stone gave a devastating summation to the jury, which left Ted wondering once again at Michael Moriarty's ability to pack passion into such a laid-back delivery. The screen jumped to an ad for senior scooters. He hit the MUTE button and went out for a coffee. He knew what the jury was going to do.

The pot held a half inch of black goo. Ted went through the cabinets and found a box of filters, but the can of Bustelo in the dorm-sized refrigerator contained nothing but a light coating of dark brown dust. He left it open on the counter and walked down to the snack and beverage machines.

Salt or sugar. Pick your poison. He surrendered two dollars and was rewarded with a twenty-ounce bottle of Mountain Dew and two quarters. The Fig Newtons whispered his name, but he put his money away and took a walk along the corridor to stretch out the kinks in his back. He wasn't tired and didn't need the caffeine—yet. The soda bottle slid into his jacket pocket for later.

The double door at the end of the hall was operated by an electronic release. Anyone who wanted to enter had to either swipe a pass or be buzzed in by a nurse, who could monitor the situation via closed-circuit television. As an added precaution, and at the Zielinskis' request, a guard was on duty, sitting on a folding chair inside the door. Only he wasn't.

Ted walked quickly to the station. "Excuse me." He didn't wait for any of the people on duty to take notice. "The guard is not there. Does anyone know what's going on?"

The women all ignored him. A male nurse looked up. "All security personnel were called down to the ER to handle a situation. He'll be back as soon as things downstairs are under control."

Ted was not reassured. "What kind of situation?"

The nurse shook his head and continued typing. He didn't know, didn't care, or didn't care to be questioned about it—or all three. Ted didn't like it. Anything out of the ordinary would have put him on the alert. A missing security guard was a screaming siren with blue and red strobe lights.

"Can you let me know if anyone tries to come in while the guard is gone?"

That got the attention of one woman. Her eyebrows met in the universal expression for *What are you talking about?*

"I know I sound paranoid, but I'd feel better if you went along with me on this," Ted said.

"Not a problem." She smiled once in dismissal and returned to her work.

Ted stood in the corridor watching the doors long enough to feel a bit pathetic. He was being paranoid. The only other visitor on the floor was the mother of a young man who'd been in an auto accident. She was asleep, despite the purposely designed discomfort of the easy chair in which she was sprawled. There was the right idea. Ted needed to relax. *The guard might be missing, but the perimeter is safe. Time to chill.* He returned to Kenzie's room.

A cleaning cart was blocking the entry, keeping the room's sliding glass door from automatically closing. The soothing twilight of the room instantly became dark and menacing. Ted pushed the cart away and stopped in midstride.

The man had his back to Ted and was wearing the one-piece dark green overalls that Ted had seen on all the cleaning staff. But the rest of the picture made no sense. Ted registered that the man was broad shouldered and tall and moved like a predator. And he was doing something with the saline bag hanging over Kenzie's bed.

63

"HEY!" TED YELLED, INSTANTLY regretting it. The man had not known Ted was there, and he whirled around and went into a fighter's crouch. Whatever benefit of surprise Ted might have had was gone. "What are you doing?" Ted demanded, putting as much authority into his voice as he could summon at that late hour.

It was the Russian. The man with the nose of a boxer. He rushed forward, stopping suddenly and swinging his leg in a roundhouse kick aimed at Ted's thigh, a blow that could have ended the altercation immediately.

But Ted reacted. He fell backward, landing on his hands bent kneed. The kick passed over him, and Ted pushed up onto his feet. In the split second that the Russian needed to rebalance from the kick, Ted closed on him, coming in low.

The guy recovered quickly and landed two left-handed jabs on Ted's head before Ted connected. Ted grabbed the man around his thighs and pushed forward with his shoulder. They crashed into the cleaning cart before both tumbled to the ground.

Having lost his fleeting advantage, Ted rolled away and up onto his feet. The Russian also came up quickly. In the moment before the next attack, Ted saw why the man seemed to be fighting one-handed. In his right hand, he held a large syringe with a needle that looked as big as a pencil.

He had been about to inject something into Kenzie's saline bag—into her IV. The realization distracted Ted. The Russian saw this and moved in. He threw three quick jabs, which Ted easily deflected, but they left him off-balance. He had too much weight on his back foot, and when the next kick came up, he couldn't move fast enough to avoid it. It caught him in the side, just above his waist. Ted felt himself falling and grabbed the man's leg as he went down. It was a sloppy defense. Never close with an opponent unless you control the action. They hit the floor together. The Russian was on top.

People had noticed. A nurse screamed. A deep-voiced man was yelling orders, but Ted ignored him. A flashing red light spun on the hallway ceiling, sending shafts of blood-colored shadows across the Russian's straining face. He may have been on top, but he did not control the action either. He was protecting the syringe while attempting to choke Ted with his free hand.

Ted bucked hard and then brought his legs up into the air. When the Russian reared to regain his balance, Ted locked his calves around the man's head and rolled to the side. They slammed into the cart again, sending it sliding out into the hallway, where it crashed and fell over. More screams.

The fight had none of the grace and elegance Ted had brought to the sport of wrestling seventeen years earlier. He was out of shape, out of practice, and outmatched. And the stakes were deadly serious. Already he could feel his energy flagging, his muscles complaining and straining, his side aching where the kick had landed.

They were flailing at each other, their punches without weight or leverage. Neither was willing to break away and risk having the other take advantage of his retreat, and so they scrambled, pushed, deflected, and hit wildly and with no effect.

Then Ted felt a searing blow land on his shoulder, both a thump and a sting. He gasped in pain and terror—what in hell was in that syringe?—but for the briefest moment, his adversary's neck was open, unguarded. Ted grabbed the Russian around the throat and squeezed. The man thrashed, for the first time showing fear, and swung his right arm in a wide arc, smacking Ted in the temple. Without the encumbrance of the syringe, he was able to inflict real pain even at those close quarters.

Ted felt another blow land and another, the last directly on his ear. He lost his grip on the man's neck and felt himself sliding away. The fight was all but over. He was losing. He drew back his hand, formed a fist, and drove it down with all of his remaining strength into the man's Adam's apple. Something broke.

Hands gripped him from behind and pulled him away. He looked over his shoulder. Uniformed security guards were filling the room, subduing both men with weight and numbers.

64

TED TRIED TO PULL free of the guards holding him, but his muscles failed to respond.

"The thing!" he yelled, various body signals announcing he was beginning to panic. The word for the medical device used for injecting liquids through a needle had been wiped from his mind.

The thug was making noise—cursing in a strangled chicken squawk and demanding to be allowed to leave, though he repeatedly hawked up globs of thick blood. The tall male nurse ventured closer in an attempt to examine the Russian's neck and earned a glancing kick to the side of his head for his trouble. The Russian croaked sounds that could not have been words and threw flailing punches. His eyes were dazed and unfocused, but he was still dangerous. The security detail backed off and let the police take over. In seconds he was facedown on the floor, his hands cuffed behind him. He kept on screaming in that hideous animal cry.

"He's Russian," Ted tried to explain to the police, believing that this simple fact would explain so much of what had happened.

"Syringe!" Ted yelled the second the word came to him.

A nurse found it tossed into a corner and held it up. It was broken. Ted gasped and tried to remember why this was important.

Two blue uniformed men took over from the security guards. They sat him in a chair. Nurses, both male and female, were shouting at one another. Ted tried to focus on relaying facts to the cops. Facts had become slippery, sliding through his fingers as he grasped at them.

The police listened to Ted's story. The broken syringe and the puffy injection mark in his shoulder lent some credence to an otherwise unlikely story.

"I don't feel well," he said. "I need a doctor." He was enormously proud of himself for getting those thoughts out. Forming sentences was a chore. He was tired. Exhausted. And at the same time, he felt on the verge of a panic attack, starting at sudden sounds and riding a whiplash of emotions. As he listened to himself explaining why he had attacked the man in Kenzie's room, he heard only the gaps and leaps in logic. And he couldn't seem to care. His voice tapered off and he went silent.

The head nurse and the police finally negotiated a settlement whereby the Russian, under guard, was delivered downstairs to the ER. The cops abandoned Ted in the ICU while the staff worked to determine what unknown substance had been injected into him.

Ted found their discussion increasingly difficult to follow, a fact that should have bothered him a lot more than it did. His world was inundated with gauzy cotton balls that blurred his vision, blocked his hearing, and sapped his energy. Minutes before, he had been wide awake. Now he wanted only to lie down.

"Can you tell us how you're feeling, Mr. Molloy?" The male nurse's eyes were filled with anxiety. Ted's anxiety spiked again.

"Is she okay?" Ted asked. He had some trouble putting the question into words.

"What did he say?" A woman's voice.

"I didn't get it. What's his heart rate now?"

"Soaring." Another nurse's voice.

"Jesus, he's sweating buckets. Where's Dr. Cox?"

"On her way."

Ted couldn't keep the voices straight. He felt as if he had

dropped off to sleep for a moment and couldn't remember or understand anything that was being said—only it kept happening, over and over. Each second was a newly erased blackboard, and the squiggles and lines that appeared made no sense.

"Whoa. Hold him. What is he doing?"

Ted realized he was lying down. Had he just been standing? Why were they all yelling? Faces swirled above him, blurred and indistinct, then suddenly hyperfocused and enlarged as though seen through a glass bubble.

"He's going into shock. Hey! Mr. Molloy! Stay with me!" It was the male nurse speaking. Yelling, actually.

"It's a stroke," another voice said, the speaker quite sure of her instant diagnosis.

One more voice chimed in. "Hypoglycemic shock. Is he diabetic? He needs sugar. Anything sweet."

Ted's field of vision was shrinking—or the kindly face of the male nurse was expanding dramatically.

"Drink this. Come on."

The man gently lifted Ted's head and forced a plastic cup to his mouth. Warm, watery apple juice. Ted spat it out in an explosive spray of pale gold liquid.

"Goddammit." The kind-faced man had been replaced by a stern woman. "What's that?" She tore the Mountain Dew out of his pocket and twisted the cap. Another spray— florescent green this time. Ted wasn't sure he wanted any right then, but the nurse had become very insistent. It was easier to go along than to fight her off.

And he was surprised at how thirsty he had become. He gulped down the cupful of soda. Someone poured him another. He didn't really like Mountain Dew. Did they have a . . . ? What was it called? The brown one.

"Root beer," he said.

"What'd he say?"

"God knows. 'Super,' maybe?"

"Good. Keep feeding him the soda. Somebody get another."

"Where the hell is the doctor?" a particularly upset voice screeched.

"On her way," a new voice replied from very far away.

Other people arrived and crowded around. Ted heard snatches of the conversation. Two women may have been arguing. The word "insulin" was repeated more than a few times. He was beginning to feel a touch more alert, better able to connect with the world, so he explained that the man he had fought with had punched him outside the elevator at the courthouse. He wasn't sure why it was important to impart this information at that moment, but he wanted to help. But the words didn't flow as easily as he imagined them coming out. His tongue seemed to have quadrupled in size and developed a primitive yet independent mind of its own.

"I'm Dr. Cox. You're going to be okay, Mr. Molloy." The speaker was a glossy-skinned woman with long thick hair the color of ebony. She was very young.

"I got shot," he said. *No, not shot. Something else. Another word.* It didn't matter. Did it?

"We think you were injected with insulin, but we don't know how much. The effects may last some time as it works through your system, but the needle did not pierce any major blood vessels. A subcutaneous dose is rarely fatal."

Rarely. He would have been alarmed, but he was finding that he didn't care. Everything seemed pointless.

The head nurse pushed her way to his side. "Here. Hard candy. Jolly Ranchers. Keep it in your mouth. Don't swallow it."

"He won't like it," said a woman's priggish voice from the back of the crowd.

"Fig Newton," he said. He hadn't eaten one in decades, but right then it was the most important thing in the universe.

"What did he say?"

"Here. Here." The nurse forced a candy through his lips.

Grape. He hated grape. He opened his mouth and let the candy fall out. He needed to get that awful taste out of his mouth. He asked for more soda.

"I'm sorry. I don't understand what you're saying." It was the woman with the nice hair. She sounded nice. But she was too young to be a doctor. "Drink this and you'll feel better soon." The cup came up to his mouth, and he gulped down another eight ounces of Mountain Dew. "Can you eat?"

"No. Please. No." Ted did not want any more grape disasters forced into his mouth.

"So? Was it a stroke?" Another new voice. Male. Older. The man's breath smelled of cigarettes and coffee.

"No. Insulin shock. Can I ask you to stand back, please?"

The nice male nurse spoke again. "A lollipop would be perfect."

The sugar in the soda was kicking in. Ted was beginning to make sense of the voices and what they were saying. He decided that he was going to live. Now was the time to convince the crowd hovering over him. "No more fucking candy!" he yelled. The words were crystal clear and met with two beats of silence.

"I told you not to give him candy," the hidden woman's voice chimed in.

The male nurse helped Ted to his feet and guided him to a bed. Ted sat on the edge and stared at the doctor, who seemed to be waiting for him to do something interesting. The world was moving much too fast—then too slow. His bodily chemistry was all askew. As clarity returned, it came with a frenetic rush of desperate energy. Changes came in waves less than seconds apart. As the adrenaline wore off, the caffeine from the soda began to give him a headache and caused an annoying buzz that left him cranky and ready to argue—about anything. And he was hungry. Monstrously hungry. He craved water and lusted for a Gallagher's cheeseburger. Or that stew Mohammed had been eating.

"Can I get any real food?" he asked.

Shortly, a prepackaged sandwich appeared in front of him. Tuna salad—that tasted mostly of chopped raw onion—on a soggy white roll. It was heavenly. He devoured it in four bites and promptly fell asleep.

65

HE WOKE MUCH LATER, temporarily confounded to find himself in a private room in the ICU. His bladder felt as if it were the size of a basketball. He pulled himself out of bed and rushed to the bathroom, where he pissed a jet-propelled stream for the next few minutes. Catching sight of himself in the mirror as he washed his hands, he almost didn't recognize the much older man staring back at him. He splashed cold water on the original until the reflection appeared awake. It was time to reengage with the world.

He drifted out to the nurses' station. "Is she awake yet?" he asked the nurse closest to him.

"Who?" She looked up, obviously surprised to find Ted on his feet and leaning over the counter. "You should be lying down."

"My fiancée. McKenzie Zielinski." Maintaining the persona seemed more important than ever.

"She's fine. Asleep. Now get yourself into that bed."

"Sleeping? Or . . ." His voice trailed off.

That earned him a sad smile and a touch of empathy. "She hasn't awakened yet, but we're all confident that it's just a matter of time. You saved her life, you know?"

He hadn't known. She explained. If he'd shown up a couple of minutes later, the Russian would have been done and out the door. A hefty shot of insulin into the IV, and Kenzie would have slid into a diabetic coma. The machines wouldn't have recognized the difference. She'd just never have woken up.

"And insulin wouldn't show up on a tox screen," she added.

A perfect murder, Ted thought. "Can I see her?"

"She's not leaving. Get your butt in bed. And by the way, there are two policemen waiting to talk to you."

"Are they here?"

"I'll tell them you're awake." She stood and took two steps toward the door.

"Wait," he almost yelled. "The guy who attacked me. How is he?"

"Sorry. I have no idea."

He turned back and was, for a moment, disoriented. Which room was his? He shuffled along, peeking in doors until he found an empty rumpled bed that had a familiar look. A clear plastic bag was hanging from the bed frame. He was wearing a hospital gown with his suit pants and socks, but there were the rest of his things. His shirt had been bloodied, but his wrinkled jacket looked salvageable, despite the small tear in the upper arm. He located his cell phone and wallet. He could communicate and provide evidence of his existence. Things were looking up.

He turned on the phone and found four missed calls. Three from Lester. One from Jill. He hit the CALL-BACK button as two uniformed policemen entered the room. He disconnected and shoved the phone in his pants pocket.

"How are you feeling, sir?" the older of the two asked.

"Good." Ted was surprised to find that this was the truth. He had not slept enough, and he ached in certain areas that had taken the brunt of the abuse the night before, but overall he felt ready to tackle another murderous Eastern European if need be.

"We have orders to keep you here until you've been interviewed by the detectives on this case," the officer said.

"Am I under arrest?"

"Not at this time. Make yourself comfortable and I will give them a call."

Ted wasn't surprised. He would need to make a statement. He imagined that the nurses and other staff would back up his story. Waiting was an annoyance but nothing more.

The phone buzzed as he was about to dial. Lester.

"I thought I might have heard from you by now." Lester's voice had lost the slushy quality.

"Kenzie is asleep, but they keep telling me she's going to be okay."

"Do you believe them?"

"Yes and no. Mostly yes. I couldn't call, because there was some excitement here last night. One of the Corona Partners showed up."

Lester made appropriate sounds as Ted spun the story of the night's events. "The nurse told me I saved her life," Ted said. "I haven't really grasped that as yet. The whole night was like a bad dream, and I'm not fully awake."

"But you're all right?"

"Yeah. I didn't get much of a dose."

"Are you going to stay and keep watch over her?"

"I don't know. The police want to talk to me."

THE TWO SUITED COPS who entered the room were all too familiar to him. Duran and the pit bull partner. Ted was immediately on guard.

"I wasn't expecting to see you," he said. Nassau County had jurisdiction there. The NYPD hadn't sent two detectives to investigate a scuffle in the hospital.

"Who else?" Kasabian said. "The Lone Ranger and Tonto?"

"No, but not Fred and Barney either," Ted said.

"You should get dressed," Duran said. "Your doctor tells us you're okay to leave."

"I'd rather hear it directly from her."

"That can be arranged," Duran said. "Meantime, get dressed. You're coming with us."

"What's happening with the other guy?" Ted asked. "Are you going to pick him up, too?"

"The Russian? Not my case. You'll have to ask Nassau County."

"Is he still in the ER?"

"Not a clue. Now get your clothes on."

"Am I under arrest?"

"That, too, can be arranged. It would be easier on you if you volunteered to come with us to answer some questions."

"I want to check on my friend before I go anywhere."

Duran checked his watch before answering. "Three minutes. Starting now."

Ted swung his legs to the floor. "I'll have my lawyer meet us there."

66

THE QUEENS COUNTY CRIMINAL Court was located on an island surrounded by highways and looked like a beached iceberg. If a criminal had any desire to escape, the bleak scene outside would convince them to surrender themself to the judicial system.

Mervyn Prestwick had a voice like an organ. When in court, he used it like a one-man orchestra, allowing a hint of his Jamaican antecedents to add color to his delivery—juries loved it. Ted had counted him as a friend in law school, and they had attended each other's weddings, but as their career paths diverged, they saw less of each other. Mervyn had spent six years in the Bronx DA's office before switching to "the dark side" and becoming a successful criminal defense attorney. He was Ted's first and only call.

Mervyn brought Ted a fresh shirt and a toothbrush.

"My client has agreed to talk to you, solely to prevent a great miscarriage of justice," he began when all the players were in place in the third-floor conference room. "But before he says a word, I need to know why we are here. Are you really prepared to move forward with these charges? Your detective"—Mervyn nodded in Kasabian's direction—"mentioned murder for hire, among other things. Is he serious? What evidence do you have that my client is involved in anything like this?"

"Let's go easy on the speeches, Merv." The ADA was an abrasive man named Petronelli. Ted didn't know him, but he recognized immediately that the ADA came from the same streets as Ted and Mervyn. He tended to apply sarcasm to every other word, a pose recognized by anyone who grew up in Queens—the Jersey defense. "Right now we are having a conversation. If we hear the right words, there is no need for this to go any further."

"Then what have you got?" Ted tossed back. He was prepared to cooperate—to a reasonable extent. Now it was time for the great wheels of justice to make some headway in his direction. The puke-green walls of the interview room were interfering with his recovery. Fainting was a possibility. Barfing on the table was a high probability.

Petronelli flashed him a smile. It wasn't meant to be friendly. "We had a visit from a Cheryl Rubiano first thing this morning. You know the woman?"

Ted didn't reply. It wasn't really a question.

"You are, in fact, intimately familiar with her, are you not?" He removed his glasses and massaged the bridge of his nose as he talked. The gesture hid his eyes. "According to the story she and her lawyer presented, you two had a brief, but heated, affair. The husband, who did odd jobs for you, blamed her and moved out. She was devastated, broke it off with you, and begged the old man to come home."

Ted's blood pressure spiked, and a world-class headache took up residence in his temples.

"You didn't like getting the brush-off. When Mr. Rubiano turned up dead, she confronted you and you steadfastly refused to deny any involvement. And you intimated that if she didn't play along, you were prepared to go to the police and put the blame solely on her. How'm I doing, Mr. Molloy? Is there any of this that you're willing to confirm?"

"My client has nothing to say at this time," Mervyn said.

Ted disagreed. He was ready to scream. But he let Petronelli continue.

"Mrs. Rubiano was frightened. She tried to buy you off. You took the money, but then later you showed up at her apartment looking to get your dick wet. She wasn't interested.

You threatened. She was frightened, so she performed oral sex on you. That's rape."

"This is all such bullshit!" Ted yelled. His headache improved the moment the words came out of his mouth. "Total crap."

Mervyn tapped the back of Ted's hand. "My client should speak only when I grant him permission, but he does raise a good question. Do you believe all this crap?"

Duran's face showed nothing during the recitation. Kasabian smirked at the sexual references but otherwise maintained a stoic Marlboro Man demeanor. Ted thought they were both too smart to have bought into this story.

Petronelli, on the other hand, didn't need to believe. He needed a story he could sell to a jury, and he thought he had it. He put the glasses on again and looked at Ted. "Maybe not all of it. I want to hear your side. I'd like to hear that Cheryl with the hair up to here orchestrated the whole deal. There was something off about her approach. Did she try to hire you to do the deed? Maybe you turned her down. Maybe you didn't."

There remained two one-hundred-dollar bills in an envelope in Ted's jacket. They would have Cheryl's prints on them, he was sure.

"What are you offering?" Mervyn asked.

Ted couldn't help himself. He gave his lawyer a hard, glowering look. The alternative story was as unbelievable as the first. Why was Mervyn opening negotiations?

"How do I know until I hear his story?" the ADA said.

Ted had no story. At least, nothing that would match the epic fictions he had just heard.

"Cooperating witness," Mervyn said.

"Of course," Petronelli answered. It cost him nothing.

"Remand," Mervyn said.

"Come on, I can't let a murderer out on bail," the ADA said.

"He didn't do it."

"That's his whole story?" Petronelli didn't like it. "I thought we were talking here."

"That's not my story," Ted blurted, unable to keep his temper in check any longer. "It's the truth."

Mervyn made a deep sound somewhere between a hum and a growl, loud enough to cut Ted off. "I'd like a few minutes alone with my client," he said into the ensuing silence.

Magic words. Petronelli and the two detectives stood and left the room. Kasabian was last out the door, and he paused there, looked at Ted, and grinned like a man who was about to carve up the holiday turkey. "Gotcha," he said softly.

"What are you doing?" Ted said the moment the door swung shut.

"They want this Cheryl person," Mervyn said. "That gives you leverage. Let me do my job."

"It's only worth something if I'm guilty."

"You're in my world now, Ted. It's not the same as the corporate legal world." Mervyn sounded both firm and sympathetic, as though imparting these realities was a sad duty he had to perform too often. "Petronelli wants you for the murder. He's not alone. You saw that cop. He's got you in his sights, and you are going down. If you tell me to fight this, I will. But as your legal advisor here, I am telling you that you are making a big mistake. Right now I can get you a deal. But if you don't appear to be cooperating, they'll do an end run around you, and your next stop will be Rikers Island."

"The story is all wrong." The words tumbled out faster than his brain could order them. "Someone put her up to this. They're leaning on her hard. Which means they're scared. If we push back, they'll bail. It's a distraction."

"Slow down. And hold off on the grand conspiracies. Just give me a simple story that I can sell."

"My bet? The Russians did Richie. The slick one practically admitted it the first time I met him. On the steps after the foreclosure auctions. Richie was following the paper trail on those stolen properties, and he ran into Corona Partners. And they killed him."

Mervyn shook his big head sadly. "Petronelli isn't going to buy that without proof."

Ted had a thought. Pieces of this puzzle fell into place. "They might already have the proof. Let me ask Detective Duran a couple of questions."

"You should let me do the asking."

That wouldn't work. The detective would never open up to a defense attorney. "No. Duran's all right. I can talk to him. Two minutes. Alone."

"You are paying me for my advice. You should take it."

Ted nodded in agreement but plunged ahead anyway. "I need an ally in their camp or I'm done. I know it's a risk, but it's my choice."

"This is not how I learned this in law school," Mervyn said. But he stood and went out the door.

Minutes passed and then the door opened again. It was Duran.

"Make it quick, Mr. Molloy. Nobody out there is happy about this." He took Petronelli's seat directly across the table from Ted.

"I've got a couple of questions for you," Ted said.

"I don't know if I can answer. You have now officially graduated from person of interest to suspect."

Again. Ted didn't feel as if he'd been promoted. "You told me you were working an alternative theory of the case. Is this it?"

"You know I can't tell you that," Duran said.

"I'll take that as a no. Cheryl didn't come up with this story until today."

"No comment. Any other questions?"

"This is an easy one. Where'd you find Richie's body?"

"Douglaston." Duran bit the word out. He wasn't happy about sharing info with the suspect.

"I mean, was he lying on the street? Tossed in a dumpster?"

There was a long pause before he answered. Ted could see him wrestling with his own sense of caution, and finally, Ted saw the detective make his decision. "He was behind a restaurant down by Alley Pond. Lying in the reeds at the back of the lot. Some doctor from Great Neck was parking his Mercedes where it wouldn't get scraped. He saw the body and made the call."

"Thanks." Ted felt embarrassed that he had never even thought to ask the question before.

"That's it? You could've found that out reading the *Daily News*."

"Let me start over. What I want to know is, What did he have with him?"

"On him? Wallet, keys, a few bucks. Not much."

"A backpack," Ted said. "He always carried a black backpack."

"Yeah, we found one at the scene. But there was nothing there. Copies of court papers. We looked at them, but there was no reason to think they had any bearing on his case."

"A standard foreclosure for unpaid water and taxes." Ted did not make it a question. He barely waited for confirmation.

"Right," Duran said.

"Do you still have it?"

"The bag? I'm sure. It was booked. But if you're looking for any clues there, you should keep looking."

"And the papers?"

"Also booked. We throw nothing away. But we looked at them, Molloy. There was nothing there."

Ted was exultant but kept his expression neutral. There would be time enough to celebrate when this was done. "Those files tie Richie Rubiano to Reisner, LBC, the tower, and the damn Russians. You've heard most of this before, but let me walk you through the updated version. Reisner needed Barbara Miller's properties to put the tower project together. One of his lawyers—Jacqueline Clavette—arranged to have herself appointed by a judge to be the old lady's caretaker. I can't prove that, because I don't have subpoena power. Your people do. Clavette stopped paying taxes on the lots that Reisner wanted."

Ted could feel that Duran's patience was flagging. The detective had heard all this before.

"Bear with me. I would bet you'll find proof of that in Richie's files in the backpack. The lots went to auction and, through a couple of cutouts connected to the Russian mob, ended up in Reisner's hands. Richie dug up enough dirt to figure out the rest. Maybe he thought he could get Reisner to pay him off. Or maybe he just blundered into it and got too close to the truth. Either way he became a problem. The Russians killed him. Meanwhile, this same lawyer is Reisner's bagman, paying politicians for little favors, like air rights and other variances he needs for the tower project. Let me look at those papers, and I'll walk you through it."

Duran was now listening. He wasn't fighting it; he was hooked. He had heard the tale before but never with the possibility of real proof. Ted was beginning to reel him in. "I still need the old lady," Duran said.

"Barbara Miller was taken—by the Russians, damn it—and moved, most likely to another nursing home. They did this so she couldn't point the finger. But I would bet they didn't take her far. It would take me weeks to find her, but the NYPD could do it in minutes. With those files and Miller's testimony, you've got a case."

"Why didn't you give me the lawyer's name before?"

"It's personal. I owed a favor."

"And what? Now it's paid?"

"They tried to kill my friend. Twice. That cleans the slate."

"But why?" There may have been a hint of sympathy in his voice. "Why was Zielinski a threat?"

Ted had been turning this over and could only guess. But he believed it was a good guess. "It's the fat Russian. Slobovich or whatever his name is. He recognized her even with the disguise. He had to be spooked. Kenzie was getting too close. If she put all the pieces together, she could go public. The deal would be dead. And fat boy would have to explain to his daddy why he'd screwed up again. I made a call to a pal in London. Orlov didn't resign from that bank. He was fired for money laundering. It cost his old man seventy million pounds to keep the kid out of jail."

If Duran was at all surprised, he didn't show it. "That's verifiable?"

"I would think so. My source said it's common knowledge."

Duran kept his poker face, but he was nodding. He saw the whole picture. Ted had his ally.

The door opened. No one knocked or announced themself. ADA Petronelli came in looking as if he'd bitten into a bulb of raw garlic. He was immediately followed by a tough-looking couple, a man and a woman both dressed in jeans, lace-up boots, and dark windbreakers. The man had the close-cropped, fresh-from-his-workout look of a Navy SEAL or a member of Delta Force. A guy you wouldn't want to have upset with you. The woman looked tougher. Mervyn came in last, missing his usual bombast and radiant confidence. His expression was worried.

Petronelli cleared his throat before reluctantly delivering a short speech. "I've had a call from the federal prosecutor's office, Mr. Molloy. You are no longer my problem. We're to hand you over to these US Marshals."

67

"CALL LESTER YOUNG MCKINLEY," Ted said to Duran as the marshals approached him. He checked his phone and rattled off the number. "He's good with the details and Miller trusts him."

Mervyn was working his phone, trying to get hold of a federal prosecutor he knew at the Eastern District. "I'll find you," he said, but his eyes said he didn't have a lot of hope for an immediate resolution.

The marshals pretended to be patient while Petronelli pretended to read their warrant. He'd been trumped and hated it. He finished playing with the document and thrust it at Mervyn, who scanned it quickly and shrugged.

"Call me when you can," Mervyn said. "I'm standing by."

The woman handcuffed Ted, patted him down, but left him his wallet and cell phone. Then the two led him out of the interview room and through the maze of offices to the elevators. Neither one spoke to him.

"Does either of you want to tell me where we're going?" Ted said, breaking the silence once they were all in a car—a monstrous SUV equipped with ringbolts on the floor, which Ted assumed were there so prisoners could be shackled in place. Apparently he did not represent enough of a risk.

The woman drove. The man watched Ted in a mirror on the sun visor. Neither one answered him at first. Just before pulling out into traffic, the woman caught his eye in the rearview mirror. "MDC Brooklyn," she said.

THE METROPOLITAN DETENTION CENTER, Brooklyn, was famous for all the wrong reasons. It was the short-term jail for the federal justice system in the Eastern District, a warehouse for all levels of alleged criminals. From drug lords and made men to white-collar suburbanites and tax evaders, all were waiting to be arraigned or, without bail, awaiting trial. Some waited years. Ted had never been there, but every lawyer had heard the stories. It was a vile, smelly, violent holding pen—one of the worst in the system. Stabbings, sexual assaults, and suicides were normal.

They were inching along the LIE when a cell phone rang from the front seat. The man answered. He listened for a minute, twice saying the words "Yes, sir."

"Change in plans," he said to the driver. "We're to deliver him into the city."

68

TED BRACED FOR A trip downtown. If he was very lucky, he would be taken to the FBI or the federal prosecutor's offices for questioning. The more likely destination was the Metropolitan Correctional Center, a federal facility similar to the MDC Brooklyn, this one located in Lower Manhattan. The main differences between the two institutions were a matter of opinion. Most attorneys agreed if the MDC Brooklyn was a zoo, then the MCC was a circus. That was metaphor, as the reality was worse. Each held dangerous animals in cages with considerably less oversight and control than any zoo or circus.

The drive into Manhattan took close to an hour; the marshals didn't bother with lights or siren, which might have earned them ten or fifteen minutes. Ted was relieved they didn't seem to be in a particular hurry. When the car turned uptown on Third after exiting the Midtown Tunnel, Ted was both relieved and confused. This was not the way to the feds' offices. In a few blocks, the woman cut over to Park Avenue and continued uptown. Ted had an odd premonition that soon became reality as they slowed and made a U-turn in the midfifties.

"Why are we here?" Ted asked.

The driver shot him an angry look in the rearview mirror. "Because someone with major juice wants you here. This is not SOP."

The SUV pulled over in front of a building Ted knew well. The law offices of Hasting, Fitzmaurice, and Barson took up most of five floors. After a quick phone consultation, the marshals led Ted to the firm's private dining room on the topmost floor.

The Judge met them at the elevator.

"Thank you both for your service," he oozed. "This is all quite unusual, I am sure. The deputy director is an old friend, you understand. He is doing me a great personal favor."

Ted could see that the marshals didn't understand—or care. But they didn't like it either.

"Please remove the handcuffs. I will be needing Mr. Molloy for approximately an hour. Two at the most. If you don't mind waiting?" The Judge held up an index finger, and Oliver, the sole waiter, joined them. "Can we get these hardworking officers something to eat? Sandwiches? Have them delivered out to their car, would you?"

The Judge smiled at the marshals. They were dismissed. They didn't like that either, but they retreated into the elevator.

"Ted," the Judge cried, feigning surprise, as though Ted's presence were the work of some second-rate magician. "Thank you for joining us. This way, please." He took Ted's arm and guided him into the dining room. There was no one else present. This was unusual but not unique. Lowly associates and junior partners never ate there unless invited by more senior members of the firm. And as everyone from summer intern to department head was billing for every eight-minute unit of time, very few people showed up in the dining room unless they were accompanied by a client. When Ted was with the firm, he had eaten there exactly once—the day that Jill's father had welcomed him to the firm.

"Have a seat," the Judge said "No, not there. There. Much better. Our client has a preference, you see. And keeping the client happy is always our first priority."

Ted took the proffered chair. "And here I thought respect for the law was what the firm was all about."

The Judge put his head back and roared with laughter.

"Well put. I miss you, young man. I do hope that we can reach an agreement today. I'm so glad you chose to come."

If the alternative had been one of the federal holding pens, Ted could have been easily persuaded to come uptown for lunch. The matter of choice, however, had never been part of the discussion.

"Who's the client?" Ted asked.

The Judge made a show of taking a pocket watch from his vest and checking the time. "He seems to be running late." Tucking it away again, he smiled at Ted. "Which gives us some time to go over a few items. Still, or would you prefer sparkling?"

Oliver was standing across the room, ostensibly out of earshot, but at these words he scuttled to the table and made a bow, deep enough to denote the presence of aristocracy but not quite royalty. He held a clear pitcher of water with lemon and lime slices.

"Still," Ted said. It was the Judge's script they were playing to, and these polite little concessions were there to put Ted at ease. They wouldn't work. He was on guard, expecting a thrust to his heart or a slash at his throat.

Oliver poured and retreated.

"The biggest challenge this firm faces is talent," the Judge said. "We are in constant competition for the best and brightest from the top schools, and yet so many of them fail to survive the first five years. They lack fire. You had that fire, Teddy. It was what I saw in you the first time we met."

Smoke. The Judge was using smoke. The thrust would come next.

"Aside from the extremely rare late bloomer, it is impossible to hire an experienced lawyer of any quality. Plodders, yes. But a star? No. And then there is you." He abruptly switched persona, throwing off the unctuous sincerity, making eye contact for the first time, and adopting the pose of a serious negotiator.. "Tell me—what would entice you to return to the firm?" the Judge finished, aiming directly for the heart.

The performance deserved applause, but Ted took his time responding. "I'd like to know what I'm selling before we start negotiating price."

"Humor me."

Fine. But he wasn't going to make it easy. "Why would the firm want me? I don't bring valuable clients or niche expertise. I don't even have a current license to practice."

"You are both resourceful and impulsive. Jesuitical in your moral reasoning. Intuitive and brilliant. At times a bit of a rogue. Piratical. These are the qualities I look for in any prospect."

The script was an old one. Ted had heard it fifteen years earlier. It no longer had the power to move him. "And don't those top schools produce such prospects every May?"

The Judge made another abrupt change in direction. "There have been some developments this morning that bear on your situation."

"You mean my visit with the Queens District Attorney's Office?"

"Indirectly. You will find that they have lost interest in you."

Ted didn't trust himself to say anything. The Judge noted his silent surprise but did not pause. "While you were being interviewed, the main witness against you recanted, under questioning by the FBI and an AUSA from the Eastern District. Cheryl Rubiano"—the Judge pronounced the name "Sheryl"—"has agreed to plead guilty in federal court to a single charge of soliciting a bribe. She will serve a year in a minimum-security federal facility. Mr. Petronelli was not consulted."

Was this their plan B? What carrot-and-stick inducements had they used to persuade Cheryl to change her story so dramatically and abruptly? What was the going rate for falling on one's sword?

"And Councilman Pak?" Ted asked.

"There is no case. He is with the prosecuting attorney now, answering questions."

Ted let the sarcasm flow. "She operated alone? Demanded cash for access? And her boss had no idea this was going on? The media is going to tear that story to pieces."

The Judge let show a touch of his frustration with Ted's attitude. "And despite the fact that there is ample evidence that you were her coconspirator—and quite likely her lover— you will not be prosecuted, nor asked to give testimony."

"Only none of that is true."

The Judge laughed again. "Facts? You've been watching *Law & Order* again."

"What about the Russian gangster?"

"You mean the man you attacked in the hospital?"

"Twice he tried to kill McKenzie Zielinski. Prior to that he and his partner assaulted me and another friend, and he would gladly have killed me if I hadn't fought him off. What's his deal? Will he have to spend a few months raking gravel in one of those minimum-security facilities? Or does he get to walk?"

"The case against him may not be as strong as you might wish."

"I caught him in the act of administering a potentially lethal dose of insulin to a comatose patient."

"It seems that your Russian is actually from Belarus and is here on an expired visa. As soon as he is strong enough to travel, he will be repatriated. He will not threaten you or anyone else again. That is a solemn promise."

Ted wanted to see the man in court being sentenced for his crimes. He wanted to see that arrogant face sag in defeat as the man realized that he was about to serve a decade or two in prison. He wanted to be able to tell Kenzie that he'd watched him being sentenced and led away.

And then he realized that in making that promise, the Judge had admitted his culpability. He might not have aided and abetted, but he had been aware of the players involved and what deeds they committed. Nothing could ever be proved, of course. But the promise was as real as the threat had been.

Ted had been outmaneuvered again.

"What happens now?" Ted asked.

"Lunch. Just as soon as our guest arrives. You must be hungry. You've had a hell of a night. I don't know what's keeping him. Oliver, could you bring Mr. Molloy a little something to keep him from fading away? Something with protein, I think."

Ted wasn't hungry. He wanted confirmation for all he had deduced. He would get it; he just had to keep the Judge talking. "What is the package? I'm not coming back to the firm to sit on my ass. What do I do? What's my future? Where do you see me in five years? In ten? Come on, this is your pitch. Make me want it."

The Judge looked down and repositioned his knife and fork, aligning them in parallel equidistant from the plate on either side. He cleared his throat and began:

"The wheel has come around, as it always does, and commercial real estate is again a major source of revenue for the firm. I can't make you head of the department, but I can see you coming aboard as a junior partner—"

"Senior," Ted interrupted.

The Judge paused long enough that Ted believed him when he agreed. "Senior partner. You will have a substantial client list. Ten years from now? You would be running the department with a seat on the governing committee."

Oliver set a small plate in front of Ted containing a tennis ball-sized burrata on a bed of fresh basil leaves. Ted ignored it. "What else? There're other people involved. What happens to Barbara Miller? I am assuming she's alive. You might need her."

The Judge allowed a slight nod of admission.

"So?" Ted continued. "Her money? Her properties?"

"I am touched. You met this person once and feel compelled to advocate for her. She is a tough old woman who, sadly, is sinking into dementia. She now resides in one of the best eldercare facilities in the country. No. In the world. She has no heirs, no pet charities, not even a close friend who would benefit. What would you want for her that she does not have?"

"I want to see her. I want to know she's happy there."

"I will arrange for you to visit her. But happiness comes from within. I cannot guarantee it, nor should you expect it. But she is content. And safe."

"The surplus money? There's a million and change sitting there."

"You won't need it. In five years you'll be worth ten times that."

"It's not for me. I have a partner. He's owed a substantial share."

"A worn-out drunk, from what I hear," the Judge said in an arch tone, which he immediately dropped. "He's not worthy, Ted," he said, ladling on an unctuous false sympathy, as though Lester were an unfortunate relative.

"I could tell you that I owe him, but that kind of loyalty to a man like Lester wouldn't make any sense to you." There was more to Lester than the Judge could ever imagine. But Ted held off. The Judge would sneer at emotion, but a reasoned argument presented by one legal mind to another might get through. "He knows as much as I do about all of this and he's smart. He'll figure out the rest. You can't scare him off. Pay him a fair cut. Or you can order a more permanent solution, though I don't think the cabal can afford another of those. The police have been struggling with the Richie Rubiano murder case, but a second body would be the thing they need to tie that to the attack on McKenzie Zielinski, and then you'd all be well and truly screwed. I don't doubt that you could do it—and get away with it again—but why? There's no shortage of loose cash lying around. Pay him."

"Who is this Richie you mentioned?"

Ted didn't let this half-hearted evasion stop him. "The point, Your Honor, is that you can no longer bear the scrutiny of the police. For a relatively small sum, you can divest yourselves of a potential threat. My way, the risk disappears. Your way, it simply shifts—and increases."

The Judge stroked the side of his long, thin nose. "We can arrange something," he agreed.

The weight of anxiety in Ted's chest lifted a touch. He hoped it didn't show. He wasn't done.

"What would you suggest?"

"Half a mil."

"Too much. One hundred thousand."

"Three hundred thousand," Ted said. "That's half of my half of what I would have recovered for Barbara Miller. That was my deal with Lester." Ted felt entirely comfortable lying about this. Lester had earned every last dollar.

"It would be cleaner if we allowed Ms. Clavette to pursue those particular funds on behalf of the client. The money will go to Miss Miller and help to pay for her care. It will leave a convincing paper trail, should it be needed. We can find another way of paying your friend."

"And speaking of Jackie, what's your proposal there? Jail or disbarment?"

The Judge sighed, indicating that any resolution of Jacqueline's involvement was going to be complicated. Not only did she have to be kept quiet, but more importantly, Jill had to be satisfied with any arrangement. "Her foray into high-level real estate transactions was not a success, I am sorry to say. However, there is always a need for a good trust and estates lawyer. She can have her old job."

"She bribed an elected official. Defrauded an elderly client. Destroyed court records. And she walks? No, even better. She gets rehabilitated with documents to prove it. What a farce."

"You and I have a special place in our hearts for someone who loves her dearly. Jill would be broken in two if we didn't do all in our power to keep Jacqueline safe."

It was the Judge's blind spot. Ted's too, he acknowledged. But there was more than concern for Jill at work. The stakes were too high. If Cheryl had balked at taking full responsibility for the bribery, the Judge would have had to toss Jackie out of the life raft. But the fierce Ms. Clavette would not have gone quietly. She could not be easily—or cheaply—bought. Ted discovered that he had a grudging respect for the woman. "You have to protect Jackie, or she'll talk and the whole house of cards tumbles. She knows all the ugly details. The firm. Councilman Pak. The Russian banker. Even Reisner, the man behind the biggest real estate deal in Queens. She'd take everybody down. Except you, maybe."

"I am only an advocate, Ted."

And the Judge was betting that Ted's love for Jill would keep him from intervening and forcing their hand. Jackie would walk and Ted and the Judge would conspire to let her.

"And the damned tower gets built," Ted finally said.

"Which will make a lot of people very happy. It is inevitable. Not only will this project attract real wealth to that neighborhood; it will provide jobs, improved amenities, and a commitment from both city and state government to upgraded services and infrastructure. Every politician in the state is racing to take credit, right up to the governor."

Ted was perhaps less enthused about the governor's support than the Judge expected. "I know at least one person who won't be happy about it."

"Ah, yes. The community organizer. How is she?"

"Healing."

"I am happy to hear that. What she does is important, though quixotic. But I am sure she is used to living with disappointments. There will be other projects to protest."

Ted took a moment to let the stink of such arrogance dissipate.

The Judge checked his watch again. "I can't imagine what's keeping him."

"And what do you want from me? What do I do to earn my place in this utopia?"

The Judge raised both eyebrows, smiling tight-lipped and cold. "Nothing, Ted. You must do and say nothing. And if you can do that, the world is yours. I believe you are a man of honor. I will take your handshake as your bond."

TED WOULD HAVE INSTANT status, money, and work he had once loved. There was the promise of power. And he would once again be a member of the legal fraternity, with recognition and respect.

Silence was a small price to pay for all that. *Too small*, he thought. What was he missing? He watched as the Judge again checked the time. That was a legitimate tell. He was worried.

"Who are we waiting for?" Ted asked, though he was sure he knew.

The Judge rearranged his face into a simulacrum of ecstatic expectancy before answering. "The first of your new clients." The facade dropped. "I can't think what's keeping him."

"What happens if I don't take your offer? Do I get to gracefully bow out? Or do the thugs bury me in the first concrete pilings that get poured?"

"I don't understand. I'm saving you from prosecution and offering you the opportunity for a meaningful career."

"No you're not. This client. It's Reisner. You want me to handle the LBC account. To keep both father and son happy and out of jail. And to do that, you'll expect me to be their bagman. I'll be the one carrying the envelopes full of cash, my stomach too tied in knots to even think about eating the fancy dinners all those bastards are wolfing down around me."

"You couldn't be more wrong."

Ted laughed in his face. The Judge was good, but he had not expected Ted to see through the offer so completely—or so quickly. For a brief moment, Ted was able to see the frightened man beneath the mask.

"Fuck you all," Ted said. They would let him come back

to the firm, but there would be no recognition, no respect. He would be nothing more than a gofer, highly paid to leave his conscience at the door. They wanted him because they truly believed that his morality could be bought and that he would be willing to do any unspeakable—and illegal—act for a price. They—the family and the whole damn governing board— would be glad to have a gonif on board. Someone they could order to do the things they considered beneath them.

If he was successful, they'd keep him around as long as he was able to dance fast enough to stay out of jail. And if he failed? If he self-medicated with booze or drugs to assuage his guilt and inadequacy, if he developed ulcers and heart problems, if he screwed up and even once disappointed the client? Then he'd be out. Essentially where he was now, only older and terminally broken. Used up. Without even a shred of self-respect to keep him from stepping off the Jamaica Station platform into the path of the express train to Babylon.

In a brief flash, he saw what Jackie had been offered and felt, for an instant, a touch of empathy. She hadn't seen it coming. They'd offered a plum assignment, and she had assumed that she'd been chosen for her skills or because she had earned a place at the table—or because of her relation to Jill. They had only wanted her because she was expendable.

And so was Ted.

The Judge was having a hard time staying on point. His eyes kept flashing down to the watch he now held in his lap. "I can't make you work for Hasting, Fitzmaurice, and Barson, though I cannot imagine why you would turn down such an opportunity. But I cannot protect you if you don't. Do you understand me, Ted?"

"I do."

The Judge's words came faster, spilling over one another. Ted had never seen him like this, and it took him a moment to realize the Judge was afraid. "Other parties argued against offering this proposal. They preferred seeing you in prison or silenced."

"I said I understand," Ted spoke ponderously, trying to wring some of the frenzy out of the air.

It wasn't working. "They will feel threatened if you are in a position that cannot be closely monitored."

"Well, I think I have a way around that, Your Honor. I could turn myself in."

"What are you saying?"

"I could claim to be Cheryl's partner. The feds would believe it. Assistant DA Petronelli already believes it. And I could give them all the names. I'd get less time than Cheryl— maybe none. At the first threat, they'd put me in WITSEC and I'd be untouchable." It was a wrestler's trick. When desperate, go limp. They never expect it.

"That would be madness." The old man's eyes were suddenly bloodshot. He was giving himself a stroke.

"Maybe so, but it would be ruthlessly efficient. You would all be so busy covering your own asses that no one would even think to come after me. You'd all be pointing the finger at each other. Reisner would fight it on television because that's what he's good at, and he might win that way. The lawyers and politicians would be stuck between the police and the Russian mob. It would be fun to watch."

"What is it you want? Name it." He was sweating. Beads were sprouting across his forehead. Ted had never imagined he would ever see Judge Cornelius Fitzmaurice break a sweat.

"Mostly to be left in peace."

"That's all?"

"No." Ted almost laughed at the eagerness of the Judge. "I want Lester to get his money."

"Done."

"I want to know that Barbara Miller is all right."

"You will see her."

"I think I'll let Lester make that trip."

"As you wish."

"I want a green card."

"Certainly not for yourself."

The Judge patted his brow with his napkin. He was becoming comfortable again, no longer negotiating with a madman. Ted prepared himself for pushback.

"I'll get you the name," Ted said.

"As long as this person is not on a terror watch list, I don't see any reason why we can't make this happen."

"I want your guarantee that McKenzie Zielinski is safe and will remain that way."

"Her position seems to put her at odds with powerful people," the Judge said, relaxing back into his seat. He was smiling again, believing that with these small concessions, he had retaken the high ground. "I can't control them all."

"I think you may need to be more proactive. If anything happens to her—ever—then there is no deal."

"That may take some arranging."

"You're good at making arrangements."

He looked away. Processing. Ted could now read him so easily. Finally, he nodded. "What else? What do you want?"

"I want Richie Rubiano's killer."

- 70 -

"WHO?" THE JUDGE'S EYES widened. For the briefest second, he looked thoroughly confused. "Richie Rubiano?" He recovered quickly. The mask of the all wise, all knowing returned. His voice registered moderately hidden scorn. "Is he connected to your friend in the hospital?"

Ted was thrown. He could not unsee that moment of nakedness on the Judge's face. Either the puppet master had not been told of Richie's murder, or something in the storyline Ted had devised was terribly wrong. Was it all wrong? No. The Judge had not so much as blinked when presented with charges of fraud, bribery, assault, and the attempted murder of Kenzie. But mention of Richie's murder had taken him by surprise. Impossible. The tectonic plates of Ted's world were in motion. He put his faith in what he knew to be true.

"Richie Rubiano worked for me," Ted said. "He was married to Cheryl. Someone killed him. I believe because he was investigating, in his own clumsy manner, Barbara Miller's surplus money. Jackie's little rainy-day fund. Her fraud led directly to Richie's death."

"I've never heard of him," the Judge said. He showed nothing more than a mild impatience. "The Reisners play hardball. Ask any of their competitors. They are capable of bending rules and making decisions that reflect ethical or moral persuasions many might find deplorable. That's their world. Saints don't prosper in the New York real estate markets. But murder? Or murder for hire? No, Ted. That is not possible."

"I don't think they control the situation anymore," Ted said. He'd witnessed two murder attempts on McKenzie

Zielinski and was still shaking off the effects of his fight with the assassin. He didn't want to hear about the ethical gymnastics of the rich and powerful. "Reisner is working with people who will use any means necessary to protect their investments. Richie got in their way."

The Judge blinked owlishly. *Processing or denying?* He mumbled something, then tried to steer the conversation back to what he knew. "The Russians are being handled. There will be no more assaults on your community organizer. You have my word."

But Ted wasn't buying. He didn't want weak promises. He was disgusted with opportunistic morality. Lines had been crossed that should never have been approached. "She's still in a coma, dammit, and you give me nothing but words." A strong, beautiful, caring human being was lying in a hospital bed, unconscious and a breath away from death, and no one would be held responsible. His stomach knotted at the outrage, and he yelled, "Who pays? Someone is going to prison for this. I swear it."

The waiter appeared at the table, almost trembling. Ted had been loud, he realized, but there was no one else there to hear. The Judge waved Oliver away, but he presented a phone. "I am so sorry to intrude, but the policeman was insistent that he speak to you." He pressed the phone into the Judge's hands and retreated.

"This is Cornelius Fitzmaurice. To whom am I speaking?" The Judge's voice held a lifetime of service on the bench.

Whoever it was wasted little time delivering his news. The Judge's face registered shock, then anger. He listened for less than a minute, then spoke calmly and coldly. "Thank you for the call, Lieutenant Bass. I will not forget your consideration." He pressed the button to disconnect and looked at Ted with a touch of confusion in his eyes. "Do you know a Stavros person?"

"I've met him. He's a friend of Cheryl's." Ted could see the Judge was deeply shaken. He kept talking to hold back the delivery of more-terrible news. "A detective told me that he's a small-time hood. An enforcer."

Coldly, his mask in place, the Judge swung an arm across the table, sending glasses, plates, and silverware flying. The untouched burrata hit the floor and slid along it, leaving a trail, like a slug on steroids. The Judge looked surprised at what he'd done. "Sorry," he said.

Ted stared in shock, not knowing how to respond to this eruption from a man who never seemed to lose control. Ted waited a moment, then finished what he had been reporting. "They call him Nicky Greco."

The Judge nodded, playing catch-up, obviously putting pieces together in his head. His words came out without inflection, as emotionless as if he were reporting the daily rainfall statistics for the past month. "An hour ago, as Ron Reisner and his son were leaving the compound in Douglaston to come here, a man approached their car and shot both of them. The father is being taken to the hospital in serious condition. The son has been declared dead at the scene. Based on a witness's description, the police are looking for this man, Stavros."

Ted thought that at six foot eight with a shaved head shaped like a basketball and the physique of a steroidal gorilla, Stavros would be easy to identify. How easy he would be to find, however, depended on his cunning and luck.

"Greco, you said? Why has this man done this?" The Judge's anger had withered, and what was left was helpless shock and confusion. "It was all arranged."

Ted was so shocked by the transformation in this man, who had never before shown a sign of weakness, that at first he missed the implication in the Judge's last words. *All arranged?*

Cheryl and her sudden confession. The light sentence. Even the payoff. The Judge would have been the one to direct all those arrangements.

And then Ted focused on the Judge's question. Why would Nicky Greco do this? Murdering Reisner or his creep of a son wasn't going to get the big Greek any closer to Cheryl's supposed windfall from the surplus money. There never had been much of a chance of that anyway. So if money wasn't the answer, what was left? Love, money, honor, or revenge. Revenge was merely a response to being thwarted in pursuit of one of the other three. Honor, in any of its guises, didn't apply. That left only love. The big gorilla loved Cheryl Rubiano.

If Cheryl was taking the fall for Reisner and crew, Stavros Nikitopoulos, a.k.a. Nicky Greco, was going to make them pay. The Judge might understand murdering for love. "Why? Revenge. He'll go after all of them. I'd have the police put a guard on Councilman Pak until this guy is caught."

The Judge blinked again. He had aged decades in minutes. "Dear God," he whispered.

Ted felt no sympathy for him. The Judge had operated as though he could control all the players, manipulating each one to secure success on his terms, as he saw fit.

A new revelation hit Ted.

"Jackie," he said.

71

TED GRABBED THE PHONE from the Judge and punched in Jill's number. She answered on the first ring.

"Where's Jackie?" Ted said. "She's in danger." If Jackie was at work, she was safe. The giant wouldn't be able to reach her. Security in the lobby would never let him into an elevator.

"I thought this was her calling. Why should she be in danger?" Jill said. She sounded arch and dismissive. She did not believe him.

Ted gave her the shortest version he could devise. "The Reisners were attacked a little while ago by a professional thug. Your grandfather and I think Jackie will be on this guy's list."

"What have you done?" she growled in full attack mode. It was family dogma: when threatened, attack.

"Jill," he cried, "listen to me." He heard the click and the immediate return of the dial tone. He hit REDIAL. Straight to voice mail. "Damn." Jill was alone and that mad giant would walk right through her if he thought he'd find Jackie there. Ted had to get there.

He tossed the phone to the Judge, who fumbled but caught it. "See if Jackie's here in the building. If she is, get her someplace safe."

The Judge was still in shock. Ted didn't have time—or the inclination—to coddle him. "Now! Make the call," Ted ordered. The Judge gasped once and dialed.

Ted dashed out of the dining room, heading for the elevators. Jill's apartment was thirty blocks uptown. A mile and a half. In college he ran two miles a day—four when he had to make weight. He wasn't a track athlete. Eight-minute miles had been his norm, and he had not run a mile in ten years or more.

There were three IT staffers—easy to identify by their blue color-coded swipe cards hanging from lanyards, as well as their identical wardrobe of khaki pants and black polo shirts—waiting at the elevator banks. The doors of a car opened as Ted approached, and he barged past the techies.

"Take the next one," he snarled. They stopped in surprise. Ted hit the button for LOBBY.

He stopped before stepping out onto the street. The two marshals were standing by the big SUV, ostentatiously taking up space in a well-marked no-parking zone. They towered over a brown-jacketed traffic cop who was having no trouble ignoring them while writing a ticket.

Ted saw his chance and took it. He walked out the door and cut to his left, walking fast like a New Yorker but not pushing it. The traffic was at a standstill going both downtown and up. If he could make it across the madness of Fifty-Seventh Street, the marshals would never even know he'd gone.

He darted between cars as he crossed Fifty-Sixth. One block to go. He risked a look back. A mistake. From a block away, their eyes met. The marshal saw him. She grabbed her partner by the arm and pointed. Ted ran.

As soon as he did, his body reminded him of the events of the previous night. He had pain when he needed energy. He hurt and felt winded after the first few running steps. The pedestrian light across the street was already counting down into single digits. He stumbled but kept moving.

And then he was in the street—half running, half walking. The crosswalk timer ticked down: 3, 2, 1. The red hand stopped flashing and turned solid. He pushed ahead, passing the centerline. He looked to his right. Taxis in the inside lane. A city bus in the curb lane, followed by a fire engine. The bus was already moving, easing through the last remains of the red light.

A siren sounded and for a nanosecond Ted thought it was the fire engine signaling the bus to get out of the way. He leapt the last few feet to the relative safety of the sidewalk before the realization hit. The sound had come from behind him. He looked over his shoulder and his heart soared. Rather than following him on foot, the two marshals were back in the SUV attempting to force their way through two solid lines of traffic. They still had to make a U-turn. They were obviously expecting their flashing lights and siren to have an effect on Midtown Manhattan drivers.

The light changed. The bus slid across the intersection and stopped behind a cab depositing a fare in front of the Citibank. Ted considered making a dash for the emptying cab but decided against it. It was already committed to continuing west on Fifty-Seventh and away from Jill's apartment. Ted quickstepped across the avenue as the fire truck edged forward and stopped, blocked by the bus and in turn blocking traffic. Flashing lights two blocks south marked the location of the black SUV.

Both Fifty-Eighth and Fifty-Ninth Streets were one-way eastbound. The chances of finding an empty cab before the far corner of Sixtieth were nil. Ted could no longer run, but he pushed himself to walk as fast as he could. Pedestrian traffic thinned out on the far side of Fifty-Ninth. He made better time, but he was afraid to check his watch.

And then a miracle happened. A taxi pulled around the corner on Sixtieth and stopped to deliver a tall grey-haired man at the first apartment building. Ted sucked in a breath and made a dash, climbing into the back seat before the doorman had a chance to slam the door.

"Uptown," Ted said, stuffing a hundred-dollar bill into the plastic tray. "I've got about two minutes to save a life."

THE CABBIE MADE IT ten blocks before the staggered lights caught them. Ted was, by this time, almost comfortable with Mohammed's driving. This ride needed the Yemeni's touch.

"Floor it, dammit!" Ted yelled. "I've seen Park Avenue before. Move it."

A long limo coming down Park made a left turn at Seventy-Eighth Street and barreled through the intersection in front of them. The cab missed its rear bumper by millimeters. Ted's driver never took his foot off the gas.

Ted twisted around to look for the black SUV's flashing lights. Far back but coming on quickly. If the marshals were still using the siren, he couldn't hear it.

"You're doing fine," he said. "But don't let up."

They made the light—deep amber—at Seventy-Ninth and flew through the next few blocks.

"There," Ted ordered. "The middle of the next block. Second canopy."

Ted knew immediately that something was wrong. There was no doorman on duty. Ted was too late. "Damn. Damn. Damn," he said in a whisper as he entered the lobby.

Ted heard a groan from the package room. Osvaldo was on the floor, looking dazed but alive.

"He's upstairs?" Ted asked, kneeling by the man and checking him quickly for wounds. He saw none, though there was a red welt on Osvaldo's forehead that promised to swell into a nasty bruise. "How long ago?"

"I tried to stop him and he hit me." Osvaldo sounded surprised.

The marshals would be arriving any minute. If Ted waited for their backup, they would waste time asking questions, demanding answers, and being careful to do things by the book. Ted wasn't going to wait. "Help is coming," he said. "Send them after me." He ran to the elevator.

72

THE ELEVATOR CAME UP from the basement almost immediately. Ted pressed the button for the sixth floor. The moment the door slid shut, the enormity of what he was committed to swept over him, leaving a liquid feeling in his gut.

Was he really prepared to go up against an armed man? A killer? In the hospital he had attacked the Russian without the benefit of reflection. He had seen danger to Kenzie and he had moved. It had been simple—and he could have died.

The elevator opened. Jill's door was splintered, hanging open as though the Lexington Avenue subway had been rerouted through her apartment. His decision became a whole lot easier.

He called Jill's name. No response. He listened for any other sounds. None. The giant had no need for stealth; he was big enough to create his own weather system. Ted called again. "Jill? It's Ted. Are you okay?"

This time he thought he heard her voice from the rear of the apartment. He eased around the shattered door into the foyer. "Jill? I'm coming in."

Behind him the elevator clicked loudly and he nearly jumped. Then it began to hum. It was on its way back to the lobby. The marshals would be here in a few minutes. The thought gave him a boost of false courage.

The living room furniture had all been overturned, but it looked like it had been done for show—to demonstrate anger and power, to engender fear and compliance. The only thing broken was the hideous glass sculpture in the corner. Shards crunched under his feet as he moved through the room.

"Jill. Are you all right? Is he still here?"

A low moan sounded quite clearly.

Ted turned and looked down the hall. The doors were all closed—the two bedrooms, the guest bathroom, the den, the entertainment room. The giant could have been hiding behind any one of those doors, waiting for some reckless St. George coming to save the maiden.

Ted put his back to the wall and crept down the hallway. His pounding heart was making a racket loud enough to be heard across town. He tried to control his breathing.

He came to the den. Translucent-curtained French doors covered the entry. He peered through. No lurking shadows hovered on the other side. He gripped the brass lever handle and eased the door open. No one was in the room. He continued down the hall feeling stronger and less afraid.

The guest bedroom was next. He could now see that the door was slightly ajar. Ted kicked it and jumped forward, half expecting to be met with a fist—or a bullet. The door rebounded off a dresser and came back at him. He put up both hands to stop it but managed to get a glimpse inside. No sign of the giant and no sign of Jill.

He took a moment to get his breath—and his blood pressure—under control before he moved on to the next door. The bathroom. He reached out to turn the knob, and the door swung open. Ted almost tripped over his own feet as he retreated, anticipating a murderous charge, only to realize a moment later that it was Jill who stood facing him.

She was holding a white hand towel to her face. It was blotched with pale pink and bright red. Blood.

"I think he broke my nose," she said. She moved the towel away so Ted could see the damage.

"Thank God, you're all right," Ted said. "He's gone?"

"You didn't see him? He broke in here, tore up the living room, and punched me."

"He's looking for Jackie," Ted said.

Concern for Jacqueline overcame Jill's own pain. "She's not at the office?" It was more a plea than a question.

"Your grandfather has people looking for her. The guy who punched you: Big? Bald? Squeaky voice?"

She nodded.

"When did he leave?"

"Just before I heard you calling me."

The elevator had come up from the basement. Nicky Greco had taken the same exit Ted had used the day before.

A trickle of fresh blood ran from Jill's nose. She seemed unaware of it. Ted took the towel and gently held it to her face.

"Keep this on," he said. "That's it. Help is on the way up right now. They'll get a doctor to check you out. When you hear them come off the elevator, yell real loud."

She grabbed his arm. "Don't let him get her. Promise me." She looked fierce. This was no simple request; she was demanding a sacred pact.

"I promise." He looked into her eyes. The nose wasn't broken, but she'd be wearing oversized sunglasses for the next week or so.

"Listen to me," she ordered. "I want you to promise me you will do everything in your power to keep Jacqueline safe."

"I did. I do. I promise."

As he ran to the foyer, Ted heard the elevator click. He ducked into the dining room and watched from behind a towering brushed-steel-and-ebony display cabinet as the two marshals came through the broken front door. They were followed by a uniformed NYPD cop. All three had their guns drawn. With an index finger and a glance, the woman silently ordered the other two to check the archways. Ted was about to be discovered and most probably shot on sight. The chase was over. He raised his hands and took a last breath before facing three guns.

"We are police," she called out. "We are coming in."

Jill started yelling. The three thundered down the hall.

Ted went out of the dining room, slunk out the door, and slipped into the waiting elevator.

73

TED RAN OUT THE basement door, knowing that he was far too late. He looked up the alley. The bottom half of the metal gate had been folded up like a piece of cardboard. It would have been a tight fit, but the giant had made his escape. Ted had held no illusions of catching the killer, but he had hoped to keep him in sight.

Ted walked up the concrete steps, ducked under the folded gate, and came out onto the quiet side street. No pedestrians waved frantically, pointing out Nicky Greco's escape route. No cars tore off, tires smoking. There was simply no sign of the big man.

Ted walked east toward Lexington. He didn't have a plan—yet. He took out his phone and called the Judge. After answering a series of maddening robot-generated questions, Ted was connected to the dining room phone.

"He's been there and gone," Ted said. "The police are with Jill now. She took a punch, but she's going to be fine. She's safe."

The Judge blew a sigh of relief before reporting his news—or lack of it. "Jacqueline is not in the building. Security has her logging out two hours ago."

"You called her?" Ted's promise to Jill, so quickly given, was already in doubt.

"Her phone goes straight to voice mail. Could she be hiding?"

Ted thought for a moment. "No. She wouldn't have known he was looking for her. Or about Reisner getting shot. It's something else." He was exhausted. He couldn't think. He needed food, rest, and most of all he needed the world to stop moving. "Keep me posted."

He turned up Lexington. When he had lived in the neighborhood with Jill, there had been a decent deli on the block. It was now a Taco Bell. The menu board was too confusing to read. Combos? Only aficionados would be able to make sense of the various permutations available.

"I need something filling. Calories. What do I want?"

The middle-aged woman at the cash register looked at him in wonder. "You never eat at Taco Bell before?"

"Guilty," he said.

"Best value is the chicken Quesarito. Six hundred fifty calories for under four bucks with tax. You want guac on it? It costs."

"Sure. Can I get extra cheese? Load it up."

"Three cheese blend, jalapenos, refried beans, fritos, dressing, salsa, and low-fat sour cream."

"Low-fat? Really? Bring it on."

"You can get lettuce, too."

"No need to overdo," Ted said.

Half a quesarito later, Ted began to wake up. His brain was functioning again, and he knew where Jackie had gone. And where the giant was headed. He called Lester.

"Are you all right?" Lester asked. "Where are you?"

"Better than ever." Ted spoke around a mouthful of restorative grilled quesadilla. Four Con Ed workers in neon-green vests were eating at the next table, their blue helmets taking up half the surface. As one, they suddenly exploded in laughter. A single woman diner looked up in alarm. It all felt so real compared to the last forty-eight hours of his life. "Upper East Side. How soon can Mohammed get here?"

"It's Friday," Lester said.

"Yeah?"

"It's the Muslim Sabbath. You didn't know that?"

"No. I didn't know." How did Lester? He and Mohammed

seemed to speak to each other only in asides through Ted. "Did Duran get hold of you? I told him to call."

"I'm sitting in the back of their car answering questions." Ted could hear an angry voice in the background. "His partner's a dick," Lester whispered, and then continued at a normal volume, "Duran's got a different take on things. About who killed Richie, at any rate."

"He knows something he's not telling you. Can you convince him to meet me somewhere?"

"What's up?"

"Tell him I know where we're going to find Nicky Greco."

74

ARCHER AVENUE AND SUTPHIN Boulevard. The redevelopment of downtown Jamaica had finally reached this crossroads. Shopping malls and new apartment buildings, many with a view of all eight Long Island Rail Road tracks, sprouted in every vacant lot. But tucked in between there were two- and three-story survivors where you could still get a pair of shoes resoled, have your hair braided, or eat a three-star lunch while standing at a linoleum counter.

Ted hugged the building side of the pavement as he walked north, letting the afternoon shadows and the crowds of pedestrians keep him hidden. In the middle of the block, he ducked into a Chinese restaurant. Lester was sitting with the detectives, Duran and Kasabian, at a four-top near the door. The cops were drinking coffee facing each other by the window. Lester had a glass of clear liquid that Ted hoped was water. As the window was half-covered in menus and photos of the delights within, the men were hidden from the street but had a clear view of the courthouse steps.

"Finally," Lester said. He was healing. His bruises, now a greenish yellow rather than dark blue and purple, looked less angry. His eyes were clear and had lost their watery dullness. And he was dressed in a bright plaid jacket only a size or so too big for him. He must have found another thrift shop. "It feels like I've been stuck with these two for half my life. They can't help themselves. Even a conversation about baseball feels like an interrogation."

"Sit down," Duran said, indicating the empty seat next to him. "And then you can tell me about Nicky Greco."

"In a minute," Ted said. His stomach felt full from the

burrito, but his nose told him he was still hungry. He went to the counter and ordered two kinds of panfried dumplings and a plate of noodles with scallion-and-fiery-beef sauce. Even with a bottle of water, the tab came to less than twenty bucks. The woman behind the counter was a perpetually smiling plump Asian woman—Chinese, he guessed—so short she had to stand on a milk crate to see over the counter. He took out the last of Cheryl's money. A single hundred dollar bill. "Keep the change," he said.

Kasabian didn't wait for Ted to sit. The moment he got to the table, the cop started talking. "Why are we here? Mr. Nikitopoulos is in Manhattan. They've got half the cops in the city looking for him."

"He *was* in Manhattan," Ted said. "That was over an hour ago."

"Did you see him?" Duran asked.

"No," Ted said. "I missed him by minutes. But he's on his way here."

"Why's that?"

"Because he's in love with Cheryl Rubiano," Ted said. "And she's taking the fall for a slew of people. I think she is getting paid a boatload of cash and promised a short sentence, but the big guy doesn't care. He just wants his Velma back."

"Give me that in small bites, so I don't choke on it," Duran said.

Ted focused on Duran, the more reasonable of the two. He filled him in quickly on the conversation at the aborted lunch with the Judge. "She's the patsy and I would think they're paying her well not to tattle."

"Who the hell is Velma?" Kasabian asked.

"Cheryl," Ted said. "Try to keep up, Detective." He looked back to Duran. "He wants Cheryl, and if he can't have her, he's going to take it out on everyone she's covering for. He shot the Reisners. Where's Councilman Pak? He's got to be on the hit list."

Duran answered. "He's with the feds explaining why he didn't know anything about his assistant squeezing developers for bribes. That's not an easy sell. He'll be there for a while."

"Who's left?" Ted said. "The fat Russian who bankrolled the whole operation? I would think right now he's in Brighton Beach surrounded by a wall of bodyguards."

"That would be my guess," Duran said. "Either there or the VIP lounge at JFK waiting for his flight out of the country."

"And then there's the lawyer. Reisner's lawyer. The one who made the cash payments, handing them to Cheryl in the ladies' room at that overpriced steak place. Jacqueline Clavette. That's the name you wanted, Detective," Ted said with a nod to Kasabian. "But you'll find, if you go after her, that she's untouchable. Any assistant DA who tries to make a case against her will find him- or herself reassigned to traffic court."

"Where does she get that kind of juice?" Kasabian asked.

Ted thought about telling him but decided against it. There was no point. "It's all about favors."

Lester had been quiet and patient throughout. But he'd been following closely. "This is the guy you asked me about? The guy who tossed your apartment."

"Right," Ted answered.

"Nick Whatever. What was that all about?" Lester asked. "Why screw around with you? Was he working for the Russians or what?"

"No. The Russians have their own muscle. I've been wrong about him all along. I think he was looking for those missing files. He wanted the money for Cheryl. He followed me for a while and leaned on me. When that didn't work, he upped the stakes. By the way, did these two get you the files from Richie's backpack?"

"Yes," Lester replied. "They're legit."

Ted turned to Duran. "And have you been able to locate Barbara Miller?"

"The NYPD has been a little busy today. This serial murderer has everybody's attention."

"So what if he comes for you?" Lester asked.

Ted had had a long time to think this through on the subway. "I'd rather not run into him—he'll kill me if it's easy—but he's on a mission. I'm only the sideshow."

The little woman behind the counter yelled something in their direction. It could have been his name. "I think my food's up." He brought the two trays to the table and dug in. "Help yourselves," he offered.

"Supposing you're right, why would he come here?" Kasabian asked.

Ted swallowed a pork and chive dumpling and washed it down with the water. "Because the lawyer is here. Nicky must have tried her at work, but he got the automatic out-of-office response. So after he shot the Reisners, he went into Manhattan to try her at home. She wasn't there either. Where else might a lawyer be found? Here. At the courthouse. Or next door at civil court. Supreme court for real estate, next door for her estate practice. This block is where Jackie does half or more of her business. He's probably seen her here. Cheryl could have pointed her out."

They all turned their heads and stared out the window. Neither Jackie nor Stavros strode by.

"Suppose he's wrong," Duran said, his eyes turning back to Ted. "Or you're wrong."

"Jackie's here," he said. "Bank on it." He reached for the noodles with his chopsticks, but Duran gripped his wrist.

"Talk first," the detective said.

Ted snagged a single noodle, put one end in his mouth, and sucked it in. He stared at the cop while he put his thoughts and suppositions in order. He knew he was right, but he needed them to believe. "Clavette doesn't know she's untouchable. It's all about family and she's an outsider. In her shoes, I'd feel the same. And she is looking at the whole conspiracy blowing up. The feds may have Cheryl, but there's no way that Jackie is going to come out of this looking good. She not only passed along the bribes; she stole from a client. Conned the old lady out of millions. But she doesn't panic. Our heroine is tough. She figures the only thing to do is to put the milk back in the bottle."

"Meaning?" Kasabian shot back.

Lester got it. "Meaning she's over at the courthouse replacing the missing files. Correcting the record. Breaking up the paper trail."

Ted stabbed another dumpling. "Covering her ass."

"And Nicky knows this how?" Duran asked.

"He doesn't have to, Detective," Ted said. "He's a predator. A cat doesn't know why the mouse runs along the base of the wall, but he knows it will. Stavros isn't smart—he's cunning. He's here because he knows one thing: Jackie was here before, and she will be again. And then he'll pounce."

75

SUTPHIN BOULEVARD WAS LINED with storefronts providing legal services, meeting rooms, and food that could be prepared and consumed in the time allotted by an impatient judge. There had to be a dozen or more spots where a would-be assassin could watch for his victim.

"So he's getting a slice or a cup of coffee and watching the street. Just like us," Kasabian said, his eyes sweeping the street again.

Duran alone was a skeptic. He was staring fixedly at Ted, arms crossed over his chest. "This is all conjecture. The guy has to know he's made himself famous. He's running. And this lawyer lady could be anywhere. Maybe she's in the wind, too."

"Molloy knows these people," Kasabian said, with a nod in Ted's direction.

Ted appreciated the surprising support and so did not disagree, but there was always a hidden price to be paid for that cop's assistance.

Duran looked out onto the street. Seconds passed before he spoke. "Fine. We need backup. We need someone in the courthouse to find Clavette and warn her."

Ted agreed. "Inside the courthouse is the safest place to be. I can't go, because Nicky knows me. And he'll pick you two out for cops from a hundred yards away."

"She'll bolt," Kasabian said. "We want her, too."

And there it was. The price. Ted wanted Richie's killer. Kasabian wanted it all.

Ted looked to Duran. If Ted could sell him on letting Jackie go, Kasabian would have no choice but to go along. "You don't need her. She's no danger to anyone. If you try to be too clever, someone's going to get hurt." How much was his promise to Jill influencing him? Jackie deserved punishment. What responsibility did he have to see her brought to justice? Did keeping Jackie safe mean keeping her free? *One question at a time*, he thought. Keeping her alive was first priority. "For the moment, can we settle for getting a serial murderer off the streets?"

Duran gave his partner a quick look. "He's right. We can't even call for backup until we know Nikitopoulos is really here, and by that time it will be too late. We keep it small, and we keep it simple. We get the Reisner shooter."

"And Richie Rubiano's killer," Ted said.

Duran shook his head. "We looked at him hard. I would've loved to put him away for that. But there was no evidence. No motive. And she alibied him."

"She knows he did it," Ted said.

"She was very convincing."

"Well, that's genetic. I don't think she can help herself. All she ever cared about was the money. If Richie could get it, she was going to go with him. When he turned up dead, she hired me. But when I pointed out to her that the money was tied to the LBC project, she freaked. Anybody pulling on that loose thread was soon going to come up with Reisner, Pak, cash bribes, and her. The tower was coming down on all their heads."

"She had to know that Stavros did Richie," Duran said. He was leaning in, arms on the table and thoroughly engaged. Ted had him.

"Not at first," Ted said. "It was only afterwards that she started thinking it through. Once she had that connection, she must have realized that very few people could have put all the pieces together. One of them was dead, and one of them was Nicky. Lover boy. Then she got really scared."

"When was this?"

"By the next time I saw her on Sunday, she knew. That's when she fired me."

"That's when she told us Nicky was with her the night Richie got whacked."

"And you believed her," Ted said.

"Nicky had no motive. He had the girl. Why knock off her ex-husband? He'd won already." Duran was arguing but Ted could tell his heart wasn't in it. He was coming around.

"Because he was scared."

"Nicky Greco?" Duran said. "I don't think so."

"No, listen to him," Kasabian said.

"Scared of losing her to an ex-husband who showed up with a story about making scads of money," Ted said. "He wasn't worried about being in competition with Richie. But he was worried about Cheryl seeing dollar signs."

Duran was nodding. "It's a good story; too bad no jury will ever hear it."

"There must be evidence. DNA? Can't you match the gun or something?"

Duran smiled grimly. "Nicky uses a revolver, so he leaves no brass at the scene. And he fires soft-nose .22 shorts. They mangle on contact, so there's no markings. You can't trace the bullet to a gun. They don't have the stopping power of a bigger bullet, but they can be just as deadly. And they're quiet. Outside of war zones, .22s are the bestselling bullets in the world."

"Would you mind if I ask a question?" Lester said. He took one of the last two dumplings and dipped it in the soy sauce. "Are we all sitting here waiting for me to volunteer?" He popped it in his mouth and spoke around it. "Time's wasting."

"I'm with you," Kasabian said.

76

TED WATCHED LESTER WIND his way through the barely moving traffic, crossing the boulevard in hops and stops. The afternoon sun was strong, and the air seemed to shimmer off the pale plaza across the street. There were few pedestrians over there, most people taking advantage of the shade on the west side of the street. Kasabian trailed him, slower, more deliberate, using his bulk and authority to keep drivers from running into him.

Jackie wouldn't know either of them, but then they might not be able to recognize her either. Ted googled Jackie on his phone and found a picture. The image was small and crowded, but Lester and the detectives had some idea of what she looked like.

"It's late Friday afternoon on a beautiful spring day. How many people do you think are in the basement of the courthouse checking out files in the records room? Look for the woman scotch-taping pages together," Ted had offered.

"Wonderful," Lester had said.

"Or you could stand at the door and call out, 'Jackie,'" Ted had said. "The woman who scowls at you is the one."

They were crossing the nearly empty plaza, Lester two steps in the lead. Kasabian's head swiveled as he scanned the area for any sign of the giant. The shadow from the subway-token sculpture reached halfway up the steps. As Lester passed it, the main door opened, and Jacqueline Clavette stepped out, briefcase swinging.

"Ah, shit," Ted said.

"That her?" Duran whispered though there was no need for quiet.

"Yes, dammit."

Lester continued up the steps, passing the lawyer seemingly without looking at her. Jackie came down, head high and alert. She noticed and dismissed Lester in a split second. Ted could read the tension in her body. Was she aware of the potential danger out there? It was hard to tell, he thought. She always looked like she had a stick up her ass.

Kasabian slowed as he approached her. He called something to Lester.

Lester's head whipped around. He stopped, turned, and called.

It was too far for Ted to hear him, but Jackie's scowl made it clear what he had said. She whirled, head cocked to one side.

Lester put up both hands in a mollifying gesture and jogged down to confront her.

"Get her inside," Duran said to himself, more a prayer than an order.

Lester was selling it hard, but Jackie wasn't buying. Body language told the story. He was a master at gaining people's trust, but his magic wasn't working on her. She said something quite final and turned away.

Kasabian showed his shield. Jackie looked startled, then angry.

Lester reached out and took her arm.

The briefcase came up fast, a roundhouse swing that any two-handed man could have deflected. But Lester had one hand on Jackie's arm and the other in a sling. He ducked his head, taking the blow on his shoulder. She was a big woman in excellent shape. And though he had twenty or thirty pounds on her, he was shorter, frailer, and barely recovered from a ferocious beating. He staggered and went down. The fall probably saved his life.

"This is going south," Duran said. "I can't wait for backup." He was out the door, gun in hand, before Ted could take it all in. Without a thought, he followed.

77

IN MOTION STAVROS NIKITOPOULOS had both the size and the nimble grace of a fullback. And the speed. He burst out of the pizza parlor down the block. The traffic on Sutphin did not slow him down. He was crossing the plaza before Ted cleared the door. Ted saw his arm come up holding a long-barreled revolver.

"Gun! Gun!" Duran yelled, running in a crouch across the sidewalk and into the street.

Kasabian heard him and turned to face the threat. "Police!" His weapon in one hand, gold shield in the other, he yelled louder, "Police! Clear the way." Pedestrians on both sides of the street scattered, but Ted thought this was in response more to the sight of the guns than to the sight of the badge.

There were at least a dozen people on the sidewalk and two lanes of traffic. Neither cop would risk a first shot. But the giant would and did.

He shot twice at Jackie and she fell.

Ted screamed, "No!" A shaft of despair pierced his heart. And where was Lester? Had he been hit, too? Ted kept running toward the scene, fear for his own safety buried under a blinding anxiety.

Nicky swung around and fired four more times—a subdued smack, smack, like the slamming of a book on a table. It surprised Ted. How could something so deadly sound so innocuous?

It was a long shot for a small handgun, across half the plaza, but more than one bullet found its mark. Kasabian staggered, hit somewhere that Ted couldn't see. Ahead of him Duran plunged into the traffic. Immediately behind Ted an older Asian woman with a wheeled laundry cart cried out and sagged to the sidewalk, blood blossoming on the front of her sack-like housecoat. A single shoe—a shearling moccasin—stood guard on the bags of laundry.

A motorist, panicked by the sight of guns to either side, revved his engine and plowed into the car ahead of him. Another driver abandoned his car and ran.

Nicky calmly watched Kasabian sink to the sidewalk, then opened the revolver, emptied the spent cartridges onto the ground, and reloaded with a device he removed from his suit pocket. His movements were quick but careful. He could have been preparing to brush his teeth or replacing the battery in the television remote.

"Drop the weapon!" Duran yelled, now across the street but with a parked car between himself and the shooter. Ted scrambled behind him, desperate to see to Jackie or Lester, willing to risk his own life to save theirs but powerless to do anything but watch and keep close.

Nicky looked mildly surprised but unconcerned to see the cop so close. Expressionless, he raised the revolver and squeezed off another few rounds. Ted was directly behind Duran. Each explosion flashed straight at him, blinding and loud, a succession of high-pitched, earsplitting cracks.

Duran fired a split second later, and the deeper boom of his weapon was a coda to the whole exchange. A double tap to the chest. The giant toppled over backward, landing on the pavement like a sack of cement. His heart pumped a geyser of blood into the air. Once. Twice. And once more. And stopped. It was over.

Almost over. Ted rushed forward, dimly aware of a burning pain in his right shoulder. There was a snail's trail of smeared blood on the steps ahead. Jackie was alive—moving—but her actions seemed spastic. As he headed toward her, Ted caught movement to his left. Lester rose from behind the big bronze sculpture.

"You're all right. Thank God." Ted was suddenly feeling winded, as if he'd sprinted a few hundred yards.

"You're bleeding," Lester said. His voice barely registered through the ringing in Ted's ears.

The pain in Ted's shoulder coalesced into a single burning lance. He looked at it. Blood was coursing down his sleeve. The world was pulling away and he sat down. Or fell.

78

"**YOUR DAD TELLS ME** they want to move you out of the ICU. They need the bed." Ted was sitting on a metal folding chair facing Kenzie. The padded visitor chairs made it too hard to keep his arm and shoulder tucked to his side and immobile. The pain pills worked, but he could feel the staples pull every time he moved, and that set off another bout of dizziness. "That's modern medicine. I didn't even rate an overnight. I'm recovering at the Marriott. They advertise a free breakfast, but it's basically a waffle machine and a Keurig."

Kenzie didn't crack a smile. He would have been ecstatic at any reaction.

"I'd like to see you get out of here altogether," he said. "And the best way to do that is to open your eyes and tell them you want to go home." He sighed. "Which, no doubt, you will get around to doing soon enough. Meanwhile, resting is good."

Kenzie did not open her eyes, but she occasionally made sounds and small movements. The nurses all expected an imminent recovery; even the doctor was mildly optimistic. Ted was hell-bent on remaining positive, upbeat, and with her, no matter what.

"Lester and I are going up to Connecticut tomorrow to see Barbara Miller. She's in Greenwich. I'm told the nursing home is quite luxurious, as these places go. Nice address, at any rate."

Someone—a woman—was crying softly from a room down the hall. It was an oddly comforting sound.

"You've probably heard the news—we were the top story on CNN last night—but I'll fill in a few of the details, if that's okay."

She didn't say no.

"They've agreed to close the Richie Rubiano case. Everybody knows Stavros Nikitopoulos— I had to practice to say that. Anyway, everyone knows he did it, but now they don't have to prove it. With all the mayhem that this guy let loose—murdering two and putting another four in the hospital, one of whom is a cop—the DA is okay to clear one more murder case. Both Duran and his partner will get commendations."

Kenzie sighed.

Ted did too. The sigh escaped him before he could stop it. Hope is hard to maintain. It requires constant maintenance. "The longer I stayed with this thing, the more I wanted to see Richie's killer in court. I wanted justice. I wanted to hear the gavel come down on a thirty-year sentence. Now that it's over, I find I don't care. I'm going to miss Richie. He wasn't my friend, or my partner, or even somebody I can say I was proud to know. But I think he loved Cheryl."

So had Nicky Greco, for that matter. Was it still love if you murdered someone? Or was it obsession? Did it matter? Both Nicky and Richie were dead, and Ted doubted very much that Cheryl had ever loved either of them back.

Ted smoothed an errant hair from Kenzie's face. The movement made him wince, and his stomach did a somersault. He took a few deep breaths before continuing.

"Lester says hi, by the way. He says he's rooting for you, but he's going to wait until you're up and talking before coming to visit. I think he's oversensitive."

Ted brought out an iPad and set it up on the wheeled cart next to her bed.

"I brought you a surprise. Think you're up for it?"

No response.

"I'll take that as a yes."

The aroma of bland chicken soup filtered into the room. Lunch was being served for those capable of eating. Ted thought Kenzie wasn't missing much.

"I know. I'm leaving things out. I guess I'm trying not to upset you. But, yes, you're right. You're tough. Tougher than me. So, yeah, you heard right. Two murders. Young Reisner and a little old lady. She was heading home from the laundry and got hit by a stray shot."

He paused for a moment, preparing for the hard part. Saying the old woman's name out loud cost him something each time. "Her name was Woo. Mrs. Woo." A sudden twinge in his shoulder made him wince, and he took a few more deep breaths.

"No. I don't know if she had any family." He found he needed to clear his throat. "And Jacqueline Clavette is alive. She took one bullet to the head. They rushed her to NewYork-Presbyterian for surgery. I don't know any more than that, but I doubt Jill will welcome a condolence call from me. I was supposed to keep Jackie safe." He paused again. This was the hardest part of all. "I don't feel good about it, but maybe I make promises to Jill too easily. I'm going to have to think on that."

He stared at the far wall for a long time. Minutes. Long minutes.

"Right. Is it time for that surprise? No? Ah. You want to know about how I'm doing. Well, I'm going to have to learn how to sign my name left-handed for the next few weeks, but otherwise I'm cleared for all normal activity. No skydiving, bungee jumping, or competition ballroom dancing, but all else is a go. Now is it time?"

Again, he took her silence for assent. He opened a file on the iPad.

"I thought a diversion might be just the thing for a long night. I will now introduce you to some of my favorite old movies. That way we can talk about them when you're feeling up to talking. Shall we begin?"

Her face moved. Was it a smile or a twitch? A smile. Definitely a smile. He took her hand.

"So? *Thin Man* or *Maltese Falcon*? Considering the fact that we're both feeling a bit bedraggled, I'm going to suggest the first. It's not as dark. And the love story is a lot less complicated. Ready?"

PAULIE MCGIRK WAS SINGING softly, something by Jackson Browne, Ted thought, though he wasn't a fan and so couldn't be sure. Meanwhile, Lili was listening to satellite radio, the afternoon DJ playing a series of Stax and Atlantic hits from the sixties and seventies. She had recently discovered Otis Redding and cranked up the volume whenever "Shake" came on. The television was muted. There was no one paying attention to the talking heads on a sleepy Friday afternoon.

"Andy Love," Lester said as he handed Ted another file folder. Lester had spent some money on his teeth and his wardrobe. He looked good—prosperous and proud of it.

"Hmm?" Ted asked. He already had three thick folders and hours of work in front of him.

"The Memphis Horns," Lester said. "Andrew Love played sax."

Ted put down the file and listened. He wasn't sure what to say. He supposed he had heard these sounds from time to time his whole life and never paid attention. Or maybe he didn't have the right ear for them. "Nice," he said.

"Nice?" Lester guffawed. "The man played with everyone from Otis and Aretha to U2 and Willie Nelson."

"Like I said. Nice. Show me why you think this case is going to work."

They continued to wade through the files, Ted alternately making notes and giving advice on how to track down potential clients. They'd arrived at a workable partnership, Lester putting in the most hours and Ted providing the guidance and legal expertise. The fifty-fifty split provided a comfortable income for both, but more importantly for Ted, the arrangement freed up his time, which he now devoted to his revived legal career.

"That's the last," Lester said.

The clock over the bar read 3:40—ten minutes fast but reliably so. "Quitting time," Ted said. He thought about getting a beer but decided to wait for his partner's sake. Lester maintained that he earned a five-day sobriety chip every week, and as soon as the sun set on Friday he celebrated each milestone. But never before.

"They should be along soon," Lester said.

"Showtime at 4?" Ted asked, though he didn't need a reminder. "Today is special." The events of twelve months earlier were as present as yesterday, today, and tomorrow. And the next hour or so was going to be tough.

"Nothing to celebrate before sundown," Lester said."

The front door swung open, ushering in Kenzie and the Preacher. Ted's day brightened immediately.

"My favorite clients," he said, waving them over. Kenzie grinned happily when she saw him. The only thing different about her was her hair. She was letting it grow out again, but it would still be months more before she would once again have that flaming wild mane.

"Your only clients," Lester said.

"Sad but true," Ted said with a laugh. Suing developers, contractors, engineering firms, and numerous agencies and departments of New York City on behalf of various community organizations—all cases unearthed by Kenzie, the Preacher, or other kindred souls—constituted exactly 100 percent of Ted's legal business outside of his partnership with Lester. It kept Ted busy.

They made room in the booth, and Lili came over to deliver drinks. "A Stella for the lady, two Diet Cokes, and a Miller Lite for the Preacher. Have I got it right?"

"Thank you," Ted said. He took a sip of his soda and hid

his grimace. "And if you would be so kind, can you turn on the sound on the television and put on NY1? There's breaking news coming in a few minutes."

"Right after this song," she said.

"It's Aretha," Lester explained. "You don't turn off Aretha."

Ted bowed to this pronouncement, and they listened through to the end of "Rock Steady."

"Very nice," Ted said.

Everyone else burst out laughing. "I'm afraid you are hopeless," Kenzie said, but she took his hand under the table and gave it a squeeze. "Are you okay with this?" she asked with a nod to the television.

Her voice had its usual effect on him. Hormones flooded his system. "Ready as I'll ever be. How about you?"

"I can bear it," she said.

The music stopped. The clock ticked to 4:10. The television picture cut away from the studio to a sunlit scene in Queens. A group of smiling men and women in business dress faced the camera. Three men in the center held goldcolored shovels. Ron Reisner, the governor, and Councilman Kevin Pak.

"Where's the mayor?" Lester asked.

"Not invited," Kenzie said.

"He lacks faith," the Preacher said.

"He doesn't take Reisner money," Ted said.

On the screen the governor stepped forward and began by thanking everyone who helped to get the project to the point of groundbreaking. It was quite a list.

"Can we do this without sound?" Lester said. "This is painful enough."

Lili turned the radio back on and fiddled with the television remote. The governor was still talking, but now his words were scrolling in closed caption across the bottom of the screen. He finished speaking and the camera pulled back and swept over the beaming faces.

"Do you see Cheryl?" Kenzie asked.

Ted shook his head. "They don't want her anywhere around. Last I heard, she left for Hawaii the day she got out. And she's not coming back."

Ted recognized two senior partners from the law firm, as well as Cornelius Fitzmaurice.

"That's the grandfather, right?" Kenzie asked.

"Yup," Ted said.

"Nasty old son of a bitch."

"Yup," Ted said. "But he keeps his word. He got a green card for Anora." And the nasty son of a bitch had kept his other promises. So had Ted. He'd sold a little piece of his soul for Anora, for Lester, and for Kenzie. And they could never know. He had traded his silence for their welfare. He wasn't particularly proud of this, but he was content. It had been the best deal he could get.

"Anora who?" Kenzie asked.

"A friend," Lester said. "She did us a solid."

This seemed to satisfy Kenzie, though Ted felt a penetrating look from the Preacher.

The camera zoomed in on Councilman Pak, who spoke about the immediate benefits to Queens, all of which were economic and most of which would not be realized for a decade or more, if ever.

"It's not even his district," Kenzie said. "My God, he'll take any chance to get in front of a camera. Why the hell isn't he in jail?"

It was, by this time, a rhetorical question. Without testimony from Cheryl or Jackie, there was no case against Pak. You could read all about his malfeasance on anonymous blogs, but no mainstream news outlet would touch the story. Neither would any prosecutor. *Yet*, Ted reminded himself. *Yet*.

Ron Reisner's face filled the screen. He, too, loved the television, but in his case the television loved him back. Having seen him in person at court appearances, Ted was always surprised at how charismatic the man was on the screen. In person, he always looked stressed and rushed, even when he wasn't. His skin had the pallor of a vampire's, and his gleaming bald pate showed odd bumps and wrinkles. On television, he glowed.

"He looks good," Ted said, "for a guy who almost died last year."

"He's wearing makeup," Lester said.

"He has to; otherwise, all could see he is a demon," the Preacher said.

"I'll give an 'amen' to that," Lester said.

"By their fruits, you will know them," the Preacher said.

Ted was now only half paying attention. He was looking for Jacqueline Clavette—and she wasn't there. As far as he could determine, no one had seen her since the shooting. He had phoned Jill repeatedly in the first weeks after, but she would not take his calls. Finally, he'd realized that she had blocked his phone, so he had called her on Lester's. She answered but hung up the moment she heard Ted's voice.

Jill had given him a single directive—to keep her Jacqueline safe—and he had failed her. There weren't words in any language that could heal the wound that had caused. Ted felt a whole lot less guilt over this than he had imagined he would. Jackie had created her own bad karma.

Reisner finished speaking and flashed $50,000 of dentistry at the camera.

"What did he say?" Lester asked. "Was anyone paying attention?"

"Who cares?" Kenzie took a long slug of beer. "None of these guys will ever mention the real cost—a whole community torn apart, lives disrupted or shattered, people homeless.

The lucky ones will survive by paying more for less and living with a two-hour commute."

"Amen to that, too," Lester said.

The camera backed off again, framing the three principals as they put the golden shovels to the ground. On cue, the three men plunged the blades into the earth, and Ted felt his stomach muscles tighten, as though he had been stabbed.

The onlookers applauded and the screen cut back to the studio. The show was over, but the replays would be on the evening news on every local channel. The governor's aspirations to higher office would ensure the scene would be repeated on national news as well. Ted felt sick.

"I need a drink," Lester said. "What time is sunset?"

"Not for four hours or so," Kenzie said.

Lester thought for a moment. "I'll wait."

The Preacher placed his empty glass on the table and rose. He sighed with a weariness that startled Ted. "So, what do we do now?"

"Nothing," Kenzie said. "We're done." She sounded crushed. Ted saw the exhaustion and despair in her face. She had lost before—it was practically part of her job description—but this one hurt. This one had become personal—for all of them. They'd put their lives on the line. She turned to Ted. "We're done, aren't we?"

"Ask me tomorrow."